Apr 2016

STRIKE

STRIKE

DELILAH S. DAWSON

SIMON PULSE

NEW YORK   LONDON   TORONTO   SYDNEY   NEW DELHI

SIMON PULSE

An imprint of Simon & Schuster Children's Publishing Division

1230 Avenue of the Americas, New York, New York 10020

First Simon Pulse hardcover edition April 2016

Text copyright © 2016 by D. S. Dawson

Jacket photographs copyright © 2016 by Thinkstock

All rights reserved, including the right of reproduction in whole or in part in any form.

SIMON PULSE and colophon are registered trademarks of Simon & Schuster, Inc.

For information about special discounts for bulk purchases, please contact Simon & Schuster Special Sales at 1-866-506-1949 or business@simonandschuster.com.

The Simon & Schuster Speakers Bureau can bring authors to your live event. For more information or to book an event contact the Simon & Schuster Speakers Bureau at 1-866-248-3049 or visit our website at www.simonspeakers.com.

Book designed by Regina Flath

The text of this book was set in Dante MT Std.

Manufactured in the United States of America

2 4 6 8 10 9 7 5 3 1

This book has been cataloged with the Library of Congress.

ISBN 978-1-4814-2342-7 (hc)

ISBN 978-1-4814-2344-1 (eBook)

For Merle, who taught me that hugging a fat dog always helps

STRIKE

1.

The thing about faking your own death is that it kills a little part of you while setting everything else free. It would feel great if not for the blood under my fingernails and the knowledge that I have nowhere to go. Everything I did, I did for my mom, and I have no way of knowing if they killed her anyway. My dad could be dead too, for all I know. I haven't seen him since he walked out when I was a little kid. All I want to do is go home, and I can never go home. My entire world is in this car: me, Wyatt, my dog, Matty, the clothes in my backpack, and the laptops I took from a double agent's burning trailer.

He told me the password before he died. He wanted me to help take down Valor, the bank that now controls the government and sent me out on a killing spree. So I guess I should use it.

I type "Adelaide," and a green glow fills the car as the laptop flickers to life.

"What is that, the Matrix?" Wyatt asks.

He's driving too fast, but I wish it were faster. The green lights flash over the dark interior of his old Lexus, and when I glance at him, the green dances over his face, leaving his eyes black slits. It's hard to see on this curving country road, and I'm grateful for every second that passes without Hummer lights blinding us from behind or the thump of helicopter blades overhead. Because soon Valor will know what we did. And they'll come after us.

I sigh. "You're such a nerd. And I don't know. The green numbers are moving too fast."

I hit return a few times, hoping something will happen, but nothing does.

"You look good in green. Like the Hulk," I say quietly, so he knows I didn't mean the nerd thing and so he knows I'm not still in shock.

At least not on the surface.

The numbers on the screen slow and stop, but even frozen they make no sense. There are no windows, no icons, no white background with discernible navigation. Not even that tooly little paper clip on my mom's old Dell. *It looks like you're trying to hack into a conspiracy network. Want some tips?* Just a black screen with rows and rows of green nonsense, ending in a blinking cursor.

"It's code," Wyatt says, and the tires eat gravel as he swerves back into our lane. My heart stutters, but will it ever stop stuttering?

"No shit, Mario. Keep driving."

He slows and corrects the car, flashing his brights in the shadowy spots where there aren't any streetlights. Deer eyes gleam green before their white tails bounce back into the darkness, and my heart can't speed up any more when Wyatt slams on the brakes because it's already going full tilt. Crashing the car over a deer in the middle of nowhere after all I've done would be an ironic end to my story. I've killed nearly a dozen people in the past few days, and now I have no idea where we're going, how we'll live, where I'll manage to get clean underwear when this pack of cheap white ones from Walmart runs out.

I thought the laptops would . . . I don't know. Have all the answers? Maybe a file labeled VALOR PLANS or WHY I PRETENDED TO BE A VALOR MURDERBOT AND THEN HID IN AN OLD SINGLE-WIDE or something from Alistair that explained what we're fighting and why we were chosen. Why I was chosen. I want to swing by my old neighborhood so bad, but I know we can't. I just have to hope Wyatt has another hiding place for us tonight, somewhere we can go and sleep off the adrenaline and drink another milk shake.

Except—shit. He can't use his Valor credit card anymore. They can track us. Every time it slides through a machine, they'll get a little *ping*. And I'm almost out of cash. I'll barely be able to cover his four-hamburger minimum tonight. I'm used to being poor but not completely bankrupt, and it's easy to see how the entire country got so accustomed to using credit cards. I'd give anything for comfort tonight, even if it meant paying it back double next month. I can't imagine living through the next week, so maybe the lack of cash won't matter. It's not like we can get jobs. No one can know who we are, or Valor will kill us—and maybe everyone around us too. That seems to be how they work.

We're on a road I drive every day, and yet suddenly I'm a million miles from home, and I slam the laptop closed to keep the torrent of tears from electrocuting my lap. All this week, and I've barely cried. All that blood, all those eyes going flat. Explosions, fire, bullets, stitches, fights with Wyatt, running and running and running. I came within inches of being shot tonight. Inches. By this boy I've known only a few days but who I trusted enough to almost shoot me, even though I killed his dad. And—I'm so soft inside, so mushed up and broken and trampled. I push the laptops onto the floorboard, pull up my knees, and uglycry so hard that Wyatt's music is almost drowned out. In the backseat, Matty whines in solidarity, her tail thumping.

The car slows, and Wyatt reaches for me.

"Keep driving," I say. "I'll keep crying. No big deal."

"That's a band, you know. From Georgia."

I stare at him, eyes hot and wet. "What?"

"Drivin' n' Cryin'. It's a band. They do 'Honeysuckle Blue.'"

"Jesus, Wyatt. How does that even matter?"

"Uh. I'm driving. You're crying. This blows? I don't know. I'm just . . . It's so surreal, right? Where are we even going? We never discussed that part."

I fit each eye into a knee and press hard to keep from flying apart. "Take us to another one of your ex-druggie hangouts. Somewhere with no lights, where the car will be hidden, where no one would ever think about looking for either of us. Somewhere with milk shakes and money trees and day-long mosh pits. I don't care anymore."

Wyatt puts on his blinker and turns onto the main highway, four lanes buzzing with late dinnertime traffic. Calm as a damn Buddha statue, he says, "Yes, you do. You say that, but you do care. That's what makes you different. You care, but you keep going anyway."

My crying falls off after that. He's right.

I'm not surprised when he turns in to the McDonald's, but I am surprised when he pulls a twenty out of his backpack. "Get whatever you need. Dad's emergency fund. Not like he's going to need it, right?"

I wince and mutter, "Milk shake."

I wish we still had the mail truck with the bed in back so that I could slither between the seats and lie on the hard bed beside Matty. It's easier to cry when Wyatt's not looking at me, when I'm not this broken object on display. He still thinks he can fix things, fix me, somehow. But now the backseat holds an aquarium full of snake and a big black dog who'd love nothing more than to lick all the tears off my face. I don't even have a sweater to wrap up in or yarn to knit a new one. In all the world, I have nothing but my dead uncle's dog and this messed-up boy who has no business caring about me because I'm the one who killed his dad.

And then he buys me three milk shakes, one in each flavor, and it's okay again.

For now.

I'm finishing up the vanilla milk shake when Wyatt turns the car down a gravel road. Branches brush the roof, and Matty springs up from the floorboard and sniffs the air.

"Where are we?" I ask.

Wyatt swallows half a cheeseburger and grins. "Just another place Mikey and I used to hang. Land that the county bought to make a park and then ran out of money."

A NO TRESPASSING sign flashes past, filled with bullet holes.

"Is it safe?"

Wyatt shrugs. "Is anything now?"

I go quiet as he navigates the overgrown road. Asphalt fades in and out. Sometimes it's just two bumpy red-dirt ruts, and I have to put my milk shake down so my teeth don't clack. Matty's pressed to the window, panting like crazy. Monty the python remains creepy and still. The lights flash over a half-blackened concrete block that might've once been a crappy apartment in the middle of the forest. Ancient barns and rusted cars pop out of the trees like sleeping dinosaurs caught in the headlights. Finally, Wyatt eases his car in between an old boat and a topless Cadillac and parks. When I squeeze out and look back, stretching until my fists brush the branches, his car has a sort of camouflage. Funny how I hadn't noticed the worn-off paint on its hood until now.

I open the back door, and Matty bounds out of the car as if she's forgotten the bullet wound in her neck and starts sniffing around. The big shadow looming over us is a huge, creepy house, one story and all spread out like they made them when my mom was a kid, before people realized that land was a finite sort of thing. Wyatt rummages in the trunk and hands me a flashlight as he hefts his backpack and a sleeping bag over his shoulder.

"Go ahead. Ignore the signs. The key is under the mat."

I stare up at the house. It looks haunted. "Seriously?"

"Unless you want to sleep in the car with Monty. He loves warm snuggles."

With a shiver, I grab the fast food out of the front and hurry to the house as if Valor guys are stalking us through the woods. We're in a clearing, and overhead the stars are as glittery as broken glass. The moon is higher and smaller than it was when I walked up to Wyatt's door in my postal service uniform just a few hours ago, mostly expecting to get shot, whether by accident or on purpose. I feel like part of me stayed buried with my Valor camera, under my friend Amber's body in Wyatt's front yard. The moon watched me then, and it watches me now, distant and cold as a frowning judge robed in black. The moon knows I walked away alive, and by now surely the Valor suits have turned Amber over and realized she's not me. The question is: Do they care enough to hunt me down?

It would be beautiful out here if I weren't terrified and shivering, if I weren't constantly expecting to be shot. When Matty's tongue slops over my hand and the oil-spattered bags, I go for the key and wrestle the door open. The sign to the right says DANGER: ASBESTOS. So that's promising.

The door creaks, and I swing the flashlight around. Matty rushes past me and starts sniffing the floor. It looks like this place got burgled during an earthquake in the sixties and everything got left on the ground to rot. The smell is musty with an overlay of moss and the faintest sprinkle of skunk, and I wish to hell Wyatt hadn't already exhausted his other, nicer hideouts. He's so close behind me that I can smell his deodorant.

"You pick the best hotels," I say.

"Five stars. You're going to love the indoor pool."

"Gross."

He trades his sleeping bag for my flashlight and leads the way down a narrow hallway with flimsy wood paneling peeling off the wall. Normally I would be too scared of getting in trouble or falling through the floor to walk into an abandoned, dangerous house in the dark. Now I'm checking for hiding places and escape hatches, should Valor come for us. After a few more turns and lots of weird crap that I barely see, we end up in a decently clean room that smells like cigarettes and weed. There's a squashy sofa in the corner that might sprout mushrooms at any moment and a big pile of records spilling out of sleeves beside an army of empty liquor bottles filled with ashes.

"You and Mikey, huh?"

"Good times," he says, kind of bittersweet, kind of sarcastic. "But no one ever came out here, not a single time. And this room is the only one that doesn't leak. So there's that."

He arranges the sleeping bag, pulls another flashlight out of his backpack, and hurries outside for more stuff, and I sit down on the sleeping bag and poke fries into my mouth and try to remember how to chew. Matty creeps close on her belly, her head on my knee, like she wants to apologize for all my trouble. Wyatt tromps back in with Monty's aquarium and hurries right back out. I keep eating. I go throw up in a cardboard box, just to make things interesting, because the floppy French fries remind me of dressing my ex–best friend's corpse in my own shirt and hat tonight. Amber's arms were floppy, just like the fries.

When Wyatt comes back, he drops his bag and hurries to my

side. I'm curled up in a ball, shaking, making a weird keening noise. Soon he's a big spoon, making me into the little spoon, holding me tight against his chest, murmuring stupid shit to me and raising my body temperature back up to the land of the living.

"It's okay. Shh. C'mon. It's going to be all right."

That makes me snort. "It's really not."

"Is this . . . ? I mean, is this the usual stuff, or something different?"

"Wyatt, if you ask me if I'm on my period, I'm going to literally murder you. And you know that's kind of my specialty."

His hand stills on my stomach. "Is that supposed to be a joke?"

"I guess. It's the best I can do. And it's all the usual stuff. I thought I would feel better now, and I don't. Nothing feels real or okay or better. It was supposed to be over, and it's not over. I can't go home." A sob catches in my throat, and I ride it out, tucking my head into his shoulder. "I can't go home."

"Nope. You can't."

"You pointed a gun at me and pulled the trigger, and it's got me all messed up, because I know what that feels like, and I thought I was hard inside. I want to be hard. But I'm all squashy and tangled. All it takes is a bullet in the wrong place. It's over so much faster than it is in the movies. All the blood. And the eyes." I dig my fists into my eyelids. "Jeremy's eyes. God, they—he was Jeremy, and then all of a sudden, he wasn't. And I was me, but now I'm not anymore. So who am I?"

"You're you. And it's not your fault."

He's so solid and real and honest that his words just double me up harder, and I am full of so many feelings that I can't hold them all, and I'm going to explode, because seventeen-year-old girls shouldn't have to kill people, and I have. A lot of people. They said that if I did what they told me to do, I was supposed to be able to go back to real life, to my house and my mom and my job and school, but here I am now, on the run. With nothing. Just a boy and a dog and a snake, lost in the woods. It was supposed to be worth it. I was supposed to get my life back.

But it's gone. Just as if I really were dead.

I keep crying.

I cry until lights flash through the window, dancing across the peeling wood walls.

Someone else is in the woods.

My hand tightens around the gun.

I never let it go, you see.

2.

My tears stop falling, and my chin stubbornly sets. I don't know how to deal with the aftermath of killing, but I'm pretty good at the actual murder part.

"You think it's Valor?" Wyatt whispers in my ear.

"Who else?"

"Second Union again, maybe?"

I hadn't thought of that—that Second Union might still be sending their own assassins after the kids, like me, who got tapped as bounty hunters for Valor. I can't believe we ever trusted banks. They sent my best friend, Jeremy, after me, and now he's dead. What else can they possibly do?

I snort. "Either way, they're going to die."

Wyatt's big body uncurls from around mine, leaving me cold. Iron seeps into my veins. I check my clip, even though I know it's full. This is my dad's gun, the one Valor didn't know about. Wyatt reaches into his backpack and pulls out Jeremy's Glock, the one stamped SECOND UNION in glittering gold. He nudges Roy's shotgun so that it's on the ground between us, and he nods and clicks off both of our flashlights, which were fortunately pointed low instead of lighting up the windows like idiots. The light from outside dances in my eyes, and Wyatt dives for the ground and pulls me with him, our shoulders smashed together and my arm around Matty.

"Shh," I murmur. "Good dog. Don't get us killed, 'kay?"

Voices chitter in the night as a beam of light cuts the darkness overhead.

"Is it safe?" says one—a young guy. Funny—that's the same thing I asked.

"Oh, for a haunted house in the middle of a creepy forest, it looks pretty safe," says another guy, smooth as butter. "I've hung out here before. It's cool."

"Idiots," hisses a third. A girl. "Shut up and point the light down. Could you be less obvious?"

"They're kids. So, not Valor," Wyatt whispers.

"Doesn't mean they don't want us dead," I whisper back. And we're both thinking about Jeremy and Roy, sent by Second Union to kill us for reasons we still don't completely understand.

"They're going to the front door."

I grab my flashlight and silently rise to a crouch. "Then let's go tell 'em we don't want any damn Girl Scout cookies."

Wyatt goes first, hurrying down the hallway. It's dark as death, so I grab the back of his hoodie and try not to step too heavily. I'll never forget the sound of that thug's foot breaking through a rotten step in Sharon Mulvaney's house. Was that really only three days ago that I got in a gang shoot-out in a meth house? I shake my head. If I can survive that, I can survive this.

White light shoots overhead as a face appears in the window by the front door.

"Amateurs," I mutter.

A high whine reminds me that Matty is at my side—stupid, loyal, doesn't-understand-guns Matty. We should've locked her in a bathroom or something. Overweight Labradors suck in gunfights. I guess she's an amateur too. It's too late to lock her up somewhere safer—I just have to hope we can end this quick, whatever it is.

My heart is in my throat again. But then, did it ever leave?

They're all on the porch now, and fingers scrabble around the floorboards.

"You said there was a key," says the young one. Baby Bear.

"There used to be," says the smooth, cool guy. Papa Bear.

"Again, you guys are idiots. The wood's rotten. One kick and the whole fucking house will fall down." Sensible Mama Bear.

"You probably shouldn't—"

The door bangs open, and I step into it with my gun up and my flashlight on.

"Can we help you?"

God, I sound like a badass. But inside I'm screaming. Matty starts barking like crazy, and Wyatt grabs her collar and pretends to hold her back, his gun pointed alongside mine. I can barely see them in the single beam of light. They're just ragged, desperate shadows in the night. Whoever was holding the flashlight on their side? They drop it.

I smell piss and gun oil, and then Papa Bear is cocking a pistol like it means something. "Yeah, you can help us. We're hiding here. So you can leave."

"Wrong answer. Go hide somewhere else or get shot."

My jaw is so tense that my teeth are about to crack like popcorn, and I can hear these kids breathing, because they're kids—they're our age or maybe even younger—and Papa Bear's gun doesn't waver and Matty is barking and when Baby Bear goes for his waistband, I spit, "Goddammit," and shoot him before something seriously stupid happens.

But I shot him in the leg, so I guess I'm learning.

It wasn't meant to be a killing shot this time.

He squeals like a baby and falls over, and Wyatt lets go of Matty and slaps a hand over the kid's mouth to stop his screaming.

"Jesus! You shot him!" says the girl. She fumbles for the flashlight and shines it on whoever the hell I just shot, and oh my God, I didn't shoot a teenager. I shot a ten-year-old, maybe. A rat-faced little kid in boat shoes, and his pants are a wet splatter of piss and blood, but at least the blood isn't gushing out, so maybe I'm not going to hell forever.

"You come knocking on somebody else's house after dark, you got to expect bad things to happen," Wyatt mutters. "She warned you."

With a deep sigh, he pulls off his hoodie and ties it around the kid's leg. I can only stand there, numb, gun flopping at my side, hating myself and feeling like shit. At some point, the kid stops shouting and passes out, and the girl is fussing around with him, shooing Wyatt away, and the weird slurping sound I hear is Matty licking Papa Bear's gun hand. It's too dark to see much, but he's leaning against the door, cool as a stupid cucumber, staring at Wyatt.

"Sup, Beard?" he says.

Wyatt's head snaps up, and he stands, suddenly twice as tall as he should be and exuding menace as he gets in Papa Bear's face. "Do I know you?"

"Haven't seen you since Mikey's funeral. You don't remember me? I'm hurt."

"Oh, yeah. I remember now. You used to have a shaved head. Pretty sure I got drunk every time we hung out because I couldn't stand you. What's your name again? Chance?"

"Cianci. But Chance is good enough for the apocalypse. Yeah, let's go with that." He tucks the gun under his shirt against tight abs and slumps against the door. "Chance," he says to himself. "And who's the chick with the itchy trigger finger?"

"I think you mean the chick who still has fourteen bullets," I say.

He just laughs like that's adorable. Which pisses me off even more.

I ram my gun against his belly and say, "Dude, I will totally blow you a new butthole. Just pick up your friends and go away."

He shakes shaggy, dark hair out of his eyes, which are just shiny black pits in this light. "They're not my friends. And no." I think he's reaching to hold my hand, but he does something with the gun, pushing it smoothly out of my grip before I can react. Holding it up, he grins. "Tonight's not New Butthole Night. It's actually Thursday. And you should never touch somebody with a gun unless you're going to pull the trigger, because you never know who spent a lot of time in juvie practicing disarming techniques."

Still holding my gun, he walks past me and into the house, whistling.

Wyatt and the girl drag the kid I shot (*The kid. I shot.*) into the house and onto our sleeping bag. Turns out my bullet (*My. Bullet.*) went right out the back of his thigh, leaving a clean wound that didn't hit anything major. Which makes me a monster but not, at least, a monster who murders little boys.

"I don't blame you, Zooey. I wanted to shoot him, too," Chance says, settling in on the squashy sofa and splaying out in the way of boys who want to seem bigger than they are. "But Gabriela wouldn't let me. So here we are. And now I ask you: Do you have any food? Because I'm dying here."

"My name isn't Zooey," I say.

"I don't want to know your real name, and you look like Zooey Deschanel's trailer-trash sister, so we're going with that."

"I wish I'd shot you instead."

His grin is so annoying that I click off the flashlight.

"Lots of people say that, Zooey."

Gabriela grabs my flashlight and props it up with hers so she can inspect the kid. It's not a pretty sight. Wyatt and I are standing just outside the hallway, watching and incompetent, and it's horribly awkward. Not as awkward as that time I wasn't wearing pants and he got a pajama boner while trying to slash my throat with a steak knife, but close.

"We can take him to the vet tomorrow," I say, and Wyatt shakes his head.

"We can't go back there. And we're broke. Except for the card."

"But a vet wouldn't turn away a bleeding kid. Hippocratic oaths, right?"

Chance sits forward, a gun in each hand, his and mine. "Zooey, do you honestly think oaths mean shit in this world? All contracts are void, and God bless Valor."

I stare at him, hard. "Were you . . . ?"

"A Valor assassin? Yep. I did my ten. Had to shoot the kid's parents right in front of him, and Gabriela McBigheart brought him along like a dumb puppy. And when we all went home to be a happy family, our house had burned down. Coincidence? I think not."

But I'm not listening anymore. My hands are fisted in Wyatt's shirt, and I'm on tiptoes, pulling him close and murmuring, "We have to go. We have to go now. We have to go to my house. My mom. She needs me. They can't. They wouldn't. Wyatt. We have to."

He pulls me close like he can hug the pain and panic away. "You know we can't go back. You knew that when we ran. You knew after Amber. Just try not to think about it. We have to keep moving. Right? That's what you said. We have to go on." His whisper trickles into my ear, and it should make me feel better, but it doesn't. He's right. We can't go back, not for good and not for bad. For the first time, it occurs to me that if my mom knew what I'd done, she'd be horrified. It was bad enough, doing what Valor demanded. But now I've shot a kid for no reason at all. Would she even recognize me?

"I'm a monster," I whisper.

"You're Patsy."

I can't unclench my fists, and he helps me, gently untangling me from his shirt like I'm a panicked kitten. My fingers shake, and I drop to sitting cross-legged, suddenly light-headed and lost. It's one thing to have hope, and it's another thing to know that you never had hope and were just fooling yourself all along.

"Holy shit! It wasn't you, was it, Beard? It was her." Chance leans down, elbows on knees, grinning at me like a shark. "How many?"

"Leave her alone, man," Wyatt warns, but Chance doesn't budge.

"How many?"

My eyes roll up to him. "As many as I had to."

"And you haven't been home."

It's not a question. His eyes meet mine like the click of teeth.

"Me and Valor didn't end things on the best of terms," I finally say.

"Valor doesn't end anything on good terms," says the girl, pushing her way into the tight circle of our conversation. She's about my age with medium-dark skin and a faded purple fro-hawk.

"You too?" I ask.

She shakes her head. "Nope. Just went with my brother to make sure he didn't do anything stupid."

I look from her to him, Gabriela to Chance, or Cianci, or whatever, and the only thing they have in common is that they're angry. He's tall and lanky; she's short and curvy. He's tan, but she's brown. His eyes are shifty gray; hers are maybe dark hazel. They can't be related.

"Yes, she's my sister. Yes, it's a long story. Point is, would you like to adopt the nerd you shot? Because we're on the run, and he can't run anymore, and it's kind of your fault."

"I can run," the kid whimpers.

Chance stands and saunters over to nudge the kid's leg with his boot tip. The kid howls and sniffles. "No, you really can't."

I look up at Wyatt, unsure what to say.

"We have plans," he says for me.

"So do we." Chance looks pointedly at the door. "And they're happening now."

"I don't want to go with the girl that shot me!" the kid wails.

"I can shoot you, too," Chance offers, flopping his gun in the kid's direction.

"No, you can't. You're out of bullets."

If looks could kill, Chance just turned the kid into pulp.

"Did I mention he's a tactical genius?" he says, shoving the gun into the front of his jeans. It's a black Glock, of course. Just like mine, which he pulls out instead. "I've got fourteen bullets now. You want one?"

The kid just sniffles and glares like he knows that Chance is an asshole but not a monster. Lucky him.

"So you've got bullets now. Take your kid and go. There's another building in the park. Stay there. But don't come back here, or we'll aim higher," I say. "We have more guns."

"Where are you headed?" Gabriela asks, too quick.

My hands go into fists. "Wouldn't you like to know? Let me guess. You want our supplies."

"Yeah. I'm just really excited about half-eaten hamburgers and a fat dog. And is that a freaking snake?" She shakes her heads and puts a hand on her hip. "Look, I'm just saying . . . if you're in the same boat we are, we might as well see if we can help each other. We have nowhere to go, no one we can trust. You don't, either. Maybe there's safety in numbers."

"I promise we won't eat your dog," Chance says, but that's obvious. Matty is on her back, licking his knuckles while he rubs her belly.

Wyatt and I lock eyes. He shakes his head no. And I know that he knows more about this Chance kid than I do, and if their only connection is Mikey, that means Chance is a connection from Wyatt's bad-boy phase. Could be drugs, destruction, or punk shows. Could be worse. But I shot this kid, and they look desperate, and I can't help thinking about what it would feel like to go home and see your house on fire. There's a connection here—a common enemy. In the new world Valor is fashioning, connections like this one might be the only way to survive. I don't trust these kids. Not a bit. But I don't know if my conscience can take three more lives, three more strike marks. If we send them away without money, without food, without medicine, with only fourteen bullets against the world, I will hate myself even more.

Chance slides out my clip, flicks a bullet out with his thumb and rolls it around in his palm. "These aren't Valor issue, are they?"

I say nothing. Wyatt curses under his breath. Chance slides the bullet back in, snaps in the clip, and aims the gun at me. "Where are the rest of the bullets?" he says slowly.

Wyatt's gun is ready, aimed at Chance's chest. "None of your goddamn business. Now, she asked where we were going, and that's nowhere. So where are you going? Because now would be a good time to leave."

Chance measures us with his eyes, stares around the dark room as if taking inventory. Roy's shotgun pinned under my foot, Wyatt's Glock pointed at his chest, our bags, our dog who is clearly not a guard dog, a glass box full of snake. He gives me a lopsided smile.

"We don't know where we're going, okay? We were going to figure that out here, tonight. I mean . . . what's left? Can't go home. Can't go back to school. Don't know who's in on the takeover and who's not. This place is turning into the Wild Wild West."

"I forgot how much you and Mikey liked crappy movies," Wyatt says. "Idiot. It's nothing like that."

"There's no law, the law there is went corrupt, and you can shoot anybody without consequences. That's pretty fucking Wild West to me, bro."

"Why don't you just go join the Citizens for Freedom?" I say, hoping to scrape them off.

Gabriela looks up from beside the kid. "The what now?"

"Okay, so we found out about this meeting—" I start.

"Don't!" Wyatt puts a hand on my arm.

"Ugh!" I wave my arms around and pace up and down the hall. "Why not? What do we have to lose? They'll see the flyers one day anyway. Let them go. Maybe the Citizens have medicine for the kid."

Wyatt leans in to whisper, "You want them to go to the meeting?" He inclines his head toward Chance. "Look, I know this guy, and you don't want him on our side."

"If I'm a bad guy, you're a bad guy, too, bro," Chance says lazily, turning the gun around like he's looking for the gold stamp.

"Why don't we all go?" Gabriela says. "If you were going anyway. Strength in numbers."

Wyatt's voice is strained. "I don't like this."

Gabriela stands and walks to me. "Okay, so let's work this out without the gorillas. Do you trust him?" She motions to Wyatt, and I nod. "Well, I trust him." She points to Chance. "So if you and I can trust each other, maybe we can all live. But if we dick around, I'm pretty sure the kid's not going to be okay. And we don't have a car."

I look at the kid on the floor, and he's so pale he stands out against the darkness of the rotten house. He's painfully small and still, just as floppy as Amber was. I don't want to be haunted by another ghost. And even if Wyatt doesn't trust Chance, I like Gabriela. And I think she's right. Maybe it's because I lost my best friend this week, but I want to agree with her. And if it all goes south, we've still got more bullets than they do.

"Seriously, you're not considering this?" Wyatt puts his arm around my shoulder and turns me away, but I notice he keeps his gun on Chance. His whisper is even softer this time. "That guy is bad news. Seriously bad news."

"He hasn't shot us yet."

"That doesn't mean much."

I turn around and raise my voice, because I'm so damn sick of this tension, of the way the temperature in a room ratchets up as soon as someone aims a gun.

"Look. Here's my final say. I don't trust them, and they don't trust us, but I'd rather join forces than shoot three more people. They can come with us to the Citizens for Freedom meeting tomorrow, or they can leave right now, or we can kill them. I just want to go to sleep and forget today happened. Prey animals live in groups for a reason. So come on or get out." I plunk down on the sleeping bag and shine my flashlight in Chance's eyes. "And give me back my goddamn gun."

Chance reaches into his pants and gives me his gun, his empty gun, and it feels all wrong in my hand even though it's a Glock just like the one Valor gave me.

"This is not my gun."

"So fill it with bullets, and then we're all on the same page. I'm not letting my sister sleep in the same room with two armed strangers and me holding my dick."

It's probably the sleep deprivation and insanity talking, but I kind of see his point.

All this time, Gabriela's been dealing with the kid, but now she's hunting around the room for something.

"If we're sticking around, we need to elevate his leg," she says.

I grab a few moldy pillows from the corner and put them under his foot.

"Blankets?"

I point at the sleeping bag. "That's our only one."

"Spare clothes?"

"Not that would fit him."

Gabriela stares daggers at me like I'm totally useless and tries to prop the kid up. He whimpers like he's having a bad dream.

Which . . . I guess he basically is.

"Yo, Cianci—" Gabriela calls.

"Call me Chance from now on. It's cooler."

I can almost hear her roll her eyes. "How about you share your bounty?"

Chance gets up and strolls to the door. Wyatt follows him, and their angry whispers carry down the hall in the still night. The slap of flesh suggests they're bumping chests or something similarly apelike. I kind of wish I could see it. I've never seen Wyatt talk to anyone our age except me, and everything about the way he walks and talks and acts changed the second he saw Chance. He's gone full silverback.

"Don't fuck this up," Wyatt finally says.

Chance saunters back in and squats beside us, tossing a ratty duffel bag on the ground. When he unzips it, the inside rattles around. Dozens and dozens of pill bottles.

"What the hell?" I say.

He hunts through them, pulls out an orange bottle, and knocks two white pills into his palm. Gabriela hands the kid a half-full bottle of water and helps him swallow the meds.

"You're a drug dealer?" I ask.

His stare is flat and judgmental. "I'm a businessman. The kid's in pain. I can help him. The insurance system is effed up. I help people, connect them with what they need. This isn't meth and crack. It's all real. I'm like . . . the Robin Hood of Big Pharma. What if your mom couldn't afford insurance to get her meds?"

My mouth drops open and I choke. My eyes are swimmy, and I'm hot and cold all over, and Wyatt hurries to me, his arm heavy on my shoulder.

"Guess I'm a telepath, too," Chance murmurs, zipping up his pack. "Your folks dead? Natural orphan or Valor?"

"She told you. She hasn't been back to find out," Wyatt growls.

The old house goes eerily silent, as if all our ghosts rushed in at once to haunt us.

"How long does it take until it stops hurting?" the kid asks.

"I'll tell you when I find out," I say.

That's not what he meant, but it's what we all want to know, really.

Wyatt's in the corner, filling Chance in on the Citizens for Freedom, or whatever Alistair and his group are calling themselves. I don't know what was said in the hall, but they seem to have an uneasy truce now. I scoot back against an armchair and slide bullets into the clip of Chance's gun. My vision is wavering, and I almost nod off before I'm done. The kid—I still don't know his name and haven't asked—his meds kicked in, and he's on his back, snoring hard, his glasses askew. His leg stopped bleeding and crusted up, so I guess it's fine for now. Matty is stretched out by his side, paws twitching as she dreams. Whenever the kid tries to move and cries out, I flinch and swallow down the guilt. Gabriela's on the squashy couch, perched over him like an awkward angel.

Chance looms over me, his stare hard. "I sleep light," he says.

"Congratulations."

"You try to take my gun or hurt Gabriela or that kid, and you die. And so does Beard. And that dog."

But I don't believe him anymore, not really. At least he wouldn't hurt Matty.

"I'm too tired to care," I say.

Wyatt returns from whatever he was doing outside and stretches out on the least nasty part of the carpet. Strong arms pull me close.

"It's okay," he says. "It's going to be okay."

Which is a lie.

My eyes don't want to close, and my fingers are clenched around Chance's gun. I can see my gun, likewise clamped in his hand. He's in the middle of the room, between us and Gabriela. In sleep, his smirk has stretched into a grim frown. His gun feels wrong, but why should any gun ever feel right?

I breathe out and settle back, ever the little spoon curled against Wyatt, both of us facing them as if for battle. This truce—it was the only choice that didn't end in somebody dying. But Wyatt's not happy. I can feel the tension in his chest, the gruffness of each exhalation. I keep trying to match my breathing to his so that I can get some sleep, but the air is full of unwelcome, unfriendly scents. Gabriela wears a patchouli perfume that mixes with the scent of old weed and the crust of black mildew and the hard tang of a kid who's soaked in piss and blood because of me.

So many people have bled because of me.

But I can't fall asleep like Chance, still and hard and unmoving.

All I can do is cry as quietly as possible, when everyone else is asleep.

3.

We sleep in—all of us. No one's anxious to be awake, I guess. The first thing I hear is the kid groaning and whimpering. He sounds like a baby trying to get attention, but then again, I guess he did get shot yesterday. Because I shot him.

Repress, repress . . . God, it's hard to repress shit when it's whining across the room.

I peek from under Wyatt's arm as Chance yawns, stretches, tucks the gun in his waistband, and rummages in his bag to get the kid some more pills. He looks concerned and worn down, not at all the cool-guy drug dealer I saw last night. The weak daylight filtering in through the dirty windows reveals the purple circles under his red eyes. He's wearing a shirt with the Joker on it. After glancing around to make sure no one is looking, he spreads a sweatshirt more carefully over Gabriela.

My got-to-pee squirming is probably what wakes Wyatt up, and then we're all up and moving around the room as if there were something to do. But there's not. Matty runs from person to person, sniffing hands hopefully for food that isn't there. I really do need to pee, but I'm not chancing whatever's left of the bathroom, and I forgot to bring any toilet paper while I was fleeing for my life. With a heavy sigh, I head for the door. Gabriela joins me, and Matty pushes past us into the kind of crappy day that has a white sky, an unfriendly chill, and the promise of a cold butt after peeing in the forest.

"Bushes?" She points at a patch of laurels, and I shake my head.

"Car graveyard. You can't see through a car, plus no surprise raccoons."

"Good point. Car graveyard it is."

There are at least twenty cars, a camper, and a few small boats out here, all rusted through on flat tires. I head between two tall trucks and hate every moment of it. Finding new undies and toilet paper is now a top priority. Poor as my mom and I were, I never considered the frustrations of being homeless. I own literally nothing, outside of the clothes on my back and a couple of guns. Even my knitting bag got left behind in my old Valor truck. If I had it, I would be wiping with a ball of yarn, because that's where I am in life.

"So that sucked," Gabriela says with a friendly smile as she emerges from beside an old camper.

I nod. "All hail Valor."

"Y'all got anything to eat?"

I shake my head. "We've been living on fast food, but we're almost out of cash."

"Us too. You got a car?"

"Yeah, that we've got." She perks up, so I add, "But you'll have a snake in your lap."

We use the last of our cash to buy crap off the discount bread shelf at Shop N Save. Turns out that eight dollars can buy a lot of messed-up cake. As Wyatt checks out, we fill our water bottles at the fountain and use the bathroom. I shove two rolls of toilet paper in the waistband of my jeans, under one of Wyatt's hoodies. Walking out between the security scanners, I wait for someone to tackle me, to call the cops. I expect to see Valor suits blocking the doors.

But very little has changed in the capital of capitalism. Business as usual. There are definitely more men than women around, and I don't see a single kid or baby. Everyone at this Shop N Save always looks desperate, but now they look desperate and wary. How many of them have seen neighbors gunned down? How many have heard the Valor voice mail after calling 911? Whatever they know, they need food as much as we do, so they're here, selling and buying. Just like Valor wants them to be.

We drive back to the house in the woods and eat a ton of stale cake with our hands, since nobody thought about forks and the kitchen was ransacked long ago. I take a walk with Matty deep into the woods and crap behind a log, expecting something horrible to happen all the while. It's like *The Walking Dead*, basically. Thank heavens for Shop N Save's single-ply toilet paper.

Most of the day, honestly, is spent fidgeting. No one knows what to do, but no one wants to talk about it. Every time someone tries to start a conversation, it just tapers off like we're all waiting for a phone to ring, listening for some far-off sound. By the time we need to leave for the Citizens for Freedom meeting, I've learned that the kid I shot is named Kevin and that Chance and Gabriela are the closest things I have to friends now. Chance is kind of a dick to everyone but cool to Gabriela, and Gabriela is cool to everyone and hates to be called Gabby. Wyatt and Matty, of course, are family now.

Sometime in the afternoon I realize that I left my gun sitting out by the sleeping bag and no one took it. Maybe trusting them is actually the right choice and not just me buying off my guilt.

There are five of us in Wyatt's Lexus, all silent and tense on the way to the meeting. I guess I lied about the snake. Wyatt left the aquarium at the old house and brought Monty along, tied up in a pillowcase in his backpack so he won't get cold and die in an empty house with no electricity for his lamps or whatever. Here is my advice: If you're ever on the run from the government, don't bring your pets. Especially not the creepy ones.

Matty is in back, wedged between Chance's knees and the front seats, her tail beating my elbow. Kevin is strained and pale, and we all know he needs medical help, and soon. We didn't have enough money to buy spare shorts or Bactine at the store, so it's just water and pills, water and pills. Maybe the Citizens for Freedom will have a doctor. Or some antibiotic ointment, at least. We tried stopping by the vet who helped Matty, but a sign on the door said CASH ONLY, AND ABSOLUTELY NO HUMANS, so we kept driving.

The meeting is supposed to be at Bear Creek High School, which is down a road that hasn't seen much action since the school closed when I was little. The asphalt is falling apart, and the streetlights are spotty. Red brake lights ahead tell us we're not the only ones here. A guy in a reflective yellow vest points us to the side, like at a concert, and we turn off the road and park the Lexus in an overgrown parking lot. Figures hurry toward the school, and I can feel my heart beating in my ears as we get out of the car and slam the doors. I have Matty tied up with a chunk of rope from one of the boats at the old house—I couldn't leave her there alone, so I can only hope we can pass her off as a service dog, if service dog laws still exist. She's way too excited to be of any actual service.

Kevin grunts with every painfully slow step, and Chance finally sighs in annoyance and picks the smaller kid up, carrying him like a baby. Wyatt is suddenly at my side, tall and solid, his backpack over his shoulder. My gun is flat against my back—Chance was okay with trading, once his had bullets too. There'd better not be a metal detector, because I'll turn around and walk right back out. Everything I saw in Alistair Meade's trailer tells me that this group, the Citizens for Freedom, or whatever they call themselves, is legit, but up until a few days ago, I thought that Valor Savings Bank and the police were legit. When you don't know what's real anymore, it's always better to have a loaded gun.

Whatever history they have, Wyatt and Chance seem like they're on the same team right now. Wyatt's in front, Chance is in back, both in gorilla mode with Gabriela and me between them. Everyone's twitchy. I subtly move my gun around to my hip in case I need to draw it. Carrying my Valor gun feels right tonight, but everything feels so wrong. Now that we're around people, I'm twitchy and raw, an exposed nerve. My skinny jeans feel like a layer of hardened sweat, and I know I look and smell as bad as I feel.

Another guy in a yellow vest is guiding people to an open set of double doors, and it's fucking terrifying. There are no outside lights, but an extension cord shows a chain of lanterns going in, almost like we're descending into a cave. It doesn't even look like a high school; it looks like the pit to hell. I would've gone to Bear Creek, but they closed it and built Big Creek when I was a kid. It was a big deal—what to do with this land. For whatever reason, no one was allowed to get rid of it and build parks or houses, so here it is, a broke-down school that's been empty for ten years. The guy by the doors has an assault rifle, which sets my blood cold.

"G'won in," he says with a thick Southern accent.

Wyatt turns to meet Chance's eyes, and I can almost read the conversation.

What the hell are we going in to?

Can it possibly be worse than where we're coming from?

Too late. More people are behind us with more headlights turning in all the time, and we don't have a lot of choice. It reminds me of being in line for a roller coaster. By the time you decide you don't want to ride it, they're already snapping down the harness.

We step into the hallway, and the scent is what hits me first—mildew and animal piss overlying that same weird smell that every school has that tells you you're in trouble, or at least that you're going to be miserable for a while. The classroom doors are closed, their glass windows pitch-black. All we have to guide us is the string of lanterns, one every twelve feet or so.

The lights lead us around a corner toward the sound of a crowd trying to be quiet. A line of people waits at a set of double doors, and at first I can't place the swoopy robot sound.

"Metal detectors? You've got to be kidding me," Wyatt murmurs, and my gun feels red-hot against my skin. I'll run before I let them take it from me.

"You're clean. Find a seat," says the woman holding the wand, and then it's our turn.

"We're not giving up our guns," Wyatt says quietly, and the woman barks a smoker's laugh.

"Then maybe y'all deserve to live," she says. "You can keep your guns. We're checking for wires and tech. Gotta make sure Valor ain't listening in. Arms out, please."

Wyatt holds his arms out, and the woman swoops the loop over him. It *bings* loudly when it hits his backpack, and she gives him a sharp look.

"What are you carrying, son?"

Wyatt shakes his head, furious. "Nothing from Valor."

A bearded guy in his forties who looks a little like a bear yanks the pack off Wyatt's arm. "You'd better hope that's not what it sounds like, kid," he says, all gruff menace. I take a step toward Wyatt, wanting to comfort him or defend him, and the guy with the beard stops me with a hand. He looks at me closely, eyebrows drawn down. "Stand back, honey. You don't want to get hurt."

Another guy shows up and points to his eyes, then his gun. *I'm watching you.* Kevin starts to quietly cry, and Gabriela mutters, "Goddammit."

As the first guy opens the backpack, the second guy points his gun on Wyatt, who reflexively puts up his hands. "That's not necessary, man. We're on your side," he says, as if that's not exactly what you would say if you weren't on their side.

"Oh, shit. Where'd you get these?"

The bearish guy holds up Alistair's laptops, and I glare daggers at Wyatt. We never talked about them, but I assumed the laptops were in the trunk of the car or maybe back at the house. We couldn't figure out the code, and then we got too busy putting up with our new friends and trying to stay alive on eight dollars to worry about a bunch of green numbers on a black screen.

But we're busted. There's no point in lying to someone who has a bigger gun.

"From a guy who went by the name Alistair Meade," I say. "Same place we got this flyer." I reach for my pocket, and the gun swings to face me.

"Slowly, girl." The guy with the gun is a big country boy with crazy eyes.

I nod and—slowly—hand the bearded guy a poorly folded piece of paper, one from the stack of hundreds I found in Alistair's trailer, along with a ton of maps, notes, and a list of the names of local kids who would make good Valor assassins. He reads it and looks at me carefully from a nest of black hair and mustache and beard streaked with gray.

"What's the story?" he asks. But not Wyatt—he asks me.

"Valor showed up at my house. Alistair was on my list. He told me to look in his trailer. I—we—didn't mean to shoot him. It was an accident. He told me the password before he—" I gulp down a cold stone of fear and regret, remembering that moment. "We just want to help. I swear."

After considering me for a few moments, he nods and says, "Get Leon," to the smoker. He tosses the pack back to Wyatt but holds on to all three laptops. "You got anything else we need to know about?"

Wyatt groans. "I've still got a Valor credit card. Does that count?"

"It very much counts, if you want to stay alive. Hand it over. Again, slowly."

I look back at Chance and Gabriela and join them in giving Wyatt the Death Glare. This is not the way I wanted to start out with the group that might be our only allies. Wyatt pulls out his beat-up chain wallet and holds out his card, and the guy pulls something out of his own pocket—looks like a battery pack. He runs it over the card both ways, throws the card in a box with dozens of others, and nods at the woman with the wand, who runs it over Wyatt again. No beep.

"You're in. But sit up front. We'll have questions for you after," the guy says. I must look as terrified and trapped as I feel, because he gives me a small, quick smile and adds, "Don't worry. You're going to be fine."

Wyatt waits as the rest of us pass the boop test, and we all sit where the guy told us to, because what else are we going to do? It's weird to sit on gym bleachers again, and the wood creaks with every movement. Nobody said anything about Matty, although they did scan her with the wand. A couple other people in the crowd have dogs, and one lady has a beaver-sized cat on a leash. Our area is mostly kids, ranging from country boys in overalls to prep kids to this tiny little blond girl who looks like she's ten. I'm between Wyatt and Gabriela, and although I didn't want these three jerks to show up at our hideout last night, I'm glad I'm not one of the confused loners. It feels safer to be in the middle of my herd. Wyatt reaches into his backpack and pulls out Monty, rolling the pillowcase between his hands without actually releasing the snake.

"Sorry," he mutters under his breath. "I forgot. I just wanted to keep the laptops safe."

"It's fine. We weren't getting anything out of them anyway."

But I'm pretty pissed, and I know he can feel it.

As I look around, I decide we're probably going to get ax murdered. The old gym is lit up with bright, cold lights like the kind they use to work on the roads at night. The corners are strung with cobwebs, and old decorations hang dejectedly from the walls, hearts and graying doilies, like there was a massacre at the Valentine's Day dance and they just locked up the building forever. The stage has glittery red bunting around it, the curtain halfway pulled and black beyond. I can detect movement on the stage, but not clearly.

There must be at least a hundred people in here with even more entering after the wand does its work. I look over every time it beeps, and I mostly just see confiscated credit cards getting deactivated and chucked in the box. Does that mean Valor can track a body with a credit card even if they're not using it? Jesus. Nobody ever mentions that in the TV ads.

A spotlight blasts on, bathing the stage in light. A thin man stands there alone before a podium, but it's clear that he's no high school principal or teacher. The dude is utterly self-possessed, oozing confidence. He's thin, wearing an overcoat and rolled jeans over boots, with the Southern version of a lumbersexual look, faded hair that's long on top but shaved on the sides and a well-kept beard; he's in his forties, probably. And he looks like he'd smile at you, so sweetly, and put ten rounds in your chest. I'm terrified of him—and fascinated by him. This must be how cobras die when they're staring at mongooses. Mongeese? Shit.

He clears his throat, and the room goes silent.

Just in time to hear the wand beep again.

"What you got, boy?" the smoky-voiced woman says tiredly.

"Nothing."

The guy at the podium sighs as if sorely aggrieved and turns to watch the proceedings, and the entire gym full of spectators does too. The kid looks to be in his twenties, beefy and utterly normal. Country-club type in yacht shoes that have never seen a yacht. He looks nervous as the guy with the gun pats him down and yanks something out of his front pocket.

"What the hell is this?"

"Looks like a phone, genius," Gabriela whispers under her breath.

"My phone," the kid says, like he's trying to act brave.

"And what brand is it, dumbass?"

"I—I don't know. My dad gave it to me. It's just a phone. Like, a normal phone."

The man at the podium leaps nimbly off the stage and stalks toward the door, his hands in his overcoat pockets. The guy with the gun throws the phone to the guy with the overcoat, who flips it open—a flip phone, really?

"Well, son, congratulations. You're the first malcontent to try to blow up our little tea party." He turns, holds the open phone toward us. "Friends, here's a little tip to ensure your longevity. Recall that Valor Savings Bank bought out Linkstream in 2009. So if you're carrying a Linkstream-branded phone, you're carrying a Valor company phone. And if you're carrying a Linkstream burner phone like this one? Well, we're going to have to assume you're either working for the enemy or too stupid to live."

The country-club kid's face is sweating like crazy, his hands up in front of him. "I didn't know, okay? It's just a phone. I'm sure my dad will—"

Overcoat guy snaps the phone in half, crushes it under his boot, whips out a gun, and shoots the kid in the chest. The pop echoes around the gym, and half the people stand up, and the other half must feel like me, cold and mesmerized and full of outrage with what the world has become. We came here for help, for community, and they're just randomly shooting kids with no warning? My face goes red-hot, and I want to scream and yell at the injustice of it. The country-club kid is on the floor now, facedown in a puddle that's become all too normal. Overcoat guy squats, pulls something out of the mess of phone guts, and holds it up.

"Oh, what do we have here? Why, it's a Valor company SD card. That means they know where this phone is, who it calls and texts, and who ends up on the camera. Now, let's see if the plot thickens." He rummages around the kid's body, and I have to look away. "Here we go! This fine young man was indeed carrying a Valor recording device." I dare to look up, and sure enough, he's holding a small black recorder. He stands and stomps it under a boot, again and again, until it's a pile of plastic. "Anybody else got a Linkstream phone or an old SD card?" The crowd whispers and rustles, folks whipping out their phones just to make sure, just in case the wand somehow missed them. No one says anything. "Well, then, I guess you all get to keep breathing tonight." As he turns and stalks back to the stage, he calls over his shoulder, "Clean that up, please."

Every eye stays with him as he hops onto the stage to stand again behind the podium as if nothing unusual has happened. My rage dissipates, and I go cold again. That kid wasn't an innocent victim at all—he worked for them. For Valor. Maybe they made him do this like they made me do worse, but I stand with the guy in the overcoat. This is the world now. You bring danger to the group, you die.

The crowd is as terrified as a flock of sheep with nowhere to run, and you could cut the tension with shears. Old women are fanning themselves, and little kids are crying. Whatever they've seen, they're still not accustomed to this kind of violence, not like I am. The man—Leon, the smoker called him—takes a long moment, watching us. Judging us. His hands finally leave his overcoat. His gun has disappeared. Tattooed knuckles wrap around the lectern.

"I'm so sorry we had to meet that way, but I'm Leon Crane. I hope you'll take care to remember this about me." He looks around the gym, meets every eye, and the moment his eyes lock on mine, it's like walking into a wall of steel. "I will kill whoever I must to keep you safe. Once you're on my side, you're my family, and I protect my family, even when it pains me to do so. I stand, now and forever, against Valor Savings and anyone who joins them in their crusade to remove the God-given freedoms of good Americans. Now tell me, friends, who here has lost a loved one to Valor's first wave of terror and anarchy?"

Every hand goes up. Every single one. All shaking. Leon nods like a preacher who feels our pain.

"So have I, friends. So have I. My cousin Lester was gunned down at his front door just a few short days ago, right in front of his young children. Now, as a veteran of the Iraq War, I know what it's like to lose a comrade in a fair fight, and I know that what we have now, with Valor Savings, is not a fair fight. Fortunately, I also know how to find the enemy. As it turns out, a certain anonymous hacking group called Incog has been on to the Valor takeover for quite some time, and when you add their technological wizardry to my talent for guerrilla warfare and blowing shit up, that means that we're one of the finest cells of the Citizens for Freedom in what's left of the United States. And I assure you, there are hundreds of other cells, like us, secretly fighting Valor together."

The bleachers creak, and an old man stands. He's wearing holsters like a damn cowboy, his thumbs tucked into his belt loops. His hand goes up, nice and slow.

Leon smiles, showing straight white teeth. "Yes, sir. How can I be of service?"

"That's all well and good, son. And thank you for your service to our country." Leon bows his head. "But I don't understand what you-all expect to gain here. Computers didn't make this land of ours free. I think we should take to the hills and wait it out."

Leon nods. "Yes, sir. Yes, sir, I can see your point there. But we do not all possess your gifts of survival. Looking at this crowd, I see widow women, old folks, and young children who've seen their parents shot in cold blood on the doorstep. Unless you're willing to support these folks in their time of need and you feel capable enough to feed, clothe, and shelter them through a brutal winter, leaving for the hills is likely to kill them, or at the very least, leave them at the mercy of Valor." Again, that grin. "And as I'm sure you'll all agree, Valor is not known for mercy."

"What exactly is it you want us to do, then?"

Leon steps around the lectern, hands in his pockets, and grins like Christmas. "I'm so very glad you asked. As it turns out, we're in contact with hundreds of other cells of the Citizens for Freedom. All across the country, Americans of every age and breed are meeting, just like we are. The fine scholars of technology are joining forces with those of us who, for all our ignorance, are pretty handy with weapons and explosives. And we're making plans." He rocks back on his heels and laughs to himself. "Oh, yes. We do have plans. And for those willing to abandon their former life and join our fight, we can promise you one thing: the chance to strike back at the company that has taken so much from you."

"And what are your qualifications, Mr. Crane?"

For just a second, Leon's smile breaks into a sneer, but he catches it quick. "That's an understandable question. No one wants to follow an unfit leader. I've lived in Candlewood all my life, as did my father and his father before him, all the way back to the War of Northern Aggression. I graduated from this very school and served my country during two tours in Iraq." He rubs his hands together, looks down, and chuckles. "Now, normally I wouldn't mention this part, but I want to be straight with y'all. After the war, I didn't much know what to do with myself, and I put some of my knowledge of explosives to use in some shady-type operations. And I got caught. But my time in prison taught me several things: how to preach the good Lord's word, how to lead men to the light, how to help the less fortunate, and how to control my anger issues. I style myself a gentleman now. A gentleman with a mission. And that mission is fighting to save the people Valor wants to enslave." He grins beatifically. "Now, does that answer your question?"

The old man nods thoughtfully and sits back down.

Leon eyes the crowd. "Anything else?"

"What if we're too old to fight?" This from an ancient woman, fat and wobbling.

Leon holds out a hand to her, as if she could take it from fifty feet away. "Every rebellion needs their Betsy Ross, my friend. We need Florence Nightingales and Harriet Tubmans. There are children without families, wounded without doctors. Helping those who can't help themselves is as true a calling as striking back at those who strike at us."

Another person stands, this one a guy in his thirties, maybe. He's disheveled and looks like he's been drinking.

"So what do we do?"

Leon smiles and throws out his arms. "All you have to do is meet us at these tables over here and help us find the best way to use your unique skills. Just like the Declaration of Independence, you sign your name and become a member of the Citizens for Freedom. Easy as that."

"And what if we don't want to join you?"

Whoever said that did not stand up. The crowd stills. Leon's eyebrows draw down, and he looks like he wishes he could call down lightning into the bleachers. His dark eyes go darker.

"If you're an unpatriotic coward who's too scared to fight Valor or support those who do, you're free to walk right out that door." He points to the open double doors where we entered. "And try not to slip on that traitor's blood on your way out." Because they took country-club kid's body away like Leon asked, but they left a big puddle of blood, which trails away into the darkness. The lantern light is gone. It's a yawning mouth into hell.

In this moment, there is no amount of money you could pay me to walk out that door, and I'm pretty sure Leon knows it.

"But I will tell you this." He's in front of the lectern now, his arms crossed and his smile wide and welcoming. "We have land. We have money. We have medicine. We have food. We have fellowship. We have weapons. And, most important, we have the fair rules and order that a free country requires to flourish. No one deserves to be murdered because they took out a loan. We hold these truths to be self-evident: that all men are created equal. And a bank, ladies and gentlemen, is not a man."

The gym erupts in applause and whistles as everyone stands. I feel it, too—a swell of pride, of fellow feeling, of belonging. Of fighting for what's right. But I'm smart enough and hardened enough to know that Leon Crane is an actor. This speech was planned. Hell, maybe that kid who died with a Valor recorder in his pocket was a plant. But everything that's happened since we walked into the school was staged to serve Leon's purpose. Whether he's good or bad or right or wrong, we have only one choice: to join him.

4.

When Leon heads for the door, the crowd follows. It's not a rush—
they clearly feel anxious and are whispering excitedly in clots. No
one wants to go first. Our little group sits back down and hunkers
together, heads almost touching.

"We're in, right?" Wyatt says.

"Not much choice there." Chance scratches the dark stubble on
his chin. "What do you figure is on the other side of the Unpatriotic
Coward doors? Execution?"

We all nod.

"He said they had medicine," Kevin says.

"What, my meds aren't good enough for you?"

Kevin takes a deep breath, as if emboldened by Leon's speech.

"No, actually. I got shot, and I'd prefer a real doctor to your stupid Vicodin before I die of gangrene." It's the most I've heard him speak yet, and he has more confidence than I would have expected. I notice for the first time that Chance didn't bring his bag of drugs, and now I'm curious about where he hid his contraband. Because he must've known they would confiscate it for the CFF if they found it on him. He's smarter than I had first assumed.

Gabriela laughs. "You get 'em, tiger," she says to Kevin.

Across the gym, they have three folding tables set up, with two people in chairs at each one and several clipboards and pens lying around. The people in the chairs look nice and friendly—they must've been chosen for their charisma. The scarier people are ranged around the room with AR-15s slung over their shoulders, fading back into the shadows against the walls so we can all pretend they aren't there. Funny how five days ago that would've completely unhinged me, and now it's the new normal.

I haven't seen anyone go through the double doors back out to the hallway yet, but as I watch, a figure detaches from the crowd and scurries that way. It's a heavy lady in her fifties, maybe, with a big bag clutched to her side. She glances around the gym before disappearing into the hall. I hold my breath as I wait to hear the pop of a gun, but there's no sound. Did they really just let her leave? What if she takes this knowledge to Valor? It's kind of scary to realize that I'd feel safer if I'd heard gunfire that signaled a problem put to rest. If she's not on our side after hearing Leon's speech or doesn't get that his offer isn't really a choice, she's definitely a threat.

I chew my lip as people leave the tables and head out into the other hallway, Leon's well-lit hallway, laughing easily. That hallway doesn't lead to where our cars are. So where are they going? When Wyatt stands, I stand too. We're about to find out.

Wyatt leads, and I slip my hand into his. Something about his size is comforting, and even though I've killed more people than he has this week, his physicality is still a shield. We're the last group to get to the table, and the small blond girl I noticed earlier trails us like a ghost. Her eyes seem dead, and something about her feels wrong to me, but everything is wrong now.

Before we get to speak to anyone, they've handed each person a clipboard and a pen. The first line is ALIAS (NOT YOUR REAL NAME. WE DON'T WANT TO KNOW.) I have no idea what to put. I've always been Patsy. I skip it and start marking off the other answers—age, prior work experience, skills. I feel like I'm filling in a job application to be James Bond. What kind of weapons can I use? Am I a computer hacker? What languages do I speak? Have I been in the army or the Police Academy? Do I have martial arts training? What is my size and build, and do I have a face that blends in? Do I have rock-climbing experience or institutional-cooking knowledge? Do I do cardio? Ugh. My answers are bland and totally forgettable, right up until it asks me how many people I've killed. Then I really have to think back.

Robert. Eloise. A rapist thug. Ashley. Dr. Belcher. Sharon. Three more rapist thugs, give or take. Alistair, kind of. That was more Wyatt. Amber. So . . . ten? Jesus.

Chance grabs my clipboard while I'm trying not to cry. "Ten? Dang, Zooey. You're a beast. I only have eight. But if Kevin dies, you get one more. Dial it up to eleven." He writes something and hands it back. In the space for my name, it says ZOOEY GODDAMN KARDASHIAN. I scribble out the last two parts, then, after a moment of annoyance, the first part. In my own writing, I put in Zooey Hemsworth and hand the clipboard to the sweet-faced blond girl at the table. Any wrong name is as good as another, right?

She scans it and turns the full force of her whitened teeth on me. "Hi, Zooey! How'd you find out about us?"

I try to remember how to smile. "Oh. Um." I look for Wyatt, for answers. But he's busy answering his own questions. "I found a flyer."

"Did one of our members approach you, or did you see it on a wall downtown, or . . . ?" She blinks, so unnaturally perky, and I suddenly don't want to tell her anything. She looks like she's maybe in her twenties—like a cheerleader for the Dallas Cowboys.

"I just saw it."

"That's great, Zooey. So did you like what you heard tonight? Leon's pretty amazing, right?"

"Sure."

"And it looks like you brought friends, so that's great."

"Uh-huh." I look away to see how Wyatt is doing. It's starting to feel like a cult. "So what's through that other door?"

She smiles, blinks, blinks again. Her face changes completely, and suddenly she's all business. "Show me your gun."

"Excuse me?"

"You said you killed ten people, and that means you got tapped by Valor or Second Union, and that means you have a gun. Probably around front, in case things got dicey tonight. You can pull it out, nice and slow, and put it on this table, or I can have Tuck and Hartness frisk you." Two big guys materialize out of nowhere, one with a pirate beard and the other covered with tattoos. Both carry guns that could turn me into a puddle of soup.

"It's in front," I mutter, slowly pulling my Valor 9mm out of my waistband.

"On the table, honey."

I give her the same flat stare she's giving me as I place my gun on the table, Valor stamp up. "Don't call me 'honey.'"

"Any more guns?" the tattooed guy asks.

I shake my head. "I only need the one."

The girl picks up my Glock and gives it a thorough inspection. On either side of me, Wyatt and Chance are going through the same process. Gabriela yanks a freaking machete out of her jacket—that I didn't know she had. Even scrawny little Kevin pulls out an apple knife.

There's a lot I don't know about these kids I spent one night and half a day with. Any one of them could've slit my throat while I was asleep.

A figure appears behind Gun Bitch Barbie, his hand on her shoulder. It's Leon Crane, and up close, by the light of the lanterns, his eyes are pools of black. "Please return this young lady's weapon. All these fine young citizens are coming with me," he says, and when she looks like she might have a comment to make, he adds, "You might recall they brought the laptops. Al's laptops."

Her smile returns as she looks up at me, my gun held out grip-first. "Lucky you."

Leon Crane walks toward the door and stops to face us, hands in his coat pockets and face inscrutable. "If the five of you will join me, I believe we have some opportunities to discuss. And some medicine for the young man with the unfortunate bullet wound." With a nod, he deliberately turns his back to us and walks out of the gym. Wyatt moves to my side, Chance scoops up Kevin, Gabriela shoves her machete back home, and Matty wags like crazy, like this is the best party ever. Tuck and Hartness move into position behind us, and we have no choice but to follow our new leader into the dark.

Well, okay, so it's not that dark. The lanterns have been moved from the other hall to this one, and old posters of atoms flutter on the walls as we pass. Leon Crane doesn't look back, and his boots are weirdly silent.

"That looks like a good dog," Tuck says, and Matty's tail wags harder.

"She is."

"I used to have a black Lab. Name was Bear. Best dog I ever had."

Crane stops and spins. "Will you ever learn the power of silence, Cousin Tuck?"

Tuck shrugs, unapologetic. "Nothing wrong with a good dog."

With a sigh, Crane rubs his temples. "Nobody talk. I'm unpleasant when I get a headache, and you're giving me one." He turns down another hall.

"Yeah, no talking," Hartness says, prodding me in the back with his assault rifle.

I flip him off. And why not? It's not against the rules.

All of the doors have been closed up until now, but one rectangle of light streaks across the dusty hall. The door is open, and the light isn't the cold, watery sting of the lanterns—it's warm and cozy, like somebody's den. Crane turns in to that one, and we step in after him. The room has all cinder-block walls, no windows, and it's not a classroom. It's the teachers' lounge, with musty couches and a few circular tables. The fridge and microwave are fossils, and the clock is stuck at six thirty. A bouquet of extension cords is plugged into a bunch of cheap, garage-sale lamps. Crane sits on the couch and throws his arms across the back.

"Sit, friends. Pull up a chair."

Wyatt and I head for one table, while Chance deposits Kevin at another. He and Gabriela bracket the poor kid, who looks like he might pass out soon, whether from pain or fear, I don't know.

Crane shakes his head. "Now, when I say pull up a chair, I do mean literally. Right up here, where we can see the whites of one another's bloodshot eyes."

We exchange glances and reluctantly do as he demands. It's Chance, Kevin, Gabriela, me, and Wyatt, all lined up in old plastic chairs in various positions of unease. I recall reading about how taking up space makes you feel more powerful, so I untangle my crossed legs and arms, spreading my legs, planting my feet, and leaning one arm over the back of my chair. The effect is mostly ruined when Matty sits between my knees and butt wiggles.

"Now, which one of you had the laptops?"

Wyatt raises a thumb, wags it between us both.

"And how did they come to be in your possession? By which I mean that whatever bullshit you told Myra is something you can skip. I'd like just the facts, if you please."

His voice is full-on Southern gentleman, slow and sweet as honey, but with the hardness of a bee's sting underneath it. Almost lulling, if there weren't such an undercurrent of menace. Avoiding his question is not an option. Wyatt looks to me.

"I got tapped by Valor. A guy named Alistair Meade was on my list. He tried to tell me he knew what was up, get me to turn off the camera, but . . ." I look down. "It was an accident. He had a gun, and we thought he was going to hurt me. He shot a warning shot, and . . ."

"So you shot him." This from Crane. It's not a question.

"It's not her fault," Wyatt blurts. "I—"

I hold up a hand. "Yeah, I did. But before he died, he told me the password to his laptops. Told me to destroy everything in his trailer. When we heard helicopters, we set it on fire. Did you know him?"

Crane's leaning forward now, elbows on his knees. He runs a hand through his wild hair. "Not as such, no. The CFF started online. Incog message boards and chatter. So we knew of him but didn't know him personally. He was a good man, though. I know that much."

"We didn't mean to kill him," I repeat, my face hot. Matty must sense my distress, as she leans hard into my leg and looks up, whining.

"But you have his computers and his password, and that's a good thing. So you tell me the password, and I'll see about finding you a new life."

I glance at Wyatt and the other kids. "All of us?"

"Well, now. That depends. How'd you-all get thrown in together?"

Chance sighs and leans back, one long boot up on his knee. "I got tapped by Valor too. My sister came with me. When I shot the kid's parents, he didn't have anywhere to go, so he tagged along."

"And?" Crane's eyes dart meaningfully from them to us.

"Valor didn't live up to their half of the deal once I'd finished my list. Burned my house down. My parents, too. So we ran. And picked the wrong abandoned building as home base."

"Who shot the kid?"

Everyone stares at me, and I reluctantly raise my hand. "I thought he was going for a gun."

"I was scratching myself," Kevin mutters under his breath. "Bitch."

Leon Crane stands and paces, looking us each up and down. "So what I see before me are desperate youth. Two are survivors, killers willing to do whatever it takes. Two of you are loyal. And one of you is a victim who's still got spunk. Well, that's what I like to see. Because I'm going to let you in on a little secret, friends. The CFF can use you. And considering you're now homeless, without resources, and cash poor, I think you could use us."

"I just want more drugs," Kevin moans. With a dramatically childish sigh, he flops against Gabriela.

"Use us how?" she asks, full-up with sass.

Leon smiles at her. "What's your name, darlin'?"

Gabriela smiles back, just as saccharine. "My real name or my play name?"

Leon's face goes flat like a shark. "Your real name is now flagged in every government and bank database in the country. So pick something that sounds nice, sweetheart, and start practicing your new signature."

"Then I guess my name is Ida B. Houston."

"Ida B. Houston, I suggest a mutually beneficial arrangement. Now, what you lot are missing are the basics of life. Shelter, food, something to do. Safety. For him, medicine. We got all of those. I won't say in abundance, but we got enough. We'll give you each some money to get started, get some clothes and niceties and a solid tent. You ever heard of Crane Hollow?"

I nod, remembering how uncomfortable Wyatt had looked the first time we drove past the back country compound, with its towing business, deer-processing facilities, and notary public.

Oh. Of course. It makes sense now. Leon Crane is a Crane from Crane Hollow.

"How come you get to keep your name?" I ask.

He holds up both hands and wiggles his fingers. "As far as Valor knows, darlin', I died in jail. My fingerprints don't match a damn thing. Crane Hollow was paid off so long ago that we're not even a blip on the bank's radar. So don't you worry about me."

I just nod like I'm giving him permission to go on. He tips an imaginary hat.

"Now, the Crane family has sixty-three acres of land, mostly forest. We got just a few dozen folks there now, mostly family and friends, but I expect our numbers will grow pretty quick after our first meeting here tonight."

"And what do we have to do to earn our spot in Crane Hollow?"

This from Chance, who's got to be even more desperate than I am but somehow makes it look like he could get up and walk out the door at any moment if he doesn't like Leon's offer.

Crane and Chance enjoy a swift staring contest, and Crane looks down first and chuckles. "You got balls, boy. And anybody who survives five days with Valor has the skills to go with those balls. Not only that, but you've got yourself a partner you can trust, which was a rare enough thing in life before things went to shit. Same for this little girl and her man." A chin nod to me and Wyatt. "We want you to do to Valor what Valor had you doing to regular citizens." He lets the silence spin out so long that Tuck and Hartness shift and sigh behind us.

"And what's that?" Chance says.

Crane's smile is as honest and sweet as can be.

"Kill bad guys and blow shit up," he says.

5.

Whatever reaction Crane was hoping to see, he just gets tense silence.

"What, you kids don't like blowing shit up? I thought everybody liked that sort of thing."

"I don't want to hurt anybody," I say. Matty whines her support. Crane looms over me, and I look up, uncowed.

"We don't want to hurt people, Zooey. That's Valor's game. We want to hurt Valor."

"Uh, didn't you say 'kill bad guys and blow shit up,' Leon?"

His smile is all angry teeth. "That I did, darlin'. But I mean kill the sort of suit who showed up at your house and threatened to murder your family and kick your puppy. I want to hurt the bastards running Valor, who are forcing good, innocent people to do their dirty work for them. Did you know they infiltrated the police and executed every police officer in the country who wasn't agreeable to the terms of the hostile takeover? You seen a sheriff's car or an ambulance in the last six days? You know most hospital doctors are being held hostage, reserved for helping Valor's people and denied from helping anyone else? Whatever you've seen of what Valor's willing to do, they're secretly doing worse."

My stomach feels like icy swamp water, a hard ball of acid. I haven't seen a sheriff's car or an ambulance. I haven't seen any police. I don't want to believe him, and I don't want to believe that it's possible, but . . . it's got the tang of Valor about it, doesn't it? Leaving us helpless.

"What do you want us to do *exactly*?" Wyatt asks. Crane sits again, leaning forward with the sort of grin that says he knows he's going to win us over. "That all depends, son. If you sign over your allegiance, I'd be happy to give you details. I can tell you that tonight I'm going to give each of you a loaded gift card to get whatever you need to wear, eat, and whack off to. And I'm going to take the young man with the bullet wound to a clinic and get that injury dressed. Hell, I'll even give your dog a box of Milk-Bones. But first I need to know you're on my side."

The silence stretches out. Chance is the only one who has the balls to say, "And what if we're not?"

Leon's shrug is a lion's stretch. "I think you know. If you're not with us, you're against us. You think that lady made it back to her car tonight?"

"It's the goddamn shining wires," Chance says, and we all stare at him. "*Watership Down*? Cowslip? The shining wires? How the rabbits get free food, but one of 'em gets eaten by the farmer every month?" We all stare blankly. "Jesus, read a book. I just mean that smart traps look like havens." When no one says anything, he leans back and adds, "Cultureless apes, the lot of you."

Leon snorts. I'm not sure when I went from thinking of him as Crane to thinking of him as Leon, but it probably has something to do with the fact that I don't want to think of him as my boss. As "Mr. Crane."

"Allow me to adjust your attitude, son. Your school told you America was a republic or a democracy, right? Well, that bullshit was never true, and now it's gone. There is no president, no Congress, no Senate. It's just the Valor board of directors and a whole lot of firepower. So either you vote for them, or you vote for us. You've seen what they'll make you do, and you know how you're rewarded for following their orders. Sticks in your craw, don't it? Wouldn't you rather see how it tastes, working for the other side? Don't you want to fight those bastards? Or, as you say, to turn their snares against them?"

"I don't want to fight anybody," Gabriela says. "I just want to be normal."

"You have to fight for somebody or die doing nothing. That's what normal means. Now, are you in or out?" Crane's eyebrows rise into his hairline as he waits for an answer.

No one speaks. I try to breathe. After everything I've done, after everything I've been through in the last week, after everything I know about Valor, there's no way I'm going to give up now. I don't want to fight, but I don't want to die.

"I'm in," I say.

Leon Crane smiles like the devil and hands me a clipboard and a pen.

We walked in like this: Patsy, Gabriela, Kevin, Cianci-now-Chance, and Wyatt.

We walk out as Zooey, Ida, Clark, Chance-for-real-now, and . . .

I nudge Wyatt in the ribs. "Hank Cobain?"

He blushes. "Henry Rollins and Kurt Cobain are my heroes. So sue me." He sticks out his chin. "It's very punk rock, thank you very much."

"I don't have a lawyer, and that might or might not be adorable."

He nudges me back, and I'm forced to giggle. "Yeah, well, I don't take shit from a girl whose fake last name is Hemsworth. Ooh, Thor, you're so *dreamy*."

We signed away our loyalty using fake names, and Leon kept the clipboard. I don't really get how signing a fake name with a fake signature can be in any way legally or emotionally binding, but if the only other option is to get shot in an old high school gym, I'll sign anything they ask.

Leon's last words were, "If you'll be so kind as to wait a moment, I'll get you your prize."

Which still feels a little like we might get shot.

Tuck and Hartness glance at each other, shrug, and start fussing over Matty. I guess we're all on the same side now? Chance and Gabriela have a furious whispering match, and Kevin—I'm assuming he wants to feel like Clark Kent, but there's no way I can call him that—collapses on the couch looking like he might die at any moment. If nothing else, I'm glad he signed, because that boy needs real medicine that we have no way of getting him. Every time I look at him, I want to throw up. I was so proud that Valor hadn't changed me, but as soon as I was free of Valor, I went and shot some innocent little kid. At least my mom will never know. Or my dad.

"Who wants a credit card?" The perky blond girl who interrogated me stands in the doorway holding a fan of random plastic cards and wearing a huge, knowing smile, like she's smug about us joining the cause.

"I just want antibiotics," Kevin whines.

"Uh, aren't credit cards why we're in this mess?" I say.

She rolls her eyes and hands each of us a card. They're not, like, name-stamped credit cards. They're those gift cards that come pre-loaded with cash and don't require ID. Mine has balloons on it and wishes me a happy birthday.

"How much is on this?" Wyatt asks.

I know I'm supposed to think of him as Hank now, but I refuse. If I'm fighting to stay Patsy, then I'm rooting for him to stay Wyatt, too.

"About five hundred to start off with," the girl says, like it's no big deal. "We have a back door into the system and just keep loading them up. You can't buy a car or anything, but you should be cool for a tent, clothes, food, whatever. We do communal meals at the Hollow, but stock up on nonperishable snack foods. Sometimes dinner sucks."

"Uh, okay," Gabriela says, staring at her card like it might bite her. "Free money. That sounds like it doesn't come with strings attached."

The blond girl ignores her. "Go shopping and bring your tent to the Hollow. You guys know how to get to Crane Road, right?" We all nod—it's famous in our town. "Just turn like you're going to the deer-processing barn and keep driving down the dirt road. You'll know when to stop. We'll show you where to set up and brief you in the morning. Oh, and this kid's coming with me." She inclines her head toward Kevin, who looks to Gabriela with wide, worried eyes.

"What are you going to do to him?" Gabriela asks.

The blond girl smiles. "Give him medicine and a bed, if that's okay with you. I'm a registered nurse. Unless you want to take a kid with a gunshot wound to the Shop N Save for some Band-Aids?"

"I'm going with him," Gabriela says.

Chance nods. "Make me a list."

She snorts and gives him her card but looks to me. "I'm a size thirteen. Get me whatever you get yourself. And a warm coat. And some Pop-Tarts and Gatorade."

With a determined nod, Gabriela stands to help Kevin off the couch. When he almost falls over, the blond girl takes his other arm, and they head for the door.

"Feel better!" I call after them, and Gabriela glances over her shoulder at me like I'm an idiot.

"We'll take care of the dog for you," Tuck says. When his huge, tattooed hand takes the rope leash, his rifle brushes against me, and my fingers jerk open. "You can't take a dog into the store, right?" He laughs.

Hartness adds, "Be sure to get your own dog food and a bowl while you're shopping. You all know the way out?"

I watch Matty trot beside them and out the door as if I didn't even exist. Just like she came to me when I shot her owner, my uncle Ashley, on his doorstep. I feel cold and empty without her, and I turn to Wyatt and bury my face in his chest.

"You think they'll be okay?" he asks, as low and angry as I feel.

Chance shrugs. "If they're not, we'll use the card to buy a gas can and set their stupid Hollow on fire."

He's trying to look tough, but I can see the fear in his eyes. They have Gabriela now too.

Looks like our new bosses, just like Valor, can hold the ones we love hostage to keep us in line. Except the Cranes give you a friendly smile while they cock their guns.

All the cars from earlier are gone, except for a shiny Audi and a new Ford Explorer with a sticker of flip-flops in the back window. Bet I know who that one belongs to. Wonder what they'll do with the cars left behind by the traitor and the deserter. Considering that the Crane family seems to own just about every kind of practical rural business there is, I'm guessing they'll end up on a Crane used-car lot or neatly sold for parts next week. Just like with Valor, getting rid of deadweight comes with unexpected gains.

I call shotgun, only belatedly realizing how lame that sounds now, and Chance sits in the middle of the backseat and pulls his duffel bag from under my seat, checking that his drugs are still there, I guess.

"Big Choice okay?" Wyatt says.

"Whatever," Chance and I say at the same time.

Wyatt turns left. "It's closest. You guys agree we need to hurry back before they assimilate our friends and dog?"

"Yeah, nerd. Let's keep the hillbilly Borg from giving your dog too many treats," Chance says. But he doesn't say anything about Gabriela and Kevin, which I'm learning means he's worried about them.

Big Choice looks so different when we have two thousand dollars to spend. We each take a cart and stop by a Thanksgiving display. The boys look at me expectantly, like my fallopian tubes make me an expert shopper.

I sigh. "Look, it's easy. We need tents, sleeping bags, flashlights, knives. Backpacks. Deodorant. Coats. Socks. Underwear. Boy Scout shit. Go."

Wyatt manages to look sheepish. "Uh. So. Do you want your own tent, or . . . ?"

I blush and join him in staring at the ground. "Not really." I spin and walk away, pushing my cart fast.

I head for the women's section and pick out the least offensive underwear in my size and Gabriela's size, plus pajamas, extra socks, fleece jackets, leggings and stretchy jeans, tees, long-sleeved shirts, knitted hats, hoodies, all in black, and two black puffer coats off the sale rack. I get myself a pair of slip-on shoes and try to remember what kind of shoes Gabriela was wearing. She didn't tell me her shoe size, and I can't remember. Crap. I hope her current shoes don't have holes.

I buy a big-ass bag of dog food and a bowl and a new leash and collar. In the health and beauty section, I get replacement packs of the same face wipes I stocked my mail truck with before going on my first mission to kill Wyatt's dad. I get fingertip toothbrushes and floss and mouthwash, a brush and rubber bands and deodorant and coconut-scented body spray and lotion—double everything, because Gabriela's got to feel as crappy as I do. And maxi pads, because I can't imagine how bad it would be for either of us to start bleeding in a tent in the middle of nowhere. Being a girl sucks even more in the apocalypse.

And then I do something insane. Something I would never have considered doing just a week ago. Something I wouldn't want my mom to accidentally find out about. Something daring.

I buy a box of condoms.

Because it's the end of the world, I have a boyfriend, and I don't think I want to die a virgin. An old man glances at me from the fiber and stool softener section, and I stubbornly stick out my chin . . . and hide the box under the coats in my cart.

In the food section, I grab crap. All crap. Pop-Tarts and granola bars and peanut butter crackers and Gatorade. Snack cakes and cookies and animal crackers in a giant plastic jar shaped like a bear. Since I know the guys will forget it, I slam a twelve-pack of toilet paper on top. I'm sure I've forgotten half the things I should be getting, and as I stand in the aisle biting my lip, I remember one thing. One small thing. Just for me.

The guys are arguing over tents as I hurry by without a word, straight to the craft section. I get a roll of knitting needles with all sizes, even rounds. Pawing through the yarn, I choose soft things and cheap things and bright things and speckled things, but nothing in that damning Valor blue that should've been a tropical teal but somehow ended up cold and ugly. I stop in front of the embroidery, but you can't hang samplers on tents. The last thing I get is a couple of backpacks on sale from the back-to-school section so Gabriela and I have a place to keep all our clothes. It's all we have now.

The guys are in line, looking smug and easy. I guess they solved whatever they were arguing about, and they each have a full cart. Perched on top of Wyatt's cart is a stuffed green turtle with big, goofy eyes like Ping-Pong balls. Which means he remembers that my stuffed-turtle collection died in the truck fire, which is possibly the sweetest thing on earth.

"Thought you might need some company," he says, and my heart wrenches.

I can't say thanks without crying, so I just wipe my eyes and hug him.

Outside of my turtle, everything else he has makes sense, including a portable plastic aquarium for his snake. I know we're missing a million things that we won't think about until we're squatting in the tent, but at least he remembered two sleeping bags and a two-pack of pillows. His stuff adds up to four hundred and something, and we all go tense as he swipes the card.

"Can you put in your passcode, sir?" the cashier says.

Wyatt gulps. "Uh. I . . . uh . . ."

We just stand there staring at each other, and the lady looks toward a stand where a thick-built dude in a manager's jacket is watching us, one hand on his radio.

The skin on the back of my neck prickles, and I look around at the other people waiting in line to check out. It's mostly men, and they all look guarded. They're staring at us like we might be trouble. Black holsters peek out from under their shirts, and they constantly glance at one another and the doors as if waiting for a shoot-out. Most people are alone. There's not a single child. Maybe Chance wasn't that off when he said it was turning into the Wild West. People have to have food and toilet paper and aspirin, but no one is sending out a pregnant wife with a little kid to fetch it, either. There's no polite conversation, no friendly banter. Just tense silence and carts overloaded with necessities.

"Just run it as credit, idiot," Chance says. He reaches past us to the machine, hits cancel, and presses credit. It goes through, no problem, and I try to look cool and not like I expected Valor SWAT to burst through the door.

I'm next, and mine is more than seven hundred. The lady gives me a pained look when I run my card. "Sorry, honey. There's only five hundred and fifty on there. How else would you like to pay?"

My face goes hot, and I start doing mental calculations about what to put back when Chance slides another card through. "You got my sister's stuff, right? Here's her card."

That card goes through fine, and once Chance is up, our cashier chews her gum like cud and says, "You kids got one of them festivals or something? We're selling lots of tents lately. Seems like a dangerous time to be out in the woods, what with the crime wave."

"We're just going camping with some friends," Chance says. He starts bagging his stuff up so we can get the hell out before we have to tell a bunch of stupid lies to someone who has no idea that she's not an American anymore. Valor must be hiding what they're doing from the media, or else she'd know exactly why we have survival gear.

A crime wave? That's what they're saying? Scared people will believe anything.

"Have fun. Watch out for bears." She's still chewing, hands on her hips, as we push our carts out.

I'm putting my bags in Wyatt's trunk when a guy gets out of a black sedan across the lot. In between the darkness and the credit card panic during checkout, I forgot to look for suits. In this country town, unless it's prom weekend or you're going to a funeral, there's only one reason to wear a slick black suit. I go cold all over and turn around, pulling my gun out from my waistband and holding it low behind my back as Chance follows my line of sight and mutters, "Shit."

But the guy just walks past us, checking his phone. No sunglasses, no ear wire. Probably not even Valor, then. Or maybe off duty. He didn't even look at me. But, well, I'm not special, am I? Just another dumb kid until I pull out my gun.

"You've got money left on Gabriela's card, right?" I ask Chance.

He eases his gun back into his jeans. "Yeah. Why?"

"Because I don't want to eat whatever they're serving at Leon's house."

The drive to Crane Hollow is quiet, the car filled with the scent of burgers and fries. I'm worried about Matty, worried about Gabriela and Kevin, worried about what a rebel camp on Leon's land is going to be like. We pass the road to my house, and my throat goes tight. The sky is dark and cloudy, but I still look for smoke. If Chance did what they asked and they still burned his house down and killed his parents, what are they going to do to my mom once they realize I opted out? Shit. I pull down the mirror and barely recognize myself. I look like I've been to war, like I'm haunted. Like I killed ten people this week, most of them innocent.

"We won't let them hurt you," Chance says, quiet.

My head jerks up. "What?"

"I'm just saying . . . I know we started off on the wrong foot when you shot my orphan, but whatever's happening in Crane Hollow, you and Gabriela don't go anywhere alone. I don't trust that guy." He scoffs. "Leon Crane. Who names a kid Leon?"

"The notary public married to a deer butcher," Wyatt says. He glances at me in the half-light. "And he's right. You need to stay close. After those guys . . ." He trails off. I don't know if he's referring to the IT robbers who tried to rape me in the back of my truck or the thugs at Sherry's house, and it doesn't matter. Men are desperate now, and there are no laws.

But I don't want to sound like a damsel, so I say, "Whatever. I'll just shoot anybody who gives me trouble. It's worked so far."

We turn onto Crane Road at a light, and there's a stark difference between the busy, well-lit highway and the curvy country road. There are no streetlights, and the grass is high on the shoulders, with heavy forest and barbed-wire fences in various stages of slow death along the sides. It's always looked like this—like anyone who isn't a Crane is unwelcome. If we kept driving down this road and made a few more turns, we'd end up at Alistair's trailer—or the ashes of it. Instead, we turn at a collection of ramshackle mailboxes covered in NO TRESPASSING signs and bump along the dirt and gravel road toward the scattered buildings of Crane Hollow.

6.

A figure steps from the woods to block our car's path. A big guy with a big gun. It could be Tuck or Hartness, but it's not. The Cranes must have an inexhaustible supply of huge, scary-looking cousins. Wyatt stops the car, and the guy comes around to the window.

"You miss the signs?" he says, unfriendly-like, stubby finger on the trigger.

"Leon invited us."

The guy nods like he already knew that. "Go on past the barn. Park in the field and head up to the house." As Wyatt rolls up his window, the guy gives a small smile and says, "You got a good dog."

And I know they weren't going to eat Matty, but I needed to hear that, that the Citizens for Freedom or the Cranes for Fucking

Up Shit or whatever they call themselves—that they're still human and can smile. I would thank him, but he's melted back into the woods and we're passing the barn and bumping into a huge field. It's got to be at least ten acres, with cars neatly parked at one end and rows of tents at the other end.

"I always wanted to go to Coachella," Wyatt says.

"You still play bass?" Chance asks.

"I did, yeah."

Silence falls. Hobbies are a luxury we don't necessarily have anymore. Even my guerrilla knitting serves a purpose.

"Maybe the rednecks will lend us some banjos," Chance adds grimly.

Which, to be honest, pisses me off a little. I can't help thinking about Jeremy, about how he proudly called himself a redneck right up until the end but would dive into a fight with any stranger who tried to use the term against him. Whatever his family situation, he was a good person, a good friend. Is it fair for me to think of the Cranes as rednecks if I was constantly chiding Jeremy for using terms like "fag" and "retarded"? And even if they act like what I grew up thinking a redneck was, they still own more land and resources than my mom and I ever did, so technically, they're more successful. How can I point fingers at anyone when I'm the one with innocent blood on my hands? They might be country, but I'm a monster.

"How about you don't call them 'rednecks' again?" I say.

"You want to hear what guys like them called guys like me in juvie?" he shoots back.

"How about we remember that everyone's packing heat and just act polite?" Wyatt says softly.

He parks in line, and we get out and stand there. The field is silent. There are no lights, and no one is here to meet us. A bobwhite calls, somewhere in the forest, and Wyatt pops the trunk, hunts around, and hands me my new puffer coat.

"You look cold."

I smile and go up on my tiptoes to kiss him on the cheek, and it's still new enough to make him blush. We've been together for less than a week, but it feels like forever.

"Blech," Chance mutters. "I'll take my chance with the Cranes."

When he heads for the main house, we follow, leaving our bags behind for now. It looks like a plantation house that no one wants to fix but everyone wants to add on to, white with four crooked columns out front and wings that just keep on going in different kinds of wood and metal. Chickens roost on a ladder behind a wire fence, their chicken house a replica of the big one and, honestly, better kept. A sharp bark becomes an orchestra of dogs, and the screen door bangs open. A pack of hounds bursts out, and Matty runs for me, yipping joyously. I squat to hug her and fend off her licks. The other dogs just jump around and bark like idiots. Tuck stands on the porch holding a fried chicken leg, and Gabriela walks out to meet us, her arms crossed.

"About damn time," she says.

"Yeah, well, we had a lot of shopping to do," Chance says, his voice high and careless with relief as he hugs her.

"Where's the goods?"

Chance inclines his head toward the car, and Gabriela jumps down and hurries toward it. We struggle to catch up.

"Everything okay?" Chance asks quietly.

Gabriela shakes her head. "Yeah, sure. Bunch of angry white folks eating KFC in their camo hats and talking about football. It's awesome. I totally fit in. By which I mean nobody talked to me and one old lady told me coloreds had to use the other bathroom. Please tell me you got the Pop-Tarts."

I paw through the bags and help her parse her stuff into the backpack I bought for her. She doesn't seem excited, but who gets excited about pastel cotton underwear? The coat fits and she's glad for the hoodie, at least. She tries to put on the hat, but her fro-hawk is too big to fit under it—but at least it gets her to laugh. When she sees the Pop-Tarts—that's when she finally thanks me.

As she tears into a packet, I make sure to shuttle the condoms discreetly into my backpack. Matty's leaping around us, and I put the new collar and leash on her and tell her how pretty she looks. The guys shoulder the tent boxes and whatever else they can carry and head for the tent city. When we get closer, we see the blond clipboard girl waiting out front wearing the same big, fake smile.

"Okay, so you can set up wherever you want, but you can see that we're avoiding the ditch and the cars. The porta-potties are over there, and the well is over there. So just pick a place, set up, and come on up to the house." She turns around and walks away, then stops and looks back. "Oh, and don't worry about thieves or anything. Thieves get punished in Crane Hollow."

"Uh, how?" Chance asks.

She smiles sweetly. "I think you can guess." And then she's gone.

"We're pitching our tents close together, right?" Gabriela says.

"Better the devil you know." Chance readjusts the tent box and keeps walking.

Watching boys argue and set up tents is boring and annoying, so Gabriela, Matty, and I head up to the house to check on Kevin.

"How's he doing?" I ask.

She exhales through her nose. "I don't know. They wouldn't let me upstairs. Said he was with 'the doc,' but I never saw anybody that looked like a doctor. This house is crazy. The clinic and the head honchos are up on the second floor, and they guard the staircase all the time. There are a few bedrooms downstairs, but most folks are in trailers out back or in tents. They've got chickens, goats, pigs. It's like its own little city. Like . . . Backwoods Disney World."

The wood porch steps creak, and Hartness holds the door open. "Welcome home, ladies. Dinner's in the kitchen, and they're waiting for you in the study." He looks past us, puzzled. "Where's your boys?"

"Tent duty." Gabriela hooks her thumb through her belt next to her machete.

Hartness laughs. "More chicken for me, I reckon."

"Where's Kevin?"

"Who?"

"The kid who came in with me. The one who got shot."

Hartness scratches his beard. "Didn't see any kid. Ask Heather."

Gabriela's eyes shoot meaningfully to mine. I can almost feel her thinking, *See?*

She nods to him, and he pats Matty as we pass. It's claustrophobic in here, all dark wood floors and narrow halls. Gabriela leads me past the kitchen, and I am definitely glad I bought a bunch of trash food, because it looks like a place where they cook possum stew in rusty cauldrons. A few older women with home perms and claw bangs stare at us and mutter under their breath, and we hurry down a different hall.

We pass a narrow sunroom with a long table full of people who look enough like Leon Crane for us to assume they belong here. Crane men seem to come in two types: whip thin with huge eyes or bouncer sized with beards. People are everywhere, in every room, eating on the floor and waiting in line for a bathroom that doesn't look much better than squatting outside. You can tell who's kin and who's a new member of the CFF—the folks who fit in are as comfortable as an old couch, while the new recruits are nervy and sleep-less, their eyes looking us up and down and their chicken-greasy hands constantly going for their guns.

At the stairs, we find the blond girl, Heather, eating a limp salad from a KFC container. Before she can stand, Gabriela pushes into her space and asks, "Where's the kid?"

Heather dabs her mouth with a napkin and smiles. "Upstairs, asleep. We gave him something to help him relax. You ever had a bullet wound reopened and disinfected? Hurts like a bitch."

"Can we see him?"

She shakes her head. "Tomorrow. We don't usually let new recruits upstairs until they've proven their loyalty."

"We're here," I say. "Isn't that enough?"

"Signing a fake name, spending our money, and showing up to a safe haven doesn't prove loyalty, honey. We're going to do the debriefing in the morning, so get some food and some sleep and come up to the porch when you're awake. Got it?"

Gabriela puts a foot on the bottom stair, and Heather's arm shoots out, striking bone on bone and making me wince. Heather's eyes narrow to snake slits, and she's not a Barbie anymore. "Look, I'd love to throw down, and I got ten cousins just aching to shoot their rifles, so I suggest you play by our fucking rules."

"Thought we were getting inducted tonight?" Gabriela says, her face hard. "Leon said—"

Heather's smile returns, sweet and deadly. "Business is happening upstairs. Leon's not available. Tomorrow's close enough. Go to bed."

Gabriela is breathing hard through her nose like a bull, so I put a hand on her shoulder. "C'mon. More Pop-Tarts. It's fine. He's fine. All right?"

Heather shoves salad into her mouth. "Don't forget we're the good guys, okay?"

Gabriela doesn't budge, so I grab her arm and haul her away. Matty dances around us, getting us tangled in her leash like this is the best walk ever and we're not all tense as hell.

Heather's reassurances don't make me feel any better, but this is the first day this week that I haven't shot anybody, and I'd like to keep up that streak. Walking away is the only option.

We approach the tent city with Matty wagging like crazy. I am not wagging. Tents feel so flimsy, and I've never been camping or wanted to go camping. There are dozens of campsites in all shapes and sizes, but they're zipped up tight. Very few people are outside, and it feels very cold, almost distrustful. This is where Valor leaves us—terrified of strangers. I don't even know how to find Wyatt and Chance, considering I didn't look at the tents they bought.

"Hey, ladies!"

Chance waves from between two big, clean-looking tents on the edge of the grid. When Wyatt ducks out of the door of one, Matty barks joyously and strains toward him, probably expecting French fries to fall out of his pockets. He holds back the flap proudly to show that he's arranged the two-room tent with two sleeping bags, pillows, and extra blankets. My new turtle, my backpack, and all my Big Choice stuff are arranged to the side. Monty is coiled in a ball in his new plastic cage beside a ridiculous plastic palm tree.

"Home sweet home," I say, nudging Matty aside and collapsing on my pallet.

"You guys see the kid?"

I flop down and immediately feel my gun biting into my back, not to mention the rocks and bumps poking through the sleeping bag. My bed at home was lumpy, and the cot in my mail truck was flimsy, but this is downright inhospitable. I sit back up and slide the gun under my pillow. Just like old times.

"Nope. They said we weren't allowed upstairs. Gabriela wanted to kick some ass."

"I think you mean whoop some ass. Or pull out a can of whoop ass? And aren't we supposed to use our new names?"

I rub my eyes and groan. "I keep trying to think of everyone by their new names, but . . . it's like my brain refuses. It feels like Leon is trying to force us into being new people. Just like Valor did. I can't think of myself as Zooey, and I'm definitely not calling you 'Hank.' I'm not changing who I am just because some crazy dude made me sign something."

Wyatt gets Matty settled down with a bowl of dog food before moving over to my sleeping bag. He gives me what can only be called a smoldering look and says, "You know you want to call me 'Hank,' baby."

I can't help it. I have to giggle. "It's a horrible word. Like a hank of hair? Look, I'll make you a deal. You don't ever call me 'baby' again, and I'll try to call you 'Hank' when it matters." I pull him to me with the scarf I knitted for him and lean close, my lips to his ear. "But I'll be thinking about Wyatt."

His breath catches, and he gives a gratifying little shiver. "As long as you're thinking of me, I think I'll be okay." His eyes meet mine, and his head tilts just so, and I lick my lips and wait for him to kiss me for the first time since I asked him to kill me. But he doesn't. "Don't move." He puts Matty's food bowl on the opposite side of the tent, and when she follows it, wagging, he zips up the partition. And then he's beside me again, so close, his fingertips brushing a lock of hair behind my ear.

It's soft at first, a brush of his lips against mine, a hand gently cupping my jaw, a thumb smoothing over my cheek. I start to melt and soften, the stress draining out and replaced with a floaty warmth and a flip in my stomach. I wanted so much for this to be what we were, to know that what we said and felt while on the run wasn't just pheromones and fear talking. I've wanted so badly to know that he could look at me as the Patsy I was last Monday and not this Zooey thing who can kill and walk away, who cries at night when everyone else is asleep, who only voices her confidence and never the regrets eating her alive. I need to know that when he sees me, he doesn't see the girl who murdered his dad but the girl who risked everything to save his brother. We both know my mother's life is forfeit now. I hope that makes us even. But we don't ever speak of it. And I don't want to feel it right now, so I don't.

With a soft sigh, I turn my head and let him open my lips with his tongue. Let his hand trace gently down my neck and shoulder to my waist, to a place that used to tickle but now makes me want to press into him, to pull him down with me, to let him pin me to the ground. And then I do, because I'm no longer able to bank on future pleasures. I'm no longer willing to be the girl who waits.

For a big guy, Wyatt is careful not to hurt me, taking his weight on his knees and elbows as he settles over my body with tender ferocity. My hands roam over his chest with new bravery, running through his shaggy blond hair and down his back and gently scratching up under his shirt. He groans and plants kisses down my neck, and I start kicking off my shoes, and that's when Matty starts barking and someone says, "Knock-knock, lovebirds!" so close that I have no choice but to remember that we're in a tent with fabric walls.

Wyatt pulls away and resettles his clothes, and I sit cross-legged and try to rake my filthy hair into some semblance of decency.

"Come in, asshole," he grumbles.

The zipper reveals Chance, because of course it's Chance. I want to punch his amused grin, but then Gabriela pops up beside him looking worried.

"War council?" Chance says.

Wyatt holds up a welcoming arm. "Fine. War council."

Chance's nose wrinkles up. "It stinks of pre-sex in here."

Wyatt punches his arm for me.

They step in and settle down on Wyatt's sleeping bag, and Matty scratches at the partition until Chance unzips it so she can flop down for belly rubs. With great ceremony, Gabriela puts an iPod on the ground and turns on some pop music. Her face is stern as she points to the diminishing battery icon. Whatever we're going to talk about here is so important that she's willing to spend her last minutes of music hiding our voices from the other denizens of the tent city. All four of us lean in, so close that our hair touches.

"So we all agree that we've basically gone from the frying pan into the fire, right?" Chance starts, and everyone nods. "But we also agree that there's nothing else for us to do right now?" More nods. "But we don't trust Leon, Heather, or any of these inbred jagoffs?" Another nod. "So what, then, is our play?"

"We have to get to Kevin. Clark. Whatever. I don't trust them," Gabriela says.

Wyatt's head jerks up. "You think they're hurting him?"

"No. But I don't think they're being totally honest with us, and I'm not going to relax until I know he's okay. Until I've seen him without any Crane goons around."

"Relax. That's funny." I shake my head. "How can we relax when we can't trust anybody?"

"I trust you guys," Chance says, and the cool-guy mask drops for a moment. "I don't want to sound like a dick, but if you go through what we went through . . ." He points to me. "Or if you stick with us and help us . . ." He points to Wyatt and Gabriela. "Then I think the best you can hope for is to stay together and pick up other people you can trust, one by one if need be. Build a new family."

"You watch too much *Walking Dead*, dude." Wyatt shakes his head.

"Yeah, I did. And that means I understand that when something seems too good to be true, it probably is. They gave us two thousand dollars tonight without a second thought." He meets my eyes, and it's like looking into an abyss. "They're going to want us to pay them back somehow."

When Gabriela's iPod finally dies, they go to bed. Wyatt politely turns his back to me while I clean up with wipes as best I can. I haven't showered since killing Ken Belcher at Château Tuscano, and if I don't find a place to pee soon, I'm going to explode. Life in Valor

Country isn't comfortable, and I start frantically counting days in my head when I remember that being a girl gets extra messy once a month. I read once that when Sally Ride was getting ready to go into space for a week, they asked her if one hundred tampons would be enough, and I tell myself that if she can deal with a stupid government and the betrayal of her own menstrual cycle, then I can, too. I should be safe for two weeks, and if not, that's why I bought maxi pads. And if I shoot anyone else who doesn't deserve it, the pads will probably be good for soaking up blood.

"Uh, I don't know if you need to go do anything, but I didn't know if there would be bathrooms, so I bought you these," Wyatt says, looking horribly embarrassed in the lantern light as he holds up a can of bleach wipes and a packet of baby wipes.

"Gross, and thank you so much, and God, yes."

He leads me to the line of porta-potties and stands guard, and it's as horrible as you can imagine.

It takes me a long time to go to sleep. Not because Matty grumbles and sleep wags, her tail thumping against my leg. Not because Wyatt snores, although he does. And not because I feel exposed as hell in this field, well aware that a Valor helicopter or Hummer full of suits could drive up at any moment and shoot us like fish in a nylon barrel.

It's because I keep seeing everyone I've killed every time I close my eyes. Like my brain is giving me a highlight reel of the last week, of each person's face flashing in surprise as I pull the trigger. Bob, Eloise, some burglar, Ashley, Sherry, two rapist thugs, Dr. Ken Belcher, Amber. I remember Jeremy's bloody sputters as I held him in the frost-covered field, the sick reek of my best friend's insides oozing out. Their faces won't stop staring at me, their wet eyes going flat and damning. I'm the little spoon to Wyatt's big spoon inside the sleeping bag, and I'm tucked in like a shrimp, my hands numb and shaking, my finger curled permanently around a trigger that I never wanted to pull. Again and I again, I flash through their faces like a book that never closes.

"Shh. It's okay." Wyatt resettles around me, awake now, his arm hugging more protectively around my hollow middle and his chin settling over my messy, dirty hair. "Bad dream?"

"This whole thing is a bad dream," I say. "I never wanted any of this. I don't want to do this, be this thing, this monster. What if Leon just uses me to kill? When do I stop being a person and become someone else's weapon? I can't do it. I don't want this."

"No one did. It's not your fault. It's over." He plants gentle kisses on my head, my ear, the top of my cheek.

I shake him off, but sweetly.

"That's the thing. I don't think it is. Over." I shudder and wipe my tears off on the slick sleeping bag. "I'm afraid it's only going to get worse."

7.

I'm awakened the next morning by an actual, literal rooster. It seriously won't shut up. And it's not nearly as adorable and homey as it seems in the movies. Roosters are dicks.

"Shut up!" Chance yells, and laughter blossoms here and there among the tents.

Wyatt uncurls around me, and the air goes freezing cold, even in my pajamas. Despite our attempted make-out session, we slept plastered together in a distinctly unsexual way, huddling together from the cold and, for me, to escape the nightmares. Those faces haunted me in my dreams, and my eyes hurt from crying. Is this PTSD? I wonder if Chance feels it, too, if he can't stop the visions and memories, if he feels hollow and twisted inside. I wonder if there are other kids here like us, kids tapped by Valor who actually managed to live through it.

That's the thought that gets me up and hunting through my backpack—people. The new ones around us, the ones in the house, and the chance to see Kevin and make sure he's okay. This is not a place where I want to be caught in my pajamas, vulnerable and still wearing tear tracks.

Wyatt gestures to the other side of the tent. "The tent divider is also a privacy screen. So you can . . . get dressed or whatever." The way the sun shines through the red tent already made his face look flushed, but now he's extra awkward. He grabs his backpack and heads to the other side, zipping it fully closed until he's just a vague shadow.

I turn my back to the divider and go through my routine, wishing I'd had the good sense to buy some dry shampoo or something. My hair is greasy as hell, and the deodorant I bought smells totally gross. The clothes aren't a perfect fit, and there's no mirror, and I feel utterly wretched, not anywhere close to ready for a briefing with Heather or Leon. Matty watches me, her thumping tail and bright eyes seeming to say that I'm beautiful no matter what.

"Thanks, girl. Even if you're a liar."

She thumps harder.

"You decent?" Wyatt's voice is a little breathless, whether because he knows I was naked over here for a few scant seconds or because it's cold as balls in the November morning.

"As decent as I'm going to get without running water and soap."

He unzips the divider and manages to look adorably rumpled in a band shirt, grandpa cardigan, and beanie. I'm kind of amazed that the tent is so tall he doesn't have to duck his head.

"Yeah, it's rough living. But you look beautiful."

I squint at him. "You're just trying to butter me up so I'll shoot that rooster."

His grin is like a sunbeam through clouds. "Yeah, maybe. You ready?"

I take a deep breath and reach for my gun. It's become second nature, like keys or a wallet used to be, in the days before Valor showed up at my door. I tuck it into the back of my pants, wishing to hell I'd had the good sense to buy a—

"I got this for you too. Hope that's not weird." Wyatt hands me a black holster. "It can clip inside or outside your pants. It was Chance's idea."

"This is possibly the most thoughtful gift I've ever received. No more sweaty gun butt. You're the best boyfriend ever."

I realize what I've said the moment the words leave my mouth, and we both kind of ignore it. I have to mess with the new holster for a few minutes, figure out where it'll be most convenient to draw. I settle for my right hip. Wyatt has his on the left. The gun fits perfectly, although it makes a weird bunch under my shirt. I practically throw myself into Wyatt's arms with so much enthusiasm that

Matty starts barking like crazy. He's just tipping my head back to kiss me when we hear a gunshot outside. My heart drops into my throat as we break apart and stare at each other. Our eyes meet, and we draw our guns and drop to hands and knees. Wyatt slowly unzips the tent and peeks out. It just goes to show what we've been through in the past week that Matty is totally unaffected by gunshots and we're ready to fight for our lives.

We're greeted by a shout. "Morning meeting on the porch. Won't you kindly join us?"

"Hell of a wake-up, Leon," I mutter. The man is standing on the front porch steps, his gun pointed at the sky. The rooster struts on the roof above him, staring at him. Sadly, he didn't shoot it. Wyatt finishes unzipping the tent, and we step through, guns in hand, to join the sleepy crowd doing a zombie walk through the tent town.

"Good morning, sunshine," Chance says, punching Wyatt in the arm. Wyatt punches him back.

"You get any sleep?" Gabriela asks me.

I shrug. "Yeah, but it's not good anymore."

"I hear that. Same in our tent."

There must be at least two hundred people around us, maybe a hundred tents in the field, some smaller than ours and some bigger. There are at least a dozen more than there were last night—some new folks must've spent a long time shopping with their gift cards. A few old-school RVs around the edge of the camp look a hell of a lot comfier than sleeping on the ground. The crowd is a weird mix of people. Mostly white, just like the city of Candlewood, but with a range of ages that I find surprising. There are maybe twenty teens; then it skips up to what looks like single parents with little kids and a lot of middle-aged folks.

If I had to guess, judging by the drawn, drained looks on their faces, these are people who watched their spouses and kids get gunned down at the front door. They look haunted, which is how I feel too. The teens are in a group, and they glare at us distrustfully. I recognize two of them—one is the small girl I noticed in the gym the other night. She's wearing camo clothes I saw while shopping the clearance rack at Big Choice, still creased, so they must've given her the same sort of card they gave us. She stands alone. The other familiar face is a football bully from school who made my computer class hell.

You'd think the fucking dystopia would free us from bullies, but now they just have guns and more ammunition.

"Citizens, I'm proud to report that last night's meeting brought ninety-three new recruits for the good work we're doing here." Leon pauses dramatically, and Tuck and his boys start clapping, so everyone starts clapping. It feels uncomfortably like a church revival. "Our cause is a beacon to those who suffer under Valor and its corrupt ways. I hope you'll all join me in giving a warm welcome to our new friends and in helping them find comfort and camaraderie around our fire." He gives a lopsided grin. "Although that fire must remain metaphorical, as we don't want to send any smoke signals to our friends at Valor, now, do we?" The crowd laughs, slightly uncomfortably. Guess nobody wants to be reminded of how vulnerable we are. "Now, if you're one of our new folks, please join us in the kitchen for a home-cooked breakfast and a brief meeting on the role you'll play as part of the Citizens for Freedom. Everyone here has to pull their weight, but when we all pull together, it's a hell of a lot lighter." He claps his hands and throws them out like a preacher. "And now, friends, let's eat!"

After the screen door slams behind him, most of the crowd disperses. The new folks file inside in about the same order as we approached the tables last night, which means our crew is last.

The small girl is ahead of me as we wait to squeeze into the crowded hallway. I catch her sleeve, and she spins on me, gun in hand. It's a Valor Glock—I can see the gold stamp. So I was right. She is one of us.

"Don't touch me," she says, her voice calm and flat.

I hold my hands up. "Sorry. I just wanted to introduce myself. You look a little lonely."

She looks me up and down, then glances at my friends. Her eyes are dark brown, her hair light blond, and she can't weigh more than ninety pounds.

"Don't talk to me, or I'll kill your dog." She turns back around, and I put my hand on Matty's head. The look in the girl's eyes—she'd do it too.

So much for making friends.

Wyatt's hand finds my waist, protective, but not obviously so. "Don't take it personally," he murmurs in my ear, finishing with a kiss on my cheek. His breath smells like mint.

I know he's right. The world, as it is—it's messed up. I can't imagine what last week would've been like without Wyatt at my side, without Matty's unwavering love. If this girl did it alone or, worse yet, lost whoever was helping her through it . . . I imagine her nightmares must be worse than mine. I want to believe that there's still a good person inside her, too, but I could definitely be wrong. When I look in the mirror or catch Chance's eyes, I see a crust of hardness over liquid pools of heartbreak and regret. In this girl's eyes, I see only a bottomless, murky swamp. But was she always that way, or is she another sin to lay at Valor's door? Did they break her, or was she already broken?

Everyone inside finally shifts enough to let us through the door, and the house is overly warm and smells like old people and fatty breakfast. There's a line in the kitchen, and we pick up paper plates and ladle on what's left of scrambled eggs, bacon, ham, and biscuits.

"I'm a vegetarian," Gabriela says, and an older lady in a housecoat grunts and dumps lumpy grits all over her plate, drowning her biscuit.

Once we've got Styrofoam cups of crap coffee, we follow the line to a den, but Tuck blocks our path.

"Y'all go on down to the parlor. Leon wants to talk to you, special."

Two doors down, we find a room with an old piano and older sofa, already taken. There's nowhere else to sit but in folding chairs. I count nine of us kids, and I sit as far as possible from the girl who just threatened to kill my dog. She's tearing her biscuit into tiny shreds and swallowing each shred one by one. Everyone eats in silence, eyeing each other as we balance breakfast on the laps of brand-new jeans. No one speaks. Matty stays at my knee, tail wagging politely, but she doesn't try to make friends. Because no one here is friendly.

"Good morning!"

Ugh. Heather. She's extra perky and dressed in a velour camo tracksuit.

"So did everybody get everything they need at the store? And a good night's sleep?"

Dead silence.

Heather's big, glossy smile turns into a sneer, and she knocks the little blond sociopath's plate to the ground and plants a foot in what's left of her biscuit. "I asked you a question."

The girl looks up at her. "I'm not 'everybody.'"

"No. You're Beatrix Kiddo, according to your form. Do you really expect anyone to call you that?"

A flat, reptile stare. "You can call me Bea."

Heather's smile is sweet as poison. "Did you have a good night, Bea?"

Bea's mouth widens in something that seems like an alien pretending to smile. "Oh, yes. I was a good little do-bee. I used my card and bought all sorts of lovely things. I feel like a princess. Now, who is it you want me to kill?"

Heather sighs. "No one. We're not Valor. But we do have jobs for you. And we think you'll actually find it pretty fun. First off, we're going to do target practice today. Does anyone have experience with survival skills?"

"Considering we're all alive after a week with Valor, yes," Chance says, and everyone smothers their laughter because Heather looks like she's going to have a tantrum.

"Can you find water in the woods? Can you start a fire without matches? Can you forage food? Can you survive, alone, with no money and no way to get money? Because that's where you're going to be if Valor raids Crane Hollow. And most of you bought fancy tents that you can't break down and throw on your back, so you're going to need to know how to make shelter, too."

Wyatt gives me an apologetic look and a shrug. I elbow him in the side to let him know that there's no way he could've anticipated the need to buy a smaller tent in case we became mountain men.

"I thought this was a briefing," Gabriela says. "I don't feel briefed."

"I'm getting to it," Heather snaps. "So, Crane Hollow. You have your tent. We provide food at meal times. You get one scheduled shower pass per week, so anything outside of that you'll have to cover on your own. The line starts early for the downstairs bathroom and can get long. There's a lake out back, or you can buy a solar shower or double up in the shower, if you have a buddy, so that you each get two showers. We've got porta-potties on the far side of the field, hidden in the trees. Don't mess with the food animals. Don't hunt squirrels on property. Don't steal the eggs. Don't steal from your neighbors or their tents, or they're in their rights to shoot you. If we catch you stealing, *we'll* shoot you. Don't leave the compound unless you're on a mission—"

"Don't leave the compound?" Gabriela says.

Heather's smile is so fucking patronizing. "We can't have people screeching in and out of here all the time. It draws too much attention. That's why there are guards. And they will take you down."

"For the Citizens for Freedom, y'all don't seem too big on freedom," one of the other kids drawls, and I can tell by looking at him that he's rich, or was. Or, at least, like Wyatt, his family pretended he was.

"We're fighting for freedom. That doesn't mean we have it right now. So shut up and listen. Where was I?" Heather looks at a sheet of paper. "Okay. So. You don't need to be in this house unless it's a designated meal time or you've been summoned. Don't hang out

· 101 ·

here, don't try to sneak into the bathrooms, and no one goes upstairs."

"Why not?" Gabriela asks.

"Because it's off-limits."

"Well, now, see, that just makes me want to go up there more."

Heather's grin disappears. "There's going to be a big ol' Crane boy with a gun at the stairs every moment of every day. They get real bored. Don't give 'em a reason to shoot."

"I want to see Clark."

"Well, here's the thing about Crane Hollow. If you want something, you've got to earn it."

"We've got to earn the right to see our friend?" I say. "That's bullshit."

Heather looks at me, all innocent. "That's funny, coming from the person who shot him."

Every kid in the room turns to stare at me.

"I didn't know him at the time," I mutter.

"Badass," murmurs one of the other kids.

"Yeah, we were breaking into her hideout at the time. Not her fault," Gabriela says, and I feel like I'm going to owe her for life for not blaming me.

"Still. Do good work at the range today, and if the weather holds, we'll have a job for you soon. Do it well, and you'll see your friend. Who, I assure you, is upstairs and doing great."

Nervous looks pass between me, Wyatt, Chance, and Gabriela.

Matty burrows her face among our knees, her tail thumping. One thing I know for sure? I'm not letting this dog out of my sight.

Heather leads us to the front porch and points us to a trail in the woods. "Follow that. Brady's waiting for you in the field." She disappears inside, and everybody eyes everybody else.

"You heard the bitch," Chance says. He takes off with Gabriela at his side looking fierce. She must've kept some of her own makeup after Valor, as her eyes are striped with electric purple today, surrounded with heavy black liner.

Wyatt's hand curls in mine, and Matty wiggles at my side, all ready to go. The small, terrifying girl, Bea was what Heather called her—she's directly in front of us. I can't even hear her sneakers on the path, like she doesn't weigh anything. Her hair is in a tight French braid, her outfit entirely in camouflage. I know from the Valor records in Alistair's trailer that she has to be at least sixteen, but she looks like a murderous doll. I slow down when it feels like we're walking too close to her.

It's a beautiful morning, full of birdsong, with the last of the leaves softly drifting down through the sun-dappled autumn forest. Matty's practically dancing on her fat paws, and Wyatt swings our hands, just a little, as if he's forgotten where we are and why we're here. He has some ability that I lack to forget the past and the future and live in the moment. I envy it. He's barely spoken of his father's death, but I can't forget it. I can't stop thinking of the thousand different ways Valor might've already tortured and killed my mom. I begin to see why she sank into painkillers after her car accident. She said the nightmares would wake her up, like she was reliving it, trapped in the crushed car and bleeding, and her heart would pound so high and fast that her fingers and toes would go cold, and then she was gulping down pills in the dark with trembling hands. If I could numb myself to what I feel in the night, I would do it. I would totally do it.

But I can't. Even if Chance has the pills, I can't. I have to be ready to run and fight, every second of every day.

The path opens up to a field like any other field, except that there's a line of makeshift targets at the other end and a big, built kid with a rifle over his shoulder at this end. He's at least seven feet tall, wearing overalls and a non-ironic trucker hat, and he's staring at us like he's trying to decide which duck to shoot in a barrel.

"Tie that dog up before she gets shot," are his first words to us, but they're spoken less like an asshole and more like a country boy who would feel really bad if Matty got hurt. I nod and tie her leash around a tree. She promptly starts rolling around on a mushroom.

"Now, y'all gather up over here, and keep your hands off your guns." We crowd up around him. The preppy kids are clustered together and snickering, as they always do when they think they're going to have to listen to someone who doesn't have as much money as they do. "I just need to see how good a shot y'all are. We don't want to waste bullets, and you're going to have to repack 'em later anyway, so just step up when I call your name and take five shots. Easy, right?" Everyone nods.

"What if we don't have a gun?" a hot Asian emo kid asks—the one who called me a badass. He looks to be alone, like Bea.

"Maybe you can borrow one from a girl," says the lead prep.

The hot emo kid gives a little snort of a laugh and barrels into the prep kid, taking him to the ground and basically pretzeling him around until he's got the kid in some sort of choke hold. The prep kid is turning purple and sputtering and flailing, and his friends don't know what to do. Guess they don't have guns either. Brady watches the scene and pulls a notebook out of his back pocket to take notes.

"Fight! Fight! Fight!" Chance shouts, and Gabriela smacks his shoulder.

"Tap my arm if you're done." Hot emo kid isn't even out of breath, but the prep kid frantically flaps his hand against the kid's shoulder and is released. Hot emo kid stands up with a sly grin. "That's called jiu-jitsu, dick. And it means that I don't need a gun to kill you."

The prep kid stands, his face red. His polo is askew, the collar no longer popped. Giggles ripple through the crowd. It's nice to see a douchebag laid low, new world order or not.

Brady gnaws on his pencil. "What's your name, killer?" After a pause, he points a finger and adds, "Your new name. Nobody here wants your birth name."

Prep kid looks like he wants to respond but can't speak. Of course, no one cares about his name.

The emo kid gives an amused grin and tosses his hair. "Rex."

I know it's a fake name, but it suits him. Rex looked cool as hell before he choked the prep kid out, but now there's a certain deadliness to his ease. His hair is dark and shoulder-length, his shirt black, and his jeans faded gray and slim fitting in the way that only certain rock stars can pull off. His boots ride the line between face stomping and fashion, and I suspect the brown stains on the worn leather are blood. As if sensing the up-and-down I'm giving Rex, Wyatt slides his arm around my waist. But Gabriela sees it too and mutters, "Meow," under her breath.

Brady scribbles some notes and points at the prep kid. "And you?"

Prep kid's finally got his voice back, but it's raspy. "Tyler."

Looking down at his notes, Brady smirks. "Oh, good. Tyler Durden. That's pretty cute. Let's see if you can live up to that name."

"I'm out of bullets," Tyler says. "So . . ." He looks around like we're going to offer him ammunition.

"This is stupid."

The quiet girl, Bea, steps past him, whips the black revolver from under her hoodie, and fires five rounds at the line of targets. Five Coke cans jump off the board. It's funny—the sound of gun-shots doesn't even register anymore.

"Can I leave now?" Bea's voice is flat. I'm pretty sure she's actu-ally a reptile.

Brady eyes her up and down. "What's your name, sugar?"

She points the gun at him, casual as you please. "My name's not 'Sugar.' It's 'Bea.'"

"Fine. Bea." The big redneck shrugs and grins when she lets her gun fall to her side. "You can leave if you're done. But you'll need to report to the house at lunch. Leon's got a little job for all of y'all. Unless you have any questions about how things are run in Crane Hollow?"

Bea's smile curls into itself like a dead bug. "I do have a ques-tion, actually. What sort of justice system do you have?"

I realize I'm holding my breath, because she's acting really god-damn creepy, and I can feel it in the air. Wyatt's arm tightens, pulling me to his side.

"Somebody steals from you or threatens you, you can kill 'em. But make sure you have proof or witnesses. Ain't a single Crane on the property that ain't armed to the teeth. Why?"

Bea raises her gun and, as if in slow motion, ever so casually shoots Tyler in the chest. We're all perfectly still and silent as he drops to his knees and his face lands in the dirt.

"Because I hated *Fight Club*," she says. "And that boy grabbed me on my way to the latrine last night and said he wanted to fuck me." She pulls back her sleeve to show a fresh bruise about the size and shape of a boy's hand. "Is that fair?"

Brady just nods and scribbles in his notebook.

She turns and walks away.

"What do we do?" one of the prep kids asks, all cockiness gone.

Gabriela hurries over, drops to her knees, and starts pumping the kid's chest, but . . . it's clear that he's dead. After a few tense moments, she stands, shakes her head, and tucks herself back into the crowd between me and Chance.

"There's nothing we can do," Brady says. "He's gone. This is a good lesson for y'all about how things work around here. You do bad things to anyone on our side and bad things are gonna happen to you. For now we're going to shoot, because that's what we were told to do. You got a problem with that?"

"Yes, I have a fucking problem with it! He was my friend, and you're just going to let that little tease shoot him and walk away?" The prep kid is crying, his lip trembling. He looks barely sixteen, and in his terror and fear I see what I must've looked like standing outside Wyatt's door, waiting for his dad to answer my knock. This kid—he wasn't a Valor kid. Whatever test they used to determine who to choose . . . he wouldn't have passed it.

"Yeah, I am," Brady says. "Unless you know for sure he didn't touch her."

In response, the kid whips out Tyler's gun and holds it, outstretched and shaking, pointed sideways at Brady. In one fierce, hard move, Brady smashes the gun to the side and drives the kid to the ground, where he sits on the smaller kid's chest and slaps him, hard.

"You done, son?"

The kid just blubbers, his eyes squeezed shut like he hit the end of his rope a long time ago. Tyler's gold-stamped Glock is on the ground, and Brady picks it up and checks the clip, which is empty. "That's what I figured," he mutters. And then he hands the gun to Rex.

The crowd murmurs and looks around. I suspect they're all as concerned as I am that they might lose their guns. Now, in this world, my gun feels like an extension of my body, and I don't want to see it just handed to somebody else. Again.

Brady stands up. "Enough fooling around. Y'all line up and start shooting. Bullets are in the box. If your gun ain't a forty-five, let me know. We don't have time for this shit."

The prep kid stands up and moves to whisper with what's left of his friends, who look decidedly less brave.

Wyatt and I line up at the far side. He hits cans with four of his five shots, which makes sense, as one of our earliest conversations revealed that he knew what to do with a gun. I hit two. I guess

I'm better at closer range. I let Gabriela borrow my gun, and she reloads it and returns it after hitting one of the cans. Some of the other kids are pretty hopeless, their hands still shaking like they're on Valor duty. Chance hits three. His hands don't shake, and he handles his Glock like a pro. Rex is decent, getting three shots out of five with his new gun. The prep kid misses all five of his shots, probably because he can't stop looking at Tyler's body, which has been left on the ground, staring up at the blue sky.

"Can . . . ? Can I at least close his eyes?" I ask.

Brady nods. And I don't want to touch this kid, but I do. Not because I feel sorry for him or feel that his death was unjust. Because I can't stand the sounds of the flies.

8.

I'm glad when Brady says it's time to leave the gunpowder hang-over of the field. After what we've been through with Valor, I feel exposed out here, sure that so much gunfire will draw attention and helicopters. When Rex stops to stand over Tyler's body, Brady steps beside him and lifts his hat to rub his hair.

"He wasn't gonna cut it anyway. Kid was already pushed to his limit."

Rex nods thoughtfully. I shiver. Where is my limit? Where is Wyatt's?

In the kitchen, they serve us cheap sandwiches—white bread, processed cheese, and bologna. Bags of off-brand potato chips gape on the cracked counters. An industrial-sized box of Moon Pies waits at the end like the Holy Grail. We serve ourselves on Styrofoam plates, and Brady herds us into the living room like a flock of dumb chickens. Wyatt and I sit on a fake leather couch, our hips glued together on the sprung seat as I sneak my bologna to Matty. I realize that until today I hadn't eaten anything in a week that wasn't fast food or Pop-Tarts or stolen from someone who's now dead. My stomach turns, but I eat anyway. It's just another new skill in my repertoire. Everything tastes like dust anyway.

"Welcome, citizens."

Everyone looks up, their jaws frozen mid-chew. It's Leon Crane, all dapper and dangerous in black jeans, a black vest, and a striped button-down shirt. He looks like the lab-made love child of a hipster, a preacher, and a serial killer.

"Did you enjoy your morning on the range with Cousin Brady?"

"Until my friend got shot," the prep kid says. His food is untouched and his red eyes leak despite his best effort not to cry.

Leon's smile is stunningly warm. "An unfortunate incident that should remind us all to keep our hands to ourselves. But I do believe we can all continue in our shared ambitions without ongoing enmity—wouldn't you agree?"

"Do you mean I'm just supposed to forget that bitch killed Chad?"

Leon is in the kid's face in a heartbeat, his fist balled up in his polo shirt.

"Why, yes, son, I do expect you to forget that. It might be a Valor world outside, but in Crane Hollow, we respect our women. When everyone is armed, such problems take care of themselves, as you've seen. Now, can you move on or not?"

The room is dead silent but for Rex crunching on fake Ruffles.

The prep kid shakes his head once and looks up, eyes steely. "When's the funeral?"

Leon's smile is cloying, but he steps back, arms wide. "We don't do funerals in Crane Hollow, or else we'd have no time to fight back. You want to do your friend honor, you complete your mission today. We have a common enemy, and that enemy is Valor. So let's strike back at the real foe."

"So what are we going to do?" asks a beefy kid in camo through a mouthful of sandwich. "Like, hold up a bank?"

Leon steps back and sits in a wingback chair that kind of makes him look like the Godfather. He crosses his legs and regards us coldly and bemusedly. "Son, what good would holding up a bank do?"

"I don't know. We could take over all the banks and show Valor who's boss."

"Now, let's have a little economics lesson. You know who works in banks? Nice folks who need jobs to feed their families. Tellers and loan officers and a policeman who's too old and slow to work the streets. Now, why would we want to go hold up those innocent, hard-working people?"

"To get the money out of the vault?"

"The vault?" Leon throws his head back to laugh. "Shit, son. All the money's digital now. This is not a comic book. The vault is not full of bags of gold coins stamped with a green money symbol. And the piddly peons working behind the bulletproof glass are not the enemy."

God, his voice grates on me. I sit back and mimic Leon's posture. "Then why are we even here? What are we supposed to fight?"

Leon leans forward and steeples his hands. When he looks up, I can see the veneer of respectability spread too thin over a pissed-off country boy who's still wearing prison tatts on his knuckles.

"You fight who I tell you to fight. Jesus H. Christ, kid. This isn't *Red Dawn*, okay? We're not some plucky group of losers that's going to take on the government and win. Do you even know what a bank is today? It's not one building run by one person with a big front door we can blow up and an easily recognized villain stroking a cat behind a mahogany desk. A bank is . . . a damn hydra. Executives, lawyers, managers, cables, servers. It's a million computers connected with shadows, each wire as well hidden as the second-smartest guys in the world can make it. That's the secret. There's nothing to fight. Nothing to rally against. No common enemy. No face you can put on the monster. Even their executive board, the people in charge— they go by code names and move around frequently so we can't track them down. We can't target their homes, their families, even if we wanted to hurt civilians. You can't hold a coup against an invisible monster. So we're doing what we can: making it damned unpleasant for Valor to keep on being Valor. They want to make money? Great. We can stop that. They want more capitalism? We'll knock off its cap. They want us to get more into debt? We'll cut up our credit cards and demagnetize every person we walk by."

"Then why the guns?" Wyatt asks. "Why were we at target practice?" He's practically vibrating by my side, his food forgotten, which is a big deal for him.

Leon eyes him as if for the first time and nods. "Because we like to get a feel for the raw materials we've got to work with. Who has a gun, who can shoot, who's going to blast a kid in the chest and who's gonna blubber like a baby. We need to know who's cool as a cucumber." He nods at Rex. "And who's got a problem with authority." He nods at me. "In short, we need to know who's smart, who's dumb, and who's dangerous. Now, where on that spectrum do you fall?"

Wyatt shifts toward me, his shoulder touching mine. "Smart and supportive."

Leon nods and grins. "Good man. What about your girlfriend? Can you control her?"

Wyatt sucks in a hiss. Before he can say anything about whether or not I'm actually his girlfriend or knock the bullshit cherry off Leon's misogynist sundae, I put down my cheese sandwich and say,

"Nobody controls me. I was told that if I did an errand, I could see Clark, the kid y'all have upstairs with a gunshot wound in his leg."

"Ah. So despite your bad attitude, you're determined and stubborn. I used to have a hound dog like that. She was a damn fine beast before she got rabid and had to be put down. Now, can you be trusted without a leash?"

I don't blink. "I can do what needs to be done."

"Well, Zooey, your friend Clark is doing just fine, and you can see him this evening after you've performed a fairly simple task on behalf of the Citizens for Freedom."

My blood runs cold, right down into my feet, and Matty whines and leans more heavily against my leg. "Do I have to kill anybody?"

With a hearty laugh, Leon leans back and slaps his knee. "You misunderstand our function, Miss Zooey. As I said, we don't want to kill anyone. We want to disrupt capitalism. So you're going to distribute these little babies." He reaches into his pocket and pulls out a cardboard box about the size of a double-decker sandwich.

"What is that?"

"This is just a little something our tech people cooked up. I know we might look like a bunch of beer-bellied, Confederate-flag-flying rednecks, but that don't mean we're dumb. We call it a Wiper." He opens the box to show us a machine that kind of looks like a homemade bomb, all wrapped wires and cylinders. There's a red button on the side, and he points at it. "All you do is press this button, and the Wiper starts churning out an electromagnetic field for about fifty feet in circumference. You know what that means?"

"It wipes credit card strips," Wyatt says, sounding impressed.

Leon tips an imaginary hat. "That's right. So each of you will be given ten of these, a grocery list, enough cash to cover those supplies, and a ride to a particular destination. As you walk around the store, deposit these devices in hidden places and press their buttons. Once you've got your list and have activated all ten Wipers, you pay for your groceries and leave, easy as pie."

"And you don't think a store will notice a nervous teen in a hoodie hiding shit behind the mustard?" Wyatt asks.

Leaning in, Leon looks deadly serious. "I guess you'd better be careful, then, huh? The police ain't answering their calls, but they're sure as hell protecting capitalist interests in the big box stores that can still pay for protection. You go to jail, and we don't know you. You lead them back to us, and you'll leave jail in a dozen chunks. And, of course, we'll have to keep your dog for you while you run your errands. And you'll want your buddy Clark to be safe."

"If you're on our side, why do you keep threatening us?" I say, almost without thinking.

Rex clears his throat, and everyone else looks terrified at having the elephant in the room called out.

"I'm not on your side, Zooey. You're on my side. I need soldiers, and just like all triumphant armies of old, I will keep you here through gifts or intimidation, whatever works better. We told you to pick a side, and you picked ours. Now, if you want to survive, you're going to be a good soldier, shut your mouth, and do what your general says. Succeed, and you'll get to keep everything you have, plus see your friend."

"And if I fail?"

His smile is a chasm. "Then you'll have a sad boyfriend and a dead dog."

After Leon is gone, everyone stares at their plate. No one eats. There are eight other kids here, and I know the names of only five of them. Considering that none of us might live through the night, I don't really want to get friendly with anyone else.

In the past week I've gotten disgustingly accustomed to walking up to someone's door and shooting them dead. It didn't get easier so much as I became numb. My hands still shook every time. I came to believe that between me and one other person, I could pull the trigger and leave alive, if less so than I'd been before. But walking into a store with a bag of dangerous-looking boxes requires a different kind of cool, one I don't know if I possess. When you're supposed to kill someone anyway, it doesn't really matter how bad you mess up. They die; you move on. Same end result.

But a task like this has so many variables, so many tiny, stupid things that could go wrong. And I won't have Wyatt by my side. As Leon said, we're each being given our own assignment. So on top of worrying about doing my job, I have to worry about Wyatt doing his job. And about Matty and whether Tuck and Hartness will feed her bad hot dogs or take her out back like Old Yeller and put one in her sweet, fat skull.

"Fuck it." Wyatt stuffs an entire sandwich in his mouth.

I tear mine up into tiny pieces and feed them to Matty. I need a milk shake, not this trashy lunch-bag food. Even the fake Coke in its Styrofoam cup is gross. Thank heavens I bought those Pop-Tarts.

"You scared?" Chance asks.

Gabriela snorts. "We're all scared, dumbass. At least you've got a gun."

"It's going to be fine." Chance puts a hand on her shoulder and looks weirdly serious. "We can do this. And then we can check on Kevin and go back to our tent."

"And then what?" I say. "First this assignment, then another one. It's not like they're going to just let us leave the compound and wish us well. At least Valor gave us the hope that we could earn our freedom."

"A very false hope." The tears in Chance's eyes remind me that his house got burned down. I start to think about my mom, my house, and push it right back down.

Repress, repress, repress.

I can't look in his eyes anymore. It's too raw. "But still. We had hope."

No one else is speaking. When I look up from our circle, everyone is trying not to stare at us hungrily. I guess even this little amount of friendship is enviable right now.

"Okay, nerds. What are your names?" Gabriela asks, looking around the room.

"Well, I'm—"

The boy in camo doesn't get to finish. Heather swoops in and interrupts him with a waved hand. "You're going to need to finish your lunch so we can get on with the mission. Security is slowest in the afternoon and goes up after dark. You've got five minutes, and I wouldn't waste it talking." No one obeys, and she adds, "We can have a campfire singalong later, if you're successful." She points at the grandfather clock in the corner. Its ticking fills the room. "Five minutes. Dump your plates in the trash and meet me out front when you're done."

When she leaves, we continue not eating. I swear I didn't hear the clock ticking before she pointed at the damn thing, but now it's Edgar Allan Poe–style maddening. Even Matty's wagging is in time with the insistent *tick-tock*. I feed her my cheese and try to drink the warm soda, but it makes me choke and cough as the minutes count down. The prep kid bolts up and runs from the room, and soon his retching echoes down the wood-paneled hall.

We all look at one another, my crew. Wyatt picks up his last sandwich and holds it up. Chance picks up his, and they do a weird sort of toast.

"To stupid assignments," Chance says.

Wyatt snorts. "To stupid singalongs."

"To Kevin," Gabriela adds.

I add what's left of my floppy white bread to the mix. "To people not threatening to kill my damn dog all the time."

Rex walks over to us and adds his half a sandwich. "To the fact that there's still homework in a capitalist dystopia. Who knew?"

I can't swallow. I drop my bread for Matty, who's been eyeing it and drooling. At least one of us still has hope.

The clock strikes, and we stand like old people too tired to go on. Out the door we file, dumping our plates and cups into the trash can. Crane women line the halls, going silent as we pass. The screen door squeaks, and we're on the front porch. The day would be beautiful, but it's not. We have a job to do. We have no choice. We have nowhere else to run. Wyatt takes my hand and holds it like he never wants to let go. When Tuck walks up and whistles, Matty surges toward him like she's forgotten I ever existed.

No, that's bullshit. She's just a dog, and he's holding a biscuit.

I let go of her leash, and he takes it, and then Heather is pointing me to a beat-up hatchback with a stranger at the wheel, the first in a long line of shitty, idling cars. My mind flashes back to my mom kneeling, introducing me to the topic of stranger danger and telling me that even if I thought a guy might be my dad, I shouldn't get in the car with him. I didn't believe her, though. I was possibly the only kid on earth who wanted a stranger to pull up and say sweet things. My dad never showed up, and not a single stranger ever tried to kidnap me. But now my danger sense is tingling.

The stranger driving my car is in his twenties and tapping on a phone. He has the bug-eyed, nervous look of a skinny Crane. I don't want to get in the car with him. There is no chance that it can end well. I cling to Wyatt, arms tight around his waist, face buried in his band shirt. His arms wrap around me, too, his chin over my head. He strokes my hair and murmurs, "It's going to be okay. You can do this. We'll be eating Pop-Tarts in our tent by dinnertime."

He says nothing of whether or not he can do it, of whether Gabriela and Chance will be there with us later, keeping us from hitting second base in a too-large tent. One day, maybe, we'll learn how to talk about the future. All we have right now is the past. The dude honks the horn, and Wyatt kisses my head and whispers, "Good luck."

I'm going to get in the backseat, but the guy opens the front passenger-side door instead. The car smells like cigarettes and spit-out gum, the heater turned up too high. I lean down to flick the lever and push the seat back from the dash, but I still feel crowded as we drive down the bumpy gravel road. Am I supposed to say hi? Everything feels gross.

The guy doesn't even look at me. "Uncle Leon says you're mouthy. That I better keep an eye on you."

I say nothing.

"So how many people have you killed?"

I turn my head and stare out the window, and he snorts, his hand tapping on the gearshift like he wants to slap me.

"Suit yourself. See those two bags? One's stuff to wear, and the other's got your Wipers. You got any questions?"

I open the paper bag at my feet and find a pink cardigan, a blond wig, and a pair of hipster glasses that probably came from the dollar store. When I pull down the mirror, I look like I'm forty, my skin angry from a week of neglect with huge purple bags forming under my eyes. My hair is a mess, greasy and scraggly. The wig, at least, seems new, and I put it on, tuck my bangs under it, and try to arrange it to look as natural as possible. I don't want to take off my coat with this dude giving me the side-eye, much less take off the seat belt when he's driving, but I don't have a choice. God, I feel so rumpled and wrong. We're on the highway now, and it's a highway to hell, which is what's playing on the fuzzy radio.

"Where are we going?" I finally ask.

"Doesn't matter. You know how to use the Wipers?"

I open the handbag at my feet, and it's the source of the

dead-gum smell, probably borrowed from the closet of one of the older Crane women. Inside is a jumble of the small boxes Leon showed us, and I pick one up as if it's the bomb it so resembles.

"Just put it somewhere sneaky and push the button, right?"

The guy scoffs, and I stare at him dully. He's just some random guy, scruffy under his beard with unkempt brown hair that brushes the collar of his puffer vest. But I get the feeling he looks down on me, and I wish I knew if it was because I'm a girl, because I recently killed a bunch of innocent people, or for some other reason. He doesn't seem to like me, probably because Leon doesn't like me. But do they know who I really am, or do they just despise the reckless, rude monster I've become? The CFF has said all along that it didn't want our real names, but that doesn't mean they don't already know exactly who I am, who we are.

"Wrong, dumbass. Wipers have a super-strong electromagnet. Do you know what that means?"

"Leon said it would mess up credit cards."

"Yeah. But what else do you know about magnets?"

"They attract metal?"

He points a finger at me and says, "Bingo. So it's got sticky tape on the bottom. Like, insanely sticky tape. Best place to put 'em is on shelves behind shit nobody buys, like fancy mayonnaise or expensive kids' toys. Then push the button and put stuffed animals or jars in front of 'em or whatever and get the hell away."

I put the machine down gently. "So how many times have y'all done this before?"

The guy grins. "Never. You can only pull this stunt once."

"So we're just, what? Like, expendable soldiers?"

He chuckles and shakes his head. "Are you just now getting how this works?"

I smooth back my wig, turn my head away, and watch the other cars blink past. So far we've passed two big stores without stopping. "Is it happening all over America, or is this a Crane-only enterprise?"

"That's on a need-to-know basis. And you don't need to know."

I watch him for a minute, watch him close. He looks the part of just another scruffy country boy, but his fingernails are clean and trimmed, his skin is clear, and he doesn't have a very strong accent.

"So you're a Crane, right? And Leon's your uncle?"

"Again, need-to-know basis."

"Is there anything I'm allowed to know?"

He shakes his head like I'm a pesky fly. "Damn, you're mouthy. Just do what you're told."

He moves into the turn lane for a Mark's, one of my favorite stores. This one's farther from home than the one I prefer, so at least no one will recognize me, like, say, the cute boy with the ponytail who always has cart duty at the other Mark's. We pull into a parking space, and he leaves the car running and reaches into his pocket.

"Here's a list. Try to get exactly what's on here and leave the Wipers as you go. There should be more than enough cash to cover it."

The list is typed on white paper and has a lot of the crap we've been eating in the Crane house but in the smaller quantities that a normal house would need. Two loaves of white bread, family-size bologna, two bags of chips, stuff like that. The wad of cash is in twenties and tens, still warm from his coat.

"How do you know I'm not going to take the cash and run?" I ask without thinking.

"You won't. You're too smart for that. And you can buy some biscuits for your dog, if you want. Leon says you're awful fond of her and that kid you shot." His smile is mocking, knowing. I wish I were allowed to shoot him. I haven't thought about my gun since target practice, but now I'm painfully aware of its weight in my waistband.

"Nuh-uh," he says, and now he's pointing a .45 at me. I belatedly realize my hand went to my gun. I don't even notice anymore. "Don't try that shit with me."

"Sorry," I say, holding my hands up, and he relaxes.

At least the holster Wyatt bought for me keeps me from sweating against the metal, because the warmth of the heater and dealing with this jerk is making me sweat like crazy. I guess I'm glad I didn't try to shoot him—now he thinks I'm cowed. The Cranes want me to believe that I've got only one choice, but that's a lie. I could get out of the car, sneak back around, and kill this guy, kick him out of the car, and drive off into the mountains with enough cash to get me to Tennessee.

But I won't.

I need Matty and Wyatt. They're all I have now. And the Cranes know it, which is why they're letting me get out of the car alive.

The guy jerks his head toward the store. "Hurry up. I'll be waiting."

I get out of the car, tuck the cash in my back pocket, and heft the bag over my shoulder. It's a plastic knockoff of the leather brand my mom used to sigh over, and the strap digs into my neck. I slam the car door without a word and quick-walk for the store, passing old men with half-full carts and dad types talking frantically on their phones as they load bag after bag between the seats of their empty SUVs. Not many women, no children. Just like with the folks at the store last night, hunting for resources has become a man's job, a dangerous job. I imagine their wives and children at home behind bolted doors, Mommy's hand on the shotgun as she feeds Junior applesauce. I stand out here; maybe that's why they gave me a wig. My heart's jacked up, but that's nothing new now. At least I don't have to shoot anyone.

Probably.

Repress, repress, repress.

A college-age guy walks by with a case of beer under his

arm and bigger bags than mine under his eyes, and I can't help wondering how Wyatt is doing. He's done some brave things this week, mostly on instinct, without really thinking. Mostly to save my ass. And I know he shoplifted some when he was younger and running with his old pal Mikey, before Mikey died and Wyatt got his life cleaned up. But is he cool enough to pull this off? To walk around a store, planting bomblike machines without getting caught?

Am I?

The automatic doors slide open, and I almost walk in through the exit—which would mean walking in through the scanners that beep at shoplifters. I don't know enough about the scanners or the Wipers to know what they would do to each other, so it's a damn good thing I looked up when I did.

"Oops," I mutter to no one, heading for the doors marked ENTER, which don't have the machines. Because shoplifting only works one way, right?

There's a police officer stationed by the carts, but she's on her phone, texting away. I don't see a gun, just a club. Her outfit is all black with the usual patches, but they could say anything or mean nothing. I wish I knew more about real police versus rent-a-cop versus whatever Valor's done to make sure all errors are in the bank's favor. I put my head down and get a cart and hurry toward the food with the list in one hand. I've read it fifty times at least, but the words slip from my mind the second my eyes skitter over them. Last week's hit list did that too.

The first thing on the list is bananas, one dozen, and I put them in the cart and move on. The fruit section is too exposed to place any Wipers. A bag of apples, a bag of oranges. I feel like everyone is staring at me, but when I look up through the wig's blond bangs, no one is. There aren't many people here at all. The next aisle is condiments, where I'm supposed to buy mayonnaise, one large jar. My hands start to sweat on the cart's handle. This is where I need to plant the first Wiper. I stop the cart in front of the wall of mayo and crouch down. No one is in the aisle, and I don't see any mirrors or cameras. I start to reach into the bag, but a squeaky cart turns down the aisle, an older woman parking herself in front of the ketchup with glasses down over her nose. I swear to God, she's reading every single ketchup bottle with the focus you can give only when you have no idea what's going on in the outside world. I do the same with the mayo, subtly clearing a space on the lowest shelf behind the industrial-sized jars.

"Excuse me."

I gasp and look up, expecting the policewoman, or a Valor suit. But it's just the old lady, mouth turned down, staring expectantly. I move my cart a few feet and go back to reading mayonnaise jars like an idiot.

"Love the bag," she says, and I make sure my arm is holding it closed.

"Thanks," I murmur.

A thousand years later, she selects her mayo and leaves the aisle, and I kneel, whip out a Wiper, rip the coating off the sticky tape, stick it under the shelf, and press the button. That makes it sound like a swift, elegant process, but it feels like I'm moving in slow motion, and my neck is sweating under the wig, and I expect to hear the clomp of boots or the clip of expensive shoes as someone, any-one, busts me for doing what looks like planting a bomb.

No one does. I move the jars of mayo back into place, put my own giant mayo jar in the cart, and hurry to the end of the aisle, fairly certain that I'm going to have a heart attack. Somehow, play-ing hide-and-seek with homemade magnets is almost scarier than killing people for Valor. My adrenaline doesn't know the difference because bodies are dumb.

In the next aisle, that same old lady is reading bread bags like she's in a library. I don't have time for that, so I skip the bread and head for the cereal aisle, where I'm to get a tall canister of quick oats and a large box of Cheerios. I have to wait for an overburdened young dad with two squalling spawn to grab his Cap'n Crunch before I can plant another Wiper, this one among the old-fashioned oats, which seem less popular because they take two minutes longer to cook.

"What are you doing?"

The voice startles me as I push the button, and I yelp and sit down hard. It's a little boy, maybe five, staring at me like I'm a unicorn.

"Um, I'm buying oatmeal."

"I hate oatmeal."

"Me too."

"What's in your bag? Are those toys?"

I'm stammering when his dad yanks him back by his arm.

"Sorry about that," he says, looking me over with angry, distrustful eyes. He tosses the kid over his shoulder and mutters, "Son, you can't go running away, remember? You have to stay in the cart. We got to hurry. Don't talk to people."

I'm just glad I didn't have to answer the kid's question. I rearrange the oatmeal canisters to hide the Wiper and stand, pushing my cart to the next aisle for cookies and crackers. It gets easier with each Wiper, as I learn how to whip off the tape cover while it's still in my bag, kneel, and trade it for the oversized boxes of crap on my list. I hide one behind the plastic bears of cheese balls and one behind the granola bars and another behind bottles of wine so huge as to seem like props or jokes. Then it's on to the paper section, where I trade Wipers for toilet paper and paper plates and paper towels. I pick out dog biscuits shaped like gingerbread men and leave a Wiper behind the boxes of Milk-Bones. The cart is getting full while the bag is getting lighter. I have one Wiper left and nothing else to take off my list, so I head down unfamiliar aisles, looking for lonely products stacked high enough to keep the damn things hidden. The cleaning aisle is empty, so I turn down it, park my cart in front of the Windex, and reach into my bag, practically laughing with relief at finally being done.

And then I feel a hand clamp down on my shoulder.

"Excuse me, miss," says the cop. "But I'm going to need to see what's inside your bag."

9.

I turn and paste on a plastic smile.

"I'm sorry. My bag?"

She nods, looking smug and sly. "We can do it here or in the manager's office."

I swallow and shrug. "Uh, okay. If that's what you need to do." I let the straps fall down my arm and hand her the bag.

She takes it, and a little furrow appears between her eyebrows as she pulls the straps apart to stare into the minty depths.

"What's this?"

I look down with her, and the box stares up from the darkness.

"It's a box."

"Yeah, I can see it's a box, miss. Why are you carrying a big bag with nothing in it?"

But she doesn't reach for the box, which makes me think that maybe she's not allowed to, that there must be laws or protocols for whatever she wants to pin on me, and she can't do it. I don't reach for it, either.

"This is my mom's bag, and I guess that's her box. I didn't want to leave it in the car because I was afraid it would get stolen. You know how things are right now. Is there a problem?"

I look up at her, trying to remember what innocence looks like. Harmless smile, wide eyes, I think? I have no idea. I am the opposite of innocent now.

"No phone? No wallet? No makeup?"

"I'm just here for groceries," I say. "Phones are expensive."

She shakes her head and closes the bag, shoving it back at me. "You understand that now is not the best time to be out alone? And that when you enter a store with a large bag, people are going to assume the worst?"

"I'm sorry. I guess I didn't think about that because I didn't plan to shoplift."

Her eyes go hard, and she looks me up and down. "Good," she says. "But know I'm going to be waiting at the doors to check your receipt."

When she doesn't move or say anything else, I slide the bag back onto my shoulder. "Is it okay if I finish shopping now?"

"Go right ahead." Which sounds like a dare.

I nod and push my cart down the aisle. She follows at a distance that's halfway between a "Watch yourself" and a "Fuck you," and I realize that I'll never be able to plant my last Wiper with a pissed-off cop on my tail like this. My list is done, and I doubt they gave me enough money for a splurge to take me across the store to the non-food sections. I kneel to read the peanut butter jars, and she leans against the end cap. I find myself missing the freedom of last week, when anyone who pissed me off this much took a bullet in the stomach so that I could finish my job. She knows I'm up to no good . . . because I am. If an actual bomb went off, she'd probably ignore it to see if I tried to steal some mustard.

Finally, I give up. She's not going away. I push my cart up the main aisle and pick an older cashier with thick glasses who looks kind of frazzled. He's wearing an old bulletproof vest over his red Mark's shirt like it's totally normal. The cop moseys over to the scanners by the exit and starts texting again, but I can feel her watching me in between whatever the hell she's doing on her phone.

"Is it nice outside?" the cashier asks, and it takes me a moment to remember. It feels like I've been in this stupid store for weeks, endlessly shopping.

"Yeah, it's pretty for November."

He scans the items more slowly than I'd like, but I get the idea that someone younger would definitely pick up on the fact that this hair is fake, the glasses are trash, and no one my age would be caught dead with this bag. At least the old guy just hums to himself as he tries and fails to stuff the oversized containers into normal-sized bags. I'm pretty sure I end up with forty bags for twenty items.

"Your total is ninety-eight dollars and sixty cents. Will you be using your Mark's card to save five percent?"

I fumble in my pocket. "Uh, no. Cash."

"Would you like to apply for a Mark's card? It only takes a few minutes, and you'll save five dollars."

I count out a hundred dollars and put it on the conveyor belt. "Nope. Cash."

"Are you sure? It doesn't even ding your credit, and it's backed by Valor Savings Bank."

I swallow down an insane laugh. "No, thank you."

He has to go through my bills one by one, counting them out, then putting the bills flat in the till and counting out my change. I had ten dollars to spare. My jaw is so tight that I can hear my teeth grinding, and I can't stop tapping my foot and scanning the area for somewhere, anywhere, to stick the last Wiper. All I see are shoppers who look like they're navigating a mine field. I'm out of shelves. The cop is waiting. Fuck.

"Have a nice day, and thank you for shopping at Mark's," the cashier says, and I'm finally free to go.

I think about leaving the Wiper in the bathroom, maybe in a

tampon receptacle, but the cop will notice if it's not in my bag when I leave, which will make me look bad, which means I have to take it out of the store instead of planting it like they told me to. So I walk toward the waiting, smirking cop, smiling behind my cartful of food I bought to feed the antigovernment rebels holding my dog hostage.

"Find everything you need, miss?" she says, arms crossed.

I nod and say, "Yes, ma'am."

"How about I check that bag one more time before you go?"

Which is the dumbest thing ever, because honestly, who's going to shoplift after the cop has identified them as a suspect? I pull one strap down my arm and let her look inside. Nothing but a box.

"Let me see that receipt."

I have it ready and put it in her hand. She frowns and reads it.

"You feeding a crowd?"

I smile, or try to. "I have brothers."

You can only read a receipt so long before admitting that it's normal food and not the ingredients for meth, so she hands the receipt back over and narrows her eyes at me.

"You might want to be more careful," she finally says. "Send your brothers for groceries. It's not safe for young girls to be out. Lots of desperate people. Cops like me are going to expect the worst. If you look suspicious, you're going to get treated like a perp these days."

"I'll be more careful," I promise. And she lets me leave.

The afternoon is deceptively lovely and warm, or maybe I'm just constantly overheated because my heart is permanently jacked up because nothing ever, ever feels safe. The Crane car is in the same parking spot, idling, and when I get close, the trunk pops open, but the driver doesn't get out to help me. I load up the groceries without checking the mysterious duffel bags lined up in the trunk and contemplate using the tire iron to brain the driver, but that's all just foolish daydreams.

Once the groceries are all in the car, I shut the trunk and push the cart to the cart return. The cop is watching me from just outside the doors, arms crossed. She sees me watching her and slowly shakes her head. I'm guessing the black-and-white cop car parked on the other side of the cart return is hers, which gives me an idea. I push the cart into place and whip the box out of my bag. The sticky tape has already been exposed, so I kneel and stick the damn thing under her car, where it nestles like it genuinely wants to be there.

Take that, ma'am.

I keep my head low as I hurry between the cars and back to the waiting hatchback.

As soon as I'm in my seat with the door closed, the guy says, "Did you get all ten of the Wipers installed?"

"Yep."

"And you pressed all the buttons to activate them?"

"Yep."

"And you got everything on your list?"

"Yep."

He gives me a sadistic grin. "Then let's go home and see who else passed the test."

I toss the empty purse into the backseat. I never want to smell mint gum again.

We don't speak during the drive back. I stare out the window, and the guy fiddles with the radio and ultimately gives up. At times like this, I fiercely miss my phone, miss having the ability to check e-mails and social media and just blank out in a way that means I'm not turning down human interaction so much as choosing it on my terms. I have nothing to say to the Crane goon, and he has nothing to say to me. A funny cat video would not go amiss. Say what you will about technology, but it's great for when you want to purposefully ignore an asshole.

We pass through a series of strip malls, and I see further evidence of the Crane family's influence. Crane Tires and Crane BBQ and a parking lot of vehicles just as disreputable as the one I'm in, Crane Used Cars. Crane businesses seem to be unimaginative but functional. After Thanksgiving, the dirt lot behind the cars will become Crane Christmas Trees, and when the Fourth of July rolls around, it'll be Crane Fireworks. Maybe that's where Leon learned to love blowing shit up.

Oh, sweet Jesus.

I put the Wipers around the store and under the cop's car, and I'm ninety-nine percent sure they're not dangerous . . . but what if they are? What if the one Leon opened for us was a plant, and the rest do something horrible? What if they're bombs? I didn't like the cop, but I know that even if she was a bitch, she was just doing her job. She doesn't deserve to die just because I was frustrated and vengeful. That little boy who hates oatmeal definitely doesn't deserve to die. Goddammit.

I look over at my driver. He's not going to be any help. Even if he turned around, it's not like I could run back into Mark's and collect and dispose of a series of stuck-down boxes that might or might not explode. So I have no choice but to do what I've been doing all along: repress these feelings. Shove them down under food and kisses and knitting. Hope for the best, hope that things will be better someday.

Wait for the sound of fireworks that aren't fireworks.

Filled with dread and self-loathing, I watch every store we pass until it disappears in the rearview mirror.

Finally we turn into the Crane compound, waved ahead by a nameless good old boy with a machine gun. The sun is going down, and people are moving around the tents carrying lanterns and plates of food. The scene is utterly normal. I scan the area but don't see anyone I know, much less Wyatt and Matty, waiting for me. My driver parks the car with all the others on the far side of the field, opens his door, and says, "Take your stuff to the kitchen and find Heather or Leon." And then he's gone.

I manage to load myself up with all the bags and tromp toward the house. Another car is coming down the drive, and I slow down to see who it is. I didn't see my friends get into their cars, but I can tell by the height of the person on the passenger side that it isn't Wyatt. Still, I wait. Could be Gabriela or Chance.

The car stops and Rex gets out, laughing with his driver, a chubby kid who looks more nerd than Crane. They share the burden of the groceries, and Rex gives me a relieved smile.

"Did that suck as much as I think it did?" he asks.

He keeps walking, and I join him. A girl can stand around a field like an idiot for only so long before someone notices.

"Yeah. Did you almost get caught?"

He shakes his head. "No. I was at Jim's Club, and everyone was too busy buying huge boxes of prepper shit to notice some kid with a backpack loading up his cart. Where'd they take you?"

"Mark's. A cop tried to pick me up for shoplifting because I had to carry this big-ass bag."

Rex looks me up and down, fighting a grin. "And they gave you a dumb costume, too. Leon must really hate you. It's almost like they want you to fail."

I had forgotten that I'm wearing a wig and glasses, and I rip them off and shove them into the bag with the oatmeal. I hadn't thought about it that way, but . . .

"They didn't make you . . . dress up or anything?"

He shakes his head. "Nope. Just me with a backpack. Totally normal."

We tromp up the porch steps, and I feel like more of a fool than ever. Maybe talking back to the Cranes isn't my best move. Maybe I'm forgetting the value of self-preservation. Maybe they really do want me to fail.

Chance is in the kitchen, drinking a beer and laughing by a stack of pizza boxes, but I can tell he's worried as hell by the way he glances at the door every few seconds, probably waiting for Gabriela. A fleet of Crane women are putting up the groceries, silent and grim. I drop my bags on the cracked linoleum and rub feeling back into my hands where the plastic handles bit in.

"Do you know where my dog is?" I ask the nearest woman, who is graying and built like a mountain behind her apron. She shrugs and picks up a bag.

Rex nudges me. "Hey, come on." I give him a suspicious glare, and he leans close. "I'm gay, and you're taken, so just come on. Get your buddy, too."

I catch Chance's eye, toss my chin toward the door, and pull the box of dog biscuits from what's left of my groceries. Rex grabs a box of pizza from the counter and hurries out into the hall, then to the front porch. When he sits down on the steps, Chance and I sit down too. The pizza box opens, and I salivate and grab a slice of pepperoni.

"How did yours go?" Rex asks Chance.

Chance holds up a finger and chugs the last of his beer, then burps loud enough to startle a nearby chicken. "Easy-peasy livin' greasy. Much better than working for Valor. You?"

"Mine was fine. But she almost got caught."

I shake my head and swallow back down the pizza that's trying to fight its way out. "Correction: I *did* get caught. But I guess since there was nothing in my bag, the cop couldn't legally pick me up. It sucked."

"Ed went in with me and stood watch."

I stare at Rex like he's grown a second head. "Seriously? Ed? You're on a first-name basis with your goon?"

Chance shrugs. "My dude offered to help, but I didn't want to look suspicious, so he stayed in the car."

I toss my pizza at a chicken, which is sick of our shit and flaps onto the roof in a huff. "Why does every goddamn person in this city want me dead?"

"Because you don't take anyone's shit, and that makes you a liability," Rex says.

I knock my head against the porch column. "It's just such a cliché. Girl speaks her mind; guys in power try to punish her."

Rex raises a sharp eyebrow. "Uh, you're talking to a gay half-Asian kid who likes guyliner and lives in rural Georgia. Don't get me started on the dumbass clichés that have chased us all into the apocalypse. At least America gave us some rights."

"Whiners," Chance grumbles.

"So you're from around here?" I ask Rex. Because he's insinuating himself into our little family, and even though my gut instinct says he's cool, I don't trust anyone anymore.

He nods. "Yeah. I went to private school, though."

"Bullied?" Chance asks.

Rex chuckles. "No. You saw what I did to that prep kid earlier. Twelve years of jiu-jitsu and three of Wing Chun means bullying isn't a problem. My parents wanted the best for me, and none of the local public schools were up to snuff. Hence, debt. Twenty thousand a year in exchange for flawless test scores and a future doctor seemed like a good deal."

"So Valor tapped you?"

He nods. "I take my truck and list, or they shoot my parents and little sister. Didn't even have to think about it. You learn to be pretty cutthroat at Bridgeton Academy."

The silence slips on, punctuated by the clucking of sleepy chickens. Finally, Chance asks, softly, "Did you go back?"

With a sigh, Rex flops onto his back and stares up at the porch ceiling. "Nope. Right now, it's Schrödinger's family. They could be alive, or they could be dead. I don't want them to know about what I've done. And I don't want to know what was done to them, either."

He cocks his head like he's trying not to cry. "Uh, why is the ceiling painted blue?"

I look up and have to smile. As broken-down as the house is, the porch ceiling is freshly painted and swept free of cobwebs. "It's called haint blue. My mom says it's a traditional thing, that it keeps spirits and spiders away."

"That's stupid. You can't keep ghosts away," Chance says.

"You can try."

The boys don't have anything to say to that, so they each go for more pizza. I pick up another slice and try to chew. We all look up as two cars rumble down the drive. Gabriela is in the passenger seat of the first one, but the second one just has a driver. No passenger. Beside me, Chance exhales and stands. But I can't swallow, and I stay seated, too tense to move.

Why is no one in that car?

They park, and Chance grabs my shoulder and shoots Rex a glare. "Come on. Better to know than not."

I let the boys pull me up, and we head for the line of parked cars. Gabriela gets out and stalks toward us with bags up and down her arms. Her driver is young and skinny and skulks behind her.

"This is bullshit," she says, handing some of her bags off to Chance.

The other driver gets out of the empty car with a black backpack over his shoulder. He looks pissed.

"Hey, man. What happened?" Rex asks, walking in time with him.

"Kid messed up. Got shot. That's all you need to know."

"Which kid?"

The driver spits in the dust. "Tall one. Blond."

My heart falls, and I hurry to keep up. "What was his name? Was it Wyatt? I mean, Hank?"

He glances back at me like I'm an annoying bug. "I don't know. Jesus."

I hurry behind him, not sure what else to ask, but he darts up the stairs. Tuck stops me by letting his gun fall across my chest.

"You know the rules."

I try to peer past him, but the dude's a megalith. "Leon said we could go upstairs and see Kevin if we did a good job. And where's my dog?"

He grins, showing a silver tooth. "Hartness took her for a walk. That's a damn good dog. But you can't go upstairs until Leon says so."

I can't see up the narrow stairs, but a door opens and slams closed, and raised voices explode. There's a heavy *thump*, and Leon's voice yells, "Goddammit, Steve!"

I strain to hear words, names. The room goes silent, as if they know I'm listening and are trying to piss me off even more.

Tuck puts a heavy, gentle hand on my shoulder. "Just go eat dinner, okay? You don't want to mess with the big guys when they're angry."

I nod, a huge lump in my throat, and go back out to sit on the front porch steps, where Rex, Chance, and Gabriela are eating pizza and watching the driveway. A car door slams, and I look across the field to where the kid in camo is getting out of a jacked-up pickup. Bea is walking across the field with her hands in her pockets as her driver trails in her wake, carrying her bags like a butler. We're still missing another girl, Wyatt, the prep kids, and the other kids that I never bothered to notice. Somebody in the tent city is playing a guitar, and I want to smash it to pieces.

Boots land beside me on the porch, and I turn. Leon Crane crouches, staring at me with fury in his dark, deep-set eyes.

"I've got some bad news about your boy," he says. "Come with me. Now."

10.

I stand up and drop the piece of pizza I was holding and not eating. Chance, Gabriela, and Rex stand up too.

"We're coming with her," Chance says.

Leon chuckles. "Like hell you are, son." He inclines his head toward Gabriela. "She can, though. You boys stay out here and eat. We'll be down soon, unless something else goes wrong tonight."

"I'm not letting you take two girls upstairs alone." Chance moves his shirt aside, revealing his gun.

Leon moves his jacket aside to show a larger gun. "Don't try me. Do you even know how many Cranes would put holes in you before you could draw? I don't have lascivious intentions, and if I did, I wouldn't be bird-dogging for underage sniff on my own front porch with my aunt Kitty watching out the kitchen window."

"It's fine," Gabriela says.

Leon bows with a smirk. "After you, then, ladies."

Gabriela hurries to the steps, and I follow her. Tuck moves aside to let us pass.

"Take a right at the top of the stairs. The door is open. Don't do anything stupid."

I'm surprised as hell when we end up in a bedroom with only one person in it: Kevin. He's propped up on flowered pillows in a twin bed, looking pathetic and pale. There are three more twin beds in here, and the dresser is covered in medical stuff—boxes of bandages and gauze, tubes of ointment, a big brown bottle of peroxide. This must be the clinic.

"Where's Wyatt?" I blurt.

Kevin shakes his head. "I don't know. Did you bring me any pizza? I can smell it, but they won't give me any."

Kevin is great, and I'm glad he's okay, if a little pale, but I'd rather be outside watching for Wyatt. Gabriela moves to his side and fusses with his pillow.

"Hot, ain't he?" I turn around to leave and find Leon Crane leaning in the doorway. "Your boy here's going septic. Needs antibiotics. Which we don't have."

"So this isn't about Wy—Hank?"

Leon shakes his head, walks to Kevin's bed, and pulls back the covers to show us that Kevin's skinny leg is going red and veiny. "This is about how the boy you shot is going to die unless you go buy him some medicine."

"Fine. Whatever. I've got, like, ten bucks left. Where do I go?"

"Well, it's not that simple, is it? You can't buy antibiotics without a doctor's prescription, and it so happens that while we have many capable nurses, our prescription pad just ran out. So unless you've got a better idea, I recommend you go to a pet store and buy as many bottles of fish antibiotics as you can carry."

"Fish antibiotics," I say. "You're serious?"

Leon nods slowly, but Gabriela grabs my arm. "No, it's legit. I read about it in a comic book. It's the same stuff as human antibiotics, but you don't need a prescription. And I've still got plenty of money on my card."

Headlights flash against the window glass, and I feel a painful pull to return to the front porch. But Gabriela's still got my arm, and Kevin groans and shifts against the bed, and I'm just so very sick of feeling guilty and persecuted.

"Fine. When Hank gets back, we'll go. He has his keys. The kid can live another hour, right?"

Kevin clears his throat as if he finally understands what we're talking about and is now terrified. "Uh, what?"

Gabriela smiles and puts a hand to his forehead. The smile dies.

"We're going to get you some medicine. Don't worry about it."

"I like the pink kind that goes in the fridge." He shakes her hand off and reaches for a stack of old magazines, but he seems listless and unfocused, and the magazine just flops on his belly.

"I think you should go now. And you'll need these." Leon tosses something at me, and I catch a key ring, my hands stinging. There's a Lexus key, a few house keys, and a Nirvana key chain. Goddammit.

"Where'd you get these keys?" I say, cold and hard. "Where's Hank? Was he the one who got shot tonight?"

"We don't have a full count yet." Leon puts his hands in his pockets and shrugs. "But we'll be down one more if you don't hurry. Gangrene sets in pretty fast, and the kid's burning up."

And he's gone.

"We'll be back soon," Gabriela says, but Kevin is half asleep and sweating, his head turning back and forth like he's having a nightmare.

I'm pretty sure I've been having the same nightmare for a week now. It's not going to end anytime soon.

"Everything okay?" Tuck asks as we tromp down the stairs and past him. In just a few short days, I've grown entirely accustomed to dangerous men carrying machine guns in their arms, cradled like babies.

"Not really," I say, and then we're back outside.

The crew on the porch steps has swelled: Rex and Chance, the kid in camo, a girl in a hat, Bea, although she's sitting by herself, over to the side, eating a Granny Smith apple.

No Wyatt.

"Has anybody seen Hank?"

Chance shakes his head.

"Have they said anything else about . . . um, more kids who failed?"

Another head shake.

"Crap."

"That's my new motto," Chance says. He's got another beer sweating in his hand, and his voice is slurred. Where the hell is he getting beer? "How's the kid?"

"Septic," Gabriela says, flat and tight. "So we're going to get meds. Come on."

She starts walking for the cars, and I drag Chance up by the arm. He wobbles and yanks away from me but follows her.

"Should I come?" Rex asks.

I shake my head. "Probably not. But will you watch out for my dog?"

"No problem."

"Thanks."

I hurry after Gabriela and Chance, because that's my whole life now. Hurrying after people, hurrying toward things.

As we get close to Wyatt's Lexus, I reach into my pocket, pull out what's left of my cash and shove it all into Gabriela's hands, along with Wyatt's keys. "Here. You guys go. I'm staying."

"But Leon told you to go. You and me."

"Screw Leon. I'm not going anywhere until I see Wyatt. It's not like you need me to buy fish medicine. And you know more about it than me anyway."

Chance finishes his beer and tosses the bottle deep into the woods. I don't even hear it land. "So what are you going to do?" he says, putting an elbow on the roof of the faded gold sedan that I used to think was fancy and now just looks sad.

"Wait for Wyatt," I say.

Chance presses a button on the key fob, but he's either drunk or can't see well in the dark, as the trunk pops open instead of the doors unlocking.

I go to close it, and that's when I notice there's a body inside.

"What the hell is that?" I whisper.

"Holy shit," Chance says.

"Looks like a Crane goon." Gabriela nudges the guy's foot. "He's breathing, at least."

"Uh, guys?"

The voice comes from the woods, and I nearly pee myself with joy.

"Wyatt? What the hell? What happened?"

There's a weird pause from the brush. "Is anybody watching?"

I look toward the house and the tents but don't see signs of anyone caring.

"Doesn't look like it."

He edges out into the light, and he's covered in blood.

"Oh my God!" I rush to him, running hands up and down his sides, looking for bullet wounds.

"It's my nose," he says, all sheepish. "I'm not shot or anything." He shuts the trunk with a frown.

"Care to explain why there's a dude in your trunk, then, bro?" Chance burps and leans against the Lexus's hood.

Wyatt steps back into the shadows of the trees and beckons for us to follow. "So my deal went totally shitty, and I ended up getting in a fight with my driver, and when I took it to the ground, he busted his head. He's not dead, but . . . well, I'm pretty sure he's got a concussion."

"You're not supposed to go to sleep with a concussion," Gabriela says, glancing back at the car.

Wyatt waves a hand. "Little shit deserves it. Just a complete tool. Wouldn't shut up about how Kurt Cobain was a fag."

"So you've just been sitting in the woods for an hour while I freaked out?" I squeak.

Wyatt tries to draw me into a hug, but I push back right before one of my only shirts is pressed up against the still-wet blood. "I didn't know what to do. I show up at the house covered in blood and having mostly killed one of their guys, I figure it's not going to go so well for me. I was waiting for you guys to come outside, toward the tent or here. I guess I was going to creep up after dark."

"I didn't know if you made it. I was worried as hell!"

"Me too. I didn't know if you'd made it, either. If maybe these Crane guys were attacking their passengers all over the place. It's so messed up. Did yours go okay?"

I peck him on the cheek and step back. The smell of blood turns my stomach now. "My guy was a dick and I almost got caught. They said one kid messed up and got shot, and I was so scared it was you."

"Me? Did they say it was me?"

"They said it was a blond kid."

Chance looks away, always toward the house. "I hope it's that prep kid, then. He's blond. And a douche."

"We have to go," Gabriela says. "For Kevin, remember?"

"What about Kevin?" Wyatt asks.

"His leg's going bad. We have to go get fish antibiotics. Long story. We're supposed to take your car." She snatches the keys from Chance.

"So maybe you can just toss the guy into the parking lot while you're out?" Wyatt says, a hand on the trunk. "Leon doesn't know I have a spare key. And if they ask me, I'll just say that I don't know where their guy is. The car he drove is here, at least, without any blood on the seats. My shirt's ruined, though."

Chance stumbles into Wyatt's space. "A good friend helps you dispose of bodies, huh?" he slurs. "Except for Mikey."

Wyatt looks like he's been slapped. "Don't do that, man. It wasn't my fault."

"You kinda look like you know it's your fault."

Wyatt bumps his bloody chest against Chance, his arms back, his hands in fists. "Did I sell him the shit he OD'd on? Did I hand him the needle?"

Chance wobbles back and pushes Wyatt's chest, clumsy but hard. "Was I standing in the room with him when he did it? Was I the one who didn't stop him when they knew he'd already had more than he could take?"

"He made his choice!" Wyatt growls. "He only did it because I asked him to stop!"

"You left him in front of the hospital! Like a flaming sack of shit!"

They start taking clumsy swipes at each other, but Gabriela steps between them, and neither of them is willing to touch her.

"You two can get into a fight about it once the kid's not dead and my brother is sober," Gabriela snaps. "We'll dump the guy in the parking lot. Whatever. We need to go. Now."

Wyatt steps away from the car and opens the door for her, looking sheepish and gory.

"Go get cleaned up and take your groceries inside before they start hunting for you." She rolls her eyes at me. "Funny how TV shows about the apocalypse always have guys in charge, but they're all actually idiots."

I chuckle before I can stop myself.

"Wait." Wyatt uses his spare key to unlock the trunk and rustles around inside. It creeps me out to see the guy lying there, limp, but his chest is still rising and falling, and at least I'm not the one who did the damage this time. "Ta-da!" Wyatt reaches into the guy's pocket and holds up a simple flip phone, a burner. But we have a phone now. And that means I can call my mom.

"You're a genius," I say.

Gabriela slams the trunk, gets in the driver's seat, and waits until Chance is buckled in before peeling out backward, just in case we want to slow her up any longer.

"Come on," I say, tugging Wyatt's less-bloody arm. "You're a mess."

"You're just trying to get me out my clothes," he teases.

"Shut up. It's not my fault you smell like old steak."

I'm glad he can't see me blush in the darkness.

When I unzip the tent, we can barely see inside, but what we see is a goddamn wreck.

"Did we get robbed?" Wyatt fumbles for the lantern, and when he flicks it on, it's pretty obvious that we did. Everything has been tossed around. The sleeping bags are unzipped, the pillows are out of their cases, my backpack's contents are everywhere.

"What could they possibly want?" I say, pawing through to see what's missing.

"Jesus. Monty. What the hell?" He holds up the python's plastic travel aquarium, and it's empty.

I edge out of the tent. That snake could be anywhere, and I don't want to find him first. Wyatt sorts through everything, puts our stuff in piles. Monty isn't in the tent—that we can see. I shake out my sleeping bag just to be sure before I sit down. The only obvious thing that's missing? Our food, bullets, Jeremy's gun, and Roy's rifle. I guess I'd be mad if I was surprised. We can't deal with it until Wyatt's cleaned up, though, so I hand him a baby wipe for his face, and it comes away mottled with brown and black. Funny how dried blood is never red. He strips off his tee, balls it up, and grabs for another, but I stop him.

"Wait. There's more blood."

He stops and stares at me, on his knees in the tent. By lantern light, I move closer, cautious as a baby deer, and gently wipe the blood from his neck and chest. He's got some blond hair scattered around, but not a lot, and it's curly and springy. He's frozen as I touch him, his chest rising and falling faster under my hand.

"I want to kiss you," he says softly, "but my mouth still tastes like pennies."

I finish with the wipe and take the clean shirt from his hand, drawing it over his head and threading his arms through it with a weird intimacy.

"Now's not the time. We've got to find our stuff. And Monty."

"Right." He nods and tries to get his breathing under control. His smile is shaky, his eyes black pools. "Not now. No kissing now." He grabs my hand and brings it to his cheek, curving my fingers around his stubbled jaw. "But soon?"

I nod. "Soon."

At least whoever ransacked our tent left the condoms in the zipper compartment of my backpack. We're caught like that for a moment, staring into each other's eyes, but the sound of laughter outside reminds me that now is not soon.

"You're going to need something dark to wear, if we're sneaking around outside." I withdraw my hand and dig around his pile of clothes, handing him a black hoodie. The scarf I knit for him just a few days ago is carefully rolled up in the middle of his stuff like a beating heart, and I smile. I would put it on him now, but I feel like we should keep it safe from all the blood that turns up whenever we're together. I mean, I just got him cleaned off, and there's still black crust around his nostrils. That would've grossed me out a week ago. Now it just makes me want to hug him tighter.

I'm already wearing a black hoodie, but I put on a hat and check my gun. Wyatt checks his, too, and gives me the nod that means he's ready. Once we're outside the tent, he zips the door and stares at it.

"I wish you could lock a tent," he says.

"Problem?"

Rex appears out of the dark like a ghost.

"Somebody stole our food and ammo," I explain. When Wyatt gives me a "Who the hell is this guy?" look, I add, "Rex is on our side. Play nice." Because after hearing his story on the porch, I've basically accepted him as one of our crew.

"I know who took your shit." Rex tosses his bangs. "I was watching from the porch. Come on."

He turns around and starts walking. Wyatt and I follow. The world is no longer a place where you forgive strangers for their transgressions or let a slight go without punishment. We need that food. We need those bullets and guns. He loves that stupid snake. Wherever Matty is, whichever Crane goon is "watching" her for us, we need to get her back. And if we let them take things from us now, they'll just keep doing it. The way Wyatt's hand rests on his gun convinces me that he understands this too. He puts up the hood on his hoodie, and now we're a gang of three.

Rex leads us to a stretch of woods between the cars and the house, the section that I think of as Crane property. There are tire tracks leading to the old barn where they supposedly do deer processing, a smaller attached shack with a sign that says TAXIDERMY, and a collection of single-wide trailers and old campers where I've assumed the lesser Cranes live while the more posh ones like Leon get to stay in the house proper. Something crinkles under my foot, and I look down to find a Pop-Tart wrapper.

"Assholes," I mutter.

Most of the trailers are dark and quiet, but one in particular is lit up with Christmas lights and blasting old-timey rock music that makes my teeth itch. Lights shine beyond the crooked blinds, shadows moving within.

Rex stops and points. "That one. Do we go in with guns blazing?"

I grab his shoulder and whisper, "You don't have to be part of this, you know."

"I'm already a part of it," he says simply, pulling his gun out of his waistband.

And just like that, he's part of my family. And I don't know how to approach a trailer full of armed thieves. But when I hear a sharp bark from inside the trailer, my blood boils.

I know that bark.

They've got Matty, too.

Wyatt pulls his gun the second I pull mine. Rex already has Tyler's Glock ready—I just hope it's loaded. They both look at me like I'm the leader. Am I? I don't know. I stare hard at the door. I don't want to knock. Things never go well when I knock on someone's door. That old familiar feeling is back—cold feet, shaking hands, jackhammering heart, blurry vision, sweaty palms. I swallow it down and set my chin.

Just a few feet away, inside the trailer, Matty starts barking like crazy. The aluminum door shudders as her claws scrape it. She knows it's me. I realize I'm pointing my gun at the door, at Matty, and let it drop to my side. As I reach for the knob, someone inside yells, "Shut up, goddammit!" and Matty yelps along with the sound of something hard hitting flesh.

They hit my dog.

They stole my shit and they hit my dog. That's all it takes.

I grab the knob and yank so hard the door flies open and rebounds off the trailer wall. The guy holding Matty's collar lets go, and she leaps out the door, bouncing around and wiggling. But my gun is up and pointed at the asshole who hit my dog, and he slowly raises his hands, all the while his eyes go narrow with sly hate.

He straightens up. "Well, what do we have here? Boys?"

Two more Crane goons mosey up to surround him, trying to look dangerous. The second one is Tuck, and the third one is the jerk who drove me to Mark's. My gun doesn't waver.

"I take it you're the assholes who stole our stuff?" I say through clenched teeth.

The lead guy smirks and starts to put his hands down. I shake my head no. He does it anyway, crossing his arms over his chest.

"If it's food you bought with Crane money, I figure it's more ours than yours. What are you going to do about it, honey?"

I take a deep breath and nudge Matty behind me. "Well, considering what Leon said . . ."

He goes for his gun.

I shoot him in the stomach.

11.

The guy doubles over as a red flower blooms on his shirt. The other guys dive away, probably for guns. Adrenaline rockets through me, and I feel like the Incredible Hulk, stretching with power. A hand reaches over to pull the moaning guy away from the open door, and Rex shoots it, right through the palm.

"I give up!" Tuck shouts. "Truce! I didn't like these assholes, anyway!"

"Come out with your hands up," I say, and his huge frame fills the door, hands up. I've never seen him without an assault rifle before. He almost trips and falls down the stairs as he steps over the guy I shot.

"Can I go?" he asks.

"Check him," I say to Rex, who obligingly runs hands over the places a dude could carry a gun. When Rex shakes his head, I say, "You going to try to get revenge here?"

Tuck shakes his head. "Hell no. I been telling Sean all night he shouldn't have taken your stuff. Little weasel deserves it. A good man doesn't kick a dog."

As if to support this claim, Matty wiggles up to him and licks his hand, and he pats her head.

"Can I come out, or are you going to shoot me again?" a guy calls from inside.

I look at Tuck. "Was it just the three of you in there?"

"Yeah. They got your snake, too. Didn't hurt it yet. Nice snake."

"This last guy—is he a Crane?"

Tuck has to think about it for a minute. "Not that I know of. He's just a tech guy. College kid. They found 'im online or something. Expendable." He leans in and whispers, "Kid's a prick, so I don't mind if you shoot him again."

"Pull out that one." I point my gun at the guy I shot in the stomach. "Please."

Tuck shrugs and yanks the floppy dude out by the legs. His head bonks down the stairs, and I know he's already dead. The smell reminds me of what happened when Wyatt shot my friend Jeremy; gut wounds are the worst, but they don't splatter as much as other places. I can't believe I know shit like this now. Tuck drags the body sideways, and I do my best to ignore him. It. Fuck. My stomach is twisted, my mouth sour. The shooting might get easier, but the aftermath never does.

"Is this your trailer?" I ask Tuck.

"Nope. I got my own place. According to the rules, it's yours now. But it's going to take some cleaning. Those boys were pigs. There's still one more that hasn't come back yet." He looks at Wyatt, and the corner of his mouth quirks up. "Last time I saw him, he was with you."

"I haven't seen him since we got back," Wyatt says, voice hard.

A voice hollers from inside the trailer. "Can I please come out? I'm not going to hurt anybody. You shot my gun hand. I'm unarmed."

Tuck looks at me, and I look at Wyatt, and Rex just looks bored. I shrug.

"Come on—" I start, and shots pop off as he runs outside, screaming.

I've pulled the trigger before I meant to, because these days, my body does that.

The guy stumbles and falls, full of holes. Wyatt and Rex were shooting too.

Tuck kicks him over with a steel-toed work boot. "Told you he was a prick."

"Did he get anybody?"

We all look down, checking our bodies and looking at one another for holes. Looks like we're safe, this time.

The air smells of pine trees and gunpowder, and the night is suddenly a vacuum of silence as I stare down at two dead men. I killed one for kicking my dog and the other for lying, and I'm starting to feel like that's fair. That this is what the world has become: a place where you do whatever it takes to keep what you love alive.

"What the hell is this racket? I'm trying to eat my dinner."

We all look up as Leon Crane himself struts toward us, five dudes with assault rifles in his wake. Hartness is one of them, and he gives me a small smile and wave before firming his mouth back up into a snarl.

Tuck steps in front of us, hands up. "Not the kids' fault, Leon. Little IT shits stole from their tent, took their snake and their dog. It was a fair fight, and the kids won."

Leon hones in on me, looking perplexed but contemplative. "How is it that you're at the center of every single pile of trouble I find?"

I shrug and put my gun back in its holster. "Just lucky, I guess."

"Like a bad damn penny."

"Why'd you set me up with the Wipers?"

His smile is amused, liked he's pleased I picked up on a subtle joke. "Now, whyever would you accuse me of setting you up, darlin'? In this war, I need as many soldiers as possible. Even mouthy ones."

He's trying to goad me, and I know it, so I do the opposite of what he wants. For once, I'm not mouthy at all. I just shrug.

He walks over to the dead guys and pokes them with the pointy toes of his black snakeskin boots before pinning me with a dark glare. "Not that I liked these particular fellers very much, but they served their purpose. And that's what we all do here at the Citizens for Freedom compound. We serve our purpose. Now, I'm pretty sure we sent you out to get medicine, so would you care to explain to me why I'm missing one driver, have two drivers dead at my feet, and am now staring at you without a single bottle of fish antibiotics to save your friend's life?"

I throw back my shoulders. "Oops?"

Leon steps close, too close, his nose almost touching mine. He smells like cloves and gunpowder. He is no longer amused. "'Oops' is never the right answer."

"You said that theft would be punished. So we saved you some bullets. Tuck says this trailer is ours now. Is that correct?"

Leon's nostrils flare with rage. He swallows it down and points at Wyatt. "Son, you want to tell me where your driver is? Because the car is here, but he ain't."

Wyatt shrugs. "I did what you asked. Groceries are in the car still. Whatever that asshole did once we got back here isn't my business."

Leon exhales and steps back, stroking his beard.

"No, I don't argue that both of those dead boys deserved what they got. Y'all are not the first guests from whom they've stolen. But I had a job for them, and as you're taking over their trailer, you can take over their duties as well."

"I don't want to kill anyone else," I say, too fast.

Leon grins and jerks his chin at the dead guys. "I'm sure you don't. But these boys were doing guerrilla work. Underhanded stuff. They're the ones passing out cards, distributing flyers, planting various instruments of destruction. That's how they earned their place here. Are you willing to do all those things?"

Wyatt and I look at each other. "So you'll give us a car and a list of shit to do?" I say.

Leon chuckles. "I'm not stupid, sugar. I know that if I gave you a car and money and bullets, you'd snatch up your dog and head off for the hills. I need you here. I need your devil's luck, if we're going to take Valor down stone by stone. So you just need to know that I have something you need, and if you want it back, you'd best do what I ask of you."

I shake my head. "I want Kevin to live, but I'm not going to kill on his behalf."

"Nor would I expect you to. No, darlin', it's someone you very much want alive."

Leon reaches into his vest pocket and pulls out a rosary.

My mom's rosary.

Or one that looks just like it. I hold out my hand, and he lets the black jet beads puddle in my palm. I breathe it in, and it's her smell, her favorite Estée Lauder perfume mixed with baby powder. My mom. The entire reason that I'm here, that I'm a killer, that I've lost everything in life that kept me solid.

My voice quavers when I ask, "Where did you get that?"

"She's alive. Do what you're told, and by December first, you'll see her again."

Leon turns to walk away, and I start to raise my gun, but Tuck shoves it back down with a meaty fist.

"Why can't I see her now?" I yell through a gush of hot tears.

"Because you got work to do first. Good things come to those who wait." He pauses, looks at me over his shoulder, and smiles. "Patsy Klein."

"Wait! Why'd you call me that?"

He doesn't even stop. Just calls, "Thanks for those laptops, Patsy."

Goddammit.

Wyatt's arm snakes around me, pulling me to his shoulder. I'm uglycrying, making my horrible snerk noise, but he's heard it before. Lots. My mom . . . is alive? I don't know what day it is, sometime in mid-November. Which means December first is close.

I want to see her. I have to see her. But if I see her, that means she'll see me. She'll want to know what I've been doing, if I'm okay. I'm not okay. I'll never be okay. And I don't want her to know about anything that's happened since she kissed me good night last week.

Would I kill every damn Crane here to get to my mom?

I think I would.

Goddammit. Here I am. Again. Willing to do whatever it takes to save her.

Because as much as he's making it sound like I'm the one in trouble, we all know it's her.

From far away, Leon yells, "Stay out of the house. Too much bad blood. I'll send your orders in the morning. Enjoy your trailer."

"So what do we do with them?" Wyatt says, and we're forced to stare at the dead guys.

"I'll take care of 'em," Tuck says. "Have a good night." He grabs a leg on each guy and drags them off toward the deer-processing barn. I watch for a moment and realize that I seriously don't want to know what happens in that stark, unlit building.

"Well, let's see what we've got." Wyatt hops in the door, gun drawn.

I drop the rosary in my pocket and hurry up behind him. Tuck said it was clear, but I don't really trust anyone anymore, except Wyatt. Matty plops in and starts sniffing around like she's inspecting it, even though she just left it.

"You coming in?" I ask Rex, who's picking his fingernails just outside. I'd totally forgotten he was here—but then again, when Leon's around, he tends to suck out all the air so that it feels like it's just me and him.

Rex looks up, cocks his head. "You guys can stay in there. But I was thinking about bringing my tent over this way. Maybe Gabriela and Chance will, too? Seems like we'll have better luck if we stick together."

"Good idea."

"I'll go get my shit."

He walks away, and Wyatt and I are alone in the trailer. I was expecting it to be filthy, but it's just messy. It reminds me a lot of Alistair's trailer actually, but instead of boxes of paper and map-covered walls, they've got laptops and an Xbox and what looks like a stockpile of stolen stuff. In the kitchen, our Pop-Tarts are lumped together with chips and soda and open bags of cookies. The bedroom has a full-sized bed, and it's not made, but it doesn't look gross. What I wouldn't give to fall down and curl up, because I haven't slept in a real bed since the night the Valor suit showed up at my door and gave me this gun.

In the closet, I find fresh towels and folded sheets and give a luxurious sigh. That's the top shelf. But the rest of the closet isn't full of clothes—it's stacked with supplies. Boxes of spray paint, matches, ammunition, M-80s, empty bottles and rags and gasoline, which must make up a DIY Molotov cocktail kit.

Wyatt squats beside me and pokes the red gasoline can. "So if a bullet had gone back here . . . *kaboom*."

I stand, grab the sheets, and close the doors. "We've got to get rid of this stuff tomorrow."

As I strip the bed, Wyatt helpfully wads up the old sheets and hunts for a laundry basket, which he finds in the kitchen. I make the bed, glad to find no gross stains; the mattress is pretty new at least. Before I can put on the comforter, Wyatt runs and jumps in the center, landing with his elbows out and his hands behind his head.

"Home sweet home," he says, and I poke him in the exposed belly.

"Not until we have our stuff and find Monty."

He jumps up like he might've accidentally sat on the snake. We eventually find the poor little guy in an old fishbowl in the kitchen, and Wyatt pulls him out and *tuts* like a worried hen.

"He's all covered in Doritos powder!"

But it could be a lot worse, and we both know it.

"Are you okay staying here while I go get our stuff?" Wyatt asks, trying to brush the orange dust off the snake.

"Sure. I have Matty and a gun. Who could ask for anything more?"

It takes him several trips to get everything, and on the last one, he's got Chance and Gabriela helping him drag our tent along to dump it beside Rex's tent. He's already got his iPod charging, the cord snaking from the trailer's outside plug through his zipped-closed door.

"Did you get the meds?" I ask.

Gabriela nods, her mouth set in a thin line. "Expensive. And hard to figure out which one was best, so I got a couple of every-thing." She holds up the bag. "I'm going in. You coming?"

"I . . . um . . . I'm not allowed at the house anymore. Apparently the Cranes don't like it when you shoot their goons and take over their prime single-wides."

She smothers a laugh. "Crane boys don't like uppity bitches, huh? Maybe they'll kick me out soon too. We'll bring you some more pizza if they have any. My dumbass brother will bring the tents over. Looks like we got our own little gang now."

"The Black Hoods," I say, considering we're all wearing black hoodies.

Gabriela snorts. "Uh, no. Y'all are as white as it gets. More like . . . the Cockroaches. Everything goes to shit, but we manage to survive."

"Gross."

"But accurate."

"We'll have a tribal council to pick a better name tomorrow," I say, and we bump fists before she heads off toward the house. "Hey, wait!" I run into the kitchen and grab a silver packet of Pop-Tarts and a sleeve of cookies. "Kevin said they weren't feeding him well."

She grins. "No wonder everybody's so scared of you. You're a monster."

It's supposed to be funny, but it's the truth.

I make a noise that sounds like a laugh. I don't want her to know I'm hollow inside.

Soon we've got our own tent city out front. Rex's black tent, one each for Gabriela and Chance, side by side, the big one that Wyatt got for us, which we figure will be a meeting place. The next time I go to take Matty out, I find yet another tent.

"Who's that?" I holler.

The window unzips, just a little bit. It's Bea. "I'm staying here."

My instinct is that no, no, she's not. She's a murderer. But then again, aren't I? Didn't I do the same thing she did today? If some guy had grabbed me, threatened me, would I hesitate to put a bullet into his chest? Would Wyatt? But we're not the same, Bea and me. I've looked in the mirror, and I'm still me. My eyes are still deep and wet and feeling. And Bea's eyes are the dead, flat black of sharks. And I'd rather have a shark in my club than outside, hating me.

"Sure," I say. "You need any food?"

In response, she rezips her window.

It's bedtime, but I'm so wound up. I never fall asleep easily after killing someone (*my God, I killed someone, lots of someones. I'm a killer. I'm a shark*), and I should've bought sleeping pills at the store when I could, something to knock me on my ass until morning. I'm curled up in bed with the turtle Wyatt got me, staring at a paperback thriller one of the guys left in the bathroom. The first word is "the," but that's as far as I've gotten.

Wyatt finishes installing his de-cheesed snake in the aquarium, checks that the trailer door is locked, and shoves a low coffee table in front of it. I guess he's forgotten that the door opens outward, or maybe he figures it would trip up anyone dumb enough to try to come inside. Matty's asleep on the floor by the bed, snoring deeply on a ragged old blanket. Wyatt sits beside me, in the curl of my body.

"You okay?"

He runs a hand down my back, rubs me gently through the blankets. I'm staring at Matty because it's easier than looking at him.

"I wanted to knit her a blanket," I say, voice tiny. "Out of really nice yarn. Bright colors. I wanted to yarn bomb my dog. I thought we could just walk away from all this Valor shit. Find a better place, a real life. But now it's like we escaped one spiderweb and walked right into another one."

"So knit her a blanket. Didn't you buy yarn and stuff at the store? I saw a bag . . ."

I shake my head. "Yeah, but . . . I can't even remember how to cast on the first stitches. It makes me dizzy now. I can't concentrate. I just stare at the needles and yarn, and they make no sense. I'm all stopped up. Like when you shake a can of Coke and haven't opened it yet because it'll explode on you. I used to make stuff to let out the pressure, a little at a time. But now . . . there's too much pressure and not enough time and no patience, and I can't even read this stupid book, much less follow some intricate pattern or count stitches." I throw the book against the wall, and Matty looks up like she's offended on behalf of literature.

I can almost feel Wyatt thinking as he absentmindedly rubs me, and then he jumps up and heads for the closet, where he holds up a can of spray paint.

"I've got it!"

"You've got what?"

His grin is insanely manic, and it reminds me that I have a heart. "You know what's faster and more explosive than yarn bombing? Graffiti."

"C'mon, Wyatt. You want me to become a graffiti artist?"

"No, *you* want you to become a graffiti artist. It's the same thing you were already doing: making a public statement with art. Making people think. But instead of working on it for four days with needles or whatever, you do it out in the real world in thirty seconds. Bigger. Bolder. Faster. Comes with an automatic power high."

"You seem to know a lot about it."

He gets that adorably sheepish look he gets when he talks about his bad-boy days. "Me and Mikey used to do a little tagging. You know that pink cow on the electric box by the church?"

"Oh my God. I love that cow."

"I totally drew that cow. I was high as hell, but it was done with love."

"That's . . ." I grab his hand and yank him down beside me on the bed. Possibilities are slamming through my head. "That's brilliant. I already had all these ideas for cross-stitch. 'Debt Sweet Debt' and 'Kill Your Valor' and 'Pay or Die.' But your way . . . it's better. We can say whatever we want." I pause, thinking. My voice drops. "Even warn people about what the CFF really is. Keep people from coming to the meetings and getting stuck or getting shot."

"But . . . the CFF might be different in other places. Like, we have no way of knowing if every cell is insane, or if that's just Leon being Leon. For some people, the CFF might be their best shot at safety. The point is: You get to choose what you say. And you already have everything you need." He puts the spray paint can on the dresser. It's bloodred—perfect for anti-Valor sentiment.

I pull him into a hug, because he's just given me the best gift. This is what I need to do. This is how I make myself useful and keep being the old Patsy instead of the new Zooey, although I don't know how much that name matters if Leon already knows my real name, already has my mom.

But where is she? I untangle myself from Wyatt, stand up, and twitch back the blinds to look at the lights shining from the big house. The trees obscure my view, but I can see people moving back and forth, lots of people. Maybe they had another meeting at the high school for new recruits. Or maybe they had a family reunion. Or maybe this is just dinner for those who haven't been ostracized.

"Do you think my mom is up there, at the house? That that's why they don't want me up there?"

Wyatt's standing behind me now, and his arms wrap around me, pulling me to his chest. "They should understand you well enough by now to know how stupid that would be. You don't let anything stand in your way when you want something."

I soften and spin in his arms, looping them around his neck and going up on tiptoe to murmur against his lips, "Is that a good thing?"

He kisses me gently, and his breath smells like mint, all the blood scrubbed away. "It is to me."

Soon my back is against the flimsy wall and my nails are scratching up his spine under the clean shirt. His thumbs plot my dimples, his hands big and warm, cradling my face, holding it just so. I arch my back into him, and he runs his fingertips down my shoulders, my back, my hips. With his fingers through my belt loops, he walks me to the bed, never breaking the kiss. He sits, and for once I'm taller, bending my neck down to kiss him. His hands rove up and down my legs, skimming over my skinny jeans, teasing up my thighs. He kisses down my neck, unzips my hoodie, licks my collarbones, and just starts to kiss under my shirt, toward my bra. All my horrible thoughts are gone, and there's nothing but him and me and closed doors guarded by garage-sale coffee tables, and I wish I'd put my backpack closer to the bed, because I don't want to break contact, and this is seriously hot, and there's a reason I bought condoms at the store.

Just as I'm pushing him onto his back and crawling on top of him, Matty lurches up and runs to the door, barking. Wyatt and I break apart—not with guilt this time, but with anger. Who the hell thinks they can interrupt this, interrupt us? I don't want to shoot someone else tonight, but I will if they keep me from Wyatt again.

"Knock-knock, lovebirds."

It's Chance. Of course. I zip up my hoodie with a sigh, and Wyatt rearranges his clothes and stands, looking adorably rumpled and flushed.

"I'm getting really sick of that guy," he mutters.

I shove the table aside and open the door to give Chance a death glare. But Gabriela's by his side looking happier than I've ever seen her, so I just sigh and step back to let them in. Chance immediately flops down on the flowered couch, and Gabriela goes straight to the Pop-Tarts on the kitchen counter.

"So Kevin's going to be okay, I take it?"

She nods as she chews. "Yeah, they said I got the right stuff. We should know by tomorrow if it's going to work. There's a small chance that he'll be allergic to whatever antibiotics I got, but we'll see a reaction fast if that's the case. He seemed pretty jazzed to have the food, too." She takes another bite of her red velvet Pop-Tart.

I perch on a recliner. "So that's one less thing to worry about." Wyatt sits on the arm, leaning against me. Things almost feel normal.

"What else is there?" Gabriela says. "We did their little hazing trip. Was that not enough?"

My jaw drops at her naïveté. "Oh my God. Are you joking? Do you seriously think these douchebags just wanted us to pass some test, and then we'd be honorary Cranes with full bathroom privileges? Hell no. They're going to use us like Valor used us. Leon already said we'd have a new assignment in the morning, and the way he said it made it sound dangerous. We're young. We're expendable. We've got no parents to stand up for us. There are no police, no laws. We're like those little kids in shoe factories in third-world countries. They are going to use us until we're dead."

I'm crying again, but I can't stop it. I keep seeing blood bloom on that guy's belly, his friend going down in a hail of bullets. It occurs to me that when he burst out shooting, I cared more about killing him in a haze of rage than I did about keeping my own body alive. There are holes in the wall behind the door. From my gun. And I need to reload in case I have to do it again. The walls of this trailer may feel safe, but they can't stop bullets. Sure, it felt cozy for a while, me and Wyatt behind a locked door, but it's all just a big joke. There is no safety.

Gabriela points her Pop-Tart at me. "Wait. Is that a new assignment for you guys tomorrow, or for everyone?"

I know my smile is wrong. "Funny, but Leon didn't say."

Chance puts his feet up on the couch, but it's not my couch, so I don't care. "And if we're supposed to be earning our keep, what are all those other people in the tent city doing? The middle-aged ones and old ones? Because they sure as hell didn't get sent out to plant Wipers."

When I think on it, he's right. There's got to be more than a hundred people outside of our group who live here, but I've never seen them do anything except line up at the house for food and showers. But I haven't really watched them closely, either, and we haven't been here long. I've been too busy just trying to stay alive. They're not out of their tents a ton, though, which makes me wonder if Leon's got them doing something quiet, masked by nylon walls, or if maybe they're doing something out in the woods, where I know the Cranes have other buildings. But the thing is—they're doing something for Leon, for the CFF.

Because in this world, nothing is free, is it?

"I guess we'll find out tomorrow," I say. "Now, unless you want to bring up any more conspiracy theories, can we please go to sleep?"

Gabriela smacks Chance's feet off the couch. "Come on, bro. I think they want to get it on."

Chance hops up and smacks Wyatt on the back. "Love in the time of capitalism?"

Wyatt turns red and shoves Chance away. "A man's got a right to be tired after a fistfight and a gunfight in one day."

Chance and Gabriela look at each other, break into laughter, and swagger toward the front door muttering, "A man's got a right," and, "I punched a man for looking at me wrong," in their best cowboy voices. I smother a giggle but am glad to close the door on them and slide the table back in place.

"Can we go to bed now?" Wyatt asks, rubbing his eyes.

I hook my thumbs through my belt loops and drawl, "A man's got a right."

He picks me up, tosses me over his shoulder, and throws me on the bed.

12.

Not that anything exciting happens in the freshly made bed. Like all our days together, this one feels as long as a week, and it's easy to forget that I was in a store being interrogated by a cop just a few short hours ago. We stare at each other, grinning, but neither of us makes a move. At the very least, I want to brush my teeth and put on my pajamas, because I feel beyond gross, so I roll off the bed and head for the bathroom with my backpack.

I look like crap, but that's become normal. My eyes are blood-shot from crying, and my hair's a filthy mess. But I'm standing in front of a shower, so what the hell? I close the bathroom door, turn the shower on hot, step out of my clothes, and lose myself in scalding-hot water. Maybe if I stand here long enough, I can wash all the grit and roughness and sadness off my skin. Unlike my last shower, stolen from Château Tuscano, the only shampoo here is the kind of crappy two-in-one that guys use to smell like angry werewolves. But I want to be clean, so I use it anyway. My armpit hair is out of control, but I doubt Wyatt's going to complain. In just a week, the stubble on my legs has grown lush, and I poke it, wishing I'd bought razors. I always figured that when the apocalypse hit, body hair would come back in style, quick.

When the hot water starts to run out, I feel a little guilty for using it all, but I guess it'll recharge if Wyatt wants a shower later. I step out and fumble for a towel, hurrying into my new pajamas. Such luxury, really, to get to change for bed, and while standing up with overhead lights. I wipe off my face, put on moisturizer, floss, brush my teeth, add deodorant, and rub in lotion. All the little luxuries that make me feel less like a murderer living in a stolen trailer and more like a girl who doesn't want to gross out the boy she's about to sleep with.

Wait. Not *sleep with* sleep with. Sleep beside. Because I don't know how to sleep alone anymore. I don't want to remember how. The nightmares are too dark.

My hair is a wet mess, but I run the new brush through it and scoot my bangs to the side. There's no hair dryer, because why would three dudes need one? I fetch my mom's rosary out of my jeans and slip it over my head, where it dangles down to my belly, a strange feeling against my skin. When there's nothing left to do, I step out into the bedroom. Wyatt's sitting on the bed, doing a crossword. The lighting is better in here, and he's not wearing his shirt, and there are bruises all over him. I don't know if they're from today's fight with his driver, from something else, from the way I smacked my fists against him jokingly when he picked up me. I hurry to sit beside him, touching the purple smudges.

"Are you hurt?"

He shrugs, as if the question makes him uncomfortable. "Not really. Still amped up a little. Fights do that to me."

I find ibuprofen in the medicine cabinet and bring Wyatt a glass of water and two brown pills. He swallows them, carefully sets down the glass, and takes my hand in both of his.

"Thank you."

"No big deal."

"No, I mean . . . for everything. I was just sitting here, staring at the page, thinking about how if you'd just killed my brother, you could've had a chance at a normal life. You could've just walked away."

I sit back against the pillows, still holding his hand. "I don't think that was ever an option. Look what they did to Chance's family. I don't think I was supposed to live through that. None of us were." A few beats later I add, "And neither were our parents."

"You think Leon really has your mom?"

I drop his hand. "I don't know, Wyatt! How could I know?"

"Do you want to drive by your house tomorrow? See if she's there?"

And that reminds me.

"Hey, don't you have that guy's phone?"

Wyatt nods, gets it out of his crumpled jeans. I just now noticed he's only in pajama pants, which reminds me of that time I didn't shoot him because he had a pajama boner, which reminds me that we are alone in bed behind a locked door, which makes me very much not want to call my mom at this exact moment, but that's what I'm going to do.

He hands me the phone, and I dial my house. My hands are shaking so hard that I actually mess up the number and have to backtrack. I press the green button and wait. After a moment, it rings. And rings and rings and rings. No one picks up, and the answering machine doesn't answer, and that's the scariest thing of all, because the answering machine always picks up. I should be hearing my voice right now, but all I get is ringing.

"No answer?" Wyatt asks softly.

I shake my head and end the call.

"Did you try her cell? Could she be staying with your grandparents or something?"

I stare at him like he's an idiot, because he keeps forgetting that I was broke-ass poor. "We could only afford one cell, and mine's gone. There's no one else. Just me and Mom."

My eyes are burning, and I wind back my arm to throw the phone at the wall, but Wyatt catches my hand and uncurls my clenched fingers. He puts the phone on the bedside table and pulls me close, and now I'm the little spoon and he's stroking my wet hair like it's actually pleasant to touch.

"It'll be better tomorrow," he whispers in my ear. "It's always better tomorrow."

"That's a lie."

"Shh. Today is better than yesterday was. Yesterday was better than the day before it. Whatever life was like before last week, now we have to take what we can get when we can get it. And today I'm just grateful that we both lived through that mission and now we have this trailer. I swear, this is the first time in a week that I've been able to lie down without my feet brushing something or stand up without knocking my head."

I chuckle. My old mail van—he barely fit in it, standing or horizontal. Matty waggles to my side and tries to lick me, and I rub her head and tell her she's a good girl. I didn't have her last week, either.

"You're trembling," he says.

"We should sleep."

His hand leaves my hip like it's sorry to go, and he walks across the room to turn off the light and edge the door closed just enough so that we're in darkness but there's a slice of illumination from the hall outside. It's funny—I can't go to sleep with the lights on, but I hate being fully in the dark now. I like to know no one can sneak up on me.

Gently, so gently, Wyatt pulls the covers down and back up over my legs to cover me, then slides in behind me, matching his body to mine and pulling me close. I slowly soften, melting like butter, until my eyes flutter closed.

My dreams are dark, twisted, dangerous things. But they always are now.

When I wake up, the roof of the trailer is clattering with rain. Wyatt is still curled around me, but he's awake and tense.

"What's wrong?" I whisper, anticipating the worst.

"I have to pee but didn't want you to wake up alone."

I giggle and plant a kiss on his hand. "Go on, then. I'll survive." But I'm touched.

With him gone, the bed is colder, and I spread out and stretch like a starfish. Matty licks my hand and whines, and then I'm puttering around the kitchen, looking for coffee. All they have is soda. But I'm not supposed to go to the big house, and I doubt a Crane could get my Starbucks order right. I settle for a Pop-Tart and a glass of water, setting out the same for Wyatt on a chipped plate from the cabinet. For, like, five seconds, I pretend I'm a wife or whatever.

It's strange how many little things I notice in the kitchen. There's a vaping kit on the counter, an open box of blood sugar testing strips, a pair of slippers with holes in the bottom. I'm suddenly very aware that I killed people last night, and not because I had to, not because there was a gun to my mom's chest or a clock counting down. Because they hurt Matty and shot at me. That's all. Leon seemed to think it was fair, but is that the kind of fair I can live with? The whole point of joining the CFF was to go back to not killing people, but it's become a habit. All this time, I was trying to hold on to myself, to Patsy. The change was subtle, I suppose. But I've become a girl who will kill strangers out of anger. And when I go through last night in my head, I don't see how I could've done anything differently. I put the Pop-Tart gently on the plate before I lose my breakfast like I lost my salad after killing Wyatt's dad.

Before Wyatt is done eating, the knock I've been dreading comes. Matty barks like she's actually threatening, and Wyatt and I lock eyes. In pajamas, neither of us has a gun, and he has to be thinking the same thing I am: The guys we shot last night weren't ready when they answered the door, and that's why we're here right now instead of outside in a tent in the rain.

We tiptoe to the bedroom and fetch our guns, but we're both in elasticized pajama pants, so there's no place to hide one. I turn my back to him and slide into yesterday's dirty jeans, and after a moment of what I can only assume to be sneaking a peek at my undies, he does the same. The knocking grows more insistent, and Leon Crane himself hollers, "Open up or we'll open it up for you!"

Wyatt is shirtless and I'm still in my pajama shirt as we approach the door. I kick the coffee table aside while he holds Matty back by her collar. Standing to the side of the door, I open it enough to stick my face out.

"If I wanted to shoot you, honey, you'd be dead," Leon says, sweet as syrup and soaked with rain even though he's holding an umbrella. As punctuation, he sticks a finger through a bullet hole in the side of the trailer. Two Crane goons with black umbrellas flank him, younger guys like the ones we killed yesterday. They're smirking, but their hands are on their guns, like they'd love a reason to shoot me. Maybe Leon wasn't lying about how going up to the big house would be a bad idea.

I open the door and wait, arms crossed, gun in hand. Wyatt is a solid wall behind me, holding back Matty, who'd love to go slobber all over Leon and anybody else. She's not smart, my dog. If she were, she wouldn't have followed me in the first place.

"Got a job for you," Crane says.

"What else is new?"

"We've been through this, sugar. You took our money, you killed our boys, and now you've got temporary possession of our trailer. You're members of the CFF now, and you have a duty in our war."

I yawn and don't bother to cover it.

"What are we doing today? Depositing nanny cams?" Wyatt asks.

I can't help smirking. Because the thing is? I would've been terrified of Leon Crane last week. But now I know that showing weakness to a man like him is just asking to die.

Also, he looks kind of ridiculous when he's holding an umbrella.

"Thanks to those Wipers, soon there won't be a working credit card in this county," Leon drawls, one thumb in his vest like a politician. Wyatt and I look at each other and shrug, unimpressed. "But we're going one further. You know how they put those little ink packets on expensive shit at the department store? We're going to make them all explode."

"So evil," I murmur.

Fast as a blink, Leon slaps me across the face, hard. I stumble back, a hand to my wet cheek. Wyatt's got his gun pointed at Leon, and Leon's goons have guns pointed at us, and my face stings, red rage filling me.

"Don't you ever forget that you're nothing but a pawn in this war," Leon says.

I spit in the dirt at his feet and see blood in it. "You can't play chess without pawns, asshole."

"Well, I just so happen to have your queen, little pawn, so you'd best get dressed and ready to roll. Now, normally I'd send you out with a driver, but we're down two of them since your little escapade last night, and Alex has a concussion." He stares hard at Wyatt. "The kid's a prick, I'll give you that, but did you have to bang him up and abandon him in a parking lot? Little shit wandered off into traffic like a lost bunny. She's rubbing off on you, boy."

Wyatt flinches, and Leon concentrates on me. "So here's what I want you to do. Take your boyfriend's car out to the new outlet mall off the freeway. There's two bags full of little cans waiting on the front porch for you. Now, they ain't like the Wipers—there's no sticky tape, no button to push. This time, all of that business will be handled remotely. All you got to do is plant one in every store on the provided list. In a shoe box, in the pocket of a rain-coat, in a bag, behind a trash can. I don't care. But I want every one of those cans planted in a store by suppertime. You got that?"

"Who else is doing it?"

Leon gives a crocodile's smile. "Everybody here's got a job."

"Even the old people in the tents?"

Leon chuckles. "Even them. Now, get on."

As he turns to walk away, I yelp, "So if we do this, can I see my mom?"

Leon turns around slowly, his grin lazy, like he knows I'm trapped. "I got one more big job for you after this. After that, you can have your mama. She's being well taken care of, so don't you worry a bit. Valor would've killed her. But me? I'm just keeping her comfortable. Making sure she gets her medicine."

He's about to head for the house when I blurt, "How do we know these cans are what you say they are?"

Leon chuckles and rubs a hand through his hair. "Now, how did I know you were going to ask me that? You Valor kids have a reason to be suspicious, I guess, but you're more irksome than most." He reaches into his coat and pulls out a can of peanuts, putting it in my hand. When our skin touches, he's cold as a snake, and I inspect the can like it holds a viper. "Go on. You can open it."

I throw it back at him. "No. You open it."

He steps close, too close, and shoves his umbrella at me, forcing me to hold it. The rain makes a curtain around us as he pries up the flexible plastic top. I flinch away as soon as the inside of the can is exposed, but nothing explodes. When I look again, he's pulling out a packet of wires and cells. I'm not sure what a bomb looks like, but I'm pretty sure this isn't one.

"You ever seen one of these? No? Well, our tech boy's a genius. So this is a radio transmitter just like the ones they put in those machines you have to walk through to leave a store. But this one is more powerful, so when we remotely activate it, all those little dye packs just splatter everything. It's gonna be beautiful. Satisfied?"

I nod. He nods back.

"You can keep that, Patsy. Do it by dinnertime."

He grabs his umbrella and leaves. Matty barks at his back as he walks away. I deflate, and Wyatt tosses the can out into the rain, gently moves me out of the doorway, and shuts it before drawing me into a hug. "At least we're not killing anybody," he murmurs, and I beat my forehead against his bare shoulder.

"Do one more thing, then one more thing, then just one more thing. I can't believe we went to that stupid meeting."

"Shh. We have food. We have a place to live. We have Matty and friends, and neither of us is injured. It could be a lot worse. It'll be over soon."

I pull back and look up at him. "Will it?"

He kisses my forehead. "It has to be."

"What do you mean?"

"He said there was one more big job. So either you finish it and get your mom back, or you finish it and he gives you another hoop to jump through, at which point you know he's lying about your mom and we hit the road."

"But . . ."

"We'll go back to your house today. Look around. Talk to the neighbors. They might know if she was picked up by a Valor car or a Crane tow truck, right?"

I breathe deeply and nod. It makes sense. But I'm terrified to see my house. It's like Rex said—my mom is like Schrödinger's cat right now. Until I know if she's alive or dead, she's both alive and dead, and I'm in this freaky limbo, trying to get her back. The rosary around my neck could mean nothing or everything. But it all starts with getting dressed and getting the hell out of this trailer. I lost my dad, and then I lost the locket he gave me. All I wanted was to see him again. Now it's the same thing with my mom and her rosary.

"Right," I say, not that it sounds convincing.

Wyatt heads for the shower, and I head for my backpack and pull out my bra, a new shirt, and new jeans. Nothing fits quite right, but at least I don't smell. When Wyatt ambles out of the bathroom in a cloud of steam, I hurry in, wipe off the mirror, and put on bright red lipstick and deodorant. Do I look like a girl who might shop at the boutiques in the outlet mall? Sure, in this economy, because credit cards mean anyone can have anything at any time. Or they did. Until Valor. Until those Wipers take effect.

Before we go, I refill my clip, grab a box of ammo, and stop in front of the closet. I pick up a can of bright green spray paint, and my fingers itch to use it. Considering I've never spray-painted anything before, I read the directions on back and shake the can, listening to it rattle. I put the can of green and the can of red from the dresser in my backpack with the ammo and slide on my shoes. Matty gets locked in the bedroom with food and water, and we step out the door to find the rain down to a drizzle with a peek of sunshine. Rex is reading in his open tent and Gabriela and Chance are gone. Bea's rain-streaked tent is zipped up, but there's a shadow inside, so I have to assume she's awake. I'm just glad she didn't slit anyone's throat in the night.

"Where are you guys going?" Rex asks.

"To do more Crane bullshit," Wyatt rumbles.

"You need a hand?"

Wyatt and I look at each other. "I think we're expected to do it alone," I say. "But I wish we didn't have to. Maybe you could keep Matty company in the trailer? We don't have a key, and we can't lock it, so I guess anybody could go in there, if they wanted to."

He grins. "Are there Pop-Tarts?"

"Knock yourself out."

Rex bounds into the trailer, calling, "Good luck with your bullshit!"

Bea's tent unzips, and she gives us her dead-fish stare but says nothing.

On the front porch, we find two bags waiting for us. One is my hated faux purse from my trip to Mark's, and the other is a ratty black backpack. Both are filled with nut cans. Almonds, peanuts, cashews. But when I lightly shake one, nothing rattles. When I try to pry the top off like the one Leon showed me, I find that it's been superglued on and won't budge. Could you even hide a bomb in a can this small? Just like with the Wipers, I'm going to have to trust Leon and the CFF, even if I never really trust Leon and the CFF. I shove the can back into the bag and figure that if Leon wanted me dead, he could've shot me on my doorstep, easy as pie.

The list on top of the bags is typed out and has thirty stores, most of them the sort of place that would assign a cashier to follow me around, expecting me to steal stuff. If I'd known that all my work at the CFF would involve pretending to be an honest shopper, I wouldn't have bought so many black hoodies. Five twenty-dollar bills are included, paper-clipped to the list along with the note, *In case they get suspicious, buy something small.*

Wyatt drives, singing along as his music blasts. I put my feet on the dashboard and watch, as always, for evidence of the Valor government, out in the world. All black cars look like bad guys now. All men in dark suits become agents. Even the black-and-white police car in front of the doughnut shop doesn't feel safe. But how many people driving around with their lattes even know that? Considering the full parking lots, Valor has to be in control of the media. Even if the poor folks at Big Choice know that something's fishy, plenty of people in town are still willing to wait in line for overpriced coffee at Starbucks.

My breath catches as we drive by the road that leads to Wyatt's neighborhood—and mine. I look for smoke but don't see any. Then again, it rained last night. Maybe all the smoke is gone. After this job, we'll check. I don't want to, but we will. Because I have to know. I pull the rosary out of the neck of my tee and roll the beads between my fingers like they're wishes. I'm not supposed to go home, but what part of my life now involves doing what I'm supposed to? If my mom's alive, she'll forgive me, and so will her messed-up God.

Too soon we pull into the outlet mall. It's a few minutes before ten on a Monday, which means that there aren't a ton of people shopping. If this were Black Friday or Christmas, we'd have to park at the closed fish restaurant across the street; this lot totally fills up in a mad thrash to buy crap. I think I've been here only once before, when my mom needed a dress for a wedding.

Wyatt stops at a parking lot stop sign. "What's the first store on the list?"

"The stupid luggage store. Over there."

"Guess it doesn't matter where we park, then, since we're going to be all over the place." He parks slightly far out, pointed toward the exit.

We think like criminals now.

Because we are criminals.

"One bag at a time?" Wyatt asks.

I pick up the stupid brown one I hate. "Yeah. One bag, then lunch, and then we'll load the cans into this bag. That backpack is just asking for a cop to search it, and I don't know how we'd explain away twenty pounds of fake nuts." I shake my head as I get out of the car. "This is so stupid. This is not how wars are fought."

Wyatt gets out and stretches, revealing a strip of tummy that never fails to mesmerize me. "I was there for the Battle of the Nut Cans," he says in a raspy old-man voice. "And I tell you, sonny, it was nuts. Pure nuts."

I giggle, and he reaches for my hand, and then we're walking toward this luggage store that I would never, ever go into in real life. Everything is monogrammed and quilted and displayed with dozens of smaller, identical baby suitcases that fit inside one another like nesting dolls. And everything, as Leon predicted, has a big dye pack attached to it.

"Can I help you?" It's an older woman, and she's eyeing me up and down as if looking for evidence of an orange prison jumpsuit.

"Just looking for a birthday gift for my mom." I give her my most innocent smile and pull Wyatt toward a sale rack of wallets. She follows us like a ghost as I pick through the overpriced wallets, any of which my mom would adore. I find one for fourteen dollars and hold it up for Wyatt's inspection.

"We have the entire matched set," the woman says, popping up behind us.

"Maybe for Christmas," I say, but she doesn't move, doesn't blink. Whatever happened to trust? I reach into my bag and pull out my cash before handing the big, brown monstrosity to Wyatt. "Hold my purse while I buy this, will you, sweetie?"

"Always with the purse," he grumbles, and the lady leads me to the counter with a resigned sigh. Along the way, just to mess with her, I exchange the wallet for an even cheaper key fob with a leather lobster on it. My mom would hate it, but it's half as much.

"You don't think your mother would prefer the wallet?" she asks, mouth turned down.

"Oh, no. She loves lobsters. She's just crazy for crustaceans. This is perfect."

She gives me my change and drops the hideous key chain in a bag, then basically herds us out of her store before we can be more annoying, calling, "I'll keep that wallet on hold, if you change your mind."

It occurs to me that if a store with six-hundred-dollar suitcases is that desperate for seven dollars' worth of business, then the economy is truly screwed.

"I stuffed a nut can into an expensive suitcase," Wyatt mutters once we're outside.

The next store on the list is full of hipster clothes, and the workers stay as far away from us as possible, as if cheap clothes are an epidemic. We leave a can of pistachios at the bottom of a bin of flip-flops. Then we're in a store full of leather jackets, and I nudge a can of almonds under a leather fedora while Wyatt talks up an aging biker about leather jackets. The kids' store is the hardest, since neither of us knows anything about anything in the entire store. I end up buying a pair of four-dollar arm warmers for my made-up cousin while Wyatt sneaks a can of mixed nuts behind a collection of sparkly snow boots.

The good thing is that I don't see a single cop, mall variety or possibly real variety. The bad thing is that I keep leaking money just to buy time, and if it keeps up at this rate, I'm going to have an entire stack of shit I don't need and no more twenties to distract an endless line of desperate and suspicious cashiers.

With one nut can left in the bag, we head into a ladies' boutique where there's nothing below forty dollars. I end up trying on ten pairs of hideous shoes, pretending that none of them are quite right, while Wyatt hides the can behind a potted plant. When I buy nothing, the middle-aged lady grumbles, "Cheap-ass kids," as we walk out the door.

We use some of the change to buy soft pretzels and drink water from the fountain in the food court. As usual, Wyatt's eaten his entire pretzel before I've even tapped all the salt off of mine. We don't talk much, because what are we going to talk about? Our lives are frozen. Our hobbies? Eating Pop-Tarts with my dead uncle's dog in a trailer full of ghosts. Turn-ons? Lockable doors and mail vans. Turn-offs? Those pesky bloodstains that never scrub off and the fact that we're never really alone. Or safe.

I'm not hungry anymore. I give Wyatt my pretzel, and we head back to the car for the next batch of nut cans, which I pack into my purse. At first everything goes fine—at this point, we're old pros. I've still got two twenties left, and it's easy enough to buy a pair of socks out of the clearance bin or some new shoelaces from the designer boutique. At one store, I manage to get a black tee with

Catwoman on it for three dollars, so in terms of my new life, that's winning.

We've got four cans left when we walk into the sort of super-expensive mini department store that can smell the poverty on me the second I open the door. The girl behind the counter gets right up in my face with offensively aggressive politeness.

"Can I help you?"

"Just looking, thanks."

"For anything in particular?"

I dodge around her and head for the clearance section, where I might believably belong. "Nope. Just looking."

Wyatt wisely says nothing and follows me. He looks like a bull in a china shop in here, among the dainty wisps of shirts and leggings hanging from clear plastic hangers like strips of discarded snakeskin. Whoever put this place on the list has clearly never been inside it. There's no place to hide something as ungraceful as an old nut can, there are cameras everywhere, and the shopgirl might as well be riding me like a jockey.

I snatch a filmy pink thong out of a bin and hand it to Wyatt, along with a twenty.

"Buy this for me, lover?" I say, batting my eyelashes. "I need to use the ladies' room."

There are no words for the look on his face. Damn, I miss my phone's camera.

"Uh. Yeah. Okay."

I head for the bathroom as the lady leads him to the counter with the thong draped over his finger; even it has a dye pack attached. At least the two-stall ladies' room doesn't have cameras, but there aren't many permanent hiding places for even the smallest little almond can. I settle for putting it in the trash can, then wash my hands with hot water and tons of soap. Just for fun, I pull out the can of red spray paint and stare at the cold, white tile wall. What to do for my first act of graffiti rebellion? I decide on DEBT SWEET DEBT. The paint is shiny red and runs a little where I was too heavy-handed. There's something to be said for the way it drips like blood does in the movies.

I pop the top back on the spray paint, resettle the hideous purse on my shoulder, and push out the bathroom door feeling like a badass.

And that's when I hear the first gunshot.

13.

I draw my gun and hold it a little behind me as I peek around the door. The shopgirl has her hands up, her mouth open but thankfully silent. Wyatt is still standing, thank God. And he's holding the gun. But I don't see blood. I don't actually realize what's up until I see a black-clad leg and a shoe on the ground.

"Hank?"

His head jerks to me, his eyes frantic. He looks at the door. And we run.

It's weird how quiet and normal it is outside, like no one even heard the shot. There are no sirens, no footsteps. Far away, a golf cart trundles toward us with its lights blinking red and blue, but the rent-a-cop inside it couldn't outrun a dead elephant. We say nothing, and our jog picks up to a run, and then we're throwing ourselves into the car and speeding out of the outlet mall parking lot.

"What happened?" I ask. I'm out of breath, and my heart is freaking out. For once it's scarier being the person who didn't pull the trigger.

"She tested the twenty. It was counterfeit. So she called the cop. He was right outside. But I couldn't leave because you were in the bathroom. And he was trying to take my gun and cuff me with those zip tie things, so . . ."

"So you shot him?"

He shakes his head and swallows hard. "No. I mean, I guess. I didn't want to. I didn't mean to. But he was trying to take my gun, and I wouldn't let him, and he was old, and we were wrestling for it, and he got shot in the leg, not even a bad hit. I think he maybe had a heart attack or something. He just fell over. Jesus, I feel bad for him."

"I'm sorry. I mean thank you. I mean . . . that sucks."

He nods. "Yeah."

"I wish you'd shot her instead."

Wyatt looks at me funny as we speed down the highway. "Don't say that. She was just doing her job."

"Yeah, and we were just doing ours. And the Cranes set us up."

"What do you mean?"

I pull the last twenty out of the bag and hold it up to the light.

It looks normal. Even has those little yellow lines in the corner from where it's been tested for counterfeit in the past.

"So she used the yellow pen, and it didn't work?"

"Yeah."

"So that means that not only are the Cranes making fake money and sending us out with it, but that they're going to the trouble of marking them up like real bills. That's probably what the tent people are doing. Turning crispy new counterfeit twenties into slightly used, wrinkled, yellow-penned cash."

Wyatt's hands are shaking on the steering wheel, and he looks like he wants to cry. I reach for his arm, and he shakes me off. "I just . . . Don't touch me right now, okay?"

"It's not your fault."

He pushes his hair back and dashes at his eyes with a fist. "He was just an old man. I didn't want to shoot him. What if he dies? We know nine-one-one isn't working."

I take a deep breath. For all the times Wyatt has talked me down from the ledge when I was losing my shit, this is the first time the tables have been turned, and I don't know what he needs. The best thing he's done for me is to hold me close until the shaking stops and tell me it's not my fault. But he doesn't want me to touch him, and even though I told him it's not his fault, I don't think he believes me.

"Do you want a hamburger?" is the best I can do.

He snorts and looks at me, half crazy. "Yeah, I do. But all we have is counterfeit money, and I don't want to shoot anyone else today."

I dig around in the bag and hold up some ones and fives. "We have the change. Which probably isn't fake."

He turns into the first fast-food place he sees and doesn't ask me if I want anything, which is okay, because I don't. He's crammed an entire burger in his mouth before we're back on the road.

"Where's your house?" he asks, mouth full.

"I . . . We don't have to do this now."

"We do. I need something to do. Something else to think about. Where is it?"

"Okay, just . . . head toward your house. Your old house."

I realize immediately that I've just reminded him that his dad is dead and he can't ever go back home. My face goes red with shame. That I've done the things I've done, that I've forced him to do horrible things too. I didn't mean to shoot my uncle Ashley, either. My hand was sweaty, and the trigger slipped. But whatever allows me to keep going anyway, to forget it . . . He doesn't have that adaptation. He can't ignore it. Can't repress it. His hands are still shaking. This is why he wasn't tapped by Valor. He's on his third burger as he turns onto the familiar road that leads to both our houses.

Everything just seems so . . . normal. It's the middle of the day, and the rain has fizzled out to puffy clouds and a cheerful sun. The old lady on the corner is in her garden of dead cabbages, and the horses in the pasture on the left are grazing peacefully. As we drive past the pink graffiti cow by the church, I smile fondly. Everything looks the same as all the other, normal days when I used to drive this way. There's almost no evidence that Valor Savings Bank has taken over the entire country. Unless you count the odd bloodstains here and there on a front doorstep. Or the spray of bullets painting that single-wide by the church. Or the blackened wrecks of burned houses, of which we pass two. I wonder which one of them was Chance and Gabriela's house.

"Turn right here."

Wyatt flinches, just a little bit, like he's still somehow allergic to poverty. My neighborhood may be on the same street as his, only a mile away, but you could fit four copies of my house into his old house. Of course, his dad's debt was six times worse than my mom's debt, but that doesn't show on the surface. I'm the only person who has held both of their Valor-issued cards, who has read the six-figure numbers and been forced to do something about it.

"Another right," I say.

Wyatt crams fries in his mouth and says nothing as he turns onto my street. I scan the houses for blood and smoke and find neither. Everything here is normal too. We pass Mr. Cole walking his dachshund, and seeing me, he frowns and waves. Wyatt slows to a crawl over the speed bumps, and I don't have to tell him that the spray paint and bullet holes in the SLOW CHILDREN sign have always been there. Much like crippling debt, we poor people do it to ourselves, shit on our own neighborhoods. Or that's what he thinks, probably. The rich kid who taught me how to use spray paint.

As we round the corner, I hold my breath. Then we're here, and I can see my mailbox now, my house. They didn't burn it. It's standing. I've been holding my breath, and I let it out in a long, low sigh. The last time I saw my house, it looked just like this, except that there was a mail truck parked out front, just for me. I thought I would drive home five days later and go back to normal. That the mail truck would disappear in the same way it appeared: secretly, quietly, easily, in the night.

God, I was so naive.

There are no outward signs to indicate what's happened here in the last week. The garage is closed, which means that my mom's crap car could be inside while she scans the job classifieds in her robe, or she could be at the hospital having chemo for the lump in her breast, or she could be slumped at the kitchen table with a bullet hole in her forehead. Dead or alive. There's no way to know. At least the house is still standing. It's eerily calm.

"Should I park outside, or in the driveway, or . . . ?" Wyatt won't quite look at me.

"Turn around in the cul-de-sac, I guess, and park at the curb. If you don't mind." Because this is how I think now: always with an exit strategy.

Thing is, my gut is telling me what it's been telling me every moment of the past week: Something isn't right.

He does as I've asked. The only Lexus in the neighborhood rolls up and sits on the curb, idling expensively despite its bleached gold paint. "Do you want me to stay here?"

I stare at my house, and it does that tunnel vision thing, both close up and far away. I've lived here for all of my life. My mom and dad brought me home from the hospital to live here, and every happy memory of my dad happened on this dingy plot of land. It's soaked with sorrow and small joys and struggle, but it's my home, and I am terrified of what I'll find inside.

Do I want him with me? Yes. Am I willing to risk him?

No.

"Just stay here and be ready to run. Okay?"

He swallows hard and puts his hand over mine where it clutches the edge of my seat. "Okay. Be careful." All I can do is nod.

I open the door and stand outside, feet on the crumbling sidewalk. My hands tremble as I slide my Valor Glock from the holster and into the big kangaroo pocket of my hoodie, just in case. For one short moment, I put my forehead against the roof of Wyatt's car, willing my heart to stop floundering. But it can't, and it won't, so I turn and step into my yard, the dead grass crunching under my shoes. The walk to Wyatt's door to kill his dad, my very first mission, was a lot longer, because his yard is four times bigger than mine. But it feels plenty long as step after step takes me up the cracked concrete to my front door.

A rustle in the bushes makes me jump, and a ragged calico cat erupts, meowing desperately.

"Get out of here," I say, but the rangy thing rubs up against my leg. We've called animal control on our neighbor ten times this year at least, but old Mrs. Hester keeps collecting diseased stray cats anyway, and they keep begging at our house because she can't afford enough food for them all. I'm not surprised when two more scrawny cats run across the lawn to meow at my feet. "Jesus. Guys. Go home." I nudge one gently away from the door as I realize I don't have my keys. I try the knob, but it's locked. Of course. "Crap." I almost knock, but something about that feels too loud.

I give Wyatt an exaggerated shrug and walk around my house trailing starving cats, my hand gripping my gun in my hoodie pocket. If my mom is alive and awake and at home, wouldn't she have noticed the car out front, watched me walk up? If so, she would've opened the door, crying, and hugged me; that much I know. So either she's here and can't reach the door, or she's not here. Or she could be sleeping off the Vicodin.

Our backyard has a falling-down wood fence on one side and a measly chain-link fence separating us from Mrs. Hester, as much as we always wish it were the other way around. The cats can jump the waist-high wire as easily as I can and do. The backyard looks sad and bare as usual, and the sliding glass doors are closed, bolted, and covered with vertical blinds, which means I can't see inside the house. Grabbing the spare key from inside the dead spigot, I hurry back around to the front door.

"Is that you, Patricia?"

Mrs. Hester waves to me as I jump the fence, and I stop and feign innocence as I look up. Standing on her porch, surrounded by whining cats, she's an object lesson in a life gone sour: Goodwill sweatshirt, too-short polyester slacks, threadbare slippers, gray hair that hasn't seen a Fantastic Sams in half a year. She frowns and picks up a random cat, glancing up and down the street as she rubs it hard enough to make it yowl.

"Yes, ma'am. Forgot my key."

"Where've you been? With that boy?"

I lick my lips, feeling jittery. She's never spoken so much to me; usually she just shouts about leaving her cats alone. Before last week, I might've been more polite, but now . . .

"Have you seen my mom?"

She glances nervously at her front door. "She's not home right now, but she left something for you." She holds up a finger and disappears inside her house.

My heart kicks up. She left something for me with Mrs. Hester? So maybe she got a job—maybe Valor helped her get a job. Or maybe she's getting chemo. The cats writhe around my legs, and I give Wyatt the same "wait one minute" finger that Mrs. Hester gave me. Before I can turn back, a gunshot cracks the air, and one of the cats yowls.

"Keith!" Mrs. Hester screams, and I look up, and she's dropping a black gun and trundling toward me as fast as she can. A black-and-white cat is on the ground at my feet, panting and bleeding. I draw my gun and step in front of the cat; there's nothing that could save him, even if Mrs. Hester could afford the vet bill. She stops a few feet from me, one hand out like Keith is going to reach out and grab it for comfort.

"Where's my mom, really?" I ask, the anger taking over.

She shakes her head, frantic. "Honey, I don't know. I don't know! Now let me help Keith!"

I glance down. Keith is gone. Mrs. Hester takes another step, and I block her.

"Where is my mom, and why did you just try to shoot me?"

She lets out a catlike yowl. "Just let me help my baby first." I step aside, and she kneels, pressing the still body with age-spotted hands. "Keith? Keith! Come on, honey. It's going to be okay."

I get the feeling that if I were dead on the ground, she wouldn't care nearly as much.

"Mrs. Hester. Last chance. Tell me where my mom is and why you tried to shoot me. Or I'll shoot another cat."

I won't. *I won't. I won't. I won't.* But she can't know that. She can't know that I've done worse. I aim at the calico, hating myself down to my guts.

She looks up, staring at me like I'm the Antichrist. "I don't know where she is. She was just gone one day, last week. But some men from Valor Savings Bank came to my door and showed me a card, said I owed a lot of money. They said that if I would just watch for you and kill you, they'd forgive it, let me keep the house and the cats. I didn't want to shoot you. I don't want to hurt nobody. I don't want . . . Oh, God. Keith. Keith!" She picks him up, rocking him against her chest.

"Did they say what would happen if you didn't shoot me?"

She looks up, like I've just slapped her. The way we're arranged—me, wearing a large black hoodie, standing with gun drawn and pointed, and her on the ground on her knees—it looks like an execution. It was supposed to be an execution. But whether she was supposed to kill me or I was supposed to kill her, that's not what's happening today.

"They said that if I shot you, my debts would be forgiven. And if I didn't . . ." She scans the ground, patting it with her free hand. "Where's my gun, honey?"

Like we're playing Ping-Pong. Like she dropped her paddle. No wonder Valor only tapped teens. Dementia makes for a poor assassin.

"Mrs. Hester, what are you supposed to do if you couldn't shoot me?"

She looks up, her chin quivering. "I'm supposed to go in your house and get something on the table."

I look down, swallow hard. "Look, Mrs. Hester. Don't go in my house. Just . . . do you have any relatives out of state? Don't you have a daughter in Kentucky? Just get in your car and go visit her for a while. Okay?"

She gives a sad laugh, like I'm dumb as bricks. "Honey, I can't leave my cats. They need me. They're going to be so upset over poor Keith. We'll bury him in the backyard with Noodles. . . ."

With a grunt, she struggles to her feet, clutching Keith to her chest like a teddy bear. "I do need that gun, though. Do you see it anywhere?"

"You dropped it on your porch."

"I need that gun. It's dangerous out here. Dangerous times. Gangbangers and terrorists taking over America. I saw it on the news. You wait here, honey. We'll go inside and sort all this out." She waddles toward her house, muttering to Keith, and the other cats trail in her wake, wailing.

I look up at my house, knowing that it's empty. If my mom were there, nothing could stop her from running outside if she saw me. And even if she somehow missed my arrival, the gunshot would've brought her to the porch, Vicodin haze or not. The house has to be empty. And whatever they left on the table for Mrs. Hester? I don't want to know what it is.

The jog to Wyatt's car feels longer than it should be, my heart pounding in my ears.

"You okay?" he calls through the open window.

"Get ready to run," I call.

Another gunshot is followed by the sound of a divot of lawn pinging away.

"Patricia Klein, you stop right now! We got to talk!" Mrs. Hester calls, like I'm one of her cats.

I dive into the car's backseat, and Wyatt hits the gas. Soon I'm on my knees, staring out the back window as Mrs. Hester jogs after us, giving up after ten steps.

"Slow down a sec," I say. It's not like she could catch us, even if we were doing five miles per hour. Wyatt obliges, and I watch as Mrs. Hester doubles over, hands on her knees, catching her breath, gun in hand. She shoots again, and it goes nowhere. Finally, shaking her head, she waddles up to my front door. They must've given her a key, because my mom would never have trusted her in our house alone. I hold my breath as she opens the door.

And the house—my house—explodes.

14.

My mouth drops open. Even from the end of the street, I feel the suck of air, the heat punching back out, almost like it lifted up my guts and dropped them into boiling water. The flames roll majestically, and black smoke races toward the sky. At first I think there's nothing left of Mrs. Hester, but then I see a scrap of pink sweatshirt and have to turn away.

"What do I do?" Wyatt asks.

"Just drive," I say, fists to my eyes. "Just drive."

I lie down in the backseat, the leather cold and hard and lumpy. I wish I had Matty, or my quilt, or anything that felt safe. All I have is this cheap, oversized hoodie, so I flip the hood up over my head and turn to face the seats. Breathing deep, I try to force my heart back down. Try to remind myself that it's just a house. Just a cheap, crappy house that was filled with disappointment and longing. A house that felt too empty after my dad left. It was always too warm in summer, always too cold in winter. Things broke and weren't replaced. It was almost like a train station, like my mom and I were both waiting forever for my dad to come back so our real life could start. It was a house where we either stared at the door or the TV screen because there was nothing inside worth looking at.

Another piece of me lost: If my dad came back, we wouldn't be there for him to find.

Nothing would.

And now it's just another black cage of burned wood, empty in the middle. Another rotten tooth in a neighborhood with nowhere to go but downhill. The neighbors will gather around and take pictures to put on Facebook. They'll find pieces of Mrs. Hester and her cats and call 911 and cluck their frustration at how the government isn't doing its job when the fire trucks don't show up. They'll say prayers for me and my mom, probably assuming that we're part of the blackened wreckage within. I am, for most purposes, dead. Twice. Little pieces of me fall away all the time. I'm surprised there's anything left at all.

I find the strength to roll over and sit up and buckle myself in like a good girl. Because there's one thing I know for sure now: My mom was not in the house.

Which means there's a chance that Leon wasn't lying, that she's somewhere on the Crane compound, or at least somewhere safe. Safer.

My house got blown up, and the demented old lady who was supposed to kill me is dead. And that means that Valor might not know what happened to me. Maybe they really think I'm dead too. I should've planted my sweatshirt behind, dammit, but it's too late to turn back. People will be creeping outside their houses to investigate now. They would notice.

Which means that my current problem, my real problem, is getting in good with the Cranes. According to their rules, Wyatt and I failed our last assignment. There are still three of those nut cans in my bag. Then again, do the Cranes have to know? It's not like I'm wearing a camera, like I did with Valor, not like there's a Crane following us around with a clipboard, checking off boxes. Surely they have no way of knowing that we planted only seventeen cans?

"What are you thinking?" Wyatt asks, and I exhale slowly.

He's seen me upset, plenty, but not like this. Before I was guilty, sad, filled with self-loathing. Now I'm angry. Valor tried to kill me. They used a sick, sad old woman, leveraging her debts against her. They killed her brutally. At least this time, as we drive away, I know that I'm not the one who killed Mrs. Hester. That was Valor, one hundred percent.

And I wish there were a better way to get back at them than

being just another Crane goon saying "How high?" every time Leon tells me to jump. So what's the one thing I haven't had since that black SUV rolled up outside my door?

"What I'm thinking about is leverage," I say.

"Leverage," Wyatt repeats. His dark eyes flash at me in the rearview mirror.

I nod and stare out the window as cars zoom by on the six-lane road we call a highway. It's funny how attuned I am to shiny black now. I never paid attention to cars before, but now I'm suddenly on the lookout for anything Valor, for anyone who looks too carefully or follows too closely. Suits, especially, catch my attention. If I can live long enough to get married, I'll have to find a guy who will promise never to wear a black suit, not even a tuxedo to the altar.

A shiny black sedan zooms around us, and I consider the license plate. I'm looking for government or Valor markings, but what I see is a limo plate. Is that how Valor does it—they pretend to be limos? Or is it an actual limo? There's no way to tell. The windows are tinted the same opaque black. Inside that car, there could be a movie star filming in Atlanta, a wealthy old woman, a state representative, or just another set of Valor suits, as stamped and rote as all the others. Hell, maybe the car is on its way to Château Tuscano.

Which gives me an idea. I know how to get leverage.

"Your gun is only missing one bullet, right?" I ask Wyatt.

His hand goes reflexively from the steering wheel to his hip.

"Yeah. So I guess that's fourteen? Jesus. I can't even remember. This shit messes with your mind."

"And I'm fully loaded. What other weapons do we have?"

"Uh. That knife. The one I . . . used on you." He takes an uncomfortable pause as we both think back to the rain on the roof of my mail van, to his knees pinning me down as he put a steak knife to my neck, on the cusp of killing me like I'd been on the edge of killing him. "In the glove box. I guess there's a tire iron or whatever in the trunk, whatever cars come with. And my lacrosse stick."

I stifle a giggle, badly. "You brought your lacrosse stick to the apocalypse?"

He exhales and coughs on a laugh. "Yeah. You'll thank me when I catch a grenade in it and lob it back into a Valor tank."

"My hero."

"Why do you ask? Haven't you . . . ? I mean, has today not been violent enough for you?"

I can't help flinching at that.

"Look, the last week has totally worn me out on violence for the rest of my life. I probably won't even like spy movies after this. But I think I know how to get us in good with the Cranes and maybe find out where my mom is."

Wyatt sighs and rubs his eyes. "Can't we just go home to our trailer and play with our dog?"

I have to hide the little thrill I feel at hearing him say "we" and "our" again. Shooting that security guy hit Wyatt in a tender place, and I wasn't sure if he blamed me for it. But if we are still "we" and Matty is still "our" dog, then we're still us, and that means I can still be me.

Jesus, nothing makes sense anymore. Not even words.

"Just one more thing," I say. "Take a left here."

My heart is racing as I leap out of the parked car and frantically wave my arms, trying to look desperate and helpless. Wyatt kneels by the back tire, struggling with the jack. Clearly, rich boys who drive Lexus sedans do not change their own tires. I know how to do it, but we agreed that I have to look like a damsel. To that end, I left my huge hoodie in the car, and goose bumps sprout around my thin tee, the November wind rattling my teeth.

The black SUV has to stop anyway, as we're blocking a four-way stop, which just so happens to be the four-way stop just outside of Château Tuscano. The denuded forest behind it shows neat rows of shiny black vehicles, which means I was right: It's perfect for a Valor compound, and that means that suits will be coming and going, and that's why we've been sitting here for two hours, pantomiming a broken-down car whenever the approaching vehicle is black. The last one was an old man who couldn't help. But this one . . . Maybe this is the one.

The SUV rolls to a stop about twenty feet behind us, and I run toward it like your average moron who knows nothing about the bank's hostile takeover.

"Please help!" I shout. "Can you please help us?"

The windshield is tinted dark and shiny—a good sign. A flash inside might be sunglasses. The SUV either has to do a U-turn on a narrow road with no shoulder, pull around us, where Wyatt's tools are sprawled and ready to pop tires, or do the decent thing and help.

A window rolls down, and a guy calls, "We can't help you. Government business. Please clear the road."

I run up closer, waving my arms, holding up the flip phone Wyatt lifted off his Crane goon. "What? No. We need help. Like, my dad's not answering. We can't get the tire off. Please?" I'm not quite in front of him but not quite to the side. I'm right where he would have a harder time shooting me, thanks to the lines of the car.

Inside, voices whisper in argument. "We're going around. Get out of the way." The window closes, and the SUV's tires twist left.

"What? No. Come on, please!" I have to play this like someone who has no idea that these guys are heavily armed, like someone who still thinks the government is here to serve and protect. I run right up to the window and tap on it.

I can barely breathe as the window rolls down, the shiny black revealing two pissed-off guys in matching black suits with the typical Valor earpieces.

"Look, kid—" the driver starts, and the passenger puts his hand on the driver's arm and leans in to whisper something.

The second the driver turns his head, I whip the gun out of my waistband and shoot the passenger. Not in the face—in the chest. And then my gun is trained on the driver.

"Nope. Hands up," I say as his hand edges toward his jacket.

"Kid, you have no idea who you're pissing off," the guy says.

"I know exactly who I'm pissing off." Keeping the gun trained on him, I add, "Put the car in park."

"Last chance, kid. Drop the gun and hit the ground, or shit will rain down on you—"

Wyatt's behind me now, his gun likewise pointed at the driver. "Put it in park," he snarls.

The driver's pissed, breathing hard through his nose. I can't see past his sunglasses, but I imagine him checking each mirror for help, for more Valor guys.

He mutters, "Charlie Tango, this is Delta-Three-Five—"

And then I remember that he's wearing an earpiece, and I don't know if that means they can always hear him or he can always hear them. Before he can finish, I reach up, rip it off, and throw it past him, into the backseat. He takes a deep breath and puts the car in park. Soon Wyatt has him in his own handcuffs and forces him to climb into the trunk of the Lexus.

"What if he kicks out the lights?" I say.

"Oh, crap. You're right." Wyatt pulls off this bracelet he wears, messes with it, and suddenly, it's a long roll of paracord, which he uses to bind the suit's feet together and tie that to the guy's handcuffs. I hold my gun to the suit's temple to remind him not to fight so much.

"You kids have no fucking idea. You have no—"

Wyatt slams the trunk, and the sound cuts off.

"See you at the trailer," he says, pecking me on the cheek.

He tosses the tools, jack, and tire iron into the backseat of the Lexus and takes off, just like we planned. As much as he didn't want to let me out of his sight, it would be suspicious if we drove together. I climb up into the SUV and arrange the front seat and mirrors so that I can reach the pedals and see what's behind me. The dead man in the passenger seat is sticking up more than I'd like, and seeing him makes me want to throw up, so I shove him down until he's all below the tinted black window. He leaves a red smear behind on the black fabric.

God help me, when I look at him, I feel guilty. Even though he's a bad guy, even though it didn't hurt to pull the trigger when I was all jacked up, now all I can see are the place he nicked his jaw shaving and the laugh lines in the corners of his eyes. A dead Valor suit seems more human than a living one, somehow. I've tried so hard not to change, not to lose who I was, but perhaps this is the first moment that I accept what I've become: a killer. Because this time? This is war. And as much as I hate to admit it, no matter what family this guy had, the world is better off without him, whoever he was. Without well-armed suits, Valor is just a bunch of computers, like Leon said.

Soon I'm driving to the Crane compound, taking back roads and following the speed limit. When I notice another black vehicle in a parking lot, idling, I snatch the sunglasses off the dead man's face and slide them on, making my face a mask. Does Valor even hire women as suits? Does the car in the lot belong to Valor? There's just so much I don't know. But maybe, now that we have a hostage, we'll find out.

But then I realize—are they tracking the car right now? To Crane Hollow?

What the hell have I just done?

I hit the gas to zoom past Crane Road, turn down the next little street, and pick a dirt road with ragged construction forms flapping against an old barn. The car bumps over the gravel and skids to a stop in a bend, where it can't be seen from the road. I can't believe I almost delivered a Valor SUV to the Citizens for Freedom without checking to see if it was bugged, tagged, or being tracked. My brain treats me to a vision of helicopters descending and shooting up the tent city, of the house on fire and Kevin trapped, alone, in his bed upstairs. All those deaths, on my head just as much as Robert and Sherry and Ken.

And then I pull myself together and pull out the flip phone. At least the goons are predictable—Leon is the last contact who called, three times, probably leaving furious messages about how the missing kid should've already reported back from driving Wyatt on the Wiper mission. I press the call button and pace in the gravel as it rings.

"Alex is right here, so who the hell is this?" Crane's voice is low and deadly, a soft chorus of men gabbling behind him.

"I've got a present for you, Mr. Crane," I say.

He exhales like he hates surprises. "I repeat: Who the hell is this?"

"This is Zooey Goddamn Hemsworth, and I just stole a Valor SUV. You want to tell me how to disable whatever tracking system they've got on it?"

"Shut up!" he shouts, and a door slams. His side of the line goes quiet. "Well, of course it's the same mouthy, pain-in-the-ass girl who seems like catnip for the Grim damn Reaper. You've gone and poked a stick into the hornets' nest, and now you want to bring it right to my doorstep?"

"I didn't take you for a pessimist, Leon. Now, do you want your present or not? There are all sorts of yummy-looking boxes in the back."

He mutters a long string of curses, and I can imagine him running a hand through that crazy hair. "Stay on the line. Let me get my tech guy."

Time stretches out as I kick gravel and toss rocks at trees. Birdsong seems so strangely normal now. Soon a new voice clicks on, this one deeper, slightly amused, and lacking the typical, honey-slow Crane accent. "Yeah, okay, so you've got a Valor car? What make?"

I walk around back. "GMC Acadia."

A keyboard clicks, and he pops gum. "Yeah, okay, so here's what you do."

Soon I'm on my back on the ground, gravel digging into my spine as I edge under the car. I'm pulling out wires and crushing SD chips and pressing codes into the front-seat computer while a dead man's blood congeals on the floor mats.

The GPS screen goes to an error message, and I say, "Got it."

"She got it, Leon," he says, voice slightly muffled.

Leon's voice, offscreen and far away, whoops. "Devil Johnny would be proud of those hackin' skills, son!"

"What now?" I ask.

"You did a good job, kid. But you're going to want to hurry back with it before they show up to investigate. They'll be on site within twenty minutes. You got any Valor guys with you?"

"One. Dead. Hank has the other one in his trunk for questioning."

"Damn. You are gutsy. Pull out the earpiece, get the card out of the battery box, snap it in half, and toss it somewhere far away from where the vehicle is. Then you should be good to go."

"That's it?"

· 228 ·

The guy snorts. "That's it? For real? I just helped you deactivate the world's most cutting-edge tech, and you want to know if that's it? Fucking ungrateful kid." But he sounds kind of impressed.

I click the phone shut and peel out.

Driving over a bridge, I roll down my window and drop both of the snapped earpieces into a creek. Last week I might've forgotten about the one I threw in the backseat, but now? That's the sort of detail that gets people killed.

Now I can go home.

I turn down the dirt road, and a Crane goon steps out from his hiding place among the trees, his gun already tucked against his shoulder. I roll down my window and push down my Valor sunglasses to give him a wink.

"What the hell is this?" he barks.

"I brought Leon a present. He's expecting me."

He shakes his head like I'm a moron, but an impressive one. "Name?"

"Zooey Goddamn Hemsworth."

After checking a small notebook, he nods. "Don't park it in the field. Take it out to the barn. They're waiting for you. Follow the tire tracks through the woods. Got it?"

I nod, roll up the window, and drive. It's late afternoon, and the tent city is awake and busy, with people of all ages moving around, laughing, talking. They all have paper plates of food and plastic cups of soda, and it looks like the world's biggest family reunion. Which one of them, I wonder, put the yellow marks on the twenty that got us in hot water earlier today? And what other seemingly trivial jobs are they doing to earn their places with the Citizens for Freedom? And is there a chance that my mom is out there right now, among them, handing out snack cakes or throwing corn at the chickens? Because she wasn't in my house when it blew up. I refuse to let myself even consider it.

A few people look up as I drive by, closer to the tents than most of the cars that go park in the field. A few shouts and pointed fingers remind me that I'm in a Valor vehicle with the windows up, and that means I look like the enemy, like the car that drove up and ruined all their lives. I roll down the window again and push the sunglasses up on my head, waving like the queen. The crowd breaks out into laughter, and one old man shouts, "Take that, Valor!" to the tune of clapping.

The forest is much quieter as the SUV bumps over the tire ruts and under the trees. A line of tense men with guns waits outside the barn, Wyatt among them. Tuck waves me toward a rolled-up garage door, and I drive in, park, and get out of the SUV. I'm shivering, and Wyatt walks up and hands me my hoodie, which I put on with a grateful smile as we stand in front of the still-warm Valor SUV.

"Where's the other guy?" Crane says, marching up with his hands in his jacket pockets.

"You're welcome. And he's in the passenger seat. I tossed his wire."

Crane inclines his head, and two of his guys hurry around to pull the suit's body out onto the concrete with a dull thud. I look away and feel like the worst person on earth. They search him and make a pile of what they find: handcuffs, a nice pen, a pocketknife, a phone, an ID badge with Delta-Nine-Nine listed as his name. Then come the guns: one on his ankle, small and stubby; a Glock like mine at his waist; and in a shoulder holster, hidden under his jacket, a long and evil-looking one with a silencer.

"Same ol', same ol'," mutters one of the guys before they stand up and look to Leon.

"You kids can go," Crane says to Wyatt and me, and Wyatt's hand sneaks down to hold mine and give a supportive squeeze.

"What about the driver?" Wyatt asks, and Crane's eyes narrow at him.

"What about him?"

"We want to know what you're going to do with him. We want to know what he knows."

Leon's smile is patronizing and easy. "Son, you get full credit for delivering enemy goods to the Citizens for Freedom. But you don't want to be involved in what happens next. The man we took out of your trunk is not a good man, and what we're going to do to get information out of him means we're not good men, either. Trust that we know what we're doing. And hold on to whatever innocence you can, for as long as you can."

"What about the laptops?"

Crane looks bored. "What laptops?"

"The ones we brought to the high school. What did you find, besides her name?"

"Nothing you need to know. Now get on."

Wyatt looks down at me, and I grit my teeth and shake my head. I wanted leverage, not to see what kind of torture a sociopath like Leon Crane is capable of when faced with enemy intelligence in his taxidermy barn. I look around real quick. The walls are covered with dead things: deer faces and flying pheasants and gun racks made of neat black hooves. A pegboard along the wall is chock-full of tools that might be handy for yanking out a dead thing's guts—or a live man's teeth. There are rags and newspapers and coils of thread and jars of needles, and my stomach starts to turn when I notice the ancient refrigerators and freezers humming along the wall.

Yeah, I bet they know what they're doing.

And I'm pretty sure I know what I'm doing.

"Leon, I've done everything you asked and more. I've brought you information and hostages and a bulletproof SUV. Now I want to see my mom."

The corner of his mouth curls up, and he rocks back on his heels. "I'm sure you do. Let's talk about it in the morning, shall we?" He inclines his head toward the door, and one of his guys snickers.

"No, let's not. Let's talk about it now. Is she here or not? Is she alive? Because we watched my house blow up, and I don't think I can relax unless I know she wasn't actually in it."

Leon steps into my personal space, and Wyatt bristles. Up close, the head Crane smells like wood smoke and clove cigarettes, and his thumb is calloused as he chucks my chin. "Just because you can shoot a stranger in cold blood doesn't mean you can tell me what to do."

I look up and mirror his twisted smile. "I guess not. But as friends working together, it sure would help keep my faith if you could give me just a little something. A pic on someone's camera phone would do. Maybe her voice. Because I can't sleep well if I'm worried. And when I don't sleep well, I get up to no good." I pause. "And just out of curiosity, when are those nut cans going to do their work?"

His eyes flick to me, sharp again. "You plant 'em all?"

I nod.

He chews the inside of his cheek like he wants to let me in on a juicy secret and can't tell if I deserve it or not. "Tomorrow. Tuesday morning. Outlet mall's supposed to have a big sale. Pre–Black Friday thing. *Kaboom!* Ink everywhere." He raises his fingers and lets them flicker down like fireworks.

"So. My mom?" I give my most winning, desperate smile. The

same one that got a window rolled down on the SUV currently being pried apart across the garage.

Leon calls someone on his phone. "Yeah. Hey. Look, can you put the Klein lady on for five seconds? Five seconds, then hang up." He holds out his phone, another burner, and I jab my ear against it.

"Hello?"

My heart jacks up and tears squirt out. "Mom! It's me. It's Patsy."

"Honey, you're okay? They said you were, but I didn't—"

"That's five," says a man's voice, and the line clicks off.

"I love you, Mom!" I shout at the dead phone.

Leon shrugs and tucks it back into his breast pocket. "We good here?" He points at the door.

"Just one more thing." My heart's yammering, and I would tear Leon limb from limb for five more seconds on that phone. And he knows it, damn him.

"Now, look, little lady. I've all but bent backward for you, so it's about time you thank me and head back to your nice, homey trailer and get some sleep. Your work ain't over yet, but it's over for today."

"Can I at least visit Kevin? The kid in the clinic?"

Leon's eyes twinkle. "The innocent boy you shot?"

"Yeah. Him."

"Well, of course. A friendship like that can't be severed, now, can it?"

"Thank you, Leon."

His eyes go dark. "That's 'Mr. Crane' to you. Now get out before things go ugly."

I don't know if he means ugly for me or ugly for the Valor suit they're escorting into the garage and dragging toward a closed door. There's a black bag over his head, and they're not being gentle. At a coded knock, the door opens, and they shove him inside. I can't see anything but a dangling lightbulb, and honestly, I don't really want to see more. So I take Leon's advice and let Wyatt tug me out into the night.

The moment the door shuts behind us, I wrench my arms around his neck and fold my body against his, kissing his neck and holding him tight.

"Uh, hey," he says, hugging me back.

"She's alive," I say. "She's alive."

He hugs me until I stop shaking, then gently pries me off and holds me away. "Can we go back to the trailer now? Before Matty pees on everything?"

"There's just one more thing I need to do."

He snorts and gives me a fond smile. "Always one more thing with you."

I go up on tiptoes to kiss his cheek. "Yeah, but this one's going to be fun."

15.

I get a couple of dirty looks in the big house, but the Cranes must learn to let bygones be bygones pretty quick. That, or they're scared of me. The dining room table is packed with thin Cranes and fat Cranes, and they stare as I pass but don't put down their plates of spaghetti. I figure all the dangerous ones are with Leon in the taxidermy shed. The big guy at the stairs is neither Tuck nor Hartness, and he won't let me pass unless I let him search my backpack.

"No problem," I say sweetly, unzipping it and letting him look.

All he's going to find are Pop-Tart boxes and sodas.

"You steal all this food?" he asks.

I shrug. "Bought it with my card. Kids like junk food."

He points his gun up to let me squeeze by. Upstairs, I knock on the first door I see. No one answers, and I push it open and go in. It's an old-fashioned bedroom turned into a conference room, with four card tables set up in the middle and maps and data pinned all over the whitewashed walls, just like at Alistair's trailer. I reach into my backpack, pull a nut can out of a Pop-Tart box, and hide it in a dresser drawer.

In the next room, also empty, I find what I was really looking for: the tech room. Laptops are ranged on every flat surface, identical to the ones I brought from Alistair's trailer—hell, maybe they actually are the ones from Alistair's trailer. In the corner is a pile of clothes, all with ink dye packets attached, which I figured they had to have, somewhere, to test tomorrow's strip mall inksplosion. I drape a coat over one of the chairs, put a pair of expensive panties in a corner, and take several shirts into the conference room, hanging them on coat hooks in a corner, facing out. The nut can goes onto a table covered with half-eaten snacks, where its camouflage has a lovely irony.

The stairs creak outside, and I duck behind the bed pushed in the corner, shrinking down as small as possible. Footsteps enter the room and linger near the biggest map. "You think it's going to work?" one guy's voice asks.

"It better," says the other. "Where's my damn chaw?"

They rummage around the tables, and one walks toward the

bed. I flinch as his muddy work boots stop, and he says, "Here it is. We're good. Hey, did you mark today's blast?"

The boots tromp back over to the map, and in the silence I hear the soft punch of a thumbtack. "Wish I coulda seen it," one of them says wistfully.

"If there's one thing Leon knows how to do, it's blow shit up. Now come on, before we miss dessert."

Once they're down the creaking steps, I creep out and inspect the map more closely. Right where my house is, there's a shiny red tack.

Right where my house *was*.

The puzzle pieces fall into place with a sickening thud in my heart. I gave Leon the laptops from Alistair's trailer, told him the password. Somewhere in all that green code, Leon got information on me, found my name and address. He went to my house, or sent his men. They stole my mom and put a gun in Mrs. Hester's hand and rigged my front door to a bomb, all the while dressed as Valor suits.

Whether he did it to control me or kill me, he's going to get the opposite.

I pull out my can of spray paint and start shaking it.

I go visit Kevin, but my mind is definitely not on his fish-medicine intake. But I did really bring him some Pop-Tarts, so he's easier to deal with when his mouth is full.

"What did you guys do today? Was it, like, spy stuff? Gabriela says you get to go on missions."

God, he looks so young in his hospital bed. At least he's not pale and wilting today. He's annoyingly perky. I guess the antibiotics worked.

"It's not like spy stuff. It's more like . . . when your mom gives you a list of shitty chores you have to do, except you might get shot while you're cleaning your room." I think back to Wyatt's face today as he watched the old security guard lying on the ground. "Or you might have to shoot someone, which is kind of worse."

Kevin snorts and shakes his leg. "Uh, until you've been shot, I don't think you know what it's like."

I feel my face go blank and numb. "Until you've shot someone and watched them die, I think you can be grateful for your time sitting in a comfy bed while other people do the hard work. Do you have any idea how many people . . . ?"

His face is slowly breaking, and he goes from looking like a pissed-off pre-teen to a lost little boy. "My folks. I saw it happen. I've got nobody. Just Gabriela and Chance, and they haven't been to see me all day. Just . . . nobody. So don't you tell me how hard it is. Because I know, okay? I know."

Without really meaning to, I'm hugging him, this scrawny little kid, and he feels like he's made of rabbit bones, quick and slender and fragile and full of energy. He starts crying, too, pressing his face into my hoodie and shuddering with sobs. I try to edge up on the bed, but I nudge his leg and make him gasp.

"I'm sorry," I say, jumping away.

He pulls up the flowered sheet to rub away the tears. When he says, "It doesn't matter," I know he's lying. Because it does matter. But if it makes him feel better, he can say whatever he wants. At least he doesn't look at me like I'm a monster—he still thinks I'm on the good side.

"Have they said when you can leave?" I ask.

That brightens him up. "Tomorrow. They said tomorrow, if I can walk downstairs and remember to take my pills. They said they might need the bed for someone else." He looks at the other three beds, all empty, and his face screws up. As little as he knows about the truth behind the Citizens for Freedom, he knows enough not to trust them.

"We'll come get you at breakfast," I promise him. "We've got a tent ready just for you."

At that, I get his real grin, his little-kid grin. "I've never been camping before," he says.

I just know that I want him out of this house before we find out why they're going to need beds. And before those nut cans cover everything with ink and make Leon even more suspicious.

That's two nut cans gone. The last one I keep. Just in case.

I never did trust the Cranes, but I sure as hell don't trust them now.

X X X

Matty barks joyously from inside the trailer, and a cluster of what I guess you'd call my friends waves from the tent camp in my front yard. The gang's all here—Chance, Gabriela, Rex, and a lantern's glow denoting Bea's presence in her zippered tent. Chance is flopped over on his back on his sleeping bag, while Gabriela looks jittery as a long-tailed cat in a roomful of rocking chairs. Rex, as ever, seems utterly relaxed.

"Where were you guys this morning?" I ask, scuffing my toes in the dirt to hide the bloodstains on my sneakers.

"Just got back," Gabriela says. "Very close call."

"Closest call yet," Chance adds, an arm thrown over his face.

"Wait. They didn't send you out on nut duty, did they?"

Gabriela hops up to pace, looking haunted. She keeps glancing at the dirt road like she expects bad news. "Yeah. Insane, right? We got sent to that strip of fancy shops by the mall. You know, the ones where the department stores off-load their unwanted crap? In the fourth store, they cornered me. Wanted to see what was in my backpack. Two workers and a policeman. I tried to run, and they grabbed me. They put strip ties on my wrists." She rubs them, and we all stare at the indentations.

"I didn't know what to do," Chance says. "I was still outside, so I stabbed all the tires on the cop cars and pulled our car up to the curb and had it running. I shot the cop and one of the ladies. Arm and leg.

They freaked out, and I managed to get her in the car and peel out. But Leon was pissed."

"Only got three cans placed out of twenty, and then the cops were everywhere. Leon wouldn't even let us have dinner." Gabriela looks up at me, eyes pleading. "What kind of fool sends a kid with a purple Mohawk into a store where the socks cost a hundred god-damn dollars? What am I supposed to do, pretend to buy a prom dress?"

I jerk my chin at Chance. "Why didn't he do it? He can act like a snob."

Chance snorts. "It was a women's store. Was I going to pretend to buy a gift for my mom?"

We all stare at him and as one shout, "Yes!"

He rubs his eyes, then pounds his fists into the dirt. "Okay, yes, fine. Well, we didn't think about that today. We'll know better the next time we fight the bank government by planting peanut cans in fancy stores. I've never done this before, okay? It's not like they gave us an instruction manual."

"Leon said we were the only ones who had to do it," I say.

"Yeah, well, Leon lies," Chance shoots back.

"Did you open your cans?"

"We tried," Gabriela says, "But they were glued shut. As long as Kevin's in the house, I figure we don't have much of a choice. Like it even matters what's inside."

The silence gets awkward, and I assume everyone is thinking back, like I am, to all the stupid mistakes we've made in the past week. I don't want to think about that, and I don't want to think about watching my house blow up or shooting the suit in the SUV, so I nudge Rex's boot with my toe.

"How about you?"

He smiles up at me, placid as hell. "Me and Little Miss Sunshine"— he jerks a thumb at Bea's tent—"had no trouble. But we were at the crappier outlet mall, down by the interstate. We fit right in, even in the stores fancy enough to have ink packs."

"Is Wyatt okay?" Gabriela asks.

I stare up at the trailer and steel myself. "I'm about to find out. 'Night, y'all." When my fingers touch the doorknob, I get a shock and draw back with a gasp. After watching Mrs. Hester at my house today, I don't like doorknobs anymore. Which reminds me . . .

"Kevin should be down tomorrow morning. I told him we'd go get him after breakfast. He can sleep in the big tent."

Gabriela smiles for the first time and stands. "I'll get it ready for him, then."

And I have no choice but to open the door.

Matty, at least, is glad to see me, barking and wriggling like she thought I'd disappeared forever. Wyatt appears behind her, his smile crooked and his eyes red.

"You okay?" he asks.

I'm too shy to touch him, so I kneel and concentrate on petting Matty. "Not really. But . . . that's kind of how it is now, isn't it?"

He breathes in and lets it out as a sigh. "Yeah. I guess it is. Hungry?"

"Nope."

"But you haven't eaten all day."

He's right. The moment I say it, my stomach lets out the most ridiculous growl.

"Come on. I made you some soup and toast."

Now the warm, comforting smell in the air makes sense. He's got the tiny table set with two bowls, two plates of soggy toast, and two Cokes poured into glasses so I guess we can pretend that we're civilized. He even pulls out my chair for me, which makes me giggle. No one has ever done that for me before.

"Wyatt, I'm really sorry—"

"I don't want to talk about it right now. Let's just eat. Can we eat?"

I nod and blow on my soup. It's the same kind my mom used to make for me when I got a cold as a kid, canned and creamy. It's like drinking a sunbeam, and I slurp up the whole bowl in a companionable if worried silence. There's so much to talk about, but I want Wyatt to have what he needs, so I just peel the crust off my toast and fold it in half twice to eat it. Wyatt notices and murmurs, "You're so weird," but like it's a compliment.

He finishes long before I do and follows his dinner with two Pop-Tarts, which I liberated from their boxes earlier so I could sneak the nut cans into the big house. When I'm done, he washes my dishes, and I throw our napkins in the trash and feed Matty. It's kind of funny, how just last week I was in a mail truck, wishing it were a college dorm or an apartment so that I could play house, and now I'm basically living with a boy in a small house. It's like someone hit fast-forward on my life and I'm suddenly twenty-four. But I never dreamed I would have a job as an unpaid mercenary. I would not have chosen this.

Now we're alone in the kitchen, and the dishes are done. The space seems small and awkward, and Wyatt edges around me and takes my hand. I let him lead me to the bedroom, where he closes the door, sits on the edge of the bed, and stares at his hands. I don't know what he wants from me, so I sit beside him. Not so close that I'm touching him, because the last time I did that, he asked me not to. But close enough, I hope, to show that I'm here and I'm listening.

"How did you get through it?" he finally asks, although he won't look at me.

The pause draws out long as I wait for him to elaborate. He doesn't.

"Do you mean . . . last week?"

He nods.

"I cried a lot and hugged my dog."

He shakes his head and looks at me, really looks at me. "No, I mean . . . how did you live with yourself? I can't stop seeing that old man's face, his surprise and confusion and shock as he fell over. I did that. And I don't want to be the kind of person who does that."

A few tears slip out, and his hands are shaking, so I sit on the bed, against the headboard, and pull him back into the cage of my legs so that he's leaning against me like I'm a pillow. It's strangely intimate, but I want to be able to answer him honestly without him looking into my eyes.

"Okay, so first of all? I'm not over it. You know about the nightmares. I relive it, all of it, while I'm asleep. Every night, every person, every bullet. And then my brain shows me all the other things that could've happened, in the truck and in Sherry's house and every time I rang a doorbell. I've seen myself shot full of holes and burned alive and left for dead on a lawn covered in frost. I don't know how long it's going to take before I go back to normal, or if I'll ever be normal again. I never had panic attacks before, and now it's like I have one ten times a day. My heart never slows down. I'm scared of doorknobs and shirt buttons. I think this is PTSD, but I don't have Internet, so I'm not sure. So don't think that I'm okay, because I'm nowhere close to okay. Okay?"

He nods against my chest. "Okay."

"Okay. So here's how I think it happens. At each moment that goes wrong, you have two choices: You die or they die. Right?"

"I guess."

"No!" It comes out as a shout, so I focus on making my voice calm again. "No. You don't get to say that. When I was standing on your front lawn and the red clock in the truck dash started counting down, you have to understand that it was me or your dad. Actually, me and my mom or your dad. There was no in-between. Valor didn't give a third choice. Okay?"

"Okay."

"So from that moment, when I chose to shoot your dad, every moment after that meant that if I let someone else go, then I was wrong about your dad. With each person I shot, I had to shoot the next, or the previous marks meant nothing and my mom and I had to die anyway. It's like I had to carry them with me." I put my cheek against his hair. "They're always with me. Weighing on me. Drowning me. So the best thing I can do is keep swimming and not sink. I want to forget them so it won't hurt anymore, but if I forget them . . ." I can barely swallow. I shake my head and whisper, "If I forget them, then I'm a monster. I let Valor make me a monster. I don't deserve to forget them. It can't get easy. The killing."

"One of my therapists taught me a trick," he says, and his voice creaks and cracks. "Have you ever heard of a memory palace?"

"Is it anything like Château Tuscano?"

He chuckles and resettles against me, relaxing just a little. "No. It's a way to remember things. Like, you build this palace in your mind, or maybe it just looks like your house, and when you want to remember things, you associate them with physical parts of the house. Like, you always put your keys by the front door of your memory palace, so if you need to remember to take your homework to school, you mentally put your homework and your keys right by the front door. He was trying to help me catch up on schoolwork and remember all the shit I had to do for Max and community service, because I kept messing up. But I sort of used it for the opposite purpose."

"You made an un-memory palace?"

"Kind of. I built this broken-down Victorian haunted house to keep my bad memories locked up. I didn't want to remember all the horrible things I said to my mom, all the bad shit I did with Mikey. I didn't want to remember him anymore, didn't want to think about the past. So every time I had one of those thoughts, I imagined using a skeleton key to unlock the front door of this old green house, I walked up the creaking stairs, and I went into this locked room in the attic that had a huge pigeonhole desk. And I put the memory in one of those drawers and closed and locked it. And then I could forget about it."

Without realizing it, I've started stroking his hair, running my fingers through it. I try to imagine this place he's built, the drawers full of locked, quiet memories.

"Did it work?" I ask.

He nods, leans into my touch. "I'm going to put the memory of that old man away now. But before I did it, I wanted to know if that was wrong. It feels good to lock up stupid, childish things I did a long time ago. I locked up taking out that Valor card in my brother's name, and I locked up watching Mikey OD, and . . . all this other stuff. But am I allowed to forget choices I made that . . . I'm still not sure were right? That's why I wanted to know. How you do it."

I take a deep breath. In my mind, I'm walking past Wyatt's old Victorian and taking a rusted key from under the mat of the house next door. This one is lavender going gray, with a tower and garrets and little curlicues on the corners. I unlock it and walk up the stairs, which creak, just like Wyatt's. I find the attic room, and instead of a desk, I have a card catalog. One by one, I open drawers and put away the people I've killed, almost like a mortician sliding bodies into the freezer at the morgue. A drawer for Robert Beard. One for Eloise Framingham. A nameless, rapist thug I left to die in the dirt, gut shot. Ken Belcher. Alistair Meade. Sherry. Two more thugs. My ex–best friend, Amber. My uncle Ashley. Crane goons who dared to steal my dog. A Valor suit. And now, even if I didn't actually kill her, Mrs. Hester and her cat Keith. I lock the door behind me and open my eyes. Wyatt's sitting up now, looking at me carefully, hungrily. I put a hand on his stubbled cheek and look directly into his brownie-batter eyes.

"I think you did the right thing today. Accidents happen, and you can't blame yourself. If you hadn't shot that guy, I might be dead. You might be dead. There's no way to know. But I do know that every time we strike back at Valor, we're doing honor to their memories. All these people, dead, are not our fault. You can't blame the gun for shooting someone. Valor turned us into weapons, and it's not our fault."

"Are you sure?"

I nod. "I have to be. I like the Forgetting House. It's a way to forget them . . . the victims . . . while doing honor to them. Putting them to rest." And I feel lighter. I do. I just hope I can keep that attic room locked for a long time. I don't want to fill any more drawers.

He goes quiet, idly stroking his flat fingers up and down my arm. After a few moments, he takes a deep, sighing breath and turns around to sit cross-legged in front of me.

"Did you lock up the old man in your Forgetting House?"

He grins and nods.

"Do you feel better?"

Wyatt licks his lips and leans in to kiss me, so gently, just a peck. "I'm working on that part. All that adrenaline today—it's still in me. It's crazy. I feel so alive."

"Almost dying will do that to you."

I go warm all over, and something rises up in me, like an animal, making me want to grab him and pull him down over me on the bed. We've never kissed with any freedom, with any time. An entire bed and all night? No one to kill on the other side? I'm starving for him. But he's going slow, so I'll go slow.

The peck turns into a long, lapping kiss that leaves me breathless, and I slide farther down against the pillows. Wyatt goes with me, his legs tangling with mine and his fingertips tracing my cheeks, my nose, my jaw. I slip a hand under his tee and stroke up his back, rubbing a thumb over the knobs of his spine and the wide wings of his shoulder blades. A groan rumbles against my lips, almost a purr.

He pulls away and looks down at me, fond and sweetly smiling. "I need you to know three things," he says. I nod, my lips parting. "For one, I'm sorry I snapped at you last week for saying you just wanted to not be alone. I get that now. You weren't trying to use my body. . . ." I blush. "You were trying to feel human again, weren't you? Trying to feel . . . real. Alive." I nod and bloom with affection for him. I didn't know how badly he'd wounded me with that one, nor how much his apology would mean to me.

"Thank you," I say, and it comes out all breathy.

"Second, I'm not a virgin. You said you were, but I'm not, and I thought you should know that."

When he says the word "virgin," I blush redder . . . and go warm all over. Does he want the same thing I want? Does he know about the condoms? All I can do is say, "Hey, at least one of us knows what they're doing, right?"

His eyes go dark, his lashes lower, and he kisses me again, slow and deep, before pulling away to say, "Right. And the third thing is that I think I'm falling in love with you."

Outside the realm of Valor, this is possibly the most unexpected thing anyone has ever said to me, and it's like what happens when you hold a piece of paper up to a match. I am the paper, and I want to be consumed by this boy. He must be thinking the same thing, because before I can answer him, he's stretched out on top of me, his weight on his elbows and his mouth on mine.

It gets awkward only once, when I tell him where the condoms are.

16.

I see now why they call it "the afterglow." Because what we just did? Was like being on fire. By which I mean it was very hot and hurt a bit, but it was beautiful, and now I feel glowy.

"Told you I was just using you," I say, stretching luxuriously, completely naked and comfortable for the first time in a long time.

"Yeah. I'm really suffering." Wyatt stretches out beside me under the covers. He's asked me several times if I'm all right, if he hurt me, if it was okay. It's weird to see him so insecure and confident at the same time. "But you never said anything. About what I said."

My mouth drops open. Am I ready to say it? Do I even know what it is?

"I think I might be feeling the same way," I say, and I nudge him with my forehead. It's easier to be physical than to match words to feelings. There was an eloquence to what we just did that I'd like to think showed him how I feel. But words help too.

He wraps his arm around me, and I settle myself in the crook of his shoulder. Even yesterday, it would've felt very, very strange to be in a guy's bare armpit, but now it feels . . . mature? Natural? At least animalistic. I belong here, up against him.

After kissing my forehead, he takes a full-body breath, relaxing against my side. "My dad once got really drunk on my parents' anniversary and told me that I should only marry someone who lights up every time I walk into a room. He said that was more important than anything else. That he knew their marriage was over when he would walk into a room and my mom would look away or sigh or look down with a little V between her eyebrows, like she was disappointed in him before he'd even said anything."

"That's so sad."

"Right? I don't even remember noticing them, how they interacted. I don't think I ever saw her light up." He pauses, and I hold my breath. "But you do."

"I do?"

His lips brush over my forehead, and I close my eyes and hum a sigh.

"Yeah. Every time you see me, no matter how horrible I look, no matter how covered in blood I am, no matter what sort of horrible things we've had to do, you light up. Like a lightbulb. Like Matty when I give her half a burger."

"I light up like a fat dog, huh?"

He laughs like a little kid and snuggles me closer.

And that's when some absolute asshole decides to bang on our door.

It's not a friendly knock, not an, "Anybody home?" knock.

It's a "You'd better be wearing a shirt and holding a gun, sucker" knock.

Matty barks at the door. When it opens, her barks turn to growls. I'm already shimmying back into my clothes, commando and braless in my desperation to be covered.

"Didn't we lock the door?" I hiss.

"We did," Wyatt says. He's barefoot and shirtless in his jeans, gun already in hand, and no wonder I light up whenever he walks in the door. He's a damn good-looking guy when he's acting lethal. And he's the kind of guy who goes first when scary knocks are at the door.

I tuck my gun into the back of my waistband and follow him as he peeks out the bedroom door and into the hall.

"Can we help you?" he shouts in his tough-guy voice.

"I'm here to speak to Patsy." The guy's voice is gruff and familiar.

"Maybe you could wait outside?" Wyatt says, opening the door just enough to show his gun, probably. "We need a minute."

I peek around Wyatt and see a bearish guy in his forties with a big beard and a beanie cap—the guy who took the laptops away from Wyatt in the high school gym the night we met the CFF. He sees me looking, and his eyes lock on mine and narrow.

"I'm not here to hurt you," he says. "I'm not a Crane. You can come on out."

But I don't see a gun. And I do not, in fact, wish to come on out.

Wyatt opens the door and reaches up with one arm to hold the jamb, his other arm dangling the Glock. I recognize the posture of a pissed-off ape showing muscles and confidence as he hides his prize from a challenger.

"You're not her boss. So who are you, and why did you break into our trailer?"

The guy smirks, blue eyes twinkling. "I'm the guy who helped her debug the Valor car today. I heard she did a good job. And I didn't break in. I've got a key." He holds it up, dangling from a carabiner. "Figured she could use one." He looks around, sniffs the air, and frowns. "Didn't know there were two of you shacked up in here. Nice dog, though."

"Not much of a guard dog," I say, feeling testy.

As if to show Wyatt that he's not scared, the guy kneels and gives Matty a full catalog of pats and rubs. "You're a good girl, aren't you?" When she shows him her belly, he looks closer, and his frown deepens. "Where'd you get this dog?" As he says it, he stands, and his hand looks like it's itching for a gun. He seemed pretty chill and friendly before, but now he looks pissed. And dangerous. And much older than I originally thought.

Suddenly, I realize why he looks familiar, and I push out from under Wyatt's arm.

"What's your name?" I ask, voice high and squeaky. "Your real name?"

He looks at me with blue eyes the same shade as mine and says, "Jack Cannon."

The air punches out of my chest, and I can only gape and blink. I've been waiting for this moment since I was four years old, since the day he left. I have a million questions, a billion words of spite, a trillion words of love. I want to run into his arms, bury my face in his neck, cry into his jacket, kick him in the shins, but I know what I smell like and there are too many guns in the room.

It's him.

It's my dad.

"How'd you know?" I squeak. "How'd you know it was me?"

"I'm the one who decrypted the files on the laptops. Unfortunately, Leon was standing right behind me at the time. He knows your real name, but he doesn't know you're my daughter. He can never know." His grin is fond and wondering and near tears. "It was hard as hell to hide that I knew it was you at the meeting the other night. I never dreamed . . ."

"I did. I dreamed it. Every day. Every day for thirteen years." My voice breaks. "Where the hell have you been?"

"That doesn't matter. I'm here now, honey. God, you're so big."

He opens his arms, and I freeze, suddenly shy and unsure. When he left, I was tiny and love was an automatic thing unencumbered by awkwardness. Throwing myself into his arms was natural then. But now I have reasons to pull away, too. Wyatt presses gently on my back, urging me forward, and then I'm hugging my daddy, just like I always dreamed of.

Well, almost. I stink of sex and I'm not wearing a bra or underwear and my boyfriend is five feet behind me, half naked with a gun in his hand. And my dad works for the Citizens for Freedom. He works for Leon Crane.

"And that's Ash's dog, isn't it? I remember when she got that scar on her belly. How'd you end up with your uncle's hunting dog, pip-squeak?"

I pull out of the hug and step back, hugging myself instead.

"I think we need to talk," I say.

His eyes shoot around the trailer, and I imagine him tallying everything he sees. Bullet holes in the wall. Me and Wyatt, obviously doing things no dad ever wants to know about, not even a missing-in-action dad. The fact that this trailer belongs to the Cranes and the guys who used to live in here are dead. They were tech guys, I heard, and on the phone today, Leon called my dad his best tech guy, so maybe he was friends with them. Hell, maybe the place is bugged or rigged with cameras, although I haven't been able to find any. In any case, I'm not surprised when he puts a hand on the doorknob and inclines his head.

"Let's go for a walk." His eyes shoot from me to Wyatt, and his eyebrow goes up. "Get cleaned up, first. And dress warm. I'll be waiting."

He watches me a moment too long, his eyes soft and wet, before stepping outside and closing the door. Wyatt and I stare at each other.

"You sure that's your dad?" he says, all cagey.

"I know my dad," I say.

"You sure you can trust him, then?"

I snort. "Of course not. But I want to."

I walk into the bathroom and close the door. The shower takes a few minutes to get hot, and I'm scrubbing Wyatt off me with harsh soaps only a boy would choose. My skin feels swollen and puffy, and I think I understand why people act like virginity is something you can lose—or, more accurately, something you can give to someone. I feel exactly the same and yet completely different. And I feel like Wyatt and I, we'll have this forever. It might be a short forever, but we're stuck together now. My mind bounces between what just happened with Wyatt and the fact that my dad is waiting outside, which is awkward and confusing. I've been waiting to see my dad every day of my entire life, and now is when he shows up? *Shit timing, Dad. Just another thing you messed up.*

The room is full of steam as I towel off and slap on some lotion. Wyatt's stubble has left the most kissable parts of me red and raw, like he's marked me. My lips are pouty and pink and my eyes are soft, the pupils as swollen as the rest of me feels. This is not the way a girl wants to look when she talks to her dad for the first time in thirteen years. This is not what I want on my mind, my memory replaying Wyatt's face and hands and body. I want to fall asleep, warm and protected, in his arms. I do not want to step outside, where it's cold and dark, and tell my father what happened to his brother.

But I've done worse things, and I can do this, too.

And isn't this what I wanted? What I've been yearning for?

Isn't this the secret, the truth I kept in my locket, right up until Valor stepped into my life?

I never imagined I would feel this conflicted.

I wrap the towel around me and bumble into the bedroom, trying to find all the layers I shed in a giddy hurry. Screw this—I have new stuff in my backpack, awkward and creased and a little scratchy. I pull out a new pair of underwear and almost fall over when stepping in. Wyatt watches from the door, silent. I'm surprised by how natural it feels, how I'm not embarrassed by the strangeness of getting dressed as he stares. But he's seen all of me now, hasn't he? Inside and out.

"Bra?" I say.

He hands it to me, and as our fingers brush, we both giggle. He had trouble getting it unhooked and he threatened to rip it apart, but it's the only one I had, so I stopped him. Soon I'm fully dressed and pulling on my hoodie and my mom's rosary, hunting for my puffer coat. My socks don't match. My sneakers are spattered with dried blood. My hair is roughly hacked and frizzy from using crap shampoo, and no matter how much water I splash on my face, I look like I've been doing exactly what I've been doing. There is no way that my father will be proud of what I am, not of the surface or what lies beneath.

Oh, but God, I want him to be.

"You okay?" Wyatt asks as I stare in the bathroom mirror.

My only response is to charge him and bury my face in his bare chest.

"No."

"You don't have to go with him."

I look up, begging him to understand. "Yeah, I do."

"But you don't want to. You're scared."

"Not of him. Of me. Of him finding out what I've done. My uncle . . ."

Wyatt holds me by my shoulders, stern but gentle. "Don't be

ashamed—do you hear me? You did what you had to do. Anyone who's still alive right now, anyone who knows what's really happening? They'll understand. Especially if they're here." He smooths my hair back and rubs a proprietary thumb over my swollen lips. "If he's not proud, he's an idiot. And an asshole."

I nod and try to swallow it down. I know he's right.

But I'm still scared.

"Take care of Matty," I say, patting her wide back as I head for the door.

"Wait." I turn, and Wyatt holds out my gun and the scarf I knitted for him. "It could be cold," he says. I don't want to hunt for my holster, so I just put the gun in my waistband, against my spine, then hold still while he wraps his scarf around my neck. The last thing he does is kiss me on my forehead. "You're going to be great. It's going to be great. He's going to love you." When I still don't touch the door, he adds, "And don't take any shit from him. Or anyone."

That makes me smile. "Thanks," I say. And then I'm stepping out of the trailer into one of those crisp November nights when the sky is dark as ink and the stars sparkle like knives. Our little tent city is quiet—most likely, they're all hiding after what they heard happen in the trailer a few minutes ago. Jack—my dad—my dad!—is waiting in the field beyond, hands in his pockets and staring up at the big house. My sneakers crunch through the cold, dead grass until

I stand beside him, humming with excitement and bursting with questions. And anger.

Was he here, all this goddamn time, all these years, just a few miles from my house and working for Leon? I want to ask, but I don't want to be the one who talks first. I don't want him to be just another shitty Crane goon, just another pawn.

"You did the graffiti by the map, I take it?" he asks without looking at me.

I rock back on my heels, trying not to smirk too obviously. I really enjoyed spraying FUCK THE CFF on that stark white wall. "Leon blew up my house. And Mrs. Hester."

My dad looks down at me. "You don't think Leon had his reasons?"

I meet his gaze, unflinching. "Oh, I know Leon has his reasons. That's what worries me. Do you really take orders from that asshole?"

He opens his mouth, then closes it. For a few long minutes, he chews on the inside of his cheek like he wants to say something and can't. Finally, he says, "We should get some distance on Leon. Have you ever seen the preserve?"

He starts walking toward the trail we took to Brady and target practice a few days ago, and I stick my hands in my pockets and hurry to keep up.

"Do you mean the neighborhood off Hayley Bridge? Across from the Estates?"

My dad snorts, the same way I snort. "No. I mean the Cannon Wildlife Preserve."

"Never heard of it." But I'm not going to tell him about going through the photos at my uncle's house. Not yet.

"See, the Cranes and the Cannons go way back. Me and Leon grew up together. Crane Hollow extends into the forest, where it meets Cannon land." He beams. "Our family's land. Leon's granddad got into some money trouble a long time ago, and my granddad offered to buy some land off him and turn it into a shared preserve, hunting land. Cranes and Cannons only."

"Okay, but I have so many questions. Where—"

"Plenty of time for that, pip-squeak. Let's just walk a bit. Get farther away."

We walk past the bullet-gouged targets and the trailer where Brady probably stays. The lights are still on. My dad holds a finger to his lips, and I nod and walk in silence. This is as far as I've been in Crane Hollow, but my dad keeps walking, taking a dirt path through the overgrown field. We pass a deer stand and the remnants of a bonfire strewn with beer cans and shotgun shells as we push past scrubby pines and into a hardwood forest. I expect it to be colder in the shadows, but without the brisk wind, it's warmer, and my shoulders unhunch a little. Normally, this situation wouldn't feel safe to me, but I've got a gun, and I'm willing to bet my dad does too. I don't know if I trust him yet, but in this moment, I know that I would follow him anywhere if it meant I got the answers I crave.

This close to my dad, I feel like a live wire, humming with emotions and energy. On one level, the little kid inside me got her wish, and everything feels right. But deep down, the grown, monstrous version of me knows nothing is right.

"We grew up back here. Building forts, hunting, running wild. All the Crane and Cannon kids, a whole passel of cousins." My heart twists. I always imagined having cousins, and I did. They were less than five miles from my house, all this time, but I grew up alone.

"So does this land belong to you?" I ask.

He holds a branch out of the way for me. "My father's trust, technically. John Cannon Senior. They called him Devil Johnny. For good reason. Did your mom ever . . . ? No." He chuckles sadly. "She just told you I left, didn't she?"

I've heard that name before, though, and then it comes back to me. Leon told my dad that Devil Johnny would be proud of his hacking skills when he helped me scrub the Valor SUV over the phone. But I don't say that, either.

"You were there, and you said you had to leave but you loved me and you'd be back one day. You gave me the locket. And then you were gone. Mom never said why."

He's just a shadow in the woods ahead, but I can feel sadness radiating off him. "Did you keep the locket?"

I nod even though he can't see me. "I did. Until last week. Lost it running from Valor. But I still have your gun."

"Probably more valuable these days."

"It saved my life." But I don't mention that it's the same gun Wyatt pulled on him earlier. I don't want him to take it back.

"So how'd you get involved with the CFF?"

My head jerks up. "How'd you?"

He sighs. "Okay, so Leon was my best friend growing up. Our families ran this town. The Cranes still do. All those businesses, all this land. They put my granddad's money to good use, turns out. As soon as Valor's takeover stopped being a threat and became a promise, it made sense to join forces. I'm the brain; Leon's the brawn. Or that's what I used to think. Like he was the mad dog and I was holding the chain. Turns out he was just playing dumb while his daddy and older brother were alive. Now they're gone and he's off the chain." He looks down at me, a little stern. "But how'd you end up here? It's not safe."

I step ahead and catch his jacket so he'll stop. "You already know. Valor tapped me. I found the flyers in Alistair's trailer. I didn't have anywhere else to go."

My dad turns and looks down at me, eyes sparkling in the low light. He's been crying. "I wish I'd known. I would've done anything on earth to stop that from happening. I thought I had. I—"

I let go of his jacket and shake my head. I'm not ready to hear his tearful apologies. Not when I still have other people to worry about.

"It doesn't matter. I'm fine now. But Leon has Mom. Dad, he's hiding her somewhere. So he can make me do things." I hold up the rosary, my throat dry and my eyes stinging with cold. "We have to find her."

"We will, honey." Something snaps in the forest, followed by a soft curse. "Goddammit. Come on, Pats. Fast and quiet."

When my dad starts running, I struggle to keep up. My heart's gotten a workout this week, but my lungs and legs are as limp as ever. He said to be quiet, but how can I be? I'm in the woods in the pitch-dark, and I'm terrified. I hear someone crashing through the brush behind us and speed up. My dad's waiting ahead, by a tree.

"Up you go. Hurry, now."

A ladder of wooden planks waits, and I scramble upward to a rickety platform, the tree bark tearing at my hands. My dad is behind me, and as I drag myself over the edge of the deer stand on my belly, he pushes me down and lands on top of me.

"What is it?"

"Shh," he whispers in my ear.

For a moment the only sounds are my heart beating in my ears and my dad's rough breathing, his weight crushing me to cold boards that smell like old tobacco and rain. Then I hear the crunching leaves and whispering down below. Ever so slowly, my dad reaches between our bodies and withdraws the gun plastered to my spine. I feel cold and fragile without it, not to mention angry and scared to have it taken so easily by someone I want to know but clearly don't. And then he slides it into my right hand.

"Loaded?" he whispers.

I nod.

"Good shot?"

I nod, jaw clenched. How does he think I lasted this long?

"Me too. If Leon sent them after us, either they die or we do. You ready for this?"

I nod and find my grip, glad I'm in the habit of reloading every time I get home.

My dad edges off me but keeps his body between me and whoever is coming after us. He's on his belly, peeking over the edge of the platform. He holds up four fingers, and I nod. The gun in his other hand is yet another 9mm. I didn't even see him draw.

"Leon send you boys after me?" he barks, and one of the fools below fires a shot that wings off our tree.

"Come on down and talk, Jack."

"We can talk from here, Hartness."

The big man chuckles below us. "Well, now, that ain't fair. I can't look a man in the eyes, I don't feel like it's a real conversation."

"Four men follow me into the woods with guns drawn, I figure they lack any real skill at conversation, anyway. Now y'all go on home and tell Leon I'll report back when I'm done here."

Down below, the sound of a shotgun cocking. "You known

Leon long enough to know that he ain't much for waiting. So are you gonna come down here, or are we gonna shoot that old stand full of holes and wait for you to fall?"

"You known me long enough to know the answer to that question, boy." Quick as a whip, my dad fires three shots. I hear one of the guys break toward my side, and I peek over the edge to shoot him in the back as he runs. He falls face-first and tries to crawl, crying and snuffling in the wet leaves. So I shoot him again, and he stops moving.

"Goddammit, Jack! You shot me in the leg!" Hartness yells.

"Only because I meant to. Now throw down your gun."

During the tense moment that follows, I shuffle around and aim my gun next to my dad's, right at the big Crane goon that I had pegged as a sweet-natured good ol' boy. Two men lie dead in the leaves. Hartness mutters some pretty foul words under his breath and throws his shotgun to the ground.

"All your weapons."

A pistol and a Glock follow.

"And your knives."

Hartness shrugs, a picture of innocence. "What knives, Jack?"

My dad groans. "The only reason I ain't shot your other leg is that I can't drag your heavy ass through the woods by myself. Now toss out all your weapons or eat a bullet." Funny how when my dad was talking to me earlier, he barely had an accent, but now it's here and hard, just as slow and twangy as a Crane.

Starlight flashes on blades that clank as they hit the ground. "I'm clean, you bastard."

"I'm coming down. You go for anything, you're going to get shot by my friend up here. You got that?"

"Got it."

My dad leans in close to whisper, "Try not to speak. Just listen. If he goes for anything, shoot him somewhere that won't kill him. You hear me?"

I nod.

I belly up to the edge, pull up the hood on my coat, and aim for Hartness's leg, the one already dripping blood as black as the sky. My dad's on the ground before I can track him, yanking off Hartness's belt to lash the man's wrists together. The big man's jaw is tense, and each touch causes him to grunt in pain. I'm damn glad I haven't been shot yet. Looks like it hurts.

My dad kicks all the weapons far out of reach and says, "Okay. So here's where we are. You're going to answer all my questions, or I'm going to leave you out here to die."

Hartness splutters a laugh. "You think Leon tells me anything? Shit, I'm just an errand boy. We're all just errand boys, to him."

"Well, big pitchers have big ears, so maybe you picked something up. Now, what happened to my daughter?"

"Didn't know you had one."

"What about my wife?"

Hartness spits and laughs. "You got a wife, Jacky boy? Well, hell-fire. And to think you didn't invite me to the wedding. I'm hurt."

"Why were you following me?"

"Leon told us to. Said you might be meeting your daddy's people for a little midnight rendezvous. Said to shoot you as soon as you crossed the line to the preserve."

My dad looks away like he's pained, wipes the sweat off his forehead, and paces like he's running out of time. "I'm the best tech guy he's got, one of the best friends he'll ever have. Why'd he set me up like this? He needs me for what's to come."

At that Hartness laughs for real, big belly laughs. "Hellfire, son. He don't need you. You already built remote buttons for all the bombs and cracked the laptop codes. What the hell else are you good for? You ask too many questions, and you know Leon Crane don't like to be questioned. Now, is that all?"

My dad steps behind the bigger man and kicks down at the back of his calves. Hartness hits his knees with a grunt and almost falls on his face. "That is not all. Now, if there's a woman named Karen Klein on Crane property, you'd best tell me now, or you're not gonna see morning." His Glock comes to rest on Hartness's forehead, and I have to look away.

My heart goes cold. This is not how a girl gets to know her father.

"You go on and shoot, Jacky boy. Because everybody you ever

loved is dead, and if I go back to Leon without your head in a bag, I'm dead too. And he'll make it hurt a lot more than you will. So go on. Go on and shoot the boy you grew up with. You go on and prove you're the bigger man."

My dad sighs sadly. "I chose your side. Leon's side. I went against my family. I defied my father. I abandoned my woman and baby daughter to join you in a bigger fight, to do the right thing. Now I want to know if Leon's holding a woman named Karen Klein captive, because if so, none of you are the good guys you pretend to be."

"Nice speech, brother. But it don't change nothing. Dead is dead."

The silence drags out, and when I peek down, my dad is staring up at me, his gun resting against Hartness's forehead, tears coursing down his cheeks like his heart is breaking.

"You understand what has to happen," he says. It's not a question.

I can only nod.

"Then look away."

I do.

He fires.

17.

The forest is strangely silent for a moment, and then a body hits the leaves. Poor Hartness. He seemed like an okay guy, and maybe Leon really did keep him in the dark, just like the rest of us. But I understand that what has just happened is the same as what I described to Wyatt: My dad looked at him and me and decided that only one of us could live. And he chose me.

"Come on down, baby," he calls softly, and I uncurl my frozen fingers from the edge of the wood and shake as I hurry to the ground.

My dad is doing what anyone in our situation should do: searching Hartness's body. When he pulls out another burner phone, he mutters, "Aha!"

I head to the other guy, the one I shot in the back, and find yet another identical black phone. You can't have too many in the post-Valor world. The dude also has a wallet with three different IDs and a wad of cash, some of which is way too worn to be counterfeit. I take the guy's Glock and check the clip. He's missing one shot, so I guess he was the one who fired first. The third guy is too messy to touch; it was a head shot. Nice aim, Pop. The fourth guy isn't here, which must mean he hightailed it back to Leon. That can't be good.

My dad stares at the woods, at the way back to Crane Hollow, and sighs. "I didn't want to do that, goddammit."

"Then why did you?"

He kneels and closes Hartness's eyes. "Because I needed to know if Leon knew about you and your mom, and once Hartness knew, I couldn't let it get back to Leon. Once he realizes I'm gone for good, he'd use her to get me back."

"So what now?"

"You know we can't go back to the CFF," he says quietly, and the words die on puffs of frost.

"But Wyatt. And Matty." I can feel it coming on—that sense of panic, of being trapped. My heart is fluttering, and the air burns my lungs.

He shakes his head. "Leon Crane will want us dead after this. Whether it's because he thinks I'm a double agent for my dad or because I shot his boys, he'll forget we were ever friends and make it his duty to put me in the ground. If I didn't know these woods and my dad hadn't been too busy to tear down that old deer stand, we might be full of holes. We go back there, they'll finish us."

"But they can't kill us in front of everybody," I say, the desperation making my voice high.

"They'll find a reason. They always do. Everybody loves to see a traitor get executed." He holds up a burner phone. "Does your boy have a phone? We could meet him somewhere."

I hold up the phone still warm from my pocket. "He gave it to me. It was our only one."

"Then we'll keep going. I know somewhere safe. It's close. Leon doesn't know about it. We'll figure out a way to get in touch tomorrow. Leon's going to be busy with Operation Nutjob."

I scoff. "That's seriously what y'all called it? Because of the nut cans? Jesus. We almost got caught, planting those damn things."

His head snaps to me, alert as a dog in a thunderstorm. "You put 'em all in the mall, right? Like the list said?"

I put my hands in my back pockets, but the urgent look on his face is making me deeply uncomfortable. "Ha. We only got seventeen of them placed, so I hid a couple around the house, along with some dye packets. Just to mess with Leon. My friend only got three done. And there's still one in my backpack."

"Where's your backpack?"

I shrug. "In my trailer."

"Oh, shit." My dad paces toward the trail to Crane Hollow, then back to me. He's looking all over like he's trying to solve math problems in his head. "Why the hell did you do that, Pats?"

I lick my lips and rub my arms, feeling cold and stupid and like maybe I've been fooling myself all along about Leon's chores. "Because it was funny. Because it was stupid. I don't know. I imagined Leon and all his Crane goons sitting around the card tables in the morning and getting splattered with ink. It was a joke."

"Patsy," he says, slowly and carefully, like I'm an idiot. "Patsy, they're bombs."

I can't speak. Can't even find words. Suspecting it is one thing, knowing is another. Mouth open, head shaking, I head for the trail, or where I think the trail might be. My dad grabs my jacket as gently as he can, and I spin around.

All I can do is shake my head and say, "No. They can't be."

"They were supposed to make the dye packets explode, but we couldn't work it out in time. So they're just bombs. Full of nails and nasty stuff. Leon's specialty."

"He showed us the inside of one. It was just . . . wires. The rest were glued shut."

"He showed you a dummy. And you believed him?" He runs a hand over his beanie and kicks a log. "Jesus, Patsy."

"I . . . I had to believe him. He had Mom. He had Matty. I

would've planted anything." Then the realization trickles down, cold as ice. "Wait. When are they supposed to go off?"

He looks up, and his face is hard.

"Six in the morning."

I spin to run back to Wyatt, but he grabs me by the shoulders and holds me back. I fight and pull, and he just holds me, tight, around the waist.

"Dad, we have to go back. We have to. There's one in the trailer with Wyatt and Matty. And there's one in the room next to Kevin, this sick kid who can barely walk. And another one—hidden in the house. But we can't let it happen. All those innocent people. Mom might be near one. I think Gabriela has a bag filled with the ones she couldn't plant. My friends. I can't . . . I can't . . . I need them. Okay? I need them."

I double over in his arms, crying, wishing to be anywhere but here, doing anything but this. In all the killing, I've never been this helpless. I was always the one in charge, the one with the mandate, the one holding a gun. But now I'm powerless to protect the people I care about.

"There has to be a way," I say. "We can sneak back over after midnight. Something."

My dad's face is right up against my cropped hair, his beard against my ear. "We. Can't. Go. Back. Once Leon Crane wants you dead, you die. Game over. He knew I was going to your trailer.

Someone probably saw us leave together. The people in the tent city—they get gifts for snitching. And the guy who ran away just now—he might not know you're with me, but he knows I'm on the way to Cannon land. And he knows I was willing to kill my friends to escape."

"Let me go, Dad."

"Promise you won't go back."

I exhale, long and slow. "Promise."

He releases me, and I stand. There has to be a way. If we can't go to them, can we make them come to us?

"Okay, so do you have anybody over there you can trust?" I ask him.

He chuckles darkly. "Not anymore. If Hartness was pointing a shotgun at me, they all are. I was the best man at his wedding."

"Can we deliver something to Crane Hollow? Like, a pizza?"

"Honey, do you honestly think anybody's getting past Leon's guard at the road? Do you know the number of a pizza place? Do you have a credit card?"

I pull the phone out of my pocket and scroll through the contacts. "Last time I called Leon, he let me speak to you."

"He didn't know you were my daughter. The only reason you're on his radar is because you brought the laptops, you lived through Valor, and you get on his nerves. He might've grabbed Karen to control you, but he doesn't know that you and I are connected. He knows we're together now, though, and that we just killed three of his boys. You call him again, you're just going to piss him off. Unless one of your friends has a phone and you trust 'em with your life, there's nobody to call."

"I wish Matty could hear me," I whine, knowing how pathetic it sounds.

But my dad cocks his head and grins. "Aw, Patsy. I always knew you were a goddamn genius." He tugs my hair and pulls a burner phone out of his coat pocket. "What's your phone's number?" I find it and read it off to him, and he programs it into his phone. "Now, for this to work, I need you to do exactly what I say. Can you do that?"

I nod.

"Then I need something that smells like your boy. Wyatt?" I nod. "You got anything of his?" He's excited, but there's this weird Dad tone to it, like he doesn't want me carrying anything that belongs to a boy, that might smell like a boy. I pat myself and pull off the scarf.

"This is his."

"Then here's what we're going to do. You climb back up into that deer stand and stay hidden. I'm going to get as close to Crane Hollow as I dare and give a special whistle me and Ash taught Matty, how we call her when we're hunting and she's too far off. If I can get her to come to me, I'll let her smell the scarf, wrap it and the phone around her neck, and hope to hell she understands that she's supposed to go back to Wyatt instead of following me back to you."

I chuckle, thinking about my fat, silly dog. "Uh, you know Matty's dumb as a post, right?"

"She's not dumb, honey. She's a hunting dog. When she's on the hunt, she's sharp. When she ain't hunting—that's when she's dumb. She's smarter than you think. Now, can you stay up there? Because if she sees you, she'll forget what she is, and this won't work, and your boy's gonna be in bits and pieces come sunrise."

I shudder, thinking about what a bomb could do in that cheap-ass, bullet-riddled trailer. "Yes, sir," I say, climbing obediently up the ladder and flattening myself on the boards. He turns to walk away, and I call, "Wait!"

He turns.

"What happens if it doesn't work? What if Wyatt won't let Matty out of the trailer? What if you don't come back?"

He blows me a kiss. "If she hears the whistle, she'll eat through the door to get to me. And if I don't come back, then you do what you've been doing. Just stay alive."

Then he's gone, and I'm alone in the forest. I roll onto my back on the platform and stare at the sky. The trees are stripped bare but for a few stubborn, crisp leaves that shake and rattle in the wind. The sky is deep ink blue, a few puffy clouds traveling fast, left to right, as if they're being chased by the slivered white moon. I find Orion, forever striding, and the crown shape that I think might be Cassiopeia. A bobwhite calls, sounding lonely and bereft. I turn my head sideways, hunting for the Big Dipper, and my mom's rosary slides down into the hollow behind my ear. Pulling it off over my head, I can't help thinking of my mom's puffy fingers counting the beads as she muttered under her breath. It calmed her, gave her a routine to help lessen the pain, gave her hope for a better tomorrow. I wonder what she's doing now, if she misses the comfort of the faceted black stone.

"I believe in God, the Father Almighty, Creator of heaven and earth," I start, my breath ragged, just barely a whisper between me and the sky. I know the "Apostles' Creed" and "Our Father" and "Hail Mary" well enough from the days when my mom used to drag me to church, but things get sticky when I get to the Mysteries and all the numbers. Whether I'm doing it right or wrong, it starts to feel right, and I keep going. The stars seem closer, brighter, like I could reach out and touch them. I haven't really thought about this process before, never had the time to stop and listen to the words. When I get to the part, "pray for us sinners, now and at the hour of our death. Amen," a chill washes over me.

I still remember being very small in an uncomfortably fancy dress and too-tight shoes as my mother let me hold her rosary and explained how it worked. We were sitting on a stone bench in the garden outside church, and she said that when you first started praying the rosary, it was common to ask for something miraculous and receive it. She told me that she met my dad after praying a rosary.

"Our Lady wants to bring you closer," she said—I remember that part. So as I murmur the prayers and run my thumb over each bead in turn, I concentrate hard on what I want most: my parents, Wyatt, and Matty, all together, somewhere safe. I can see it in my mind, this big group hug. Chance and Gabriela and Kevin and Rex are suddenly there with us like actors walking onstage. All these people—I want them safe. I lost Jeremy and I lost part of myself, but I want everyone else to walk out unscathed.

Something howls far off, a dog or a coyote, and I forget where I am and hold the rosary to my chest, tears filling my eyes. "Please let them be safe," I say. "Let us be okay." And then, so small under the yawning sky: "Please forgive me for what I've done."

The howl turns into barking, and I know it's Matty, and I roll over and sling the rosary back around my neck and under my shirt to watch. But she doesn't show up, and that's because she's not supposed to. She's not supposed to see me, to smell me. Her bark carries far in the still night—that's all. It feels like forever before I hear boots in the leaves, and then my dad is calling me down from the deer stand.

"It worked?" I ask, bouncing on my toes.

"The first half of it did. I got her to come out to me, and I tied the phone up in the scarf and tied that to her collar, then sent her back. Thank God for a fine hunting dog."

"Was she okay? Did she seem happy?"

"She's a dog with a job. Of course she's happy."

He rubs my back through the jacket and inclines his head toward the woods. The whole time I was here, I forgot there were three dead men lying on the ground beneath me. Everything feels haunted, all of a sudden, and I'm all too glad to follow my dad deeper into the forest, away from all things Crane.

"Where are we going?" I ask.

"It's a secret."

"Um, aren't I going to find out sooner or later?"

He chuckles. "Yeah, but I want to see your face when you do. Keep close, okay? It gets a little tricky in here. Lots of pricker bushes. At least the snakes are asleep, right?"

I hurry, trotting on his heels, close enough to touch his jacket. I have no idea how he's navigating in the dark. The starlight gives everything a blue-white glow, sharp shadows cutting the forest floor into strips of black and blacker black with silver edges keen as a razor blade where frost glints on wet leaves. There are no marks on the trees that I can tell, no orange flags or carvings or the typical ruined fences and outhouses to mark our way. But my dad walks steadily on as if we were following a GPS in broad daylight, holding branches out of my way and pausing as I duck under fallen trees or edge around thick clusters of laurels. At one point, he hops onto a mossy tree to cross a creek, and I almost slip and fall into a gleaming pool surrounded by jagged rocks.

"Whoopsy daisy," he says, like I'm still five. Who knows? To him, maybe I still am, even if I stank of sex the first time we knew each other for who we were.

He's stuck in the past for me too. He was godlike, then, and now he seems smaller, tenser. Just a man. And I want to ask him so many things, but I'm out of breath and running for my life, even if we're not actually running. Until I talk to Wyatt, until I know our people are safe, I can't just dive into thirteen years of *What the hell, Daddy?*

My lungs feel thick and sluggish from pumping the chilled air. My stomach is empty and acid-sour. I want nothing more than to lie down somewhere soft and warm and sleep forever. And that's when my phone rings.

I fumble for it and open it, and my dad grabs it out of my hand. "Who's this?" he says, all gruff. When I try to grab it, he turns away, one furious finger up in a "wait a minute" stab. I hear Wyatt's voice frantically gabbling on the other side, and my dad rolls his eyes and hands me the phone.

"Where's Patsy? What did you—"

"I'm here! Wyatt, I'm here. Are you okay? You have to get out. Okay? Right now."

"What? Out of where? Where are you? What the hell? There were gunshots, and Matty clawed the door until I opened it and then ran off, and I thought she just had to pee, and now she's back with my scarf, and you're gone, and—"

"Wyatt, listen. I don't know how many minutes this phone has. Those nut cans are bombs. There's one in my backpack and two more in the big house and Gabriela has a bag full. They're going to explode at six in the morning, and if you can't get the cans out or the people out, they're all going to die. Kevin's in there with one, and there's one in the room next to him, and . . . I don't know how to get you into the house, but you've got to get Kevin out, if nothing else."

He swallows audibly as Matty whines and slobbers in the background. "Bombs? You're sure?"

"My dad says so. Leon built them."

"But why would Leon lie about that?"

He sounds so innocent. Just like I did before Leon sent goons with guns after me. "Because we wouldn't have planted them if we knew for sure. The ones at the mall, at least—the workers won't be there when they go off. Maybe they're just supposed to blow up the stock. Like, so people can't buy stuff. An eff you to Valor, or whatever."

"Patsy," my dad says gently, twirling his finger in a *"wrap it up"* gesture.

"So here's where they are." I tell Wyatt where all the cans are and to write down my number, just in case something happens.

"Give me the phone," my dad says.

I turn around like a hunching vulture, but he snatches it from me.

"Okay, so the blast radius is pretty big. You can't just toss the can out of the trailer—you need to get it at least a football field away from anyone. They're made to shred everything in their path. Don't open the can. Don't try anything stupid. Just get the cans away from people. We're going somewhere safe. We'll call you tomorrow for a rendezvous point. You're going to run when they start exploding. And one more thing." My dad glances at me and tugs at his beard. "Leon's got Patsy's mom Karen somewhere. We don't know where. Not in the big house. And we need to get her out. When you come find us, I want her with you." He pauses, frowns. "I don't know, kid. Figure it out. If my daughter likes you, you must have a brain. So use it."

Before my dad can click the phone shut, I yelp, "Be careful! I love you!"

He slides the phone into his pocket and gives me a dangerous glare. "You love him?"

At first I look down, embarrassed. But then I remember who I am and what I've been through, and I square my shoulders and meet his eyes. "Yeah, I think I do. Wyatt's saved my life a dozen times. Shot a guy who was going to rape me, charged into two gunfights, paid a vet to fix my dog. He's done a lot more for me than you have, so you don't get a say in it. Now, where the hell are we going?"

My dad looks me up and down like I'm some weird new species he's never seen before. I can't tell if he's going to lecture me, hug me, or slap me. And then he points at the ground.

"We're here."

"If this is the surprise you were waiting to see on my face, prepare for disappointment."

That gets an actual laugh out of him as he sweeps leaves and pine straw away with his feet to reveal the last thing I expected to find out in the middle of the forest, in the middle of a small clearing: a manhole cover. Soon he's got it pried up to reveal a hole into the ground. He flicks a light switch, and fluorescents buzz on, leading the way underground.

"There we go. That's the surprise I was looking for," he says. "I'll go first."

He starts climbing in like it's totally normal, and I find my tongue.

"Dad, what the hell is this?"

"This is your grandfather's nuclear fallout shelter," he says. "On the other side of this hill is the old Cannon house where me and Ash grew up. Now, watch your language and come on down."

18.

It's cold underground but not nearly as gross as I was expecting it to be. The fallout shelter is like a long, metal pill, and it has a built-in ventilation system that hums as it churns fresh air through, although it does smell a bit musty. As soon as he's made sure everything is safe and functional, my dad climbs back up to close the cover and lock it. And that's when it begins to feel like we're buried alive.

"Should I ask why you have a fallout shelter?" I say, leaning back on a narrow bed set into the wall. It's as flat and crisp as a hospital cot, and the guns stuffed in my waistband are instantly uncomfortable, so I put them on a little shelf set overhead. Everything in here is white or beige and strictly utilitarian. As soon as I see the brown marks my muddy sneakers are leaving, I shuffle them off guiltily and curl back up.

"My father was a very paranoid, vindictive man. He had this shelter built back in the nineties in case something happened. Y2K, zombies, whatever. He wanted a place to hide. I think it was left over from the fifties. I only know about it because there was a land dispute and I managed to hack into his files." He brushes off his hands and ducks farther back to open and close doors. I hear a toilet flush, water running. I guess he's making sure everything works. A few moments later, he reappears with a flat package in each hand.

"What are those?" I ask, and he hands me one.

"MREs. Meals ready to eat. They're for troops in combat. Twelve hundred calories to keep you fighting, including dessert. Open it up. You've got to be hungry."

I flip the package around and dump a pile of dark brown plastic squares on the bed. "What's it made of? Is this even food? Is it safe? Wait. How old is this thing?"

Of all the questions I'm dying to ask him about where the hell he's been, I can seem to focus only on the immediate. Maybe I'm not ready for what he has to say.

My dad's already flopped down on the identical bed across from mine, eating something that smells like tuna out of one of the bags, and I want to gag. He shrugs and gives me a crazy grin. "Oh, it's safe. Would the government do something that was bad for you?"

I poke through the bags. No way I'm touching that chicken à la king. I pull out some crackers and a bag of M&M's that looks weirdly off. The first piece of candy is yellow, stale and dry, but still chocolate enough to work. I dump them out in my hand and look up at my dad.

"Since when do they make tan M&M's?"

"They stopped before you were born."

I pour the candy back into the bag, tuck everything back in the package, and decide I can wait for real food. My dad watches me, his eyebrows scrunched down, and abandons his meal to bring me a bottle of water.

"At least stay hydrated."

I check for weird inscriptions before drinking it.

The shelter is strangely impersonal, quiet and cool. I get the idea that anyone trapped down here for very long would go insane, despite the bookshelf set into the wall and boasting hundreds of slender paperbacks, mostly science fiction and thrillers. I don't really know what to say, don't know where to start, but my natural instinct is to let my dad go first. Let him do the work. After all, he's the one who left.

I expect him to apologize, to tell me how good it is to see me, or to ask what my hobbies are or if my grades are good or what I want to be when I grow up. But I'm dead wrong.

"So why do you have my brother's dog?" he says, eyes locked on mine over his bag of tuna.

I swing my legs over the side of the bed to face him.

"This is how you want to start? You're gone for thirteen years, and you want to know about your brother, who you saw six fucking months ago?"

He puts down the tuna, wipes his mouth on a paper napkin, and turns to face me.

"My brother would die before he let that dog out of his sight."

"Then I guess you know what happened."

He pulls off his beanie and runs a hand through wolfish hair gone salt-and-pepper, though still mostly pepper. I can tell he's chewing the inside of his cheek just like I do when I'm pissed and at war between what I want to say and what I should say. This is not how I dreamed our reunion would go, every word fueled with anger, suspicion, and blame.

"How'd he die? He was supposed to stay out of this mess."

"You want the full story?"

He chuckles like he can't believe we're doing this, kicks off his muddy boots, and lies back on the bed to stare at the ceiling. "Well, we've definitely got the time."

"Don't you want to know about me? Or tell me where the hell you've been?" I dash the tears away, wishing it weren't so well lit in this goddamn underground courtroom.

"If you killed your uncle, for Valor or otherwise, I need to know why."

"But I'm the one who's still alive!"

"Honey, this is a war. We are in a war, and people are dying. We both killed people, not even two hours ago. And as much as I'd love to do the hugging-and-laughing thing, I'd rather do everything in my power to keep you alive. And that means I need to know what we're up against. So. Tell me about Ash."

I take a deep, petulant breath and lean back against the wall so I don't have to look at him. I know he's right, but it still hurts.

"It all started when a Valor guy knocked on the door," I say.

"I know. But tell me anyway."

So I tell him the entire story. Mom's cancer, the gun pointed first at her and then tossed in my lap with my knitting. The envelope of cards, the list of ten names, the mail truck waiting outside, freshly painted just for me. When I get to my first kill, to Wyatt's dad, my mom's ex-boss, he sits up and faces me, reaches for my hand. I shake it off. I don't want this to be what connects us.

"What'd you do after you shot him?" he asks.

I swallow hard. "Wyatt came after me, shoved me up against the truck. He didn't know what was going on then—no one did. But I didn't shoot him. I drove away and threw up."

He looks like he wants to reach for me again, but I've got my arms drawn in tight, my hands clasped. "It took me that way too. The first time," he says softly. "What happened next?"

I know he wants me to get to his brother, but the words just tumble out. Like a confession. Here, underground, after midnight, I need someone to know everything, someone who'll have no choice but to love me anyway. I tell him about Eloise Framingham, dying from the same cancer my mom has. About parking the mail truck in an abandoned lot to get some sleep and waking up with Wyatt on top of me, a knife to my throat. It's awkward, recounting how Wyatt and I fought off the suburban thug rapists, leaving two dead. But the worst part is telling him about the third name on my list, the one he thinks he wants to know about.

"I thought it was a girl. Ashley Cannon. I didn't know it was your last name. When I knocked, he cocked his shotgun. Matty was barking, and she actually sounded mean from the other side of a closed door. But he . . . he recognized me. Knew I was Jack's girl."

"But he wouldn't take the deal?"

I bow over, head in my hands. "He didn't get a chance to. I didn't mean to shoot him. My finger was sweaty on the trigger, and I was holding this stupid basket, and he knew me, and I was scared, and . . . it just happened. And he was gone."

Silence settles, still as a tomb. My dad sniffles, a manly sniffle, and I keep my eyes trained on the cheap, thin carpet.

"And then what?" he finally says.

"I went inside. For clues. I don't know. I didn't remember having an uncle, and I thought there might be stuff inside that would tell me about where you were. I found a photo of you and Ash and an old guy that's maybe y'all's dad?"

"That was Devil Johnny. My dad. He died two months ago."

A small part of me snaps, knowing that my family is growing smaller by the day.

"Uncle Ashley—"

"Ash."

"He had all my school pictures. And he had a lot of bills, owed a lot of money. And I didn't want to leave Matty there, so I took her. She's . . ." The tears fall, hot and heavy. "She felt like all the family I had left. I didn't think I'd ever see you again. I didn't know if Mom would make it. She's a good dog. She ran into a gunfight for me. I just . . . I'm sorry. I'm so sorry. I didn't know." When he doesn't say anything, doesn't reach out, I add, "They were going to kill Mom. I didn't know."

He stands slowly, like a much older man, and sits beside me, one arm around my back.

"I don't know much about being your dad, but I know you did what you had to."

"I had no choice!"

He rubs my arm, puts his cheek against my hair. It's strange at first, but he smells the same as he did when I was a little kid, and I slowly thaw and relax against him.

"I'm sorry."

"It's not your fault."

We say these words, again and again, in a circle. Parents to kids, kids to parents. Maybe one day I'll believe it.

I finally stop crying, and my dad gets up to bring me a carefully folded wad of cheap toilet paper. I blow my nose, wipe off my eyes. It's time to ask the question that's been bugging me for days.

"Do you know why Valor would send me to my uncle's house?"

He's wiping his own eyes as he sits back down across from me. "You said you saw bills. He used to work for a bank, but then he quit. We both did. Our dad was a shark of a businessman, and his business got too shady. So maybe Ash got fed up and just quit paying. He didn't get anything from Dad's will except a big-ass television. Almost like it was a joke."

I give a sad chuckle. "Yeah, I noticed that. It was worth more than pretty much everything else in his house. But here's the thing . . ." I look up, meet his eyes with cold resolve. "I had some kind of connection to everyone on that list."

"Tell me," he says.

"Robert Beard was the guy who fired Mom. We were doing pretty well before him." I can't help shooting him a reproachful glance. Does he know how hard it hit us, his leaving? "Eloise Framingham had the same cancer as mom and was dying. Ashley Cannon was my uncle. Kelsey Mackey looked like me in five years, happy and with everything I ever wanted. They got her for college loans. Ken Belcher—Dr. Ken Belcher—lived in that stupid Château Tuscano, the richest mansion in the city. Sharon Mulvaney was the mom of this girl I used to be friends with. Tom Morrison was a great single dad to a little girl who looked just like me, and he went into debt trying to give her everything. Alistair Meade was a double agent, working as a Valor suit. A conspiracy theorist, I guess. Amber Lane was my best friend until she dumped me for being too poor. And Maxwell Beard is Wyatt's brother. Wyatt took out a credit card in his name when he was younger, but he's been paying it back, trying to make it right."

He lies back and looks up at the ceiling. "So why you?"

"Jesus, I wish I knew. The conspiracy guy's trailer had all these lists taken from the results of a career aptitude test we took at school. My name was on there. But my results just said I could be a secretary or a dental hygienist. There was nothing on there about . . . whatever this is. Being an assassin. I'm not important at all."

My dad chuckles at the ceiling and puts out his elbows. "You're more important than you think."

I blow a raspberry. "Yeah, you're only saying that because you're my dad."

"That's part of it. But this thing is bigger than it looks. My father started working for Valor when they were still just a local bank. Ash and I did, too, like I said, for a while. But the dealings got too dirty. Valor got too big, started cannibalizing other banks, other businesses. The presidents of rival banks had a nasty habit of dying under mysterious circumstances. Me and Ash needed some distance, so we quit. That picture you saw of us hunting—that was our last-ditch effort at reconciling with our dad. He wanted us to work for Valor, wanted to pull us into this takeover. We both turned him down. He cussed us out, cut us out of the will, and died a few months later. He was a hard, evil son of a bitch. Neither of us went to his funeral."

There's a crumbling feeling inside me, everything suddenly clicking into place with a sick finality.

"So you're saying that maybe they targeted me because I was your daughter? That it was, what? Revenge from beyond the grave?"

"That sounds like something Devil Johnny would do. To us both."

"Why? Why would my grandfather do that? God, none of this makes sense. Everything is so messed up. My life was good until you left." I pop to sitting and then stand to pace the shelter. "All of this. It was all your fault. If you'd stuck around, Mom wouldn't have always been behind on bills, working her ass off. I wouldn't have been pulling thirty hours a week and bringing home pizza to feed us when the peanut butter ran out. We wouldn't have been in debt at all." I face him, hands in fists. "So why did you leave? Why didn't you care?" I want to hit him, to rake my nails across his face, but I can't unclench my fists, and if I do, I'll just collapse into his arms. "Why didn't you love me enough to stay?"

He sits up, unnaturally calm. "Did your mom ever say anything about why I left?"

I shake my head. My throat is all closed up with regret.

"That's because she didn't know. I never told her. We met at a sandwich shop and fell in love. But I couldn't marry her, because my dad's lawyers would've been all over us. So we kept it secret. All *Romeo and Juliet*, right? The old-Georgia-money banker and his rags-to-riches waitress. We spent every weekend together, and she thought I was at conferences all week, but I was really reporting home to the Cannon compound, pretending like I was a good little boy. When you were born, she stopped working to stay home with you. I paid for everything and visited as often as I could with presents, but it was hard. And then my dad started asking some pointed questions about where my money was going, and I realized the dream was over. That he would find out about y'all and force you to join the family, and you and your mother would become pawns in his game. You were the only heir. So one day I left her a letter, kissed you on the head, walked out, and . . . never came back. My phones went dead; my e-mail bounced. Jack Cannon simply disappeared."

"You . . . asshole."

Jesus. No wonder I thought he was magical. I saw him only on the weekends, when he dropped by with toys and money.

His eyes are full of tears, but they can't touch my anger.

"It wasn't easy for me, either, Patsy. I missed you so much it was like a physical illness, like I couldn't breathe all the way. I learned how to hack computers just so I could keep track of you. Get your school photos, check your grades. I can't believe you got busted for selling fake pot in the bathroom, by the way." He allows himself a small smile but quickly sobers when he looks up at me.

"Everything I did was to protect you from my dad and what eventually became Valor. Ash was the only one who knew I was still around. That hunting photo was the last time I saw my father alive and the first time he'd seen me in thirteen years. He was more power hungry than I'd ever seen him, said he was on the verge of something earth-shattering. That I needed to come home to be a part of it or else."

"I'm the 'or else,' aren't I?" I say tiredly.

He nods. "That's what the puzzle pieces are saying. When Devil Johnny died, I thought all my ties to Valor were severed. His lawyer said that Ash and I were written out, and I figured I could just go back to being a Cannon. I sent your mom a little money. Not enough, but some. I actually stopped by your work one night to talk to you, but I couldn't figure out how to start, so I just paid for my pizza and left. It was a hell of a jolt, seeing you at the high school with Al's laptops and not being able to show any emotion with all those damn Cranes around."

He couldn't hide it from me, though. I saw it in his eyes that night. But when I rack my brain, I can't remember ever seeing him at my work. To think—he was that close.

"But where were you, all that time?" *All that time I needed you*, I don't say.

He shrugs. "All over. I learned how to siphon off Valor cash using the systems I'd developed to protect them. Hacked in a little deeper and started to see that nasty stuff Valor was planning and decided I had to help fight it. The deeper I got, the more determined I was to stop him. I hooked up with the darknet and Incog, then the CFF, hoping to fight back. When my old friend Leon turned out to be the head of this cell, I decided to come work with him."

I snort. "He fooled you, too."

"He wasn't always bad. We were practically brothers, growing up. But he's stubborn. Don't underestimate a man who grew up with a chip on his shoulder and a fondness for gunpowder. The Cannons went into banking, but the Cranes went into business. They may look and act like rednecks, but that's just part of the front. Devil Johnny and Lawrence Crane became two blowhards trying to outdo each other in a giant game of Monopoly with Candlewood as their board. Lawrence favored Leon's older brother Larry as his right hand, and that meant Leon never lived up to his potential. Went into the army, was in and out of prison. Being in charge of a guerrilla organization is basically the most fun he's ever had. No law. No government. Just pure anarchy while he pretends he's the good guy. I was going to get out soon, next time they sent me off property. Operation Nutjob took it too far."

"So here we are."

He throws out his arms and gives me the saddest smile. "So here we are. I've finally got the thing I've wanted the most for a decade of my life, my sweet baby girl by my side. And now I learn my brother's gone and my former best friend wants me dead. It's a hell of a week." He tips back his head and guzzles water like it's whiskey. "And now Leon'll want to get you, too. Up until tonight, he had no idea we were connected, or he would've done anything to keep us apart."

"But he has Mom. Somewhere. And you were in the big house. So if you didn't see her . . ."

"Honey." He shakes his head sadly. "The Cranes are a big family with hundreds of acres of land and a dozen businesses spread out around town. Just on the compound, they've got the big house, about ten different trailers out in the woods, a shotgun shack, the taxidermy barn, the notary house. If you weren't looking for someone, chances are you wouldn't see 'em. If she was in the med trailer instead of the clinic, I had no reason to go there. It would have taken pure dumb luck for our paths to ever cross."

"You think he's figured it out yet? You, me, and Mom?"

He shrugs. "He will soon. Once the fourth guy makes it back and he knows you and I are on the run, he should be able to put it all together. If he asks her the right questions under the right threat of violence, he'll know everything. Your mom isn't the type to hold up to torture."

I swallow. "Torture?"

"He'll do anything to get what he wants. And he wants me dead or on his side."

I throw myself back on the bed and stare at the curved white ceiling. "So we can't go back."

"Not if we want to live."

"Out of the frying pan, into the fire."

"More like out of the frying pan, into the fire, out of the fire, into the wilderness." He stands up and ruffles my hair. "I thought you were dead. I'll take the wilderness with my little Patsy any day."

"But we need Wyatt. And Mom and Matty and Kevin, and . . ." I grunt and slam my head against the pillow until I can't stand it anymore. "We have to get them out. Before the bombs go off and everyone goes batshit."

And that's when I realize what needs to happen next.

There's no cell signal in the bunker, so we climb back out of the tube. It's the middle of the night, and I can only hope that Wyatt hasn't yet done what I told him to do. I walk up a nearby hill until I have a few bars and call him.

"Patsy?" His voice is quiet. "Are you okay?"

"I'm fine. Did you do it yet?"

A tiny sigh. "They won't let me in the house, but they sent Kevin down with Gabriela. He's in our tent. Everybody's jacked up around

· 302 ·

here. Some guys went out and only one came back. Actual Cranes. Leon is pissed. He put a gun to my chest but said there were too many witnesses and he needs me to get you back."

A tiny moan escapes me as my heart clenches. I may have put a gun to Wyatt's chest last week, but that doesn't mean other people can.

"But he didn't hurt you?"

"No. Patsy, why does he want you dead?"

"It doesn't matter. Point is, they came to kill us, and they failed. But the plan changed. Did you get rid of the can in the black backpack, at least?"

"It's way out in the woods, away from all the people. Do you want me to tell Leon about the ones in the house?"

"No," I say. "Leave them right where they are and then do exactly what I say. I want to see the smoke."

19.

It's almost dawn now, and I feel like I drank twenty cups of coffee. What was in that yellow M&M? Dad said I should try to sleep for a few hours, and I tried, but it was impossible to relax in a fallout shelter. Lights on and it's like being in a doctor's office. Lights off and it's like being in a crypt. So we're walking up the deeply forested hill in the dark, following an old trail that zigs and zags ever upward. My dad has a flashlight, but he uses it only when the shadows make the way impassable. I trip. A lot.

We pass remnants of a handmade rock wall and a cave that my dad points out as the spring house. He tells me stories about the time he fell down the hill and got a splinter four inches long in his thigh and the time Ash got bitten by a copperhead down by the creek. He smiles fondly when he points out the tree house his sister, Valerie, built to show the boys she didn't need their help.

"Guess she won." He chuckles. "Ours fell down years ago."

"What happened to her?" I ask, still hungry for more family.

"She died young," he says, flat and faraway, as he helps me over a log.

We're silent for a few moments, using smaller trees to pull ourselves up the hill. I'm out of breath, my hands cold and raw from the climb.

"Okay, so here's the family history. Cannon House was built in 1897," my dad says with some pride. "The first one, that is. Big plantation. It stood until the 1920s, when it burned down, and a bigger, grander home was built in the same place. And that one burned down a few months ago with my dad inside it. Here's what's left of it."

We crest the hill, and the most beautiful and haunting scene spreads out before me. The house is a black skeleton of grand beams and crumbling fireplaces. It must've been huge, a mansion. Tiny shots of white still struggle up where the flames somehow didn't reach. The fire's wrath seems fickle—half the staircase survived on one side, but the other side is entirely gone. One side of the grand porch is still gleaming white while the other is black and powdery.

"It looks like the aftermath of *Gone with the Wind*," I murmur.

My dad nods. "It was a great house to grow up in, except for the fact that my dad was in charge of it."

"What about your mom?"

"She died when I was little. We had maids and aunts around, but mostly we just ran loose. My bedroom was up there, above the kitchen." He points to the top right, where black trees jab the coming dawn. That entire side of the house is gone. "I'm sorry you didn't get to see it before now. We lost all the family records, the photo albums. They said my dad got up in the middle of the night, turned on a teakettle, and just . . . forgot. He didn't trust anyone in his later years, and he lived alone. The maid slept straight through it in the carriage house. That's where we're going."

The air smells of doomed majesty, char, and ice, and I tiptoe through the frosty grass, silent. Around the other side of what's left of the house, there's a garden gone wild and dead for the winter, a huge stack of fire wood, an empty chicken coop, garden sheds, a dry fountain, and a two-story building that looks like the newest thing for miles. The bottom half is old brick, the top half freshly painted white with French doors and a balcony. My dad turns on the flashlight and hunts around under flowerpots until he finds a key. I watch and worry. The night is disturbingly silent; even the birds are asleep. When he opens the door, the smell of rot makes me gag, even in the chill air. Narrow steps and new carpet lead up to a small apartment. His flashlight lands on a kitchen table, where a bowl of black, wet fruit sits beside a vase of dead flowers and a sprinkling of mouse turds.

"Don't know what happened to the maid," my dad says. "I lived here for a while, when you were a baby. It smelled a lot better back then."

Everything in the apartment appears to have been abandoned by someone leaving in an unexpected hurry, including several pairs of small orthopedic shoes lined up by the door and a black-and-white maid's uniform of the frumpy, not saucy, variety hanging from a chair. The bed is still made, and my dad unlocks the French doors and throws them open, giving us a beautiful view of the sweeping valley below.

"I bet it's beautiful when the leaves turn in October," I say.

"You should see it in spring."

He checks his watch, and I check my phone. I want to call Wyatt, but I can't. Not until it's time. I pull up the list of contacts and let my finger rub over the button. But I don't press it. Not yet.

"Five fifty," he says, looking at his flip phone. "Ten minutes to go."

So close.

"Where is it?" I ask.

He points to a random section of land in the valley below. Last night's hike felt like it lasted forever, but it was really just a mile, maybe less. I can see flashes of roof through the barren trees, and I try to identify the different buildings of the Crane compound. I think I see the big house, but it's hard to tell.

My phone buzzes, and I fumble to check the text.

It's from Wyatt: `We're in place.`

"Five fifty-three," my dad says. He looks as nervous as I am, checking his phone repeatedly and tapping his fingers on the banister.

"Come on, come on, come on," I mutter. "Are you sure the time is right?"

He gives a sly chuckle. "Yes, actually, I am. I'm the one who programmed it, remember?"

I look at him, curious. "Why?"

"Why what?"

"Why'd you rig bombs to blow up a bunch of strip malls?"

He looks down at his work boots, scuffs them on the ground. "Long story. It's easy for a little rebellion to suddenly get big. It started out with the Wipers, shutting down credit cards, rerouting new cards in the mail, and hacking into the system to program gift cards. It was fun, finally messing with Valor after all the times they'd messed with me. And we did try to do the dye pack thing, but it's a lot harder than it sounds. When Leon suggested bombs to go off when the buildings were empty, it seemed like a fun challenge. It's not like you're hurting actual people, you know? Blow up overpriced clothes, businesses that can't pay their rent. Things people don't actually own, things owned by the bank. He never said he was using kids to plant them, you know? Once you're headed down a path, once you start saying yes, it's hard to decide when to start saying no. And Leon is . . . especially hard to say no to." He flips the phone around. "Five fifty-six."

"Did you know about what Valor was doing? To kids, I mean?"

He shakes his head. "If that kind of information got out in advance, it would never have happened. Do you know what they did to the police, speaking of which? And the armed forces?"

"Leon said . . . it was bad."

He takes off his beanie and rubs a hand through his hair. "It's kind of brilliant but really evil. They started high up. Invited the highest-ranking people to a special meeting. Either they signed on with Valor or went to another room to be 'debriefed.'"

"Which means dead?"

He points a finger gun at me and says, "Correct. They used a nerve gas so they could claim it was some disease, not something quickly identified as a weapon. Remember that Ebola scare? So then they made sure they only had true believers in positions of leadership, guys on the Valor payroll, and they kept going down the line, each leader on Valor's side bringing in their subordinates and weeding out the rebels and the Dudley Do-Gooders. Right before they activated the assassins, they took down the regular Internet and all the functionaries who might oppose Valor. More than half the police force and armed forces, gone. By the time the assassins went out, nine-one-one was sent to voice mail, the Internet and media were all run by Valor, and the police who were still around had Valor bank accounts and weren't working in the public's best interest. Five fifty-eight."

I shiver. "Jesus."

He puts an arm around me and rubs my shoulder, and I gratefully lean against him, glad for his warmth. "An elegantly silent takeover. And lots of the victims on the Valor lists were people they wanted gone. Members of the bank boards who knew too much, double agents, people who'd been stirring up too much trouble on the old net. Just . . . *bang*. And then silence."

"One of the guys on my list was a double agent."

He looks up sharply. "Al and his laptops. What happened to him exactly?"

I pull away and look down. "Wyatt thought he was going to hurt me, so he shot him. It wasn't me that time. I swear. I burned his trailer. And my mail truck."

My dad is . . . glowing with pride?

"Well done. That's really fantastic. I can't imagine what would've happened if Valor had gotten access to all his intel. Just . . . well done."

I shiver, my teeth chattering. "Dad, I killed a bunch of people. It wasn't well done. It was . . . horrible."

His arms go up like he wants to hug me and doesn't quite know how, and I want him to but can't take the extra steps to get there. He finally settles for clearing his throat and saying, "I'm so sorry that happened to you. If I had known, I would've done everything in my power to stop it. I would've gotten you and your mom out. I swear."

"I know."

"This is going to work, Patsy."

"I know, Dad."

The silence stretches out for a moment, and I want to cry but can't.

"Five fifty-nine. Get ready, honey." His hand lands on my back. As if I needed him to protect me.

I nod and flip open my phone. My finger hovers over the call button, and then an explosion rocks the valley. I don't feel the heat like I did when it was my house, but I hear screams as fire and smoke rise above the trees. I press call.

The phone picks up immediately. "Who the sweet hell is this?"

"Hi, Leon."

He takes a long breath, and the chaos in the background is insane, screams and bangs and crunching. I guess he wasn't in the house, then.

"Miss Patsy. I should've guessed. Do you know how many innocent people were inside when the bombs you planted went off in my family home? Because it was you, wasn't it?"

That strikes hard, just like it was meant to. But I refuse to show him any softness. It's just something else for me to cry about later, another nightmare to wake me, screaming, at night. At least I don't have to see the aftermath this time.

"It was mostly women, though. Me and most of my men were still in the barn torturing your suit, thankfully."

I know he's trying to find a soft spot to hurt, but I ignore the prodding. "What's funny is that I was told those nut cans were harmless little machines that would make dye packs explode. Nobody ever said anything about bombs. I can't believe you would lie to me. I thought we were on the same side."

A gabble of shouts calls for Leon, and his voice is muffled as he says, "I don't care how you do it. You get in there and save what you can. Rafe's a volunteer firefighter. Get him a damn ax and follow him in. Now go!" He sighs heavily and asks me, "What the hell are you doing with Jacky boy, anyway? Are you two lovebirds? Is this a Lolita thing?"

I let the dead air speak for me, then say slowly, "Whom?"

He cusses under his breath, and I imagine him running a hand through his rooster-spiky hair. "You are causing me a damn sight of trouble, little girl. And when I find you, I'm going to kill you slowly. Your boyfriend and dog too. And your mom, and your friends, and that little boy you shot. Do you know what it feels like to be tortured, Patsy? Like that man you delivered to me yesterday? To have your fingernails pulled out one by one? You ever seen a dog with no tongue try to drink water? It ain't pretty."

"Ooh, Leon. I'm sooooo scared," I say. "You're sooooo scary."

"I'm not a man you want to anger," he says, slow and deadly.

"And you've already made me angrier than most. Now my life is dedicated to enrolling more soldiers to take down Valor, and God help me, I will use them to take you down too."

My fingers curl around the banister as I watch the smoke rise, white and curling, from Crane Hollow. "The thing is, Leon . . . I'm not your soldier. You lied to me from the start, and I think at this point you're basically just getting kicked in the ass by karma. Or bombed in the ass by karma." I giggle, mainly because I think it will piss him off.

"Do you know what a soldier is, Patsy Klein? A soldier is someone too dumb to be in charge. So you go on and pretend you're dangerous, and I'll keep commanding people smarter than you."

My dad's phone buzzes with a text, and he touches my sleeve and nods.

"Well, it's just been lovely talking to you, Leon, but I'm afraid I've got to go."

"I'm not done talking to you!" he shouts. "I'm gonna—"

I flip the phone shut.

"I bet you are," I say. It rings, and Leon's number flashes up. I hold it out to my dad. "Can he track us with this phone?"

"Not if there was a nut bomb in the war room. I hate that we lost Al's laptops, but . . ." He sighs. "I need to buy a new laptop and a few new SD cards, and then I can tap back in and see what Leon's next step will be."

That makes me frown. "Why do you care? I thought we were leaving."

My dad looks from the smoke spiraling against the dawn sky to me. "Because Operation Red Thursday was a big deal, and I can't imagine Leon's going to let a little explosion at home stop him."

"What's Operation Red Thursday?"

He puts a heavy hand on my shoulder. "I'll tell you later, if it's still on. For now, we've got people who need us, and they'll be waiting."

We walk around the burned house and down a long dirt and gravel road that swoops through the woods. Trees meet overhead, the birds singing at one another excitedly as the sun thinks about rising. It's oddly tranquil out here, especially compared to the bustle of the Crane land and the madness I heard happening in the background behind Leon.

God, I would've loved this place when I was little. Our shitty little fenced-in yard and rusted-out metal swing set back home can't compare.

"Did you guys ever have, like, family reunions?" I ask.

My dad looks at me in surprise. "Well, sure. I mean, we got together with the cousins for Thanksgiving and Christmas and Easter, that sort of thing. Dad had a cabin on Lake Lanier. Sometimes I'd go along with the Cranes to their family parties—we were close enough cousins that nobody blinked. Why?"

My sneaker toes kick the gravel a little harder than necessary. "Guess I grew up figuring I had cousins somewhere having parties without me."

His hand lands on my back. "It was for your own good, honey. Devil Johnny used everybody he got his hands on. He's the reason Leon went into the army in the first place—because Devil Johnny wanted the smartest Crane out of the way. I wanted you to have a chance of growing up without your granddad's ambition hanging over your shoulder, pushing you toward whatever end suited him."

"You could've sent cards. Or money."

He stops and stares at me, incredulous. "I did. I sent birthday cards every year. To both of you, from all over the world so no one could find me. You never got them?"

I shake my head slowly. "Nope. Mom refused to talk about you. Ever. But why would she hide that from me? And why didn't you send her money?"

"I sent some. Clearly not enough. I didn't think to hack into her finances, you know? She was always responsible, frugal. I just assumed everything was okay."

I turn a sniffle into a cough. "Yeah. No, everything was great. I mean, well done. Thanks for checking my grades but not her debt. That was thoughtful."

We have to step around a fallen branch, and he says nothing, just keeps walking. I wipe my nose on my sleeves and try to sound like I'm not crying.

Somewhere in my now-exploded house was a box of cards from my dad. Maybe he told me he loved me. Maybe he sent ten bucks. And I never knew. And now I don't know who makes me more furious: the father who left me and failed to provide for us or the mother who hid his random and insufficient love from me for her own reasons.

Why can't I just have two good parents to love without reservation?

"I can't imagine how you're feeling right now, and I don't expect you to understand or to forgive me, Patsy. But I want you to know that everything I did, I did for you. I've been miserable and heartbroken all this time. Finding you again has been a gift. And from this moment on, I'm never going to leave you. We're in this together now. I promise."

Up ahead, there's a break in the trees, and I see a flash of burgundy and speed up. I don't hug my dad. I don't forgive him. I don't tell him it's okay.

I don't know if I believe him.

The burgundy sedan is idling in a small dirt turnaround hidden from the road above. I wave, and Wyatt jumps out of the driver's seat. We run at each other, arms outstretched like two idiots in a movie. I'm scanning his face and chest for wounds, but he looks totally fine. Not until I'm crushed against his body, wrapped in his arms, do I look at the scene unfolding by the car.

"Patsy, I—"

"Hold that thought."

I break away from him and run the last few steps to the car, where my mom is getting out of the passenger seat. She looks the same as she did last week, bloated and tired and worn down. But when she sees me, she lights right up, and I can finally relax.

I can't believe she's here. I can't believe she's still alive.

"Patsy!" she says, a little weakly, and then we're hugging and crying. I pull back and notice the deep hollows under her eyes.

"How do you feel, Mom?"

She laughs sadly. "Like crap. That Heather's a tight-fisted little thing with the Vicodin."

I glance over her shoulder and am surprised to see Heather sitting in the back of the car beside Kevin. They look like they're arguing, but not a warden-prisoner argument. More like a big sister–little brother argument.

"Why is she here?" I ask.

My mom looks back at the car, then at Wyatt's gold Lexus just behind it. Chance and Gabriela are staring at us from the front seat, while Rex and Bea are tuned out in the backseat, him on his iPod and her staring out the window. Her eyes, as always, give the impression that no one is home.

"Heather wouldn't leave me," my mom says, sounding fond. "When everything exploded, she grabbed my meds and dragged me out of the trailer. When your friends found us, she just came along."

"And you let her?" I ask Wyatt.

He fidgets and frowns. "She's actually pretty nice, now that she's away from the Cranes." He leans close and whispers, "And she knows how to help your mom and the kid. She's a registered nurse."

"But what if she's loyal to Leon? What if she tells him how to find us?"

My mom shakes her head and tucks my hair behind my ear. "Nobody likes working for Leon, honey. He's not a nice man. Heather's on our side, I promise."

"Is that true, Dad?" I turn to him, and he's looking at me and my mom with tears running down his face.

He just shakes his head and says, "Karen."

My mom swallows hard and shakes her head in disbelief. "Jack?"

He nods. "I'm so sorry."

"Why did . . . ? You were . . . this whole time?"

He shrugs and gives a weak smile. "Only to keep my girls safe." When he steps toward her, hands out like he wants to touch her, I watch for a second but can't handle how my mom's mouth is shaking at the corners. Instead, I tip my head at Wyatt, and we head to the car.

I pull my gun and open Heather's door. She looks grim, like she was expecting this to happen.

· 318 ·

"Do you have a phone?" I ask.

Wyatt holds out a burner phone, black and identical to all the others. "Already took it off her."

"Do you have any other Crane tech?"

She shakes her head. "You think they allowed me to keep anything?"

"You were there that first night. You were smiling."

She holds up her hands and rolls her eyes, looking much closer to twenty than she did in the Crane house. "Yeah, that's kind of the point. Leon needed a nice little blond girl to make people feel at home. I mean, would you have joined up if it was nothing but big dudes with Uzis?"

"So why'd you stay? Why were you mean to us?"

She gestures to the cooler at her feet. "I told you—I'm the nurse. Your mom, Kevin, anybody who got hurt. I was in nursing school, so I was the only person who could help. There are more than a hundred people currently on Crane land. It's hard to walk away from people who need you." Her smile seems genuine, apologetic. "I was mean because if you didn't do what Leon told you to do, you'd get shot. It seemed better to pretend to be a bitch than have to patch you up later when you were full of bullet holes."

"Why should I believe you?"

She throws her hands up. "Do you want to search me? I ran out of that trailer carrying your mom's meds, so it's not like I had time to grab all my stuff."

I nod. She huffs and gets out of the car. I give Wyatt my gun and step close, running my hands down Heather's arms, over her ribs, around her waist, down her hips and legs and up her inseams. I've never searched anyone before, and I'm very aware of how awkward and intrusive it is and how uncomfortable it's making both of us.

"I'm telling you—I'm on your side," Heather says. "Ask Kevin."

I look to him, and he's already nodding. "Mr. Crane was really mean to her. He made her cry. She's pretty okay. Except for the broccoli."

Heather laughs. "Yeah, I make him eat his vegetables. You can't heal if you eat nothing but Pop-Tarts."

When I searched her, I found nothing. If she's hiding something, even a Post-it note, she's hiding it well. She sure as hell doesn't have a gun or a knife . . . and then I think of something.

"Wait."

I drop to a knee and run hands inside her beat-up cowboy boots. Sure enough, I find a knife in a clip-on sheath.

"Were you going to tell us about that?"

She looks at me dead-on. "If you were suddenly taken hostage by a bunch of teen assassins with guns, in the world we live in now, would you offer up that you had a knife?"

I fold the knife up and put it in my back pocket.

"I don't know if I can trust you, but I know that we need you. So just remember that if you make one false move, if we catch you with a phone or trying to contact the Cranes, I will shoot you. And not in the leg." I look pointedly at Kevin. "I shot him for the wrong reason. It's a lot worse when I do it for the right reason."

She sighs. "Look, I'm just here to help people who are hurting. So just know that I never took the Hippocratic oath, and don't piss me off."

I hold out my hand, and she looks at it a moment before shaking it.

The morning's quiet is shattered by the sound of a slap. I look to my parents, and instead of the tearful reunion I'd kind of hoped to see, she's crying, and he has a red print on his cheek.

"You bastard," my mom says, her normally frail voice loud and angry. "You could've stopped this. It's all your fault."

"Karen," my dad says, pleading.

"Go to hell, Jack."

She walks to the car, gets in the front seat, and slams the door. Everyone is staring at my dad.

"Everything okay?" Wyatt asks. He steps behind me, a hand on my shoulder, and I want to melt into him, into the relief of a solid body behind me, someone I can trust completely.

My dad just shakes his head, so I answer.

"I guess when you walk out on your girlfriend and daughter and then show up thirteen years later working for the enemy, things aren't easy."

"You can say that again," my dad says, his eyes pinned to where my mom sits in the front of the burgundy sedan, carefully staring straight ahead. I realize that it's the same car Wyatt brought back from his Wiper assignment. I didn't even think about that part of the plan—that if they managed to get everyone out, there was no way we would all fit in Wyatt's old Lexus.

"Dad, do the Cranes track their cars?"

He snaps out of his freak-out and looks at me in confusion. "Just the regular cars? No. Anything we can track, Valor can track too. They even switch around the license plates so that they're harder to find. Plus . . . well, you blew up all of their laptops."

"I totally did." I grin, remembering how good it felt to spray-paint the wall. "Did you bring my backpack?" I ask Wyatt. He nods. "And food for Matty?"

His face falls, and he shakes his head and swallows hard. "Yeah, but . . ."

"But what?"

He turns to look back at the cars, or maybe he just turns away from my stare. "We lost Matty."

20.

I go cold all the way down to my toes. How did I not notice it before? I guess I was so busy being totally overjoyed that my mom was alive and my dad was here that I didn't notice my dog was gone.

"What the hell happened?" I want to shove him, hard. But I'm not that far gone yet. "How the hell do you lose a dog? Is she dead? Oh my God."

He turns back, hands on his head. "No. I don't think so. You don't understand. You weren't there. I had to get all our stuff, get rid of the last bomb, get Gabriela and Chance and the other kids, get in position so I could see everyone running out of the woods once the shit hit the fan. I had to look for your mom, just wandering around the woods in the dark. I couldn't find her. And I was holding Matty's leash, and then the bombs went off, and she bolted."

I take a deep breath through my nose. "She bolted. That's it?"

"You don't know how big the explosion was. I mean, they must've been hiding C-4 in one of those rooms, because it wasn't just, like, *BOOM*. It was this huge chain of explosions, windows blasting out and nails and wood and fire everywhere. People were hurt, kids were screaming, the old ladies in the kitchen were dragging themselves out the door with their bones sticking out. It was a nightmare. So I watched the crowd and found your mom, and we ran for the car. I had to hit the guy guarding the road on the way out. Like, I hit a guy with the car. There's a dent in the hood." He walks over to the car, runs a hand over it.

I'm crying again. I used to fight tears, control them, tamp them back down. But now they just flow whenever they want to, hot rivulets down my cheeks. I wake up like this every night, crying before I even know where I am, but this is worse, because I can't count on Wyatt to stop it. I don't want him to touch me now.

"So what you're telling me," I say slowly, "is that Leon Crane has my dog?"

He nods. "Maybe. I don't know. I'm so sorry, Patsy. I just—"

"You're driving the red car?"

"Yeah. Why?"

I walk to his gold Lexus, open the back door, sit next to Rex, and shut the door.

X X X

It's a tight fit, crammed in with Rex and Bea, and I put my arm along the window and my head on my arm. My dad and Wyatt are arguing outside, but I don't want to hear it.

"May I?" I ask, pointing to Rex's ever-present earbuds.

He shrugs, pulls one out, and hands it to me. I shove it in my ear and feel a wave of vertigo as pounding, thumping beats travel down my ear hairs. Normally, I would yank out the earbuds and enjoy silence instead, but I'll take techno, or whatever it is, if it means I don't have to hear Wyatt's voice right now. For good measure, I stick my finger in my other ear and give myself up to Rex's music.

The other car has my mom in the passenger seat, Heather and Kevin in the backseat, and Wyatt in the driver's seat. I'm too furious with him to even stare in that direction. I want so much to be with my mom, to hug her and never let her go, but at the same time, something holds me back. Does she know everything I've done? What will she think about the gun that's left a permanent indentation against my spine, the one I used to shoot Kevin? Does she even know that was me, or does she just assume he was the victim of another faceless monster?

What happens when she realizes that I'm the faceless monster, and that it was done out of love for her?

That's what keeps me in this car. The other one is too heavy with rage and love.

Chance is at the wheel, and he keeps giving me an apologetic smile that just reads fake on his smug face. Gabriela's frown is real, though it could also be that she hates being the one holding Monty's aquarium. So he brought his snake but let Matty go? And he didn't find my mom before the bombs went off. Jesus. He messed up big-time. We almost lost them both.

I guess my dad would rather hold a snake than ride in the car with my boyfriend and my mom, as he switches places with Gabriela, sends her to the other car, and settles in with the snake box in his lap.

"Where to?" Chance asks, not even bothering with introductions.

"Start driving, and I'll tell you," my dad says gruffly. "Take a right out of here."

"You're a cheerful bunch," Chance says as he turns the car around and leads the way. "Like, you survived a hostile takeover of the entire country and then you survived a crazy backwoods dictator, and then you instigated a bombing as cover for a rescue, and now you're all *boo-hoo, woe is me. I'm a little puss.*"

"Leon has my dog, you ass," I mumble into my arm, "and, by the way, this is my dad, who abandoned me when I was four. It's complicated."

He whistles. "Yeah, okay. I deem that a just cause for whining. Why's Wyatt so pissed?"

"Because he's an idiot who lost my dog."

He starts to chuckle and clears his throat. "But he did save your mom, so . . ."

"Barely. So he gets to live, but he's not going to enjoy it for a while."

I stick my finger back in my ear and watch the trees flash by. My dad gives terse directions to Chance, and even though I thought I knew everything about this area, the same ten square miles where I grew up, we take unfamiliar streets, back roads that keep us off the main highways. We hit a busier road, and I finally see what I've been hoping to find: evidence of anarchy. The windows of a Second Union are broken and covered in plywood. A check cashing store belches smoke through a door torn off its hinges. A church billboard reads MONEY IS THE ROOT OF ALL EVIL. PRAY FOR REDEMPTION.

We have to slow down through one section, thanks to a protest bleeding into the street, the crowd wearing ski masks and holding handmade signs that say FUCK YOUR VALOR and MY SON DIED FOR YOUR DEBT and THE WAR IS HERE and THE END IS NIGH. When a police siren screams behind us, my dad shouts for Chance to turn off at the next intersection. Two shiny black SUVs follow the cruiser, and I don't want to see what happens to the protesters. They still think they're safe probably. That the Constitution and courts still count. That free speech is free.

They think they only have to worry about what happens at their front doors.

Fools.

The back roads take forever, but I'm glad we're away from the chaos of the city. I don't trust groups anymore. I'm pretty surprised, actually, when we wind up at a big box store, one of the ones that's open twenty-four hours for people who just really need to spend money they don't have at midnight.

"Shopping?" I ask.

My dad adjusts his pull-down mirror to stare at me, eyes strained but somehow twinkling. "I always wondered what it would be like to have a sarcastic, eye-rolling teenage daughter who questioned my every decision," he says. "And, yes, shopping. Everything I do requires a computer and Wi-Fi. We've got nowhere to go, and that means I have to find us a place." He points to a spot far away from the store and says, "Park here and wait. Be ready to run."

"Anticipating trouble?" Chance asks, gamely pulling through the space and into the next one so he can take off quickly if necessary.

My dad snorts and pulls down his beanie. "In Valor's world, a smart man always anticipates trouble."

"Or smart woman," Bea chimes in, her voice, as always, sounding dead.

My dad looks at her like he's only just noticed her. "That, too. I'll be back."

As he stalks toward the building, he pulls a packet out of his jeans pocket and starts sorting through cards held together with a rubber band. I can't see what they are, but I'm willing to bet they're more of the CFF's fun-time gift cards, stocked with all sorts of cash that draws from Valor's vaults. Wyatt parks two spaces over in the red car and glances at me, eyes full of worry and guilt and hope. He looks like a dog who pissed on the couch and is ready to be let back inside. Then his jaw tightens, and he gets out of his car and leans against the trunk.

"You gonna go talk to him?" Chance asks.

I stare at Wyatt, and he looks like a stranger now. My dad's in the store, and everyone in the other car is looking somewhere else, pretending that we're not all completely messed up. I'm amazed that even after a week of Valor anarchy and state-sanctioned murder, there are dozens of cars in this parking lot, just tons of people out spending money at seven in the morning. Like they think that hitting the store before normal business hours is safe. Like they haven't connected the random killings and unrest to the bank stamped on their checks. Like the workers still value minimum wage over staying alive. Not everyone is cut out for the truth, for living on the run. Maybe they think playing along is the best way to pretend it isn't happening.

It pisses me off, actually. Everything that's happened to me? Is basically their fault.

And that gives me an idea, one way to help the rage bleed out.

"Where's my backpack?" I ask Wyatt as I get out and lean against my door.

Without a word, he pops the trunk of the burgundy car and

hands it to me. When I unzip it, I see that he packed everything of mine that could fit, from my toiletries to most of my clothes and a couple of Pop-Tart pouches. My heart melts, just a little, as I paw everything aside and pull the two cans of spray paint from the bottom. One red, one green, right where I left them. Just like my fingernails were painted the day I stepped into my Valor uniform and tucked a Valor gun into my waistband.

"Tell me if anyone's driving by or whatever," I say, not meeting his eyes.

"Okay."

I kneel in the empty space between the cars on the cold asphalt, pop off the top of the red can, and shake it while I think of the best thing to write. At this point, am I more furious with Valor or the Citizens for Freedom? More important, which one should the innocent people fear more? The CFF, at least in our area, should be mostly crippled now, so I opt for the original enemy.

Carefully, in block letters, I write VALOR SUCKS. For good measure, I make the *A* into an anarchy symbol and go over the $ with green paint. Not bad for a rallying cry.

"Nice," Wyatt says, but I'm not doing it to impress him.

It does make me feel better, though. I'm going to leave this everywhere I go from here on out. Yarn bombing took time, patience. But this artistic rebellion takes just sixty seconds and someone to stand guard.

"Your dad's coming back in a hurry."

I pop the tops back on the cans, shove them in my bag, and stand. A flush of guilt flashes over me, but then I realize: I don't care if my dad approves. I nod at Wyatt and get back in my car.

"Trouble in paradise?" Chance says with a fake-ass sigh, and I punch his shoulder.

My dad gets in the car with a bag in his arms and says, "Take a right onto the highway and head for the doughnut shop about a mile from here. Park close to the door."

"Aye aye, Captain." Chance drives away, and my dad starts pulling boxes out of the bag and unwrapping a laptop and a bunch of accessories. I don't know a ton about computers, but it's the pricey kind, and he probably just dropped a few thousand dollars on all this junk.

"More Valor cards?" I ask.

He gives me a quick grin. "Who do you think hacked that little trick in the first place?"

He pops the laptop open, and it turns on without being plugged in. The damn thing is sleek and silver, the sort of indulgence my mom and I could never afford. My old laptop was big and clunky, bought refurbished, and it held a charge for only, like, three hours. It's weird how I spent my whole life wanting to meet my dad, but now everything he does, from smiling to buying a stupid computer, makes me resent him.

Chance pulls into the doughnut shop as requested, and my dad's fingers fly over the keyboard. I watch over his shoulder as he taps into the free Wi-Fi, and he's definitely not going to the normal sites that the rest of us use.

"What is that?" I ask.

"The darknet," he says, still typing. "Shadow Internet. Not regulated."

"What are you doing?"

"Finding a safe house."

He hops from forum to forum, and finally a list of addresses pops up. Some have big Xs on them, and most have several weird codes under them that make no sense to me. He scrolls down, muttering to himself about Valor and goons and squads.

"Can Leon and the CFF do this too?"

He shakes his head. "Not after my daughter blew up their war room and shot their top three tech guys, no."

"I thought you were their top tech guy."

He turns, meets my eyes. "I was never really theirs."

After some more scrolling, he points to an entry. "Let's try this one." He gives Chance directions and settles down for more typing.

"So these are, what?" Rex asks, leaning forward. "Anti-Valor safe houses? But how do you know they're actually safe?"

My dad looks back at him as if seeing him for the first time. "Whenever someone uses one or drives by one they're familiar with, they leave notes. Like the old hobo codes. A toilet works if you bring water, or you can steal Wi-Fi from a neighbor, or they left some food there in a cache. I've stayed in a few before, and some are definitely better than others. But this one is decently stocked and has plenty of room."

It's a longer drive than I was expecting, but no one seems to want to talk, especially not me. My dad acts like he wants to say something a couple of times, but he takes a deep breath and then remains silent and goes back to typing. Finally, he exhales with purpose.

"So I've been thinking about what you told me, Pats, about how you had some connection to everyone on your list. Do you know any other kids who had a hit list?"

"I did," Chance pipes up.

Rex just nods, and Bea manages to look vaguely interested.

"Good," my dad says, looking at each of them in turn. "Did all of you get through your lists? All ten names?"

They all nod.

"And did any of you know anyone on your list or have any connection with them whatsoever, that you know of?"

"Nope," Chance says. And he's trying to sound like it doesn't mean anything, but his hands are tight and white on the wheel. It's funny—we've been together almost a week, and none of us have ever talked about how we lived through it.

"Me neither," Rex says.

Bea shakes her head.

My dad continues, looking grim. "So what that tells us is that Patsy is different. Now we just have to figure out why. One or two connections would be understandable, considering that everyone's list is confined to their immediate area. But nine out of ten is . . ."

"A sick joke," I say.

"Do you know anyone at Valor, pip-squeak? Did you have an account there? Did your mom work at any banks?" He stares pointedly at the paint on my hands. "Were you doing graffiti before the takeover?"

I shake my head. "My checking account is at the credit union. I've never set foot in Valor. Mom didn't even bank with them. She worked for some businesses downtown, but I don't think any of them were banks. And, no, I didn't do graffiti until I had a reason to."

"There has to be some connection."

I glare. "Um, like the fact that my grandfather and father both worked for Valor?"

"Burn," Chance mutters.

My dad sighs. "I quit a long time ago, and your grandfather is dead."

"Still. Doesn't seem like a coincidence to me. Did you piss off someone there? Someone who knew about me?"

"The only person who knew about you," he says carefully, "was my brother, Ash."

My eyes go hot. When I blink, I see Ash's dead eyes, my eyes, my dad's eyes, Cannon eyes, staring back at me.

Repress, repress, repress.

"I think you actually mean 'suppress,'" Bea says, her voice cold and distant. "'Repress' means you do it automatically, but 'suppress' suggests you're trying really hard. It's not working, is it?"

I didn't even realize I'd said it out loud.

I ignore that and attend to my dad's last statement. "My picture was on Ash's mantel. Maybe someone else saw it? My name was on the back."

He shoots back with, "Unless it included your last name and the words 'my beloved niece,' I still don't see the connection. You saw Ash's house. It's not like visiting Valor dignitaries were stopping in for tea."

"But you told me your real name. Maybe someone who knew . . ."

He holds up a hand. "Yeah, I told *you*. Because I knew who you were. No one else knows my real name or that I have a daughter." When I roll my eyes at him, he adds, "Yeah, okay, so the entire Crane family knows my name. But for all that they're assholes, they're against Valor. They weren't involved in the process of selecting assassins and sending them out after debtors. That was all Valor. Most of what the Cranes know about Valor is from intel I brought them. I've got a list of aliases a mile long, and most of my business is done on the darknet, anonymous and hidden by layers of misdirection."

My head drops, and I look at my cheap, stained shoes. I've had enough of this. I am so sick of pretending that everything is fine. "Look, the connection is either you or me. And as I was just a normal, poor, fatherless bastard living in a crappy house, going to a crappy school, and working a crappy job, and you're the heir to the Valor throne and an Internet hacker or whatever, I'm kind of guessing it's more about you than me. So maybe stop being a defensive dick and, I don't know, ask your hacker friends about it? Because I'm too busy trying to figure out how to get my dog back to figure out if maybe I shortchanged a customer at the pizza restaurant and it began this nightmare."

My dad, this strange man, looks down and flexes his fingers over the keyboard in his lap. His mouth opens and snaps closed before he shakes his head and says, "Okay, honey. Okay."

Soon Chance is pulling into another unfinished neighborhood, all lovely streets and empty foundations and streetlights that were fancy until someone busted out their glass. It reminds me of the one where Wyatt tracked me down to kill me and then ended up saving my life, back when I still thought I could just curl up and go to sleep alone in an empty lot without any consequences. My dad points down a houseless street, just an asphalt edge fading to gravel and dirt, and Chance slows and carefully bumps down the long, winding drive to a house hidden in the woods, big enough to rival Château Tuscano. We're all quiet, and I imagine everyone is hunting for signs that it's already occupied. But when we get to the circular drive, there are no other cars and no lights, not even the bounce of flashlights or the flicker of a fire in the fireplace.

"Is it safe?" Rex asks.

My dad closes his laptop, hands it to me, hands the snake terrarium to Rex, and pulls out his Glock. "Keep the car running, pointed out, and I'll go make sure."

"Do you want backup?" Chance asks.

My dad pauses in his open door. "From here on out, let's just assume that if someone's going to do something stupid and get shot, it's me. Agreed?"

"It's your funeral," Chance says, all flippant, but when he sees my face, he mutters, "Sorry."

Wyatt tries to get out of the burgundy sedan behind us, and my dad stops him with a hand on the door, motioning for him to stay inside. They get into a whispered argument, and I'm guessing my mom's calm hand on Wyatt's shoulder is what keeps him in the driver's seat. Before I realize what I'm doing, I unbuckle and bolt for the other car. When I open the back door on Gabriela's side, she gives me a weird look, then nods and gets out, heading to the other car. I slide in to take her place, careful not to bump Kevin's leg, and put a hand on my mom's shoulder, which she covers with her own. I couldn't stay away from her a moment longer.

"How are you feeling?" I ask.

She turns partially in the seat, and she doesn't look good, but her smile is real. "I've been better, but I've been a lot worse. At least I haven't started the chemo. Yet."

I lean forward, hug her around the seat, and put my cheek against her shoulder, and she pats me. I didn't realize how tense I was in the car with my dad, but this . . . I know how to do this. I know who I am when I'm with my mom, taking care of her. I tell myself she doesn't know what I've been through in the last week, everything that I've done. Even if she tried to guess, even if Wyatt's already told her some of it, there's no way she would get it right. To her I'm just Patsy. And there's a comfort in that. The look in her eyes is still one of love.

For now.

"What about you, honey? How are you? Did you do . . . ?"

There's no good way to phrase it, is there?

Did you go kill your ten people like the bank told you to?

Yes, Mom. I sure did.

"I took care of it," I say.

"Have you been back to the house?"

I look away. Right, as it happens, at Wyatt. At the tendons in his neck, standing out, and the curls of his blond hair over his ears. He's looking straight forward, hands clenched on the wheel of the idling car. Like he's trying to pretend this isn't happening. I know that look well.

"Yeah. I'm really sorry, but . . . they blew it up."

Her head turns to me slowly. "Who did what now?"

I rub my eyes. How much does she need to know? And why does it matter? She owed more on it than it was worth anyway.

"Our house blew up. They had Mrs. Hester waiting to kill whoever showed up first. She tried to shoot me. And they told her to go in the house if she saw me, and when she did . . ."

"None of this makes sense," my mom says, sounding less like she's in her forties and more like an old, tired, confused woman. "Why would you blow up a perfectly good house?"

"Nothing Valor does makes sense," Wyatt says.

"My dad said it did," Heather says. "It's all based on deadweight and how far in the hole you are. It actually costs them less to blow up your house and collect on the insurance than to keep trying to get you to pay it. I'm betting that all the houses that exploded will actually be categorized as acts of God. They'll have the insurance adjustors in their pocket. And it frees up resources."

"Um, what?" I say.

"My dad was a statistician. Probably why Valor targeted him. He'd done some CPA work for one of the smaller banks that Valor subsumed—and for the Cranes, of course. That's why I went to Crane Hollow after. He was writing a study of the subprime mortgage collapse and had sold a book on the politics of debt."

"Did he have debt himself?" I ask.

She shrugs. "Nothing unusual. A thirty-year mortgage. Valor just wanted him quiet. Permanently." She looks out the window and wipes away tears. It's getting pretty hard to hate her.

"So, Mom. I have a question for you. Did you ever work for Valor? Or do any business with them?"

She sighs and taps her lip. "Hmm. I never worked for them. I filled out an application once, but they never called back." She pulls her purse into her lap and digs through it, releasing the scent of her perfume into the air. "I guess this is all I have," she says finally, handing me a credit card. It's bluish green and has Valor's logo on it. "It had such a low interest rate that I thought it could help."

I turn the card over in my hands, and even though I've held guns and bombs this week, the unremarkable piece of plastic feels like the most dangerous thing I've ever touched. On the front it says in red DIAMOND ELITE, with my mom's name beneath that. I flip it over and find her signature in the signature strip and all the usual things I guess you'd expect in a credit card. It doesn't say, "Owner can be murdered at any time," anywhere on it. The closest thing I can find is the phrase "By activating this card, user agrees to the complete terms of service outlined in the credit card application."

That line leaves a lot to the imagination these days.

"Wait. Heather. Is this trackable?"

She looks up, eyes red. "What, the credit card?"

"Leon mentioned getting rid of cards at the meeting. Can Valor use it to find us?"

I put the card in her waiting hand, and she looks it over. "Only if you use it. Leon might've lied a bit to keep people in line." She hands it back.

"How high was the balance on this card?" I ask.

My mom looks away, her cheeks red. "I don't remember."

"It doesn't matter," Wyatt says. "It's over."

"But I'm trying to figure out why they picked me. Why I knew everyone on my list."

"You knew everyone on your list?" Heather asks, suddenly interested.

I lean back and pull my gun out of my waistband so I can slump. The gold letters are starting to rub off a little. "I mean, I didn't know them personally. But they were all connected to me or Valor somehow."

"I don't think I've ever heard of that before," she says, looking troubled.

"So what does it mean?" my mom asks.

My dad appears at the top of the grand staircase and motions us inside.

"It means that I'm special," I say. "And not because of my test scores. Let's go."

I get out of the car, grab my backpack, and head for the open door.

21.

The house smells like incense and BO, which is not good, but at least it doesn't smell like blood and bleach. It's kind of amazing how low my standards have fallen in just a week. There's no electricity, but there's a battery-operated camping lantern in each room and jugs of dirty-looking water sitting beside the toilets.

"Cisterns out back to flush the toilets without city water. It's kind of genius," Rex says.

My dad's already found a worn piece of paper hidden in one of the huge, fancy kitchen cabinets that explains how to tap into a neighbor's Wi-Fi. He's on the floor of one empty bedroom, legs out in front of him, typing away. I've had a dad for twelve hours, and I already know what it's like to be neglected for work.

Our shoes make strange echoes in a house that's big enough for twelve people but was probably just haunted by two people who constantly planned new renovations. The walls are all high and white, the floors wood and stone. It is not a soft place. Even though it's still morning, I feel like I'm supposed to claim a bedroom and go to sleep, because what else is there to do in an empty house? Without a mission or a list or any way to access media, sleep seems like the most interesting option anyway.

I feel like a little ghost, going from room to room, looking for something that isn't there. In the basement, there are rows of chairs facing an empty wall, bolted down like a movie theater. There's also a bar and an entire apartment that's bigger than my old house. Most importantly and strangely, though, is the pool table. I guess it must've been too big and heavy to move, or maybe the house was just built around it, because it's massive. And even in the post-Valor world, even though the people who lived here must've fled months ago, every cue and ball is still here, along with the rack and a row of blue chalk.

"Want to play?"

I spin around, mouth open. Wyatt snuck up on me, which makes no sense until I see that he's in his socks. That's the kind of guy he is—he would take off his shoes in an empty, foreclosed house so that he wouldn't mess up the floors.

"You don't want to play me at pool," I say, a beat too late for it to sound relaxed.

A ghost of his old smile. "Except maybe I do."

I stare at him, and I want nothing more than to run into his arms, except that it won't be the same if Matty's not slobbering all over us. My anger has cooled, but I'm not ready for hugs yet. I guess we can play pool. It's better than talking, at any rate.

"I'll rack."

He tips his head to me as I gather up the balls and put them in order, rolling the rack and snapping them into place before backing away. He's already got his cue and is chalking it up and rolling the cue ball under his hand in exactly the place I like to break from. Just when I think he's still rich-boy, honor-society Wyatt, he does something to remind me that he's also smashed-a-window-with-my-bass-and-watched-my-friend-OD Wyatt. His break is flawless and sharp, and the balls rocket around the felt. He pockets a stripe and a solid.

"Stripes," he calls, and suddenly he's all business as he moves around the table.

"Did I hear pool?" Chance calls, barreling down the stairs.

Wyatt turns to face him. He always seems a foot taller and wider when he stands like that, and whatever Chance sees on his face sends him right back upstairs, shouting, "Never mind, bro."

Wyatt misses his next shot and steps back with a small bow to me. I take an easy shot and pocket the two.

"So," he says.

"So," I say. I miss my next shot and step back.

"So I'm going to assume that things are going to be weird until we get Matty back."

A small smile tugs at my lips at the word "until." "You learn quick."

"When I pay attention, yeah. But I know I won't feel okay until we have her back, either. So how are we going to do it?" He misses his next shot, too, and it was an easy one.

I miss my shot and scuff the felt. "I just can't believe you let her go. She's the closest thing I have to—"

"That doesn't work anymore, Patsy. Your mom and dad are in this house. Like, right upstairs." He points at the ceiling, angry. "I get that Matty's important. She's important to me too. But how would you be treating me if your mom had died in the explosion but I'd brought our dog? You're not being fair here."

Panic clutches my chest, and I double over with my hands on the pool table. It feels like there's a sucking hole in my gut, as if all the horrible feelings I've been repressing are rising up like an overflowing toilet and choking me. I just want to hug my dog. Matty can make this better. But what if they kill Matty? Leon would do it. I know this instinctually: Leon would kill her for nothing. I can't even imagine where I'd be if my mom had died in the explosion. Either of the explosions, Klein house or Crane house. But that doesn't make it any easier to tamp down the panic.

My heart is hot and hammering, my stomach a cold rock, and

the world goes fuzzy and starts spinning. I think I might be as angry at myself as I am at Wyatt. If I'd just told him to grab Matty and run, or if I'd never planted those stupid nut cans, maybe we'd all be together. But now Leon is furious, and it's all my fault. And he knows it.

"I think I'm having a heart attack," I whisper, and Wyatt wraps his arms around me, his chest against my back and his cheek against my hair like he's a second skin, like he's armor.

"You're not having a heart attack. You're having a panic attack. It's the same thing that happens at night. You just have to breathe deep, in through the nose and hold it and out through your mouth. You can do this."

"Panic attack?" I squeak. I can barely draw in any air at all.

He lifts me like a baby, one arm under my knees and the other around my shoulders, and sits down on the ground with his back against the carved wood of the pool table. I manage to swallow down a breath, but my heart is still beating in my ears, my eyes darting madly, my thoughts showing me all the horrible things I've done. All the horrible things I've seen, all the things that might have happened if I'd pulled the trigger a second later or aimed a little worse. All the horrible things Leon could be doing to Matty right now, her tongue flopping bloody on the ground like he promised.

"This is a panic attack, Patsy. Once you understand that, it loses its power. It's just your body sending the wrong signals. Nothing is wrong. You're safe. Breathe with me. In-two-three, hold-two-three, out-two-three-four. Good. Now let's keep doing that. Just think about breathing, okay? Think about your lungs expanding like balloons."

It's stupid. Breathing is one of those things you should just do automatically, and thinking this much about it feels like a complete waste. It's hard to inhale in that long and hold it and then exhale so long. But he's right. After a few minutes, I feel calm and relieved, and my heart stops beating in my ears.

"You good now?" he asks. He's been rubbing my back all this time.

I pull away a little. "Yeah. Thanks. How'd you know what to do?"

"Uh." He looks away, blushing. "Pot makes me paranoid. Some strain Mikey found made me have panic attacks. I thought I was having a heart attack, but I couldn't go to the hospital, so I looked it up online. Turns out it's just easier to quit smoking up than it is to feel like helicopters are going to bust into your garage at any moment, you know?"

I can't help thinking back to Alistair's trailer in the old orchard and the sound of helicopters rushing to where we were. "I wish I could quit this feeling that easily."

"Soon," he says. "Soon. We just need to get Matty and hit the road, and we'll be cool."

"You make it sound so easy."

"Oh, yeah. Well, I'm a liar."

That gets my first laugh, even if it's a sad, weak one.

"But to go back to your original question, I think we all know who's the brains of this operation, Patsy. You've been calling the shots, and you're really good at it. So I figure you'll find the best way to get our dog back, and then I'll do whatever you ask." He rubs my back, and I grin into his neck.

To think—me! I'm the brains. I've never been the brains before.

But he's kind of right. After everything I've been through in the past week, I should've died twenty times. Valor tried like hell to kill me, and then the CFF sent me into all sorts of impossible situations with Leon's passive-aggressive attempts to screw me over. And I paid them back by blowing up their house.

"I think we need to talk to my dad," I say.

Wyatt pulls back with a frown. "Yeah, I don't think he likes me."

"Good," I say. "I'm getting to like being a rebel."

Upstairs, my mom is in the empty kitchen, sorting through more of those stupid MRE things as if she's trying to put together an actual feast. All the cabinet fronts have been removed, like maybe the old owner sold them, along with the faucets and doorknobs conspicuously missing from every room. Even the outlet covers are gone, and I imagine them made of solid gold, a middle-aged woman with a French manicure flicking the lights off with a discontented sigh. Kevin and

Gabriela and Heather are playing cards on the floor of what used to be the dining room, Rex is sitting outside in the dry fountain, reading a book, and Chance is shooting hoops with a beat-up basketball and a backboard that looks completely unused. I slip out of my sneakers, line them up by the front door, and go hunting upstairs to find my dad.

As I would expect, I find him high up in a wood-paneled study hemmed in by empty bookshelves. He's so invested in whatever he's typing on his new laptop that he doesn't even notice me standing at the door.

"Dad?"

He looks up and stares through me, slightly lost. "Huh?"

"Earth to Dad."

"I'm here. Just trying to figure out . . ." He looks down, types for a minute, then rubs his eyes. "Everything. I'm not seeing any reports about coincidences like yours among Valor mercs."

"Among what?"

"That's what everyone's calling you kids—mercs. Short for mercenaries. Most of the first wave didn't live, according to the forums. The ones who did had nothing to go home to. Most of them have been absorbed into CFF cells. You guys are like war orphans." I give him a dead stare, and he adds, "Well, not you, I'm glad to say. Did you need something, honey?"

His eyes are on his screen, and I sit down facing him and wait a few beats until he looks up again.

"Will you close your laptop and actually listen?"

He sighs like this is a huge pain in the ass and gently closes the laptop, setting it aside. He folds his hands in his lap and stares at me as if to say, *This had better be good, young lady.*

Not that I care.

"Do you know what's happening in Crane Hollow?"

He gives me a sly smile. "Nope. Radio silence. You guys must've taken down all their laptops, or at least their Wi-Fi. There's nothing since five thirty this morning. Why?" He puts an awkward hand on my shoulder, as if this is the thing he's been told good fathers do. "Are you worried, honey? They're not coming after you."

I snort, pull my Glock out of my waistband, check the clip, and slide it home. The noise echoes in the open room. "Yeah, I'm not scared of the Cranes. I want to go back."

"You want," he says slowly, looking into my eyes, "to go back?"

"Leon has my dog, and I want my dog."

"Your uncle Ash's dog."

I glare at him, the hard glare that mostly ends up with people being dead. "My dog."

He starts to open his laptop, and I give a little *cluck* that stops him.

"I was going to check the satellites for a photo, but chances are that place is a wreck. From what Wyatt described, they had a lot of injured people, and you took down most of their house. They're not going to be happy to see you." His face goes hard to match mine.

"And if Leon's as mad as I figure he is, that dog might already be dead, and it won't be pretty. But let me check around."

He rubs my shoulder, and I shrug away, so he pulls the computer into his lap and falls back into the screen like I'm not even here. As much as I want his time and attention, as much as I want to ask him more questions and get to know him, I don't have that luxury right now. Still, I wish he'd try again, reach out somehow. I hate the smooth clicks, the sure way he types so quickly that I can't even keep up. It's so useless. Talking about what's happening instead of, you know, changing it. Working against it.

This is not how problems get solved.

I stand, walk a few steps away, turn on my phone, and press call.

22.

He picks up on the first ring.

"Let me guess: You just realized who's got your dog. Doesn't she, girl? Can you speak? Can you tell your shit-town owner that you're a Crane now? Speak, goddammit!"

Matty's joyous bark tells me that they're at least treating her well . . . for now. But the snickers in the background tell me they've already planned something pretty bad.

"Drop the crap, Leon. Just tell me what you want for her."

My dad's on his feet in a second, but I notice he's pretty careful about setting down the laptop first.

"Give me that phone," he growls, and I shake my head no. When he makes a clumsy grab for it, I turn away and hold up a finger. The look in his eyes tells me he wants to wrench it out of my hands but knows that that would be the end of any hope of a relationship.

"Well, now, Miss Patsy. Any interest in telling me how you know Jacky boy?"

"No. What do you want?"

He laughs, slow as poisoned molasses. "Plenty of things. I want to know why you disappeared with my tech boy and killed three of my cousins. I want to know why you blew up half of my house and killed seven of my people. And I want to know where you are right now."

"If I tell you all that, how do I know you'll give me my dog back?"

"You don't."

"Then . . . no?"

"Interesting answer." Matty whimpers like someone's hurting her, and I double over like I've been punched.

"Don't hurt my dog."

A meaningful pause. "Then don't tell me no, sugar."

"Tell me what you really want. What's it going to take?"

My dad stares at me, arms crossed, shaking his head in disappointment. Leon's self-satisfied sigh makes my skin crawl, and I imagine him leaning back, hands behind his head and ankles crossed, feeling smug.

"I don't want anything special, really."

"Bullshit," I hiss.

"But I will tell you how to get her back. You still got my tech boy?"

I look up at my dad. "Yeah. Holding him hostage. Got him hog-tied. You wanna hear him squeal?"

My dad stifles a laugh.

"You tell Jacky that Operation Red Thursday is still on. And your dog's gonna be part of the festivities."

"What does that mean? What's Operation Red Whatever? What festivities?"

My dad's on the floor on his laptop immediately, and he'd better hope he's looking up Operation Red Thursday.

"Let's just say that your little pooch is going to be in one of the boxes."

"Where?" my dad mouths.

"Where at?" I ask.

"Jacky knows. Make sure you hurt him a little, and he'll tell you."

And then the bastard hangs up on me. It takes everything I have not to snap the phone in half and throw it at the wall. I spin and point it at my dad like it's a gun.

"What the hell is he talking about?"

When he pats the floor beside him, I slide down the wall and slump. I'm suddenly aware of how very exhausted I am and how much I miss the simple pleasures of a crappy trailer. A bed. A shower. I need one. But I don't want to stand in an empty Jacuzzi tub while people pour cloudy cistern water over me.

My dad doesn't look up or stop typing as he speaks. "Okay, so Operation Red Thursday is this thing the CFF is planning for Thanksgiving. Not just Leon's CFF—the entire network, all across the country. You know how people used to wake up the morning after Thanksgiving and go crazy shopping for crap, and they called it Black Friday? And then, in the past few years, they've started offering insane sales on Thanksgiving itself? Well, the best the CFF can figure, Valor is part of what's been pushing the movement. They want people out and spending money. And this year, from what we can tell, they're going to have the credit machines rigged. People will run their card, and there'll be a tiny line above their signature that commits their allegiance to the Valor government. We're talking conscription, draft, agree to search and seizure, all that good stuff. You sign a credit card receipt, they've got you."

I exhale and slump further. "It's so stupid. Why does it even matter? They can do whatever they want. They can send tanks into the streets. Why is it still about plastic and signatures and credit?"

My dad sets his laptop aside and slumps down beside me. "Because people . . . hate to look stupid. How many people have ever refused to sign a terms of service agreement? How many people have thrown away their phone because they thoroughly read the TOS and didn't agree with the terms? Nobody. You point to someone's signature and tell them they signed it without reading it, what are they going to do? They can't take it back. You've got the digital signature. Most people will click 'accept' so they can get on with their day. They're basically becoming complicit in the bloodless rebellion." He leans over to whisper, "And here's the part that Leon doesn't know: Eventually, once Valor has weeded out all the deadweight, they're going to forgive debts in return for servitude. Can you imagine—you've got a hundred thousand in debt, say, and the government says it'll all be forgiven if you just agree that they're your government and start sending them your taxes and giving them your votes? If you'll join the police force? If you legitimize what they're doing with your support?"

"Oh my God. We're so desperate. So lazy. We won't even fight back." I groan.

"Yeah."

"So where does the CFF come in?"

"Well, you saw what the nut cans can do. That was Leon's idea—just local. Just for fun. Not CFF sanctioned. Red Thursday is even bigger, taking it to the next level to cripple Valor's holiday-shopping plans. You can probably guess what the 'red' stands for." He holds his hands together like he's cupping an aluminum can, then mimics an explosion.

I sit up and push my bangs out of my face. "They're going to bomb . . . the malls?"

He nods. "Yep. All across America. Or Valor Nation. Every mall." He must see the panic on my face, as he adds, "Before the crowds are there. The CFF, especially outside of Leon, doesn't want to hurt innocent people. They just want to mess up Valor's plans, and you can't shop in a mall that's on fire."

"And you helped with this."

It's not a question.

"Ever since I saw where Valor was headed, yeah. And Second Union is no better. They just want to piggyback on everything Valor does. You know about their recon kids?"

I look down, close my eyes as the tears threaten and I remember the glitter of gold on Jeremy's gun. "You mean the part where they send kids out to kill the Valor mercs? Yeah. They came after me."

"What happened?"

"I had to kill my best friend. Or Wyatt did. But . . . it was him or us. And we chose us."

"Screw this," my dad mutters, and then he's got his arm around me, fierce and rough. "I'm so sorry, Patsy. The only reason I left you was so this would never happen, so you wouldn't be a part of this bullshit. And you've had it worse than anyone."

I do not, do not want to melt into the comfort of his hug. I cannot even begin to pretend that my daddy can make everything okay. For so long, I carried that little strip in my locket, my childish cursive reading, *I want to find my dad*. When Valor came calling, I changed it to *I want to survive the next five days*. I got both of my wishes, and it's still not enough. Now I wish that none of this had ever happened. Because this man, hugging me? He's not worth everything I've lost.

I stiffen and wiggle away from him and stand, rolling my toes to crack them against the wood floor. "So he's going to take Matty to a mall and blow her up inside it? That's what you're saying, right?"

His eyes are as red as pickled eggs. He doesn't bother to wipe away the tears, and he looks wounded, I guess because I'm rejecting him. For just a second, I wonder if he had dreams of me just like I had dreams of him, of what it would be like when we met again. Whatever he pictured as his daughter—it couldn't be what he found.

"The Crane cell of the CFF is supposed to hit the Candlewood Mall. And, yes, I helped them plan it. But that means I know what they're doing. And it also means that I suspect a trick. Leon wouldn't just give you the truth that easily. He's got something else planned. He wants you in that mall."

"Is it just more nut cans?"

He shakes his head. "That's too small for what they want. More like . . . giant nut cans. Huge boxes in wrapping paper with shiny bows. Dozens of them. The plan is to ring the fire alarm to get anyone out of the mall at five in the morning. CFF people—all the ones they've recruited—will be in place in custodial jumpsuits with dollies to bring in these giant presents and put them around the big tree in the center of the mall and in all the anchoring department stores. They're . . . It's actually pretty brilliant. They look like really expensive decorations, the kind of thing that none of the mall workers would actually know anything about or question. Then we detonate from a safe distance, and no one will be able to shop, much less run a credit card through the machines."

"Oh God," I mutter. "Oh no."

"What?"

I look up through the tears. "They're going to put Matty in one of the boxes. And we won't know which one."

He stands and shakes his head. "Or at least that's what Leon wants you to think."

"You're wrong," I say. "It's just horrible enough to be exactly what he would do."

"You don't know him like I do," my dad starts, and I hold up a hand.

"Enough. Whatever. Go play on your darknet and do whatever you do. But I'm going to be in that mall before it blows up, and I'm coming out with my dog. With or without your help."

He sits down and fiddles with his laptop. "How'd you live this long, charging headlong into trouble?"

I pause at the door on my way out. "I always pull the trigger first."

Back downstairs, I find my mom resting on a sleeping bag,

reading a fashion magazine. I curl up beside her, and she wordlessly, lovingly strokes my dirty hair until I fall into an uneasy sleep.

As the sun is setting, we gather in what used to be the dining room to eat crappy MRE meals that my mom thoughtfully prepared for us while I napped. The lantern-lit room smells like baby vomit, like all these horrible smells mixed together and blood-warm. I do not want to eat fake food at this last supper. What I really want is a milk shake.

"What day is it?" I ask.

"Tuesday," Rex says.

I count in my head. "So we've got two days."

"Two days for what?" my mom asks.

I ignore the question. She doesn't want to know. "Does anybody have any cash?"

"Like, seven bucks," Rex says.

"Still got my card, or what's left of it after fish drugs," Gabriela says, tilting her head toward Kevin, who's snarfing up the MRE like it's actual food.

"You had some cash left in your backpack," Wyatt says.

My dad gives me a measuring look. "What do you need?"

"Tampons and condoms," I say, because I'm still pretty pissed at him for dozens of reasons.

"Sorry I asked." He shovels a bite of MRE brownie into his mouth and looks away.

Wyatt looks adorably horrified, which is how I realize that I'm totally thawed toward him.

"Milk shake?" he asks.

"God, yes, milk shake."

My dad holds out a card with a teddy bear on the front. "This has five hundred bucks on it. I'll give it to you if you promise to never say the word 'condom' in my presence again."

"Now, Jack. If she's going to do it, I'd rather she be safe—" my mom starts.

My dad and I both stick our fingers in our ears and say, "LA LA LA LA LA."

Wyatt takes the card and stands up. When he holds out a hand, I let him pull me up too.

"Uh, did you say milk shakes?" Gabriela glances meaningfully at the MREs, and I hold out my hand to pull her up. Chance stands up too.

"Anybody else want something?" Wyatt asks.

"Ice cream!" Kevin shouts.

"Salad," Bea mutters, not looking up.

"Coffee," Rex says wistfully.

"Better painkillers?" my mom asks, only half joking, and Heather puts a concerned hand on her back.

"You sure this card's going to work?" I take it from Wyatt and turn it over, inspecting every detail. It looks ratty and stained, like it's been in the bottom of someone's purse for a year. Any time I see the Valor logo now, it turns my stomach.

"It'll work," my dad says. "We haven't had one turned down yet."

"Just in case"—I look around at my friends—"everybody got your gun?"

Chance holds out his Glock, which matches mine. Wyatt's got my dad's gun, which I hope my dad doesn't recognize or expect to see returned. I know mine is fine, considering I checked the clip in front of my dad just a short while ago to make a point. Gabriela doesn't have a gun, but she still has her knife, and she wears it casually as a regular part of her wardrobe. In our matching black sweatshirts, we look like we're about to go fight zombies and we know exactly how to do it.

"Team Milk Shake, away!" I say, and they follow me out the door.

As we're getting into Wyatt's car, my dad rushes out, waving a burner phone. "We all need each other's numbers," he says.

I roll my eyes. "God, Dad. Protective much?"

"It's not safe out there."

"I was being sarcastic. I know exactly how unsafe it is out there."

The look he gives me is sobering. "If you can't find this place, or if Valor shows up and we have to run, we might never find each other again. You've never lived in a world without the Internet." I don't make any more jokes as he puts his number in my phone. "And here's a car charger. Stay charged."

I hadn't even noticed that my cheap little crap phone was almost out of juice.

"I would make fun of you," Chance says quietly, "but he's right. This is not a world I want to be alone in."

I plug my phone into the car and watch the little green light glow. Wyatt, at least, has a good sense of direction, and we're soon back on the highway. The mood is somber, but then again, no one got enough sleep and we're on the run from two sets of high-powered enemies. Wyatt looks like determination alone is driving him, and Gabriela slumps back against her seat and starts snoring softly. Even Chance is pretty quiet, just staring out the window. It so happens that I'm watching him in the rearview mirror when he flinches and looks like he might start crying, and I glance back quick enough to notice that we passed a charred house, still smoking. I remember the night we met, how cocky he was. And here he is, on the verge of tears. As time passes, all of our walls are breaking.

Wyatt knows where my favorite milk shakes are, and he's soon ordering half the damn menu. Number ones and number threes and salads and wraps and sundaes and brownies and, as he says, "The biggest coffee you can give me. Seriously. Just fill the bag with sugar and cream, thanks."

I've never seen so much fast food at once, and my legs are soon buried in bags, my lap full of giant drinks. Wyatt hands the girl the card my dad gave us, and I dig my fingers into the seat. What if it doesn't work? What if my dad's wrong? I feel a panic attack creeping in, all the what-ifs.

And then I realize—the worst thing that could happen is that we drive away, tires squealing, and disappear into the night. If we can't call 911 when we need help, they can't call 911 when we break what used to be laws. But the card goes through, and she hands it back with plenty of cash left on it and a super-long receipt. The look she gives Wyatt tells me she'd shove me out of this car and take my place in a heartbeat. Not everything has changed—although the recently installed safety glass on the drive-through window suggests that regular businesses are catching on to new dangers.

Gabriela wakes up, sniffing the air. "Hey, can you park a minute? I bet they have toilet paper."

"God, yes. I need to make a deposit," Chance says, and Wyatt obliges them, although he's careful to park in the darker edges of the lot instead of right under a light.

"You need to go?" he asks me.

I shake my head. "You?"

"I'm good. But there's your milk shake. Uh, milk shakes."

He's got a four-pack of large shakes in his lap, and it's got to be freezing. I take the chocolate one and sip, feeling some amount of tension unspool. The last thing I ate was that M&M, and it wasn't even good. I dig in a bag for some fries and barely taste anything as I gulp them down. This feeling is eerily familiar. Food is just fuel to keep me running now.

"I worry about you getting dehydrated, but I worry more about you biting my head off," he says. "You can't drive on an empty gas tank."

"The anger keeps me going."

He pulls out a sandwich and swallows half of it. My belly feels comfortably sloshy. If I weren't so nervous about waiting in the parking lot, I'd be getting sleepy. Through the brightly lit windows, I don't see the usual families, Little League teams, or old people. The seating area inside is empty, although the drive-through has a hell of a line. All the cars are expensive, shiny, new. I've never even been in a car as fancy as the Infiniti SUV that's pulling up to the speaker box and rolling down a black-tinted window.

The world's falling apart? Don't worry. Daddy will get you a deluxe Happy Meal.

"I hate this place," I say.

"So leave your mark," Wyatt says.

That makes me smile. It's nighttime, after all, which means I'm harder to see. I dig my backpack out from beneath all the food bags and yank out my red and green paint cans. The air outside has gone full-on November, dry with a cold, crisp wind that lashes my bangs into my face. The parking lot behind us is empty, the strip mall mostly gone bankrupt in the last few years. And there's no cover at all. I open Wyatt's door and hunch behind it to scrawl VALOR SUCKS. I get spray paint on my shoes, but who cares? Everyone who parks here will have to see it.

I'm back in the car by the time Chance and Gabriela return to paw through bags. I get Wyatt to stop at a drugstore so I can buy some shampoo and conditioner, and Gabriela promises to help me wash my hair in the sink back at the empty house. I grab a few gallons of water, too, because I bet the cistern water is full of larvae or spores or something. The card goes through, and back outside, I sneak around to the side of the store and leave my mark on the unlit brick wall. With every spray of paint, I feel more powerful, take back some measure of control.

And as we drive, I see evidence that other people are getting in on the graffiti too. FREEDOM AIN'T FREE. GREED KILLS. FIGHT BACK. THANKS, OBAMA. SCREW VALOR, THE BANKS ARE THE ENEMY. They're scrawled with varying levels of skill on the sides of buildings, in parking lots, and in the middle of the road. Someone made a stencil of the Valor Savings Bank logo and spray-painted it on every stop sign we pass so that they now read STOP VALOR. It's beautiful. And it makes me feel giddy to see people waking up to what's happening.

On the way back, we're about to pass Wyatt's high school, which has this huge boulder out front that anyone's allowed to paint. Every few days, there's something new, HAPPY BIRTHDAY, KATE! or GO, TROJANS! Or CLASS OF 2016. And now it's my turn.

"Pull over at the boulder, okay?"

Wyatt grimaces. "Uh, are you sure? Just on the side of the road like that?"

"It'll only take a second. Block me with the car." I shake my paint can as he slows and the tires crunch gravel on the shoulder. "Besides, at least this time, it's totally legal."

I leap out before the car stops and start spraying.

"Hurry up," Gabriela calls. "This is freaking me out."

I'm done with VALOR $UCKS and the red anarchy symbol and into the green dollar sign when lights come around the corner.

"Come on!" Wyatt calls.

I add the last green slash and jump into the car, and Wyatt squeals back onto the road before the encroaching car sees me.

"At least we know it's not a police car, right?" I'm breathless and high on adrenaline, and it feels good. I did this. I chose to do this. Suck it, Valor.

But then our car fills with headlights, too bright, too big, too fast. The car behind us honks. I look in the rearview mirror and see that it's a shiny black SUV.

23.

"Jesus, girl. What have you done?" Gabriela moans.

I strap on my seat belt. "The rock is there for painting!" I shout. "People do it every day!"

"'Class of 2016' is not the same as 'Valor Sucks,'" Chance says. "I mean, full points for brass balls, but let's keep the antigovernment graffiti a little more quiet next time." If I didn't know him as well as I do now, I would think he was totally blasé, but he's scared to death.

The SUV is so close now that I can't even see its lights in the rearview mirror. Wyatt floors it, and the SUV speeds up and swerves to pace us in the other lane of the four-lane highway.

I pull my gun and aim as the SUV's passenger-side window rolls down to reveal . . .

"Tuck?"

The big Crane goon points at the window with one hand while shoving his AR-15 out his window to suggest that if we don't roll our window down, he'll shoot it out.

"Goddammit." Wyatt rolls down the window and leans his head back against the driver's headrest as if he's ready to avoid a gunfight. Or maybe he just doesn't trust me not to start one.

"Slow down, dumbass!" Tuck yells.

"You're the ones chasing us!" I shout back, waving my Glock.

Wyatt slows down to almost the speed limit, and the SUV keeps pace. I don't put down my gun, and Tuck's rifle barrel is staring at me like the little black hole to hell. My heart's hammering, and Gabriela is on the floorboards, and the scent of grease and chicken and pickles in the air is making me want to barf.

"Y'all head over to Crane Hollow right now and nobody gets hurt," Tuck hollers in his mean-guy voice. Then, in his regular jolly-guy voice, he adds, "Matty misses you."

"We're not going back," I shout. "Leon'll kill us."

Tuck shakes his bald head. "Not true. You took out a lot of good folks. We need more bodies. You come back now, and you can have your trailer back. I promise."

The cars race, neck and neck, toward a red light, and I look back at Gabriela and Chance. "Raise your hand if you're pretty sure Leon's going to execute us if he ever sees us again," I whisper.

Everyone's hand raises.

"Raise your hand if you think we need to get the hell away from that gun," Wyatt says. Again, everyone's hand goes up. "Okay. Here we go. Check your seat belts and hold on."

"Let's talk at the light?" Wyatt hollers, and Tuck smiles and waves like we're all friends.

Both Wyatt and the SUV slow as we reach the stoplight. It's a decently busy time of night, and even with the sweeping sense of caution Valor has inspired, cars are just doing their thing. I look ahead and do the math. And I realize what Wyatt's going to do. I lean back against my seat, test my seat belt, and turn my face sideways. Like that would help.

"Patsy, I need you to . . ." Wyatt starts, but he can't finish it. "I need you to do it. On three."

"I'll do it," Chance says.

"It has to be her." Wyatt pushes his seat back, just a little, as we coast to a stop. "If you roll down your window, they'll know."

"It's okay. I got it," I say.

And my hands are shaking and my stomach drops out and everything is cold and bloodless. Before the car comes to a complete stop, I bite my lip, sit forward, take a good look at the Crane goon in the driver's seat, and wait for Wyatt's word.

"One . . . two . . ."

Before he can say three, Chance knocks my gun down, half

dives between the front seats, and pulls the trigger three times. I can't see what's happened, and Wyatt floors it, and the car squeals through the red light, fishtailing around a sedan. A spray of bullets pings off the car, and everyone but Wyatt ducks. Chance falls into the back, breathing hard. There's a huge crunch and a ton of honking right where we were. We're already through the light and doing ninety up the highway. I look in my side mirror and see the messy aftermath, the Crane-driven Valor SUV T-boned by a white van. I'm pretty sure Wyatt was just planning on taking out the driver, but a complete crash is even better. Tuck is standing in the street, shaking his gun at us.

"That was really effing close," Gabriela says, breathless. "Jesus, bro."

"I think that was the SUV we stole," Wyatt adds.

"Lesson to self: Do not give Leon Crane new playthings." I pick up my milk shake and suck in enough to give me a brain freeze.

"Did you get him?" Wyatt asks.

"I got the driver," Chance says quietly. "Right in the temple."

"I didn't need to know that," Gabriela mutters.

I look in the mirror and see him put a hand on her shoulder. "You always need to know that. Otherwise, it stops mattering. We can't let it stop mattering. Then we become like them."

I turn to look Chance in the eyes. "Thank you," I whisper. "It still matters."

Wyatt exhales, long and slow, and turns down a side street. The air in the car relaxes once we're off the highway and away from the SUV. I don't want Chance to be right, but I think he might be. It's so much easier to forget. But the more I let myself forget, the easier it becomes to kill people. I don't know why he knocked down my gun and did it himself. I don't know how to pay him back. "Thanks" does not feel like enough.

"You want a milk shake?" I ask. "It helps."

He chooses strawberry.

We're silent for the rest of the drive home.

Back in the house, we drop all the food bags like we're returning from an expedition with unexpected and welcome treasure. The general mood is jovial and light, but I can't get there. I didn't see the driver's head, didn't see the bullet, didn't see its aftermath. I didn't even recognize him. But he's dead because I just had to stop and play rebel. And what about the people in the van that T-boned them? For all I know, it was an innocent family on their way to church to adopt a puppy. It looked like a work van, though, but why should a bunch of painters be worth any more or less than a busload of children?

No matter what I do, people die. Whether I see it happen or not, they die.

"Honey, are you okay?" my dad asks.

It throws me, at first, because how should he know I'm upset?

My mom's the one who lives with me, who understands my moods, but she's just laughing with Heather and eating a sandwich. She knew the old Patsy, but my dad's the one who recognizes the new one.

"We, um . . ." Suddenly, the fries are stuck in my throat, and I have to find a soda to wash them back down. "We ran into some Crane goons. Tuck and some other guy. In the SUV we stole from Valor. They wanted to take us back to Leon. So we ran."

My dad puts down his sandwich and leans forward. "Did they follow you here?"

Wyatt shakes his head. "We shot the driver. They crashed about two miles away. Tuck lived, but he couldn't follow us on foot."

I smile at him. He always knows when to use "we" to make me feel more human.

"So they're looking for us," my dad says, and his fingers twitch like he wants nothing more than to start typing on his dumbass laptop.

"Or they were driving around and recognized a familiar car full of familiar kids," I counter.

"Were you guys doing anything suspicious?"

A blush creeps up, and I dig through the bags for napkins. I say nothing.

"You were, weren't you?"

That accusing tone—like he's going to slap my wrist.

"I was spray-painting the Haven High School boulder, and they just drove around the corner and saw us," I say into the bag.

"Patsy, come on. That's incredibly risky and stupid. You can't do things like that."

My head snaps up, and I'm surprised that he's not shaking a finger at me. "If you'd like to talk about doing things that are incredibly risky and stupid, what about having a daughter you can't take care of with a woman you can't marry? What about leaving me? And my mom? What about giving bombs to a psychopath like Leon Crane? What about playing around with your bullshit anarchy on the Internet? Oh, excuse me, the 'darknet.' You don't get to show up after thirteen years and start telling me what to do. You're just a suburban hacker trying to get back at his daddy."

I stand up and rub the fry salt off my hands.

"Patsy, stop. The most important thing right now is keeping you safe."

"All I ever wanted was to find you. And I was so worried you'd be disappointed in me. But you know what, Dad? I'm disappointed in you. And I'll spray-paint whatever the hell I want."

I stand, grab a lantern, a random food bag, and the drugstore bag. "Gabriela?"

She stands, too, following me to the grand, echoing marble stairs. My dad watches us, and I would say he lets us go, but nobody "lets" me do anything anymore.

My mom just calls out, "Honey?"

"I'll be fine, Mom."

The last thing I hear from them when we're upstairs is my dad muttering, "I just don't get her at all."

And Wyatt, a little louder, a little angrier, saying, "Yeah, and how could you?"

I find the master bedroom and close the door behind us. It doesn't have a doorknob—none of the doors do. Gabriela turns on the lantern in the corner so that we're each carrying one, both our faces eerily lit from below. It's so weird to be this far from light, from streetlights or fluorescents, surrounded by a dark forest and endless nothing. I feel so far from home, from humanity. I want to be the child of one of those happy idiots sitting in the restaurant drive-through tonight, oblivious to anything but a loving daddy who brings treats.

"Will you wash my hair?" I say. "I don't know if it's dirt or blood in there." Realizing what I've just said, I add, "Or I can wash it and you can just help pour the water, because that sounds gross."

She smiles, a gruesome monster face, distorted by the lantern. "No, it's fine. I used to work for a vet's groomer and had to wash the nastiest, angriest dogs. Not to say that you're a dog—just that I don't mind."

We set out the supplies in the bathroom, and there's a painter's bucket of cistern water and a rough towel by the sink. My dad says that the polite thing to do in a safe house is to leave it like you found it while adding value somehow. I guess whoever was here before us thought towels would help us feel like humans again, and I wonder what we'll leave behind. I don't have anything extra, anything that would bring comfort to anyone else. Maybe we'll leave this shampoo and conditioner so someone else can enjoy the fleeting feeling of cleanliness to go with their rainwater.

I hop on the long granite counter and lie back with my hair in the sink, and Gabriela opens the gallon of water from the drugstore.

"You ready?" she asks. I nod.

The water is colder than I expected, possibly because we're in an unheated house in November. I hiss and try to turn my head to help the water soak in. I guess I never thought about how much water it takes for a simple task like washing blood out of your hair. At this point, I can't even remember how it got there. From rifling Hartness, maybe? I don't think there's enough water in the world to make me feel clean again, even if I just walked into the ocean and lived there. Soon Gabriela is massaging shampoo into my scalp and scrubbing me clean.

"You have nicer hair than most of the dogs I bathe, if that makes you feel any better," she says.

"Can I ask you a question?" She nods. "Are you glad you went with Chance?"

She snorts. "I wasn't, at first. It was horrible. I felt like some superhero's sidekick, but my superhero turned out to be a villain. And then we went back home, when he was all done, and our house was gone. Just . . . a black crust. And then I was real glad. I can only pray that our parents and the other kids weren't there when it happened."

"Your . . . ?"

"Yeah, I guess we never explained that. Our parents were this older couple who took in troubled teens who were getting hassled in the foster care system. Good people, not like the ones you hear about on the news. Chance and I, we got there about the same time, when we were both thirteen, and made a good team. Some kid at school made fun of my hair, and he just about ruined that kid's life."

"So he didn't ask you to help him?"

A laugh. "Oh, hell no. He begged me not to. But our parents would never have forgiven either of us if he hadn't come home. They turned him from a junkie into a good kid. Really cared about him. About us both."

"What about that bag of drugs?"

"It's not what it looks like. He was a dealer, a few years ago. But he wasn't lying about what he does now. Medical marijuana, pain meds, prescriptions. These days most of his customers are old folks with no insurance." She pours water over my hair and says, "You asking all this because you're curious, or because you're worried about Wyatt?"

"Both," I admit. "I'm just trying to . . ." I choke down a sob. "Does Chance have a hard time living with himself?"

"Talking about feelings is not his jam. But it bothers him more than he shows."

I sit up to towel off my hair. "Has it changed him, what he had to do?"

She turns away, looking out the picture window into what can only be more darkness.

"Of course it did. It changed us all."

"You think we'll ever be okay?"

She takes the towel from me and starts rubbing my head roughly but efficiently, like I'm a rogue poodle. "I've lived with seven different families and never met my folks. Been on the street, in the system. I've never been okay. But at least this way, anybody who tries to hurt me gets killed. That's more than America ever gave me."

"You next?" I ask, pointing at the sink.

But steps are echoing up the hallway, and we both stop and wait.

"Patsy?" my dad calls.

I roll my eyes, even if no one can see it.

"What?" I yell back.

"We need to go back to the bunker. We need the guns we took off Hartness."

"Why?"

He pushes the door open, and the lantern makes him look like an angry ghoul.

"So we can get your dog back on Red Thursday."

Finally he has my attention.

"I thought you said Leon was just playing me. That it was a trick."

"I still think that. But I also know that he wouldn't miss out on an explosion that big, which means he'll be there personally. And I'm more interested in putting down the rabid dog than in saving the good one. So I'll leave that part up to you."

"Fine. Let's go," I say.

Not because I want to. Not because I want to have the conversations that I'm sure he wants to have when we're alone and away from my mom. I agree because I owe it to Matty. And because I don't want to be a coward.

My dad is quiet while he drives, like he's still trying to figure out exactly what he needs to say. He takes back roads, diving down narrow dirt lanes and cutting through sleepy subdivisions. I lean against the window, my eyes heavy. I'm about to fall asleep when he pulls down a dirt road and stops the car.

"Where are we?"

"Nowhere important. We need to talk."

I yawn, my jaw cracking. "So talk."

In the darkness under the trees, he's just a disembodied voice, and I wonder what he sounded like when I was tiny and called out for him in the night. "We're going into that mall, but we're walking into a trap. I know Leon Crane, and there's no way that this trip is going to be simple or easy. He may talk like a preacher, but underneath that is a hardened criminal who was murdering people before murder was legal."

I shrug. This is not news.

"I don't know how to make you understand. Look, when we were kids, Leon came up with this plan to steal booze from my dad's liquor cabinet. He wanted to replace the clear ones with water and the brown ones with tea, then sell sippy cups of booze to the other kids. My dad caught us doing it, sent Leon home, and beat the shit out of me. Broke my arm and gave me a black eye. I told him it was Leon's idea, that it wasn't my fault, and he said, "That's why I'm punishing you. You should know better than to do anything Leon says. I don't trust that sticky son of a bitch. And now you'll never forget it.""

"Okay."

"Just okay? That's all you have to say?"

I shrug. "A broken arm can't really compare to everything that's happened this week."

"When we were older, Devil Johnny found out that Leon was breaking into his dad's own businesses to get back at his brother,

Larry, trying to make Larry look incompetent so he could weasel his way in as Crane consigliere. Instead of telling Lawrence Crane or calling the police or even confronting Leon, my dad had him enrolled in the army and shipped out. We still don't know how Devil Johnny pulled that one off, but Leon got pulled as AWOL and ended up doing two tours overseas."

"If you don't know how he pulled it off, how do you know your dad did it?"

"Because the day Leon got back, he shot Devil Johnny. Right in the kitchen of Cannon House while I was eating my cereal. Shouted, 'That's for sending me to Iraq, you bastard' and everything. My dad was wearing a bulletproof vest at the time, always wore one, and he had Leon arrested and put away. As the witness, I had no choice but to take the stand. So, technically, I was the one who sent Leon back to jail. And even though he was glad to use me for the CFF, happy to welcome me home and forgive me and hug me like a brother, it's been an uneasy truce. So you can maybe understand why Leon would just love to have me back under his thumb and you in his service. Or either of us dead."

"What's your point?"

"My point, honey, is that Devil Johnny and Leon Crane are the two craftiest, meanest bastards I ever met. And all this happened before Dad was on the Valor board and Leon was in charge of an antigovernment anarchy cell. After all the heartache and trouble I've known keeping you away from my father, I'd hate to lose you to Leon, especially when I know that this is another one of his bait-and-switch games."

"So we're not sneaking into the mall?"

He sighs. "No, we're going in. But we're going in knowing it's a trap. We're not going in to save some dog that probably won't even be there. We're going in to kill Leon. Are you with me?"

I swallow and tamp down my rage at the thought that he would just let Matty die. "Sure. Whatever. Let's just get the guns and go home so I can sleep."

"Patsy."

I exhale slowly through my nose. "What, Dad?"

"Just promise me you won't fall for Leon's bullshit again."

Even though he can't see it, I smile sweetly. "I try to avoid as much bullshit as possible these days."

He turns the car on and backs up into the road. I let my head fall against the door, and my eyes close, heavy as lead. When I open them again, the headlights flash down the long lane to Cannon house we walked up together just . . . Was it yesterday? It's so hard to keep track of time. I've slept for only five minutes, but it feels like hours. My entire body aches, and I've drooled on the arm of my hoodie.

We slow down as we start up the last hill, and my dad turns the car around laboriously on the narrow drive, almost hitting a tree.

"What's wrong?" I ask.

"Someone's in the carriage house," my dad whispers, as if they could hear us from this far away. "There's a light on. And two cars by the porch. I'm going to go up there on foot. You stay here."

I shake my head and stretch. "No way. I'm not sitting in this creepy car alone. They could be Cranes."

"That's exactly why you need to stay here. Get in the driver's seat. If you hear gunshots, drive away, fast."

I stare at him, then up at the house. It looks sinister, lit by the moon. Hard to believe that I was saying a rosary to that same moon a short while ago, the last time I heard Matty.

"Okay," I say with a smile.

My dad smiles. "Thanks, honey. I'll be back soon."

He gets out and shuts his door softly. As he stalks up the dirt road, he pulls a Glock from his waistband, from the same place where I carry mine, flat against my spine. He holds it like someone in an FBI movie, cupping the bottom and pointing it ahead with both hands. It's actually kind of funny. When he's halfway up the drive, I pocket the car keys, get out, and follow him.

It's so crisp and cold and dark that it feels like swimming at night, and my lungs burn as I take the hill. My dad spins around, gun pointed right at me, and shakes a fist at me. He's too smart and scared to say anything. I just smile and nod at the house, and he mouths something that I can't read that probably describes how much trouble I'm in now for disobeying him.

Whoop-de-do, Dad.

What are you going to do—break my arm?

Side by side, we creep up the driveway, making as little noise as possible. The lights move in the carriage house—lanterns or maybe candles. There are two cars parked just outside it, and they appear to be empty. One is a big ol' country-boy truck, tricked out and sky-high with truck nuts, and the other is a sleek sedan, like the kind rich guys use as limos. A Valor car. I don't get what my dad thinks we're doing—are we going to kill these guys, or hold them hostage? Is he just doing that country-style "trespassers will be shot" thing because they're on his dad's land?

A lantern bobs out of the carriage house and moves toward the big truck. The truck door opens, the dome light clicks on, and the breath catches in my throat when I see the bearded figure standing there.

It's the guy from the photo in Uncle Ash's house.

It's my dead grandfather. Devil Johnny.

24.

My dad hisses through his teeth, shakes his head, and points back to where our car waits. When he runs for it, I follow. We're not jogging now—we're running full speed. My lungs and calves burn, and my heart pounds, but I know one thing for certain: My grandfather is part of Valor, and I don't want him to know I'm still alive.

My dad must feel the same way.

Back at the car, he opens his door and holds a finger up to his lips. When I get in, I shut the door extra gently. He cranks the engine and leaves the lights off as he rolls down the hill, not fast enough to spray gravel. It feels painfully slow, and I expect to hear them screech after us, but I understand what he's doing. I grit my teeth and lean forward, wishing I could move the car with sheer will.

Come on, come on, come on.

When we turn onto the road, he flicks on his lights and goes back to driving at a normal speed. He takes a different path back to the safe house, as if he thinks he's being followed. We both glance back constantly, waiting for headlights and gunshots. It feels like I don't exhale until we're on the highway—the same one where we lost Tuck earlier. This highway connects everything in my life— before Valor and after Valor, the CFF and the safe house and every mission, every trip for a milk shake. I want to move away and never see its cracked, patched asphalt again.

"So I guess Grandpa's not really dead," I finally say.

My dad shakes his head, looking more spooked than I've seen him yet, which is saying a lot. "That was him, yeah. And he didn't look dead."

He turns into a busy parking lot and parks the car amid hundreds of others. It's a movie theater right next to a pizza place and a big box store, and the marquee lights make me ache for simpler times. Will I ever get to see movies again? I'm pretty sure that if I sat in a theater right now, I'd spend the entire movie checking the seats behind me for suits with guns.

My dad puts the car in park and turns to me. "I think we know now why Valor's after you."

"He doesn't even know me. He's my grandfather. Why would he want to hurt me?"

"To get back at me."

I cross my arms and snort. "Is that how family is supposed to work? Not that I would know anything about family."

"It's like the mob, honey. The Cranes and the Cannons. Valor. Everybody wants power and revenge, and they don't care who they hurt to get it. That's why I opted out."

"Okay, so then why would Devil Johnny fake his own death?"

My dad's smile is sad and pitying. "For the same reason you did. So that no one can anticipate what you'll do next."

I don't know what to say to that, and he seems lost in his own thoughts, so I grab my backpack and hop out of the car. Behind the open passenger door, I squat and paint my mark. Every instance of VALOR $UCKS feels like another middle finger at the people who ruined my life. It's not healing, it doesn't help anything, but it makes my heart feel a little lighter, and I need that feeling like it's a drug.

My dad doesn't stop me, but he doesn't look pleased when I get back in the car, either. I lean over to tuck the cans back in my bag, and he puts the car in reverse and backs out of the space.

"You should stop doing that," he snaps.

"You should stop acting like you have any right to tell me what to do."

"I'm your father."

"Funny—my birth certificate doesn't actually mention that."

We pull onto the highway in a fuming silence that tells me he knows he has no case. I lean back and put my feet up on the dashboard.

"So my dad and my grandfather are still alive. All my dreams are coming true. Yay."

"Yeah, keep being sarcastic about it, Patsy. That's going to help."

I cross my arms and tuck my chin. "I was trying to help. I love being helpful. I've had a super-helpful week. And thanks, by the way, for how your entire generation screwed over my generation. Credit card debt is a fantastic inheritance."

He snorts and shifts lanes to pass a slow car. "You know how much debt I have? None. How many credit cards I hold? None. So that's at least one thing you can't blame me for."

I nod slowly, the rage building. "Well, that makes sense. Considering you contributed absolutely zero dollars to your abandoned girlfriend and baby daughter, you'd have ample opportunity to live debt-free. But you know what? Mom and I didn't have that option."

I dig around in my bag, way down into the bottom, and pull out two things. One's the photo of my dad, his brother, Ash, and their dad, which I stole from Ash's mantel. And the other . . .

"One hundred and sixty-seven thousand, eight hundred and ninety-two dollars and thirty-three cents," I say, flapping the printed card from Valor, the first one I ever saw, the night the suit pointed the gun at my mom's chest. "That's how much my mom owes Valor."

"I sent her money."

"Not enough!"

"You don't know that. You can't blame me for your mother's bad decisions."

"No, I totally can. You got her pregnant and left. Everything that happened after that is your fault. That's the definition of the word 'fault.'"

"Are you saying you're sorry you were born, Patsy?"

I stare out the window, a fist to my eye. "No. I'm saying I wish you had been there, asshole. It would've been different."

I didn't even notice it, but we're back at the safe house. He's silent as we navigate the long drive, but when he pulls up by the fountain, my dad leaves the car running and turns to me, his face lit up by the glowing dashboard lights.

"Patsy, I don't know if it helps or even means anything to you, but I'm sorry. It broke my heart, leaving, but I truly thought it was for the best. Everything I did after you were born, I did to keep you safe. I left to keep you safe from my father. And now that we know he's alive, I'm serious about not taking any more chances. Don't go joy riding. Don't go out for ice cream. Don't stop to spray-paint rocks. Just . . . stay close. Devil Johnny is a very bad man. I can't prove it, but I'm pretty sure . . . I'm pretty sure he killed my sister, Valerie."

"And you're sure that was him we saw?"

"Let's just say that when his favorite truck is parked outside of his house, I don't think what we saw is the old bastard's ghost."

When we get inside, he goes straight upstairs. Of course.

"Did you get the guns?" Chance asks from the floor. He's lying on his back by the bags of food, his hoodie pillowed under his head. From what I can tell, he's in a food coma. All of them are.

I shake my head. "Nope. There was someone there."

Wyatt sits up. "Who?"

My dad and I didn't discuss this part, and I'm not sure how much of the information is relevant or if we can trust Heather with it, so I just shrug and say, "I don't know. Two cars."

"Is the red car unlocked?" Rex asks.

"I think so?"

He hops up with way too much energy. "Sleeping bags are in the back." Bea trails him outside like a ghost, and I shiver. It's easy to forget how cold a drafty house can get at night in November without any heat.

"Can we start a fire?" I ask, looking at the fireplace with naked longing.

I'm surprised when Heather answers. "You don't want to do that. This house is too remote. Anyone looking for something out of the ordinary would notice hearth smoke."

"Is that how the CFF finds people?" I ask sharply.

She smiles at me like I'm a stupid little kid. "The CFF doesn't find people. They wait for people to show up. Plenty of people are more than happy for the safety Leon provides."

"Maybe the people he doesn't send on one-way bombing missions," I grumble.

Rex and Bea are back, dropping armloads of rolled-up sleeping bags on the ground. Without a word, they go back out for another load. When they return, Rex says, "That's everything."

I do a quick count, and there's no way it can add up. I'm counting the sleeping bags in my head a second time when Wyatt puts a hand on my shoulder. I didn't even notice he was gone.

"Come on," he says. "You have to sleep now."

"But there's not enough, and what if Devil Johnny comes?" I mumble.

"Then I'll take care of him," my dad says from somewhere nearby.

And then Wyatt is carrying me, and I'm limp as a noodle. My feet sway. We're on stairs. I'm flat on my back, something soft under my head, the coolness of a plump sleeping bag cushioning the hard floor.

"But we never decided what to do," I protest.

Wyatt pats my back, and I smile and snuggle down.

"We'll figure it out. You sleep," he says.

And I do.

X X X

When I wake up, there's a big square of golden sunshine covering me, and I stretch and roll around like I'm coated in hot butter. I'm alone, a cold chicken sandwich and a watery soda by my side. I hear voices echoing from downstairs, but I'm going to take this gift of time and plenty. Tomorrow morning, just before dawn, the Citizens for Freedom are going to blow up the mall where I got my ears pierced when I was eight, and if we can't stop them, they're going to blow up my dog, too. Whatever my dad thinks he knows about Leon, I heard the glee in his voice, and I know he's going to put Matty right where he wants me to go. And I'm going to go there anyway.

That means that we're going to have a late night that will involve fighting people who would be more than happy to see us dead, the kind of people who claim to be good guys but would blow up a good dog just to make a point.

But for now . . .

Sunshine is nice. Food is nice. Caffeine and sugar and grease and tapping up the crumbs with my fingertips are nice. All I'm missing, really, are Matty and Wyatt.

As if on cue, he appears in the doorway, looking worried. But he always looks worried, doesn't he?

"Did you get enough to eat? Do you want something else? I know the Coke is watery, but there was no way to keep the ice from melting—"

"It's fine." I suck up the dregs so he can hear it. "Thanks."

"We're making plans downstairs. For tonight. Or tomorrow morning. If you want to . . . ?"

I shake my head and flop back down on the sleeping bag, rolling over onto my full belly. "Not yet. Just a few more minutes."

Wyatt sits beside me, and after a moment of what must be hard-core interior debate, places a gentle hand flat on my back. I allow it. Welcome it, even. We're in one of our bubbles, in one of these rare, miraculous moments in which no one wants us for anything, and we're not running away from or toward anything, and no one is shaking with fury, and no one has a gun drawn or a heart beating out of their throat. No one is bleeding. No one is driving. No one is shooting.

Not like last night, on the highway.

Repress, repress, repress.

"Last night, when I was sleeping. Did I do the thing . . . ?"

I'm asking the wall, but Wyatt knows what I mean.

The thing where I scream and cry and thrash in my sleep, where my eyes are open but I'm not there. I'm not anywhere. I'm in the past, holding a gun.

"I don't think so. I was outside the door. I wanted to be here if you needed me but not really close if you didn't. I wasn't sure if you were still mad at me. Plus, your dad read me the riot act about sleeping beside you."

"Screw him. He's not in charge of my body. And I'm not mad. Much."

Gently, slowly, he starts rubbing my back. There's nothing sexual about it—he's as careful as if I'm a cat that might purr or bite him, and he doesn't know which. It's nice.

"Will you scratch my back?" I ask. Because I fell asleep in my bra, which means there are hard, red, itchy lines pressed into my flesh.

He obliges, although his nails are stubby things. He's been biting them, I think. Everyone's picked up bad habits. Rex with his earphones, Chance with his cockiness, Bea with her creepy stares. My bad habit appears to be shooting anyone who gets in my way.

I relax down further.

"Do you want to know the plan?" he asks.

I'm kind of annoyed that I wasn't involved in forming it, but I'll wait and see what it is before I protest. I nod.

"So your dad says we need to be in the mall before it closes at ten. We'll each have a backpack with a jumpsuit in it, like the mall's custodians wear. So we're supposed to go to the store today and buy new clothes and get haircuts and do whatever we can to not look like ourselves. And we need new shoes, work boots, to go with the uniforms. Your dad's going to get a couple of hotel rooms within walking distance of the mall, and that's where your mom and Heather and Kevin will be, where we'll meet afterward. And anyone who wants to be part of the rescue will be in different corners of the mall, hiding until the CFF has placed the boxes. We get Matty and get out."

"And what's my dad going to do?" Because, honestly, this doesn't sound like the plans he was making last night.

"He didn't say."

"Yeah, I bet he didn't." I frown at the wall. "Because he's going after Leon. I don't like it. This is not a party. We don't need a bunch of people. Just you and me. She's our dog."

His hand is gentle on my back. "That's what I said. But your dad wants to be there. And Gabriela and Chance want to help. Even Rex. Heather wanted to join, but your dad was too worried about her still being on Leon's side, so he wants her to stay with your mom." He leans closer, his breath grazing my ear. "I still don't trust her. I think we should tie her up until it's done."

"Smart," I say. "I don't trust her either. What about Bea?"

"Who knows what she's thinking? She was there while we talked about it, but she didn't say anything. I don't know if she's in or out. I don't even know if she's human. And I don't know why we trust her, either."

"Because she chose us, maybe." I drop my voice down to whisper in his ear. "I think she's like an attack dog. For now she's on our side. And if we tried to get rid of her, she'd turn on us, and it would be really, really bad."

"I definitely don't want to be on that girl's bad side."

"When do we head out?"

Wyatt stands. "Whenever you're ready. We're just waiting on you."

25.

I'm in Mark's—a different Mark's that's farther away and not packed with Wipers—and my cart is full of crap. Clothes that aren't my style, heavy work boots, organic peanut butter biscuits and a dog bed for Matty. It's kind of funny how I've had more leisure to shop in the apocalypse than I ever had when poor and in debt in the normal world. I've been standing in front of the hair dye display for five minutes, the tension growing as the clock ticks down. My hair is dark and thick and wavy, which means that the only way to make a drastic change involves bleach. But I've never bleached my hair, and I'm starting to think that deep down I'm terrified of how much of myself I'm losing, inside and now out.

I don't act like Patsy. I don't feel like Patsy. Soon I won't look like Patsy either.

"This one's actually better." Gabriela appears with her cart and hands me one of the three bleach boxes. "Works faster."

"Thanks." I read the box, but the words no longer make sense. "Is it that obvious that I have no idea what I'm doing?"

"I'm an assistant dog groomer with a purple Mohawk. I can spot virgin hair a mile away. I wish you could go blue or green, but since we're supposed to blend in, maybe ash blond?" She hands me a box with a thin, boring woman twirling her dull, mouse-brown hair.

I hate this woman, and I don't want this hair. I put that box back and select a different box. The redhead on the front has gorgeous freckles and looks like she's enjoying the hell out of her spunky short hair.

"Blondes have more fun," Gabriela reminds me.

"But redheads have more confidence," I retort. "What are you going to do with yours?"

She puts a hand to her fro-hawk and frowns. "Shave it. All the way down. I guess I can always grow it out afterward, right? I'm getting the nicest clipper set they have here, so I can do your hair. I was supposed to go to beauty school, but I guess that's out. Maybe I can become an underground barber. Cut all the rebels' hair. Trim their rebellious beards."

She picks up a box of turquoise dye and reads the back.

"That would look pretty kickass," I say.

"Mall custodians probably aren't allowed to have blue hair."

"So don't go. You don't have to. You don't even have a gun. Just hang out in the hotel and dye your hair blue and make sure my mom's okay."

She puts the box back on the shelf and turns to face me, hands on her hips. "First of all, you're not my boss. Second of all, don't you think that's exactly what I want to do? She's a nice dog and all, but she's not worth dying for, and it's not my fight. But my brother is determined to help, and that means I'm coming along to make sure he doesn't do something stupid. You understand that doing stupid shit is his thing, right? I'm beginning to think he might be suicidal. So I'm coming whether you want me there or not. And you'd better get that dog out safe, because I don't give up my 'hawk for just anybody."

It chokes me up, hearing her say that. I want to hug her, but she doesn't look like she'd welcome a hug just now. I settle for squeezing her hand and saying, "I will. We will."

We drift together through the store, picking out Pop-Tarts and tossing makeup in each other's carts. The bubblegum-pink lipstick she recommends for my new red hair is most definitely not my style.

"Yeah, that's the point," she says. "So you're getting it."

When we get in line to check out, our entire party is spread out with carts full of bags. My mom and Kevin sit in the food court as he slams down pizza and slushies, and when she sees me looking, she smiles and waves like she still can't believe I'm alive. I feel a wash of gratitude—that she's alive, that she's here, that she has someone with her who can give her chemo once we're on the other side of this bullshit. I leave my cart behind Gabriela's and race to the card aisle, where I pick out one with pearly hearts and flowers on it "Wishing My Beloved Mother a Happy Birthday." As the cashier rings me up, I use her pen to write, *I love you, Mom!* on the inside. I want to write so much more. But the simple truth will have to do.

That little hitch of worry is back as soon as I slide my gift card through the machine. It's accepted almost immediately, and I can breathe again. Soon we're all out, stuffing bags into the car trunks, trying to figure out where to put the huge dog bed I just had to buy, and waiting for my dad, who's still sitting in the in-store coffee shop, borrowing their Wi-Fi to reserve the hotel rooms where we'll spend the rest of the day becoming different people and quietly freaking out.

I slide into the backseat of Wyatt's Lexus, next to Bea. I still can't get a read on her, especially why she left the CFF with us. She bought just as much crap as the rest of us, although most of her food selections are, oddly, green. She looks the same as she did that first night in the high school: petite and dainty, pale and washed out, eyes big and dark and empty. I don't know if she's coming tonight, but I do know she took and spent the gift card my dad offered. I'm sick of treating her like a murderous doll, so I turn to her and ask, "So are you coming to the mall tonight?"

She meets my eyes for longer than is comfortable.

"Yes," she finally says.

"Why?" I have to ask.

She blinks slowly, like an owl. "Because everything is an army now, and this army pays the best and demands the least."

"How old are you?"

"Sixteen."

"Oh. I thought you were younger."

"Everyone does."

"So why did you join us? I kind of feel like . . . you don't like us very much."

"I don't like anyone, Patsy. But I got bored with Leon's little pranks."

"Okay." Because what do you say to that?

Her head swivels to face forward again. "I'm pretty sure I'm a sociopath," she says softly. "But probably the least dangerous kind." She glances at Rex, who's bopping his head to whatever music is currently on his iPod and can't hear us. "I don't want to kill innocent people, eat anybody, or dissect them. I'm not very fond of blood. I only like to eat green food, and I don't know why. Green just tastes better. It's clean. I'm telling you all this because I think you and I have the most in common, but you still manage to understand people. You can tell everyone else what I said so I don't have to say it again. They probably already know."

"You think we have a lot in common?" I ask, a chill zipping down my spine.

She nods and gives me the coldest, sweetest smile. "That's why Valor selected us. We're very good at killing."

I desperately want to switch cars, but that would be way too obvious. I'd rather the murderous sociopath think nice things about me than put her in the car with chatty, obnoxious Kevin or my fragile mom. Wyatt bought his usual crossword puzzle book and is on page one, the tip of his tongue poking out in that adorable way it does when he's thinking. Bea keeps staring straight ahead like a robot in sleep mode. And my dad is taking his damn time getting back from the café. When I finally see him, laptop under his arm, I'm ready to hug him again just because I'm that glad we can drive away. I don't like Mark's anymore. But, then again, nowhere feels safe. I never noticed how many video cameras there were in the world until Valor took over.

My dad looks up and hurries into the car.

"Don't drive," he says. "Wait until the choppers pass. Nobody get out."

I hear them now and scan the sky. They certainly look Valor when they appear, black and sleek with no discernible logo. They zoom in from one side and keep going.

"Do you think they're looking for us?" I ask.

My dad pulls down his mirror and gives me a reassuring smile.

"They're always looking for something. If you see Valor out in the world, just treat 'em like a bear: Don't run. Don't cower. Just walk away. Or, better yet, don't ever let them see you in the first place." He thumps the dashboard to get Wyatt's attention and gives him directions to the hotel.

The ride is quiet. My dad turns on the radio and scans a few stations, but it's just pop and country music and the usual inane commercials. I'm still surprised that we're not getting emergency broadcasts and news reports about Valor's wave of violence, which just goes to show you how powerful they are, how completely they're controlling the media. Neighbors get shot on their doorsteps and houses get burned to the ground, but no one is publicly talking about it. It's kind of brilliant, really. The flashes of anti-Valor graffiti we pass as we drive are the only real signs of the war being waged behind radio silence.

"I wonder when Valor is doing the big reveal," I say out loud.

"You're not the only one," my dad says, warming to the topic. "There's been lots of chatter about certain signs. Media buy, blocks on the cable guides, Internet URLs going dark in anticipation of a redirect. The first wave was supposed to take around a week as the mercs activated and spread. Despite the radio silence, fewer kids and debtors are living through their shifts now. Whenever the clock counts down on a van, it explodes, and that means there aren't many vans left. People are scared."

I remember those red numbers on the dash and shiver.

If I'd waited a few seconds longer to knock on Wyatt's door . . . *kaboom.*

"It's a flawed system. You see your neighbor get shot when he opens his door, you either stop opening your door or you buy a bigger gun," Wyatt says.

My dad nods in approval. "If I had to guess, I'd bet that Valor has planned their big announcement for after Black Friday. Everyone would've already signed their credit slips from Thursday and Friday morning and would be at home, inside, with their families, watching TV."

"But no one shops on Thursday, do they?" I ask.

"They will now. Valor-owned stores are offering even crazier deals on Thanksgiving than they do on Black Friday. Game consoles for ten bucks for the first ten people in the store, buy-one-get-one-free phones." He points to a billboard offering one-dollar plasma-screen televisions if you sign up for a year of E-finity satellite TV. "Valor owns E-finity. It's just more signatures. They're trying everything they can to get people out and shopping or signing their terms of service agreements. All Valor devices will force a new terms of service agreement on Thursday morning. Either join or lose your ability to text."

"And what about Cyber Monday?" Wyatt adds. "They wouldn't want to miss all the home shoppers and everyone who's too scared to leave the house."

My dad sighs. "Guys, if I knew everything Valor was doing, I wouldn't be here. I would be somewhere else, planting bigger bombs."

We go quiet, and my dad hunts through his bag, pulling out a burner phone and flipping it open. He must not see what he wants, as he shakes his head and tosses it back in. I get lost in a thought spiral, trying to figure out how Valor can even function as a government. What about Congress? What about wars? If you already have all the money and everything is motivated by money, why could you possibly want more money? Doesn't money stop meaning anything at some point? Then again, what my history teachers called either a democracy or a republic never made sense to me in the first place. If your vote doesn't count, what's the point of a vote? It all ends up in the hands of greedy old men anyway.

Soon Wyatt is turning in at a hotel so close to the mall that I can see the glass dome over the carousel from the hotel parking lot. My dad goes in without us and comes back out with a stack of key cards. I'm about to say something about the expense, but that doesn't matter anymore, does it? He just pulls more dollars out of Valor's back pocket whenever he wants to.

"Patsy, you're with the girls." He points to Bea and Gabriela. "Wyatt, you're with the boys." He points to Chance and Rex. "Karen . . ." His voice cracks, and he coughs and settles for giving the card to Heather. "Y'all bunk together with the kid. And I'm alone."

"Why do you get your own room?" I ask.

His smile is grim. "Because I'm the one with the laptop, and if they come for me, I want to be alone on a different floor when it happens. Go on up, and do whatever you want to. Eat, sleep. If you're going to the mall, we're going to meet in the hotel lobby at nine tonight in regular clothes. Bring your stuff in your backpack. Everybody got that? Nine."

Everyone nods. My dad turns and walks away.

Heather looks down. "We're in 247. See you!" As she helps Kevin limp through the door, I slip the sappy greeting card into my mom's hand and hug her as hard as I think she can handle.

"I love you, Mom," I say fiercely.

She hugs me back. "I love you too. And I'm sorry—"

"Don't be." I reach under the neck of my shirt and pull out her rosary. When she sees it, she gasps. I hold it out. "This helped me when I needed it most. I wanted you to know. I think Mother Mary is on our side."

But she won't take it from me. She just folds my fingers over it and says, "Keep it. Keep Mary with you. Keep me with you. I don't understand why you're doing what you're doing, but I want you to come back. When I came home that morning and you were gone . . . I never thought I'd see you again. I kept praying it was some sort of nightmare, that you were just at school, like normal. I called your phone again and again. Nothing. I thought you were dead."

I nod, tears in my eyes. "I thought you were, too."

She reaches in to hug me, and I'm flooded with comfort and love. Everyone else leaves, going to their separate rooms.

"We're in 315," Gabriela says. "See you later."

We're alone now in the lobby, and I have one more question, so I hook my arm through my mom's and pull her to sit on one of the hard leather sofas. "Mom, did Dad ever send you any money?"

She pats her pockets, blushes, and acts all flustered. I frown.

"A little," she allows. "He sent a fifty in your birthday cards."

"What else?"

My mom's eyes wobble with tears. "I didn't touch it, if that's what you're thinking."

Rage starts to build in my chest. Of all her failings, I never thought my mom would lie to me. Or steal from me. "Mom. Come on. Tell me the truth."

She steels herself, exhales, and sits up, her chin just as stubborn as mine. "I saved it. Every penny. It's in a college fund for you. They used to match it, when I worked for Haverford and Sons." I stare, hard, in shock. "There's around forty thousand in there right now," she adds weakly.

I'm back in her arms in an instant. "God, Mom. You idiot. You unselfish moron. You could've used it. To pay off Valor. For your meds. Or whatever. Why didn't you?"

She relaxes against me, back shaking with sobs under my hands. "You deserved so much better than you got. So much better than what I could give you. I didn't want Jack's money, but I wanted you to have a future. It was the most important thing. I didn't know Valor would do this. Who could know? It was the best I could do. I'm so sorry, honey."

I shake my head against her, my tears falling on her sweater. "Forty thousand still wouldn't have been enough, Mom. Not even half of enough."

"I love you, honey. I would give everything I ever had to make this okay. I made so many mistakes—"

I pull away, dash away my tears, and smile. "Mom, no. It's just . . . All this time, I thought he didn't care and wasn't helping you. And then I thought you had just used up all the money. Turns out you were both trying to help all along. Valor is the bad guy here. Not you." I look toward the elevators. "And not him, either."

"He was a good dad," she says, as if it pains her. "Right up until the day he walked out."

"He was trying to be a good dad then, too," I say.

X X X

After some more tears and hugs, she looks exhausted, like the crying cost her. I urge her upstairs to rest. She'll get chemo soon, but I've got to keep her functional until then.

I scan the restaurants around the hotel and text Wyatt.

Patsy: `Sushi buffet. 7?`

Wyatt: `Sounds good.`

Patsy: `Tell all the kids.`

Wyatt: `Cool.`

Then, as I step into the elevator, my phone buzzes again.

Wyatt: `We're going to get her back, Patsy. I promise.`

Patsy: `Don't promise me things. Except sushi.`

Our hotel room is soft and brightly lit, the puffy white comforters defiled by our purchases. Gabriela is in the bathroom, the sound of her clippers buzzing through the closed door. I'm next, and I'm not excited. I don't really trust a junior dog groomer to give me a good haircut, but how bad can it be? I cut my own hair, after all, and my grown-out bangs and ragged, asymmetrical bob aren't going to be hard to improve on. She told me to wait with the bleach until after she was done, and I'm not looking forward to that, either.

Bea is in the uncomfortably square chair by the window, reading a paperback romance with a half-naked cowboy on the cover and drinking a green smoothie with a dancing head of lettuce on the front. She's not smiling, and I wonder if she's getting anything out of the crappy-looking book, but I'm not about to ask. Our conversation earlier was unsettling. I long for my knitting, but I know my stitches would be tight as hell right now. Maybe I'll find something good to spray-paint on my way to the mall later. It's the only way I have to scratch this itch.

The bathroom door opens, and Gabriela steps out, shouting, "Ta-da!"

Her hair is cropped close to her head, revealing beautiful, fierce lines and making her cheekbones pop.

"You look fantastic," I say.

"Thanks. It'll do. Catch!" She throws something at me, and I dodge and fall off the edge of the bed. When I pick it up, it's a big ball of her purple Afro, fluffy and light as a puff of cotton candy.

"Your turn." She holds out a hand to the open bathroom door, and I step inside.

"What do you want?" she asks.

I start to shrug, then lift my chin. "Short. Whatever you think best. Just make me look like someone else."

She has me take off my hoodie before she wraps a crunchy hotel towel around my shoulders. I've never had my hair professionally cut, so it's not like I know what I'm missing. When she turns on the clippers and does the first swipe, I want to cry. She must notice.

"Turn around," she says, confident and tough, two things I don't currently feel.

I turn my back to the mirror and close my eyes as strip after strip of thick black hair falls to the ground. The buzz of the clippers grates on my nerves and tickles my neck, and it seems to go on forever before she turns it off, snips me with scissors for an eternity, takes my shoulders, and turns me around.

When I open my eyes, I have a rough pixie cut. And I feel twenty pounds lighter. Before I can really enjoy it, though, she's pulling packets out of the box of bleach I bought and mixing up a white paste that burns my nose. Soon I'm spackled in grit, my scalp burning.

"How long?" I ask.

The set of her mouth is grim. "As long as it takes."

While we wait, she calls Bea in.

"What do you want?" Gabriela asks.

"I don't care. Hair is just another disguise," Bea says placidly.

Gabriela reaches for the girl's long, white-blond hair, her hand hovering in the air. "May I?" she asks carefully.

She doesn't actually touch it until Bea says, "Yes."

"Did you buy any hair dye?" Bea nods, leaves the room, and comes back with the most boring brown I've ever seen. "This and a long bob, and no one will ever notice you."

Bea smiles, a real smile. Almost. "Good."

A few hours later, and we emerge. Bea is mousy and invisible. I have red hair in a pixie cut, and bubblegum-pink lips. I can't stop smiling. Not because I feel pretty or hope Wyatt will like it. Because I look nothing like myself, which means I might get to shoot Leon Crane before he even notices me. But I don't tell anyone that. It's my own little secret.

26.

And then we wait. We take turns showering, steaming up the bathroom and trying not to get our freshly dyed hair on the towels. Gabriela and I do our makeup, aiming to look as normal and boring as possible. Bea reads her book, looking even less like a human and more like a robot. I'm pretty sure she bought her striped leggings and flowered shirt in the little girls' section. For a sixteen-year-old, she's tiny. But what do you expect if you only eat green foods? She's by far the strangest person I've ever met.

Time drags slowly. I sweep everything off one of the beds and lie down, but you can only stare at a white ceiling for so long before you start to go insane. Gabriela's charging her iPod, and my phone is plugged in, and when it buzzes, I just about leap across the room.

We have to conserve our phone use, since we don't know how much data or time is on them.

It's Wyatt's number. **Meet me ten minutes early?**

I answer, **On my way.**

I stop for one last mirror check, and it doesn't even register as me. I'm in leggings and a flowy gray tunic, mostly as an ironic nod to all the YA dystopias I used to read, in which everyone wore gray tunics all the time for no good reason. Maybe I should kiss Chance and start a love triangle, too. I think the bleach is messing with my mind. On the way out, I grab my new flowered denim backpack.

"Lobby in ten," I remind my cellmates.

And then I'm hurrying to the elevators and toward Wyatt. His back is to me when I step off in the lobby—he's reading the breakfast menu, not that we'll be here to try it. When he turns around, we just stare at each other, mouths agape.

"Holy shit," he says. "You make a cute redhead."

"You look like a lumberjack," I say. He's got that hipster haircut, with the sides shaved and the top long and messy. With his stubble growing out and the plaid shirt he's wearing, I worry that he's going to be too eye-catching for what we've got to do tonight. Because I would notice him, wherever he was.

The gawking gets so awkward that I just go in for a hug so we can stop standing here, staring like two idiots in a rom com.

I pull away and rock back on my heels. "So . . . what's up?"

He looks sheepish, like the old Wyatt. "Uh, I just needed to see you. The wait's been killing me. We all went and got haircuts, and then it was like the clock stopped moving. Chance is asleep, and Rex is watching some movie with a ton of explosions, and if tonight goes crazytown, I wanted some time alone with you first. Even if you're still a little mad at me."

He holds out his hand, and I lace my fingers through his. We walk out the front door and follow the sidewalk around as I struggle for the right words. "I'm not mad at you. I'm just mad. Like, at everything. In general."

"Me too."

"Now that we have a plan, I'm a little better. At least we're doing something."

"We're going to get her back, Patsy."

"I know. But keep telling me that."

He sits on a bench and pulls me into his lap, wrapping his arms around me.

"Your hair smells weird," he murmurs into my ear.

"There isn't a normal anymore," I say. "Will you just hold me?"

"For as long as I can."

We kiss wildly, madly, passionately, desperately, as if trying to devour each other. And then we just sit like that, plastered together, not talking, looking like strangers, forgetting the world, until our friends come down for dinner.

X X X

It feels a lot like the Last Supper, but with Styrofoam cups of soda instead of wine. The six of us sit around the sticky wood table at the sushi buffet, alternately stuffing our faces and staring down at the planks of fish and rolls of bright orange eggs as if realizing that eating is pretty dumb if you're just going to explode in a couple of hours. Because isn't that the crux of it? Whether we fail or succeed, if we're not out of that building on time, we'll be burnt crispier than a salmon-skin roll.

We don't talk much, because what's the point? We can talk tomorrow—whoever is left to talk. There's another table of kids nearby, and they're all seniors talking about the colleges they've applied to for next year and early acceptance and frats and which bars serve warm beer without checking IDs, and I want to jab all their eyes out with my chopsticks. College just means more debt, which means Valor wins. Again. Do they seriously not know what's going on?

"You guys want to-go cups?" Chance asks, and everyone shrugs noncommittally. "Coke Zero?" he asks Gabriela, and she just shrugs again, her eyes far away.

When Chance goes to the hostess to charm her into more drinks, Gabriela stares at his back like she's trying to change his mind telepathically. He shaved his head, and he doesn't even look like the same guy. He looks haunted, like a war refugee. Maybe she's right about his death wish.

The waitress brings our check and another round of sodas, and I slide my Happy Birthday gift card over, because who cares which of us pays with stolen Valor money? Everyone but me and Chance heads for the bathroom, and as soon as Gabriela's out of view, he pops the top off her to-go cup.

"What are you doing?" I ask.

"I'm putting roofies in her drink," he says, like it's the most normal thing ever.

"You know I'm not okay with that. I'm going to tell her."

He shakes his head, and I can see the cracks in his cool-guy facade as he stirs her drink with his chopstick. "Look, I don't want her to go into the mall today. I might be dumb and invincible, and I might deserve to die for all the bad shit I've done, but she's too good for this kind of thing. She couldn't pull the trigger, even if she had a gun. So she's going to be asleep in the hotel while it goes down." He puts the top back on and meets my eyes, fierce and angry. "And you're not going to tell her because you know I'm right."

"Do you have any more?" I ask.

"A whole Baggie full."

I lean over and check the route to the restroom.

"Put some in Rex's drink too."

"What about Wyatt and Bea?"

"Wyatt needs to do this, or he'll feel guilty forever." It's selfish as hell, but I don't care. I need him there.

"And Bea?" He holds a tiny pill over her drink, waiting.

"Bea can handle the risk."

And the world might be better off without her, I think but don't say.

The pills go into Rex's drink, and Chance recaps it, right as the bathroom door opens.

"I would be really pissed at you for selling roofies," I mutter, "but right now we need roofies."

"I don't sell them," he whispers back. "I found them on the kitchen table of one of my marks and figured they'd be safer with me than with whoever broke into his house after I left. But you're welcome."

A guy who thinks like that doesn't deserve to die, but I don't know how to tell him that.

Gabriela picks up her drink and takes a deep sip, and I smile at her.

Chance is right. It's better this way.

As we walk back to the hotel, Gabriela and Rex get noticeably clumsy. We're lucky it's only a block from the restaurant, because by the time we're in the elevator, Chance is pretty much carrying her, and Wyatt's got an arm around Rex, half holding him up.

"Thought caffeine was s'posed to make you wake up," Rex slurs.

"S'not working," Gabriela adds.

I've already tossed the remains of both their drinks.

Wyatt gives me a look that says he knows damn well something is up, and I give him an exaggerated wink and murmur, "The eagle waits at midnight."

Bea seems totally unconcerned and continues to nurse her Mountain Dew as if this is totally normal.

When we get in the elevator, I push the button for my floor and say, "Just bring him, too."

I lead the way to our room and clear all our crap off the beds. Wyatt helps Rex crawl into one, although the kid won't get under the covers until he's managed to slip off his shoes. Chance tucks Gabriela into the other one, leaning down to kiss her forehead.

"Don't wake up, Sis," he says, more sweetly than I imagined him capable of.

It's only eight, which means we've got another hour before it's time to meet downstairs, but I want out of this room. It still smells of bleach and hair dye, and every second I spend here makes me want to pace back and forth like an animal trapped in a zoo. I grab my backpack and nod to the remaining three people on my team.

"Let's go be rebellious."

Wyatt and Chance grin, and Bea tries to.

This hotel is perfectly situated for anarchy. We start at the closed-down seafood place next door, and I leave my mark on one brick wall, my biggest one yet. I buy some big markers in the hobby store, and we head to the mostly empty bookstore, where we sneak into corners with the bestsellers and scribble VALOR SUCKS and FUCK YOUR VALOR and READ THE FINE PRINT and PAY OR DIE inside. When one of the bookstore employees starts watching me in the big mirror, I grab the others and run.

We hit a busy coffee shop next, and with the guys standing at the table like they're trying to pick me up, I scrawl VALOR SUCKS across the fake plastic wood. In the bathroom, I get out my paint cans and write, VALOR IS YOUR NEW GOD on the wall.

We run away laughing, and the sound is wild and mad, like dogs on the hunt for meat.

When I check my phone, we've got ten minutes left, and we hurry back to the hotel lobby. I realize that we lost Bea somewhere along the way. She's probably still in the bookstore, looking for a new cowboy erotic romance. One by one, people are dropping off. And that feels right. The fewer people who walk into that mall tonight, the fewer people who can get in my way. And the fewer people who can die fighting my fight.

We're a minute late, and my dad is furious.

"Where are the others? Aren't there six of you?"

"Not anymore," I say, and he doesn't ask why. It's just Chance and Wyatt, now.

My dad leads us out to the burgundy sedan and pulls a big duffel bag from the trunk. Inside are crisply folded jumpsuits, gray and creased. He hands one to each of us, and we stuff them in our backpacks on top of the identical tan work boots we bought at Mark's today. When my dad gets in the driver's seat, Wyatt and I get in the back, and Chance sits in the front.

"It's almost an hour until the mall closes. I'm going to drop each of you off in a different department store. There are four of them anchoring the mall, so we'll go to one each. I'm parking the car closest to Nickel's, which is by the hotel. I don't care what you do until nine fifty, and then I want you in your department store's bathroom, putting on your jumpsuit and boots. Dump your bag and find something to do that a janitor would do. Push a garbage can, carry a mop, squeegee a window. It doesn't matter. You have to be out of your store and in the mall at ten, or else you get stuck behind the cage and can't help. Got it?"

We all nod. We're outside the yawning mouth of the Mr. Goodbuy store, and Chance grips the handle of the passenger door, but my dad stops him with a hand on his sleeve. "I'm not done. As soon as you're out in the mall, find a place to hide. A bathroom, whatever. We have to give the CFF time to bring in the boxes. Stay on the lower level. Leave the upper level to me. I'm going to take out all the guards. And do not let them see you." He reaches into his bag and hands Chance a beat-up burner phone. "You're the only one without a phone, right? Only use this for emergencies. I have all your numbers. Once the Crane guards are gone, I'll text each of you, and then we've got to find the dog and get out before five a.m. Don't stay late. Don't do anything stupid. Just wait, get the dog, and get out. You guys need to check the boxes in each atrium and near the Santa-photo setup. Got it?"

And I watch him, realizing that everything he's just said contradicts what he told me in private about this entire mission being a trap. But I don't say anything, because I'm going in anyway.

Chance nods and gets out. Turning back, he says, "Break a leg, nerds."

Walking into the department store, he looks like any other eighteen-year-old boy. Tall, gawky, trying to walk with swagger that he doesn't quite possess. My dad drives around to the next store, Oxford's.

"You're up, kid," he says to Wyatt.

Wyatt takes a deep breath and opens his arms, and I want to hug him forever. If everything goes wrong, this could be our last hug. Or my last hug. Or his. I don't want it to end, but my dad gives a pissy little sigh, so I tilt my head up and kiss Wyatt on the lips. Not like our earlier kiss, not half crazed and desperate and hard. Just a soft, long peck, a sigh into his mouth. Wyatt goes still, probably mortified that my dad is watching us kiss, but I'm not done with him. I put a hand on his cheek and say, "Be careful."

He goes to kiss me on the cheek and whispers, "Fuck that plan. Meet me by the popcorn shack at ten."

And then he's out and walking toward the store where the rich girls buy their prom dresses, looking like a dapper kid on the hunt for some plaid.

"Last one." My dad's voice is strained, whether from the stress of going into a soon-to-explode mall or the pain of watching his daughter kiss a boy.

He pulls up in front of Frills 2, and I wince. In my old clothes, I would've looked so out of place here, where they import all the high-fashion crap that didn't sell at the fancier mall downtown. But now, with my red pixie and pink lips and flowing tunic, I belong. I put my hand on the door, and my dad says, "Patsy, wait."

"Don't worry. I'll be fine."

He takes his foot off the brake and parks nearby. When he turns the car off—that's when my alarm bells start ringing. What is he going to say to me that he didn't say to anyone else?

"Dad, what?"

He purses his lips, thinking. "We never talked about what would happen after this."

"We get Matty and drive away into the sunset. Or sunrise, I guess."

His grin is boyish and sweet. "Even after all this, you still think you're gonna get a happy ending, huh?"

"I'm counting on it."

"If you get out of here, with or without the dog, with or without anybody else, you keep this card." He hands me another gift card from a stack of cards with a rubber band around them. "It's got . . . well, a lot of money on it. I'm leaving my real bag and the laptop in the trunk. You don't wait for me. You drive away, you hear? And keep these." He hands me three drivers' licenses, one from Georgia, one from Texas, and one from Canada. Each one has a different name, and the faces on them look enough like me to work. "You're going to need those to rent an apartment or get a hotel room. And for driving. Here's an extra key to this car." He hands me that, too. My palms are starting to feel heavy, weighed down. "The tank is full."

"Seems like you were pretty busy this afternoon," I say.

He snorts. "Yeah, well, we can't all spend our time defacing private property."

I clear my throat and try to rub some green paint off my hand.

"Doesn't matter," he says. "Point is, we're not vigilantes anymore. We've got your mom and the others to look after. I don't know what Valor's next move is, but I know that things are going to be hard for a while, and the best thing anyone can do is find some mountain house where you can grow vegetables and dig a well and just stay off the goddamn grid until the government sorts out its shit. I know you don't know how the darknet works, but when you open the laptop, there's a tab for a Canadian pharmaceuticals company that will mail you any meds your mother needs. Chemo drugs, needles, Zofran, medical marijuana." I blush. "Whatever she needs," he repeats gruffly. "The password is 'Patsy' and your birthday. No spaces."

"But I don't need to know all that, because you're going to be fine, Dad."

"We can't count on that, honey."

And damn if he doesn't look like he thinks we're going to fail. I want to tell him everything—from the past fourteen years and from right now. But what comes out is what I need him to know.

"Mom got the money. Put it in a college fund for me. She had it all along."

His smile is fond as he shakes his head. "Oh, Karen. Of course she did."

"And I forgive you. I'm sorry for everything I said."

The car suddenly feels too small and warm, and I lean in to him, wrapping my arms around his neck. This is the dumbest good-bye, awkward and sideways with a parking brake in my hip. We've barely had any time together, and it's all been borrowed. He never got to know the real Patsy, the one who collects stuffed turtles and does yarn bombing and dresses in the nasty dinosaur costume for little-kid birthday parties at the pizza place. The only Patsy he's ever known is a killer who couldn't quite smile, and I've picked a fight with him every chance I got. I guess, at least, our relationship is pretty typical. Dad doesn't understand daughter; daughter rebels to get dad's attention. Except that, on a lot of levels, he does under-stand me. We both know how to shoot people if it means our loved ones get to keep going.

"I love you," I say for the first time, my words muffled against his shoulder.

"I love you too. And don't ever forget that everything I ever did since you were born was meant to keep you safe. I might've failed, but goddammit, I tried. Now let's go get your dog."

"I thought you didn't care about the dog."

"I care about *you*."

He kisses the top of my head, a benediction, and I get out of the car and look back.

When I motion for him to open the window, I say, "See you tomorrow morning."

"See you, honey."

It's a quick walk to the mall, stuffing the four cards and the car key into my padded bra. I don't want to use them, don't want to think about what it means that he's given them to me. Is my dad plan-ning something even more stupid than what I've already planned? I should've had Chance sneak pills into his drink. At least then I'd know he was safe. At least I'd know he wasn't going to mess up.

27.

The moment I push open the front door of Frills 2, I start to feel queasy. I don't know if it's the cloud of perfume, the overheated air, the effects of bargain sushi, or the fact that I'm walking toward a big pile of bombs, but I'm pretty sure I'm going to lose my dinner. I guess that's at least one sign that the old Patsy is still around—I'm scared shitless, shaking, and close to puking.

"Can I help you?"

The perfume lady blocking my path holds a glittering jar of pink liquid in my face like a threat, and I hold up a hand.

"No thanks. Just browsing."

I keep walking, and she follows me. She's like the Disney version of my mom, thin and overdone with teeth so white they're almost blue.

"And what are we browsing for today?"

"A faster way out of this store."

She stops following me after that, but I don't feel any better. It was ridiculous, to think I could ever fit in on the marble floors of Frills 2. I should go hide out in the Jerky Haus. At least it smells better.

I've got thirty minutes left to kill and two cards loaded with cash, so I decide to do something I never had the guts to do before. I head for the jewelry store, march up to the counter, and ask to have my nose pierced.

I'm the only one in the store, and the mall's pretty quiet, despite the posters promising extra mall police armed to protect the safety of "our valued guests." The girl looks around nervously. She's got multiple earrings in each ear, a nose ring, and a lip ring.

"I'm not supposed to do that," she says.

"I'll tip you twenty bucks." She nibbles her pierced lip. "Fine. I'll tip you fifty bucks."

She grins. "Damn. Can't pass that up. Promise you won't tell anybody?"

I grin. "Promise."

I almost chicken out when she loads up the bedazzled gun, but it's not the scariest thing I've seen this week. It barely hurts, and then I've got a stud in my nose and some off-the-record healing recommendations.

"You're supposed to have this done in a tattoo parlor with a needle," she says. "But I did mine here, and it's fine, so whatever." I leave with a bottle of saline solution that I'll probably never get to use, but I feel pretty badass. And maybe she'll use her tip to help pay off a Valor credit card.

Without a ton of time left, I buy a slushie and pour an energy drink into it, slurping slowly as I walk back toward Frills 2. At first I figure I'll skip it and just use the public restroom, but then I have an idea.

I hurry around the silk scarves and straight into the ladies' room, which is absurdly posh, with couches and ottomans and flower arrangements. I check under the stalls, but no one is here, and I don't see a camera anywhere, either. With an evil laugh, I lock the door out into the mall, get out my spray paint, and do my biggest and most beautiful VALOR SUCKS across their huge, well-lit mirror. And then I spray dollar signs on all their fancy chairs and a giant red anarchy symbol on the painting over the fake fireplace. When I look at myself in the mirror, I barely recognize the miscreant I see grinning back with short red hair, a pierced nose, and fingers splattered with red and green.

And that's when I hear someone yank on the door I've locked.

"Hello?" a woman calls, jiggling the door with increasing force. "Why is this locked?"

My heart goes crazy, because I've just done something totally stupid. I was supposed to be invisible, and instead I've committed a major act of vandalism and locked myself in with the evidence. I don't want to hurt this woman, and even if I did, gunshots would bring people running, including those armed mall police. I passed several on my way to and from the jewelry store, and they looked a lot tougher than the frail old man who tried to take down Wyatt at the strip mall.

The only thing left to do is run.

I wet a paper towel and wipe my fingerprints off the spray cans as the woman's yells get louder. The cans go in the under-counter trash can, and I shoulder my bag and step behind the rattling door.

"Whoever is in there had better open this door right now!" she shouts.

I scrunch into the corner, take a big breath, and turn the bolt.

The door flies open, and a woman rushes in, and I slip out behind her and run.

"Hey!" she yells. "Stop right there!"

But I'm fast and full of fear and caffeine and high on vandalism, so I keep going. It's exhilarating, running away from someone who doesn't have a gun. I'm out of the store before I hear her shout again, and I turn the next corner and head for the public restroom by the tea shop. I pick a stall and lock the door to change into my mall jumpsuit. The filmy tunic gets wadded up and stuffed into the tampon box, but I keep the tank and leggings on, because I plan to take off this jumpsuit at some point and don't want to be naked when that happens.

The whole time I'm changing, I'm shivering with nerves, waiting for the door to bang open and another basic saleswoman to start hollering. But no one shows up. When I leave the stall, I put the flats in my bag and slip on the thick socks Wyatt recommended I buy for the work boots. He said I'd get horrible blisters with my usual argyles. The boots feel huge and clompy and stiff, and I zip up the jumpsuit and straighten to glare at the stranger in the mirror. I look totally bizarre, like a bird in a bear suit, so I wipe off the lipstick with a wet paper towel and shove on a baseball cap.

Putting my bag on the counter, I dig through it for the things I can't live without. The photo I took from Uncle Ash's house, my mom's printed Valor card with that damning number printed on it in green, the two halves of Amber's same card. I have the rosary around my neck where my lucky locket used to be, the cross hanging low under my jumpsuit. My burner phone goes in my jumpsuit's chest pocket. I'm not sure what to do with my gun, as it would be pretty useless in my waistband when the jumpsuit is zipped, so I stick it in the extra-large front pocket. The hideous gray sack is pretty big on me, even though it's an extra-small, so there's plenty of room.

Everything else in my bag can be replaced, so I stuff it down the trash can and walk out the door with empty hands. I turn down the hallway marked EMPLOYEES ONLY and grab the first rolling trash can I see. Feeling obvious as hell, I push the garbage through the empty mall, toward Wyatt and the popcorn stand.

If I look silly, so does he. Wyatt's jumpsuit fits well, but his haircut and general handsomeness don't go with the drab gray aesthetic. He's leaning against a push broom, fully focused on me like a daydreaming lumberjack.

"Everything smooth?" he asks.

"Nope. I almost got caught."

"Wait. Is that a nose ring?"

I turn my head to show it off. "Yep."

"Is that how you almost got caught?"

"Nope." I hold out my hands to show him the flecks of paint, and he cringes.

"You've got to stop doing that."

I shove my hands in my pockets. "I did. It's done. What now?"

He must sense that I'm still riled up, as he reaches out to delicately touch the little green jewel in my nose. "I like it. It's cute." His smile is fond and sweet, and I tuck it away in my memory palace. "I don't know what now. We've got a long-ass time to wait and hide, and it's not like we can get into any stores or anything."

I look around the mall and see nothing but bored kids with earbuds cleaning up behind half-lowered cages. No one gives us a second glance. A mall cop is headed our way, but he's still far off and bopping his head to his iPod.

"I forgot the Windex," I say, loud enough to carry. "Come on."

I take off in the opposite direction from the cop, back toward the center atrium where the Santa-photo backdrop is located. As we walk, I glance up at the second floor. I don't see any other janitors or Crane goons; nor do I see my dad. Just to be safe, I stay as far out of sight as possible, walking close to the stores and behind every thick column.

There's a sixty-foot-tall fake tree in the open center of the mall, giant ornaments dangling from the ceiling, and dozens of creepy elf statues that look like rip-offs of Dr. Seuss. I guess the mall got tired of people just taking whatever pics of Santa they wanted to, as he's now in a small, cheerfully painted cottage with two bright red doors. You wait in line, they shove you in, Santa does with you what he will, and they shove you out. It's kind of creepy, actually. Even the windows are painted on. I can't help imagining some Dr. Ken Belcher type of jerkoff at Valor getting a bonus for making sure the poor kids never even get to see Santa if their parents can't pay.

We walk around the cottage, and there's an employee door hidden in the back, painted to blend in with the rest of the house. When I turn the knob, it opens, easy as that. Wyatt grins, and we abandon our broom and garbage to go inside. I expect it to be dark, but the back of the roof is open to let in air and light. There's a huge, cushy Santa throne, a red carpet, and an extra bench, like maybe they let primping families wait there until it's their kid's turn to pee on Santa. Everything is utterly pristine and untouched.

Of course. Because Santa doesn't show up until after Thanksgiving, does he? Not a single filthy kid has flicked a booger in this fake-ass room.

I walk right up to Santa's chair and plop down in it, draping my feet over the armrest.

"Is it just me, or has Santa gotten bigger since we were little?" I say. "Too much milk and cookies, I guess."

Wyatt grins and scoops me up, sitting down in the chair himself and holding me in his lap.

"Ho, ho, ho," he says softly, right by my ear. "Have you been a good little girl this year?"

I freeze for a second.

No, I have not been good. I have been, in fact, the opposite of that. But that's not what he means.

Repress, repress, repress.

"Oh, no, Santa," I say. "I've been very, very naughty."

He swallows and shivers, and I know it was the right answer. Thus begins possibly the most passionate kiss ever between two jumpsuited murderers while sitting on Santa's throne. Time stops, as it tends to do when we're alone and touching each other, and for a while I forget completely who I am and what I've done and what

I'm waiting here to do. For a while I'm just a seventeen-year-old girl with a slightly painful new nose ring, making out with her super-hot boyfriend with the messed-up tattoo and fancy hair. We don't talk because we don't want to talk. We want to kiss, and the kiss says everything we need to say. About passion and desperation and caring and fear and whatever drives humans to bang before battle.

Not that it goes that far. Jumpsuits and the threat of impending explosions are good at keeping such things above the waist.

I lose track of time completely. The phone in my pocket falls to the ground when the top of my jumpsuit slithers down over my shoulders. My tender nose hurts like hell from rubbing up against Wyatt's skin, and my lips feel puffy and scratched. Doesn't matter. I need more Wyatt.

And then we hear it—a noise that shouldn't be there. Hurried shoes slapping on mall floors, low voices, the sound of a squeaking wheel. Wyatt and I pull away, and our eyes meet, and we have to be thinking the same thing: *What if they come in here? There's nowhere to run.*

We scramble to zip up our jumpsuits, and I grab my phone from where it's fallen on the floor. Without many options and with the squeaky wheel getting closer, we hide behind Santa's massive chair, which is the only real thing in the room. The feet and wheels stop just outside, and a guy with a familiar voice who definitely isn't Leon says, "These three go under the tree. Hurry up."

I'm holding my breath, straining to hear the sound of muffled barking or an extra grunt as someone moves a box full of my poor dog. I don't hear the sound I want to hear, and that makes me angry. Why can't it ever be easy?

They shove heavy boxes around, and then the guy says, "Next two over there, by the train," and I keep listening for a sign of Matty and not hearing her.

Wyatt's hand lands on my arm, his lips brushing across my temple.

"We'll find her," he whispers.

We stay like this until we can't hear their shoes anymore. I open my flip phone, and it's a little after two in the morning. If they're done this fast, we should be able to leave and find Matty soon. At least, hiding here, we know she's not in any of these five boxes.

Of course, I don't know how many more boxes there are. There could be hundreds.

"Patsy. Stay with me. It's going to be okay."

My head jerks around. "What?"

"You looked like you were about to have a panic attack."

"I was thinking about the odds."

He gives me a big, dorky grin. "Never tell me the odds." When I stare at him blankly, he mutters, "Wherever we end up next, I'm going to force-feed you *Star Wars* until you understand all my jokes."

Every time he uses the word *"we,"* every time he expands that *"we"* out past the next hour, it's like a tiny Band-Aid on my heart.

"As long as I get plenty of gummy bears and popcorn," I say.

It's quiet outside now, so I unfold from behind Santa's throne and stretch as much as the jumpsuit allows. Wyatt does the same. When my phone buzzes, there's a text from my dad.

`No dog in Frills 2 or food court. No sign of Leon. 7 guys down upstairs. You?`

He must have a silencer, then.

I text back, `No dog at tree and train.`

A number I don't know buzzes with, `not @ carosel or osford`, and I grin. So Chance is still with us, then, and his texts are as careless as he is.

Nothing from Bea. Does she even have a phone? She's probably still in the bookstore. At least Gabriela and Rex are safe. Even if they were awake and functional, they couldn't get into the mall right now. Unless they figured out where the Cranes were getting in—some random loading dock somewhere, most likely. But surely whatever Chance put in their drinks will last longer than that. I hope.

There are just too many variables.

I need to focus. We need to find our dog.

I open Santa's door slowly, peeking out to scan the area. No people are visible, and the broom and trash can are where we left them. I give Wyatt a shrug that says, *What now?*

He points toward the other atrium of the mall, where the stage and toy store and candy kiosks are grouped, close together in a riot of kid insanity. It makes sense—after the Santa area, we should keep checking the places where there's the most stuff to break. We pass an older woman sweeping in a dirty jumpsuit, but she doesn't even look up as we pass. Down by the stage, three figures in identical, clean jumpsuits are arguing. Two large boxes sit on a dolly, wrapped in bright paper with bows on top. Even from this far away, I can tell that one of the guys is Tuck.

"Leon said the gold one goes by the purse store with the glass damn doors. So why's there a red one by the purse store?"

We hide behind a kiosk to watch.

"I didn't know it mattered. You guys never tell me anything," says a skinny Crane goon with a greasy ponytail.

"Well, it matters. Now fix it."

Tuck heads toward us, and we hide around the other side of the kiosk. The ponytail guy is grumbling and cussing, and an older man in a baseball hat says, "Just pick up the damn box and shut up, kid," and then I hear the noise I've been praying to hear all along: muffled barking.

"What the hell was that?" the older guy says, and Tuck spins and stomps back.

A gun cocks in the silence, and Tuck says, "Don't you worry about what it is. Just do your damn job."

Tuck storms off, and the two guys shove the box across the floor with grunts and groans. The box keeps on barking, but they don't mention it again until Tuck is past our kiosk and walking as fast as he can. I creep closer, always hiding behind a kiosk or cart, with Wyatt right behind me.

"Hey, Richard. You think that dog can breathe in there?" the older guy asks.

"Not my problem," Ponytail Guy, Richard, says. "I just want to get out of here without another hillbilly asshole pointing a gun at me."

After a few minutes of heaving, they get the box into place and pick up the red one to carry it back to the cart.

"Whatever's in the regular boxes ain't nearly as heavy as the one with the dog," the older guy observes.

"Just do your job and put the red one somewhere else," Richard says before storming off in the same direction as Tuck.

As I peek around the kiosk, the older guy walks around the box, probing the sides with his fingers. He looks up and in every direction before pulling out a pocketknife and slitting the gold wrapping paper carefully, right under the wide ribbon on top. Right where the seam would be.

"You okay in there, buddy?" he says.

The barking is louder now, joyous through the slit he's made in the box. A rhythmic thumping suggests that Matty's doing her usual happy tail wagging.

"Whoa! No, buddy. No. Stay in there."

I move from this kiosk to the next one, the closest one. When I stop, Wyatt catches the back of my jumpsuit. I check the halls, listen for more footsteps, but all I hear is wagging and barking and a kind-hearted idiot trying to stuff eighty pounds of happy dog back into the box where it belongs, according to Mr. Leon Crane.

"No! No, no. Stop. C'mon! Goddammit!"

Wyatt yanks me back behind the kiosk as the clawing, ripping sound of tearing cardboard is followed by totally unblocked, joyous barking. I hear claws clattering on the marble, the man's footsteps clumping around ineffectually.

I whistle low and whisper, "Come here, Matty. Come here, girl."

Because dogs have a really fantastic sense of hearing, right?

Claws skitter frantically, and then she's racing toward me, faster than I've ever heard her move, barking and yipping like crazy. I can't stand it anymore. My eyes are tearing up, and my heart is beating, and we might all get out of here alive before things even get bad.

I have to step out from behind the kiosk and see my girl.

28.

She barrels into me, jumping up and pawing.

But . . .

But . . .

It's not Matty.

This is a black Lab, but it is not *my* black Lab.

This black Lab is younger, floppier, skinnier, and has jangly balls.

"What?" I say, trying to fend off the happy dog's claws and slobber.

The guy walks up but doesn't make any attempt to grab whoever this dog is.

"That's not her," Wyatt says.

"I'm sorry." The guy glances around nervously. "This dog just ran up . . . I don't know what it's even doing in the mall. You should probably call the police or something." His face freezes, almost comically, when he realizes what he's just said. "I mean, never mind. I'll just take him outside." He grabs the crazy dog's collar and tries to drag it away, but it breaks free and takes off for the other end of the mall, slipping and sliding on the polished floor. The guy rubs his crew cut and stares at us.

"Are you guys . . . ?"

"Goddammit," I say, and I walk away. It's stupid, but I follow Tuck's path. Not only because he's Leon's goon, but because he appreciates a good dog and might be headed to where Matty is. She must be somewhere else.

My phone buzzes, and I check it.

Not at stage. Decoy dog. WTH? Wyatt's number, sent to me, my dad, and Chance. I didn't even notice him texting as he trailed me.

Not at Mr. Goodbuy or Nickel's. Running out of options, my dad texts back.

not @ plyfround. i dont even know whr iam. From Chance. Of course.

The mall is laid out like a giant cross, a two-storied X with one long arm that I'm currently walking down. My dad checked upstairs. We checked the stage and the Santa setup.

But was my dad checking for Matty upstairs, or just looking for Leon?

"Goddammit!" I take off running for the escalator, which is frozen into stairs.

Laughter rings from overhead, and I look up to find dozens of faces.

"Well, that was a charming scene," yells Leon Crane.

This is what I get for trusting my dad to take care of business.

As we run, bullets *ping* off the marble behind us. Clearly, no one is trying to kill us, because we'd be dead. Whatever Leon has up his sleeve, he wants us alive for this next part.

Or at least he wants *me* alive.

Somewhere, a dog barks, and I don't know if it's Matty or the fake dog, but I have to run faster. I don't think as I sprint past dozens of wrapped packages and up the escalator with Wyatt panting by my side, a trail of lazy bullets in our wake. As we barrel upstairs, a bullet hits the glass wall of the escalator, and it cracks into a spiderweb but doesn't break. When I reach the solid floor, I see an audience of janitors in jumpsuits just like mine. Some are clearly Crane goons, laughing, with automatic rifles slung across their chests and pistols in hand. Some are nobodies, nameless members of this perverted cell of the Citizens for Freedom, coerced and forced and led into doing whatever Leon Crane wants, whether or not it's actually helping the fight against Valor. Like the guy with the crew cut downstairs, they look confused, like they're not sure why they're here or who they're rooting for. Among them are the kids from the shooting range who didn't join our little group, and they look like they just got back from war.

This audience is definitely not rooting for me.

"Well, step right up, Miss Patsy. Let's have us a little chat."

Leon Crane sits on a big gold package wearing a jumpsuit identical to mine. A shotgun rests across his knees, and he's smiling, as my mom would say, like a possum. With this many guns pointed at me, I've got nowhere to run, so I throw my shoulders back, stick out my chin, and walk up to him with my hands in my pockets and Wyatt right behind me. My fingers tighten around the grip of my gun, and I give him a smug grin.

"I thought I blew you up," I say.

He tips his head. "And I look forward to returning the favor. Now, if you'll stop squeezing that Valor gun in your pocket and gently place it on the ground between us, I'd be most obliged."

My smile dies. "What gun?"

At least a dozen more guns point at me.

"Guess," Leon says. He flops his gun toward Wyatt. "His, too."

Without my gun, I have nothing. But full of holes, I have even less.

I start to pull it out, and Leon whips out his own Glock, saying, "Oh, careful. Trigger fingers can get mighty sweaty. They taught us trigger discipline in the army. You ever learn trigger discipline?"

I show him my gun, my finger nowhere near the trigger. "I'm

a little more into trigger anarchy." Slowly, carefully, I put it on the ground. Every second, I'm one twitch away from shooting him anyway and taking the punishment of dying in a hail of bullets. But if I go, Wyatt goes too. I can't do that to him. Maybe I deserve it, but he doesn't.

"Now kick those guns a little closer to me. Gentle as a light breeze, you hear?"

Our two black guns twirl across the tile. When Leon tosses his head, a Crane goon more nimble than Tuck hurries over and collects them. The box under Leon rustles and barks excitedly. What kind of an asshole sits on someone's dog like this?

"That's better." Leon resettles himself on the box. "Now, where were we? Oh, yeah." He leans forward, eyes burning. "You blew up my family's house. And several of my aunts."

Inside, I feel like I'm going to fly apart. Outside, I shrug and say, ". . . sorry?"

He ignores it.

"Now, normally, I could forgive that sort of transgression. I never did like my aunt Kitty. But . . . well, let's see. Your boy there gave one of my boys a concussion and left him to die on a simple wipe job." He jabs a finger at Wyatt. "Now, son, don't you even draw breath to tell me that's not what happened, because he remembers. Then y'all shot several of my tech boys in a trailer for stealing your Pop-Tarts." Now he aims his finger at me. "And then you disappeared into the woods with my childhood best friend and the best hacker this side of the Pacific, killing three more of my cousins on the way. I'm guessing you ended up killing Jacky, considering he has such a smart goddamn mouth. And then, after all that, you went . . ." He stands and strides over to poke me in the chest with tattooed fingers. "You went and blew up my goddamn house! And when you add it all together like that, it's un-fucking-forgivable." His face is red up to the roots of his hair, and he purses his lips as if he's thinking about hitting me in the face until I don't have a nose, but I do not turn away. "Normally, I would just shoot you and be done with it, but I spent too much time torturing hostiles to let you die that easy. And I know how to hurt you most."

He makes his hands into fists, opens them, and returns to sitting on his box. "But you are an elegant force of destruction, and I can still use you, so I will give you one more chance to do the right thing. Now, I am a simple patriot leading these good people in a righteous fight against the real bad guy here, and that bad guy is a bank that calls itself Valor." He picks his gun back up, points it at me, and cocks it. "You're either fighting on my side, or you are against me. So which side do you choose, Patsy? Mine, or Valor's?"

"She's on my side," my dad says, stepping around the corner.

He shoots Leon Crane in the chest.

29.

I turn my face away, pretty sure that I'm about to go down in a blaze of glory, but a rolling trash can zooms in front of me, careening into the front row of guys with guns.

"Come on, morons!" Chance shouts, and Wyatt and I dive for the corner where my dad came from.

Bullets *ping* off the marble wall and shatter the glass of a cooking store, but we're behind a thick stone column, safe and sound. And behind my dad, who's ducked back with us. He shoves an open duffel bag at us with his boot, and I reach in and pull out guns. Not our guns and not the guns we took from Hartness the other night. One says SECOND UNION, and one says VALOR, and now I'm guessing my dad must've figured out where the Cranes were unloading their boxes. I slide out my clip to check it, then shove it home and get ready. Funny how someone else's gun can feel the same as yours when you really need it.

"How much longer are they going to shoot the wall?" Chance asks.

"They're Cranes. They'll shoot it until it's dead," my dad says.

All of a sudden, the shots stop, and the mall goes quiet.

A throat clears, and a voice I didn't expect to hear again calls, "Nice try, Jacky. And yet you constantly say I'm the dumb one."

My dad puts a fist against his forehead, looking defeated.

"Bulletproof vest, huh?" he calls. "Or just too stubborn to die?"

A single bullet *pings* off the stone. "A little trick I learned from your daddy."

"God rest his soul."

"How'd she win you over, Jacky? You two walked away into the night, left three dead bodies and kept going. The fella who survived didn't even see y'all together before he ran away from your hail of gunfire. Is this a Lolita thing? Were you guys getting hot in that deer stand when Cousin Hartness found you?"

My dad shakes his head at me. Wyatt looks pissed.

"I bet it was sweet. I bet that tall blond bastard got her all loosened up for you, and you just swooped in and—"

"She's my daughter, Leon. So shut your goddamn mouth for once."

Leon laughs in surprise and delight, and it fills the mall, echoing off the columns.

"Oh, crap, Jacky! You got a kid? How'd you manage that? Where you been hiding her all these years? You do recognize, old friend, that I would've sent a silver rattle if I'd known."

"You were in prison when she was born, asshole."

In that moment, I realize that my dad is just as dumb and prideful as everyone else. Just as easily riled up as his dad. Because he couldn't let Leon assume the worst. And now Leon knows everything.

Leon chuckles as if he's realizing it too. "Oh, well, yes, I did spend some time behind bars, didn't I? No thanks to you and your son-of-a-bitching daddy. He was the most evil human being I've ever met. My only regret is not going for a head shot when I had the chance. I learned how to nurse a grudge in those long prison years. I learned that children can suffer on behalf of their parents, and that can be just as satisfying to a man who craves revenge. And as much as I used to love you, Jacky, I hate your dark-hearted daddy and bad-luck daughter even more."

My dad sighs. "It's over, Leon. Just give us the dog, and we'll disappear. You'll never see us again. You can have Candlewood, the Cannon land, the whole state of Georgia. Blow up whatever you want. Forget we ever existed."

"Oh. Oh, that's how it is? You waltz in and waltz out with the kid that blew up my house? Like father like daughter, just leaving a wide swath of ruination behind you?" His laugh gets madder and more manic. "Oh, I don't think so, Jacky. I don't think that's going to happen at all."

"What do you want, Leon?"

"I want both of you working for me, doing whatever I say for as long as I say."

"That's not gonna work this time."

Leon gives a dramatic sigh. "Now I'm tired, friend Jacky, of hollering at you with this symbol of capitalism standing unyielding between us. This little dog-in-the-box game was certainly more fun than I'd ever dreamed, but we're running out of time. When I come to terms, I like to see a man's eyes. So you walk out here, and let's work it out as men. As blood brothers."

My dad pauses, eyes closed. "And if I don't?"

"Then all twenty-nine of us will rush you, and if there are less of you than that, you're likely to die. Come on out. The kids, too. Admit you're treed, and let's talk."

Something booms behind us, a chunk of the column explodes overhead, and I turn to see a Crane goon with a rifle standing in front of an employees-only door, grinning.

My dad stands, and panic shoots through me. Surely he's not going to trust Leon Crane? But he doesn't have a choice, considering there's an armed Crane behind us, too. Holding his gun easy in his hand, he walks right out there and motions for us to follow. I shove my new gun in my pocket. Wyatt is watching me and does the same. My dad's eyes tell me everything is going to be fine, but every cell of my body tells me it couldn't be more wrong. Leon slides off his box, and they hug each other like mortal fools, each with a Glock in his right hand.

"We're not coming back, Leon," my dad says. "What's your next offer?"

"You're not going to like it, Jacky."

"Hit me."

"You join me now or the dog dies. You don't want to make your little girl upset, now, do you? I know how attached she is to that poor mongrel."

I spin, my eyes already wet. "Dad, no! You can't."

He puts a hand on my shoulder and shakes his head sadly.

"Patsy, do you really want to give your life to a man who would shoot a dog just to prove a point? Do you think he cares any more about us than he does about her? If we give in now, we're as good as dead."

"I guess that's a 'no,'" Leon says.

He turns to the box and shoots it twice.

30.

A squeal, and then a whimper, and then the box goes quiet.

I cry out and rush forward, but Wyatt catches me and pulls me back against him.

"Matty! Honey! What did you do? What have you done?" I focus on Leon now, my hands in fists. "What the hell did you do?"

But he's not looking at my face. He's looking at my new gun—which he didn't know I had and isn't prepared for, considering he already had me kick my gun away. So I point it at him and shoot him. Again and again, and into the crowd behind him, and then they're all turning tail and running because Leon Crane is a mess of blood and he's sliding to the floor in a puddle of red. When you know a man's wearing a bulletproof vest, you find better places to shoot him.

I'm surprised that we're not being shot at, but as I turn slowly, I see my friends and I see what we've done. The goon behind us is on the ground. The Crane boys with the AR-15s are down. The crowd is either on the ground or running away. My dad and Wyatt and Chance are up and unscathed. Four people with four little guns can do a ton of damage when they're angry and have the element of surprise.

When I see that there's no one left to shoot me, I run for the box and rip open the paper. I can't get the bow off, and Wyatt's suddenly there, helping me tear down to the plain brown cardboard. I claw at the packing tape and feel my bitten fingernails shred. Finally, we get the flaps open, and I look down, and I'm crying and screaming and it's not her.

It's not Matty.

It's not even a black Lab. It's some kind of mix, brown and black and still, and I keep crying. Because this dog didn't deserve to die. And because Matty's still alive somewhere. And because I'm just so, so sick of pulling the trigger.

Something is ticking in the box, and I move the dog gently aside and see an actual bomb for the first time. A big one.

It's not set to go off at five a.m. It's set to go off in thirty minutes.

31.

"We've got to get out of here," I say.

My dad must hear the panic in my voice, as he hurries over and looks in the box.

"You're right," he says. "That bomb's not one of mine. That's Leon's. And I don't know how to disarm it."

I stand and wipe my hands off on my jumpsuit. Looking in every direction, I see dozens of big, wrapped packages. Maybe hundreds. I bet if I put my head up to each of them, they'd all be ticking.

"What if Matty's in a different one?" I ask.

My dad shakes his head sadly. "We've checked all of them that we could. We'll try one more thing, but we've got ten minutes before we have to be outside, in the car, driving away." I nod eagerly. "And you get that there are still Cranes in this mall who will shoot you if they can?"

I shrug.

It doesn't matter. Without Leon to rally them, they're nothing.

"You remember that whistle I used to call her before?" my dad says, and I nod. "I'm going to do that now. Y'all spread out and get to where you can see and hear as many boxes as possible. If one starts to wiggle, open it. When we find her, we run. But we're only going to do this once. Thirty minutes is a lot less time than you think it is."

I'm already running. I haven't been upstairs yet, so I get to where I can look down on the atrium and see the whole line of boxes, up and down the hall and clustered at every corner. If I were a kid and my mom brought me here to see Santa, it would seem so magical— all these big, bright boxes full of surprises. But now? Jesus. They could all be full of bombs or dead dogs or both. Leon Crane is a monster.

Was a monster.

My dad puts two fingers to his lips and blows one long, high screech of a whistle. In the echoing silence, just after, I strain my ears, praying to hear a tail thumping against cardboard or a happy bark. I clutch my rosary through my jumpsuit. Wasn't Mother Mary supposed to bring me a miracle? Living through this ordeal isn't enough. I need my dog, too.

But nothing happens. Not a single one of the boxes so much as ticks. My dad looks at me and shakes his head sadly.

"I'm sorry, honey," he says.

That's the last thing he says before the crumpled form of Leon Crane shoots him from the ground.

32.

No.

This is not happening.

I'm running and running and shooting the broken mess that was my father's best friend, the lying bastard who just shot him with fingers dipped in his own blood. I get there first, and I shoot Leon again, in places where he'll never recover, and it feels good, and I hate this, and I hate how good it feels to end him once and for all when I thought I already had, and I'm nothing but a monster now and I don't care anymore.

When my clip comes up empty, I'm on the ground by my daddy. Wyatt helps me turn him over, and it's a gut shot, and I'm crying so damn hard because I know what that means. Because I know what it meant for Jeremy and Alistair, and I know what it means in a world where 911 goes straight to voice mail.

"We have to carry him," I say firmly, and Wyatt and Chance look at me like I'm a stupid little kid who still believes in magic and Santa Claus.

"Patsy," Wyatt starts, and I bolt to standing and point at the empty garbage can they used to distract the Cranes from shooting me.

"Put him in there. We'll wheel him out. There has to be a vet—"

"Patsy," Wyatt says, even more gently. "You know how this works."

"No!" I shout, and my voice echoes back at me. "No! We can fix this. It'll be okay. I know I said I needed Matty, but I need him. Okay? I always needed him. I just . . ." My dad reaches for me, and I take his hand and focus on his eyes. "I need you, Daddy. Just stay awhile longer. I don't hate you, and I'm not mad at you, and I'm sorry I didn't do a good enough job killing Leon. Just . . . please. Please, Daddy."

"Patsy," he says, like it's his favorite word in the entire world.

"I'm here, Daddy."

He smiles, innocent sweetness, and strokes my hair, or what's left of it. "Got to keep you away from Devil Johnny." His eyes go unfocused, like he's looking over my head. "Got to keep you safe."

"You did, Daddy. You did." I press his palm to my cheek and close my eyes. "I'm fine. I'm going to be fine."

"Good girl," he says fondly. "My Patsy."

I shake my head and stand up, trying to pull my dad up by his arms. Wyatt and Chance stand to the side, and I bare my teeth at them.

"Pick him up! Pick him up now! Stupid goddamn idiot boys just can't . . ."

"Patsy," Wyatt says, the softest he's ever said it.

"What?"

"He's gone."

I don't look down. I don't want it to be true. I don't want to be holding my dad's hands if he can't hold mine. I just got him back, and he's already left me again.

"Guys, the time," Chance says, low.

"I'm sorry, Patsy," Wyatt says, and I look up at him, completely lost.

"For what?"

He picks me up, tosses me over his shoulder, and carries me away.

33.

I don't know where we are. Dark walls, fluorescents, concrete floors. The boys are carrying me, and I sometimes go limp and sometimes kick and scream and sometimes turn my face into Wyatt's shoulder and sob. They're lost, trying to get us out of the mall. When Chance finally kicks open a door, cold night air chills my wet face.

"That way," Wyatt says, and I claw for the door, to get back to my dad, but they pry my fingers off the handle and kidnap me into the darkness.

"Shit," Wyatt says. "We don't have the key."

I pull the key out of my bra and throw it on the ground, and they scrabble for it and open the burgundy sedan. Wyatt places me on the backseat like I'm breakable and struggles to buckle me into my seat belt.

"Help me," he begs. "There's not enough time for this. You have to come back to me now. Okay?"

I buckle the seat belt and say nothing.

The car drives, headlights cutting the mist. Too fast, too fast, away from my dad. The road curves around a bend.

"That was a stop sign," I say absently.

They didn't stop.

The car parks, and someone carries me inside and up an elevator and puts me in a bed that isn't mine in a room that doesn't smell like bleach and hair dye and anxiety.

"You don't have to watch," Wyatt says.

But I do.

The lights are off, and the hotel room blinds are open on a square of black.

I wait.

Nothing happens.

And then it does.

I feel it in my chest before I hear it, like it's sucking me in. Like it wants me near. The feeling comes before the explosion, before the fireballs that erupt at the same time all over the mall except also at barely different times. *Pow-pow, pow-pow.* It's like watching a crystal ball explode in a riot of flame, and I swear I can feel the heat through the extra-thick hotel window.

"There went my dad," I say. "There went Matty."

I lie back down and turn my face away from the window.

Someone is banging on the door, and it makes my head hurt worse than the explosion.

"Open up, you dicks!"

Chance opens the door, and Gabriela barrels into him from the yellow-lit hallway, yelling good things and bad things about what he did and did it work and what the hell did he give her and what the fuck is wrong with him, but then they're hugging and crying, and it's okay again.

"Patsy?" Her hand is on my shoulder, but it feels like it's miles away.

"They killed my dad," I say. "They killed my dog."

She tilts up my chin with a finger and grins.

"Dude," she says. "Your dumb dog is in our room."

34.

That's what finally wakes me back up.

"Show me," I say, and I find my feet and remember how to walk to the door.

Gabriela leads us down to our room and opens the door, and being knocked over by a happy Matty is the best thing that's ever happened to me.

Because it's her. Really her.

"How?" is all I can say.

Bea is sitting in the same chair in the corner, another cowboy romance in her lap. She looks up, her eyes as dead as ever. "I couldn't find you, so I walked around the mall parking lot to find the car. I heard a dog barking, and some Cranes were drinking beer in the back of a van with her tied to the tailgate."

"And they let you have her?"

The newly chopped brown bob swivels to me and tilts like a praying mantis. "I didn't ask. Just shot them all and took her. It seemed easier that way. She's a very polite dog."

I take great pains not to show her the horror I feel. This alone tells me I'm not the monster I dread becoming. "Thank you," I say. "That really means a lot to me."

Wyatt and Chance are on their knees, roughhousing with Matty, and the phone buzzes in my jumpsuit pocket. When I look down, I see that I'm covered in blood, and I can't believe we made it into the hotel without anyone saying anything. I pull out the phone and flip it open.

PATRICIA LOUISE KLEIN, WHERE ARE YOU?

I smile. My mom remains unchanged by the apocalypse.

Room 315, I text back.

Soon we're all here, except Rex, who's still sleeping off his roofie cola. My mom, Heather, Kevin, Chance, Gabriela, Bea, and Wyatt— we're all giddy and broken and exhausted. My mom demands that we get out of the jumpsuits, and that leaves the guys running back to their room in tees and boxers to get more clothes.

"What happened?" Kevin asks, all excited like we're going to tell him about a movie we saw.

I just shake my head. "We got out alive."

"It was amazing! It was all BOOM BOOM BOOM CRASH." He makes explosive noises and jazz hands, right up until my mom sees my face and puts a gentle hand on his shoulder. "Sorry," he mutters. "But it was."

"Where's Jack?" my mom asks, but her face says she already knows. She always did.

"Leon—" I start. But I can't go on. I just shake my head and let the tears fall.

My mom covers her mouth with her hand, and for just a moment, she looks like a girl only a little older than me and in love with a dashing rich boy who shows up every weekend with gifts. Then her face squeezes shut, a mess of wrinkles that arrived too early, and we're both crying.

"And what happened to Leon?" Heather asks.

I look up, swallow down the sorrow, and meet her eyes, hard. "I shot him ten times or so. Pretty sure it finally killed him."

She nods. "Don't think anyone would blame you for that."

My mom pulls me back into the hug, and I melt into her. The sobs jerk out of me, and I let it all out into my mom's shoulder. All the things I repress, suppress, whatever—they're burbling up. All the faces I've watched as they passed over, the eyes suddenly gone far off. Every pull of the trigger, every splatter of blood across a shirt, every mouth so surprised to find that it can't talk anymore. Some of the people died angry, some died fighting, some died sad or crawling away. A few died laughing, as if at some private joke. Leon died satisfied, I think. I saw it on his face. He knew what he'd done.

And that's what I don't want to become.

I've been trying, so hard, all this time.

And the fact that it still hurts this bad, that I still cry like this, like my heart is breaking . . . I'm no Leon Crane. I'm a Cannon. And I'll never see my daddy again.

35.

We've got the two cars packed up and ready to go. I was able to choke down some breakfast at the free buffet, and so far it's staying put. You can only live on milk shakes for so long before you have to eat your damn fruits and vegetables again, especially when your mom's breathing down your neck. I don't mind a bit, even when she brings me tomato juice with a stern frown.

Everyone else at the hotel is talking about the explosion last night, about the mall sales they're missing today. The news keeps showing fire trucks at dawn, bright lights and smoke. They don't mention the Valor logo painted on the trucks' shiny red sides. No one managed to capture the actual event on camera, and no one seems to know what happened. I'm already sick of hearing the words "gas leak."

"Can we get out of here?" Chance asks. "The waffle bar is great and all, but I'm losing my appetite." He points at the screen, and it's a commercial for Valor Savings Bank with Vikings riding eagles toward a pile of gold.

We all stand up and walk out, although Wyatt gets so sick of waiting for Kevin to hobble along that he scoops him up and carries him like a baby. It feels like a million years since I shot him, but really it's only been a week. Outside the hotel, we just stand under the awning like idiots, because we haven't discussed this next part.

"So where are we going?" Kevin asks, like we're planning an awesome road trip.

"Hold on, and we'll find out," I say.

I grab the keys from Wyatt and pop the trunk of the burgundy sedan, and everyone gathers around me. The bag my dad showed me last night is right where he said it would be, along with a bunch of other crap. He left so much stuff, in fact, that I'm starting to think he walked into that mall expecting to die. We have more guns, more Valor gift cards, and printed directions to a cabin in the wilds of North Carolina. Scrawled across the top in unfamiliar handwriting is SAFE HOUSE. BRING WATER.

"Works for me," Chance says.

"I just want to get out of Crane country," Rex adds.

But now everyone is looking at me like it's my call, so I nod. "Let's do it."

Wyatt is driving the burgundy sedan, and I'm in the passenger seat. Gabriela and Chance are in back, plugged into their iPods. I flip through the radio stations for a few minutes, hoping to hear some more informative news about the mall. When I finally find something, they confirm that it was a gas leak. An act of God. A horrible accident, and right before one of the biggest shopping days of the year. There's no mention of other malls across the country. Who knows how many cells took down their local Black Friday shrine to capitalism? Maybe when I fire up my dad's laptop later, I'll finally learn the real news. When I hear the Valor jingle, I flip the radio off.

"Wait. I almost forgot. Happy Thanksgiving!" I say.

Wyatt puts his hand over mine. "Happy Thanksgiving to you, too. I guess that means we can stop for lunch someplace that serves turkey?"

"You are a walking appetite," I say.

"Your milk shake brings all the me to the yard," he answers.

Something buzzes, deep in my dad's bag, which is on the floorboard between my feet. I dig down and pull out six identical burner phones, each marked with a number scrawled on a piece of masking tape. Figuring out his phone system is right up there with figuring out the darknet: something to do later, when everything is calm and safe again. I have to open several of the phones before I find the one that has a *1* on the text icon.

When I click it, I see that `Welcome back to the land of`

the living, old man was the last text my dad sent from this phone. The time stamp is 10:13 p.m. on the night that we saw the figure by the truck at the old Cannon house and turned around. It's a 404 number, which means Georgia. Atlanta. Possibly Candlewood.

Thanks, son. Glad to be back, it says. Now when do I get to meet my Patsy? She puts on a good show, even without her Valor camera. Love, Devil Johnny.

I go cold all over and stare at the phone like it's a bomb. For just a moment, I'm aware that my dad was the last person who touched it, that our fingerprints are overlapping now. And that he actually contacted the most dangerous man in the world, as far as I'm concerned.

A dangerous man who's supposed to be dead and clearly isn't.

A dangerous man who just implied that he knew Valor had tapped me for assassin duty and that the button on my old mail shirt was actually recording or transmitting my every word the entire time I was on Valor duty. And that maybe he was watching all along.

Well, before I faked my own death and buried it in Wyatt's yard under the body of my ex–best friend. And there's something else I have in common with my dad: I killed both of our best friends. And that gives me an idea.

I waited so long to respond that the screen went black, so I reactivate it and text back, She's dead. Leon Crane killed her. Died in Candlewood Mall last night. Sorry.

"Who is it?" Wyatt asks.

I don't want to lie, but I'm not ready to tell the truth, so I tell a half-truth.

"I'm not exactly sure."

The car speeds through the sunny morning, swooping past farmhouses and valleys and trees and up the biggest mountain I've ever seen. I open the window enough to smell the crisp air, and when I look down, I feel a little scared, but in the good way—the way a roller coaster or really high elevator might scare you. But when the phone buzzes in my hand, the real fear descends, heavy as a thick blanket.

Did you kill yourself again, Patsy? Did you learn that trick from me?

And then the phone . . . rings.

My heart is going to burst out of my chest, and everyone but Wyatt is staring at me, and the phone won't stop ringing and ringing and ringing.

I snap the phone in half and throw it out the window.

Find me now, Devil Johnny.

I'm free.

ACKNOWLEDGMENTS

Books are like pajama boners, by which I mean they can be very troublesome to deal with. Thankfully, I had help with mine.

Big thanks to my family for support, enthusiasm, hippo hugs, and the gift of heated mattress pads.

Big thanks to my agent of awesome, Kate McKean, for constant supervision. I mean *guidance*.

Big thanks to the publishing team at Simon Pulse: Liesa Abrams, Sarah McCabe, Regina Flath, and everyone else who had a hand in setting this baby on fire.

Big thanks to everyone who bought, read, gifted, reviewed, rated, touched, checked out, or otherwise interacted with *Hit*. I hope this book makes you happier than Matty with French fries.